Acclaim for Renée Manfredi's *Abov*

"*Above The Thunder* is passionate, wise, drawn to books with rich, memorable characters and contemporary stories will find this remarkable debut novel not only irresistible but impossible to put down."

—Tony Ardizzone, author of *In the Garden of Papa Santuzzu*

"A stunning debut novel. . . . To describe [it] as a brilliant, issue-oriented drama shortchanges Manfredi's accomplishments; the medical writing recalls the early works of Ethan Canin, and the combination of smooth storytelling, compassionate and probing narration and imaginative plotting makes for a heady blend. . . . Amazingly accomplished."

—*Publishers Weekly* (starred)

"In this moving, engrossing family drama about journeys taken willingly and, for the most part, not, relatives' and acquaintances' lives intersect, and tests of family loyalties and friendships spur growth and insight. Meanwhile, Manfredi handles each character confidently and credibly."

—*Booklist*

"Read any paragraph of Renée Manfredi and you will hear a voice of rare authority and verve. What is even more rare, and worth celebrating, is her compassion for her characters, her willingness to reach out into lives quite different from her own, her honesty in dealing with loss, loneliness, and grief."

—Scott Russell Sanders, author of
Hunting for Hope and *Secrets of the Universe*

"Manfredi's disciplined command of language combined with her intricate plot and compassion toward her characters make [*Above the Thunder*] an absorbing read."

—*Rocky Mountain News*

"Thoughtful and complex. . . . The reader is transported through the truly significant emotions that govern our days: joy, grief, compassion and love."

—curledup.com

Renée Manfredi

Above the Thunder

Renée Manfredi received her MFA from Indiana University, a fellowship from The National Endowment for the Arts and was a regional winner of *Granta*'s Best American Novelists Under Forty. She is the author of the story collection, *Where Love Leaves Us*, which won the Iowa Short Fiction award. Her short stories have been published in *The Mississippi Review*, *The Iowa Review*, *The Georgia Review*, and the Pushcart Prize anthology and were featured in NPR's Selected Shorts series. She lives in Santa Rosa, California.

Also by Renée Manfredi

Where Love Leaves Us

Above the Thunder

Above the Thunder

A Novel

Renée Manfredi

Anchor Books
A Division of Random House, Inc.
New York

FIRST ANCHOR BOOKS EDITION, MAY 2005

Copyright © 2004 by Renée Manfredi

All rights reserved under International and Pan-American Copyright Conventions.
Published in the United States by Anchor Books, a division of Random House, Inc., New
York, and simultaneously in Canada by Random House of Canada Limited, Toronto.
Originally published in hardcover in the United States by MacAdam/Cage, in 2003.

Anchor Books and colophon are registered trademarks of Random House, Inc.

Cataloguing-in-Publication Data for *Above the Thunder* is on file
at the Library of Congress.

Anchor ISBN: 1-4000-7850-4

Book design by Dorothy Carico Smith

www.anchorbooks.com

Printed in the United States of America
10 9 8 7 6 5 4 3 2 1

We must be the change we wish to see in the world.
— *Mahatma Gandhi*

Above the Thunder

PART ONE

THE UNDERGROUND POPULATION

ONE

HAIRPINS AND NEEDLES

Staring at specimens of the Ebola virus was not how Anna had envisioned spending her birthday. It was already early evening, and she'd wasted the entire day in this dingy office looking at slides of diseases. She wanted challenging exam questions—these were her advanced students—though of course nothing as obscure as this hemorrhagic fever. Most of the medical assistants this junior college graduated would be funneled into plush suburban offices in Massachusetts, not the Ivory Coast. Still, Anna had never been able to resist a visit with cell pathology.

She looked through her chosen slides: Six diseases of white cells and two of red—sickle cell anemia, and the good old-fashioned pernicious kind. That ought to do it. For the sheer beauty of the cytology, she added acute lymphocytic leukemia as the last and final question—an easy one. She peered at this slide, adjusted the focus for the lens. Microscopically, this was one of the loveliest illnesses around, the cells plentiful and shapely, as festive as confetti from a burst piñata.

She turned off her desk lamp, started to pack up, but got sidetracked again by the rare specimen box. Why not? Better to look at Rift Valley Fever than fifty-plus candles on a cake. Her friend Greta had tried to talk Anna into a party, but Anna had never allowed a celebration in her honor, and certainly didn't want one now, three years past the half-century mark.

Anna supposed she'd had more than her fair share of what made for a wonderful life, although she'd never have imagined this—an instructor at a junior college, widowed, estranged from her only child, living in a town-house that was, as of yesterday when the Goodwill truck came, completely empty except for a desk, her cello and chair, and a bed. She didn't have so much as a saucepan or a throw cushion now.

When Anna moved into the townhouse a year ago, the previous owner had abandoned all of her belongings and moved to Korea. The realtor promised to have everything cleared out and cleaned if Anna took the place, but Anna wanted everything left exactly as it was, down to the dead hyacinths and tacky collections of pirate cookie jars and clown figurines. At the time, she couldn't bear to have her things there, the beautiful china and furniture that had filled the Tudor home she'd shared with her hus-band on the North Shore. After Hugh died, Anna stored nearly all her household goods and rented a series of furnished apartments.

The townhouse was full of cheap and tacky things, which Anna had found comforting at first; everything here was expendable and replaceable, and nothing around her carried the burden of memory. Nobody she loved had ruined the finish on the coffee table with a hot mug. The stray socks behind the dryer would never be paired to anything in her drawer. Even the photographs were of strangers, clumps of women in self-conscious groupings at a ski lodge, and—Anna guessed—the previous tenant herself with a man probably a brother-in-law, or husband of a friend. She had the uncertain smile of someone asked to a party at the last minute.

Two weeks ago, when she remembered her upcoming birthday, it seemed even more depressing to be fifty-three with paint-by-number velvet clowns and pirate cookie jars that declared, *Aye, aye matey!* every time the lid was opened. She'd called in the Goodwill truck.

"Now what?" Greta had asked when she walked into Anna's empty apartment after it had been cleared. "What are you going to do about this?" The kitchen was absolutely and completely bare. Not so much as a salt shaker. "You can't live *this* way, either."

Anna shrugged. "We'll see." But Greta was right, of course, and for the past two weekends she'd been dragging Anna out to estate auctions, though Anna didn't want cat-clawed sofas or scratched-up tables.

She opened her desk drawer and found the hairpins she bought with Greta last Saturday. Twelve of them, morbid brooches made of the de-ceased's hair to adorn the dresses of the living. She didn't want them, certainly, and bid on them only out of suspicion that the hair of all twelve pins was from the same DNA pool. That interested her most of all: how the woman who wore them bore such prodigious loss. Most women would have stopped at one brooch, letting the first death stand in for all the others. Anna admired this long-dead mother, the fact that each death was particularly commemorated and not swept under one general heading of grief.

She turned the microscope back on and slid a few strands of what was surely baby hair under the lens. Blond and feathery, the cuticle smooth as a quill. Definitely infant down. The child had either died at birth or shortly thereafter; this was hair that had never been exposed to the sun. Not one telltale pit in the shaft or cuticle. She looked at the remaining eleven. Nine of the samples undoubtedly came from one family, and all twelve, she hypothesized from the minimal UVA damage, were under the age of ten. Illness, probably, a devastating turn-of-the-century disease that took all of this woman's children.

She swept the pins into the trash, then feeling guilty, fished them back out. She'd take the collection to an antiques store later.

Someone knocked and opened her door. Nick Mosites, an internist at the hospital who was occasionally a guest speaker here at the junior college. "Hi," she said.

"Sorry to bother you, Anna, and tell me no immediately if you want."

"Okay. No, and thanks for stopping in."

He smiled, perched on the edge of her lab chair. "I'm coordinating a support group for AIDS patients and their families at the hospital, and I need to start a second group. I had someone lined up, but she backed out at the last minute. I was hoping you could find me one of your brightest students to run the event. There would be an honorarium and experience, no real salary."

"Oh," she said, relieved that he hadn't asked her to run it. Anna didn't believe in such things as support groups. She followed Nick's glance to the nest of brooches on her desk. "Hairpins," she said, when she saw his baffled stare. "Brooches made with the hair of the dead. I bought them at an estate sale because I couldn't bear to buy a couch."

"Interesting," he said, but she could see that he wasn't in the mood for banter.

"Support groups are outside my area of expertise." She picked up the most beautiful of the brooches, a wreath of silver forget-me-nots inter-laced with strands of impossibly soft chestnut hair. "I'm a med tech. I know pins and needles."

He nodded. "Exactly. And they tell me you also teach a class in medical ethics."

"Not really. It's just a one-credit class on office and hospital proce-dures. Glorified bedside manner. How to calm a patient who's afraid of needles. How to reassure parents when you're doing a needle-stick on their screaming baby."

"Perfect. I want someone with a working knowledge of virology. Basic medical skills and an unflappable manner. What this group will be is just overflow from the meetings at the hospital. Most of these patients know each other and just need a place to gather on a Saturday afternoon."

"Oh," Anna said. "So, it's not really a support group."

"Well, yes and no. I need someone to be there to run interference, and I'd like it to be someone who has a basic grasp of immunology and can also handle a few temper tantrums. I know you're turning out exemplary clinicians. The two you put in my office on externships were outstanding." He picked up one of the pins, Anna's second favorite. This one was smaller than the others, unadorned except for a thin blue ribbon that held the strands together. It was made from the hair of two people. From the near identical similarities in texture and shade, Anna guessed that this brooch marked the death of twins.

"And what about the running interference part? What does that mean?"

"Just that most of these patients know each other well, and can get into...well, dysfunctional family dynamics. Anyway," Nick said, "there's a psychiatric resident who will drop in when he can. All your student will need to do is commit to one hour on Saturdays, and write up a few notes about who was there and general topics discussed. The student will get a small honorarium, and of course, something to put on a résumé."

"You don't think you should ask one of your residents? Or a med student?"

"I did ask, but they're so overworked I can't in good conscience make them do it. Look, I'd run the thing myself, but Saturdays are the only day I have with my family." He paused. "I promise it's only temporary."

"I'll see what I can do," Anna said.

"Great. I really do appreciate it." He turned to go. "Oh, one more thing. I know anybody you send over will be an excellent student, but I hope you'll be able to find one who is compassionate and patient."

Anna looked back at him, but before she could ask him anything further, he was out the door.

She looked through her class roster after he left. How would she gauge something like compassion from the contact she had with these kids? Compassion, in Anna's view, was a personal thing, a quality that emerged in a case-by-case basis only; what moved you about one person left you cold with the next. At least that was her experience. She circled two names in her grade book. She'd call these students tomorrow.

But enough today. She reboxed the slides. It was her birthday, after all, and what she wanted suddenly was to get a little drunk—a good sign, she thought, since that meant she wasn't too old to enjoy the finer pleasures of a good Scotch with a good friend. She picked up the phone to call Greta.

"What are you doing?" she said when Greta picked up.

"Well, I was about to make dinner, but Mike called and said he's working till nine, so not to bother."

Anna could sense her friend's mood immediately. Six months ago Greta had quit her job as vice-president of a software firm to devote herself full-time to the business of trying to get pregnant. Her tripartite obsession these days was conception, making elaborate dinners with ingredients she drove all over Boston to find, and coordinating a music and dance group for deaf children. Greta called the ensemble The No-Tones, and had already been written up twice in the Boston papers. Both of Greta's parents, German immigrants, were deaf. Anna was awed by Greta's childhood stories, the way, without a trace of self-pity or bitterness, she described leaving the silence every morning and moving slowly into sound, "like I was the light on water, and had to reach one shore in the morning, and the opposite every evening."

Greta's moods these days, Anna knew, were a rope bridge, swaying this way and that with emotion of even the slightest weight. She spoke softly. "So, anyway, since my wayward husband is missing dinner yet again, why don't you let me cook for you?"

"Better yet, meet me in the city. Let's go get drunk."

Greta laughed. "You paranoid thing, you. You don't believe me when I said I called off the surprise party?"

"Yes, I do. Mostly. But I just don't want to go home right now." Greta's townhouse was right next to Anna's.

Greta agreed to meet her at a working-class bar in Back Bay, a place she'd never been but had noticed on one of her drives. "It's across the street from a Korean Deli," Anna said. "I'll meet you there in an hour."

By the time Anna was on her second martini, Greta still hadn't shown up. She got out her cell phone to call Greta's house, but the battery was dead. Anna ordered a San Pellegrino, to sip along with the drink, though she was less afraid of drunkenness than she was of maudlin emotion.

A little more than a decade ago, she turned forty at the summer home in Maine. Hugh had arranged for a surprise dinner party—the one and only time Anna didn't mind, since he'd invited only people she truly loved. He had taken her for a two-hour walk on the beach and when they returned, there on the front porch were their friends at tables set with snowy linens and pink roses. There was a string quartet on the lawn, and hired servers to fill champagne flutes. Sometime during that evening Anna wondered where she would be for future birthdays and vaguely imagined that it would be right in the same place, with Hugh beside her, maybe just the two of them drinking wine on the beach after a quiet dinner in town. This, this sticky-floored bar with its torn vinyl booths and damaged-looking characters—of which she supposed she was one—was the last place she would have guessed.

Greta walked in finally, grabbing two pool cues on her way over to Anna's booth. "Sorry I'm late."

"Is everything all right?" Anna said, noticing Greta's bloodshot eyes.

"No, but I'm not talking about my problems right now. This is your night." She gave Anna a pool cue. "Follow me, Fifty-three."

Anna laughed and walked with her friend over to the pool table, then watched as Greta racked the balls. The look on Greta's face was precisely the reason Anna was done with relationships.

Other than Greta, she didn't even especially want friendships. The older she got, the more any successful human relationship seemed impossible. There were men around when she needed or wanted them—Anna thought of them as white cells; whenever she felt a little low, the monocycles and leukocytes attacked the virus of loneliness until she felt better.

She'd had a few dalliances in the years since losing her husband, but no one had truly held her interest.

"Your turn," Greta said. "You're stripes, and we're playing slop."

"Naturally," Anna said, and her shot sent two balls thumping off the table. "Oops."

Greta gave her an exasperated look, then signaled to the waiter for another round.

"I shouldn't," Anna said. "I teach tomorrow and I still have quizzes to grade."

"Oh, bull. It's your birthday. You need to be self-indulgent. If you were a man in mid-life you'd be buying supersized SUVs with equipment racks for sports you don't even play."

Anna studied the table for a decent shot. "I need to do something out of character. I think I'm in a rut." The third martini was a mistake: Alcohol never had the mellowing effect on her that it seemed to on others. She didn't need to be stirred up, didn't want to think about regrets or mistakes. She didn't get the career she'd wanted, but she got an unexpected bonus in her husband who made her life just as fulfilling—more, probably—than if her plan to become a surgeon had worked out. She had things in her life now that satisfied her—her music, her teaching—and if her world was smaller and more lightly made than it had once been, it was also easier to let things go and let small pleasures step in for any epic striving after happiness, whatever that was.

Anyway, what satisfied her these days were quiet, low-key things— hanging out with Greta, rehearsals for the community chamber orchestra, helping out with an occasional charitable event.

"Earth to Anna," Greta said. "It's your turn."

Anna lined up a sure shot, but it went wide of the pocket.

Greta laughed. "What's the matter, granny, got the shakes?"

"Give me a break. I'm almost a senior citizen. In some states, I'm old enough for a retirement community."

"Sure. Any minute now you'll be breaking a hip and taking in stray cats. Watch my youthful dexterity now: six, corner pocket."

Anna watched Greta concentrating on the game, along with, she saw now, most of the men in the bar. Greta was in her late thirties, though she looked much younger. She commanded attention wherever she was. It was her hair, partly, the shimmering length of gold, but there was something else, too, something intangible, as though she carried her own weather with her, changing the air from cool to warm, from low pressure to high, whenever she walked into the room. Greta was a big woman, not heavy or especially tall, but outsized somehow, awkwardly postured, as though she were constantly bumping her head against the ceiling of her life and coming away wounded. It was this air of bruised vulnerability that made her more beautiful.

Anna was grateful that she didn't worry about losing her looks as she got older. Men were attracted to her for reasons other than physicality, she knew. Hugh once said it was her aura of aloneness the first time he saw her at the freshmen mixer, her cool blue dress and watery drape of dark hair, the proud tilt of her chin, as though dancing or standing alone made no difference to her at all. Anna believed that the ideal world would consist of two physical types of women: those powered by estrogen and maternity, and those who functioned on the rational hormone of progesterone, cut with a little testosterone, for a competitive edge. She'd have chosen the latter, hands down.

Greta sank the eight ball and ended the game. "Another?" she asked.

Anna said no, but agreed to a nightcap at Greta's when it became clear that her friend didn't want to be alone. "I'll see you at home then," Anna said, and ducked into the ladies' room to wash her face. She felt a little sick, light-headed with a sudden dread. She put her hands under the cold water. A man was speaking Spanish on the pay phone just outside the door. He was angry, whoever he was. He looked her up and down when she came out.

"Señora," he called.

She turned. He held out something to her. One of the hairpin brooches. She took it from him. "Gracias," she said, and saw that he was breathtaking. Beautiful dark eyes and lovely hands, lean and elegantly dressed in closely cut trousers and a yellow shirt that looked like raw silk. She turned the pin over in her hand. The one with the silver forget-me-nots. She put it back in her pocket. She might keep this one.

Back at Greta's, Anna put on a pot of decaf while Greta checked her phone messages. Anna ran her hands over the smooth blue and white tile on the butcher-block island. Greta's things were nice, of the highest quality. Beautiful copper-bottomed pots hanging on a rack above the sink, wonderful smells in every part of the house—cinnamon and dill in the kitchen, eucalyptus and lavender in the living room. Greta usually had a vase or two of daises or baby tulips, but wandering now through the rooms, Anna counted no fewer than ten vases of exotic flowers. "Who died, anyway?" Anna said, nodding toward a huge arrangement of pink orchids and Asian lilies.

"I know. Isn't that something? Mike's been bringing them home. Every other day. I suppose I should be suspicious."

Anna raised an eyebrow.

"Birthdays, anniversaries, or forgiveness. Is there any other reason a man brings a woman flowers?" Greta opened the linen drawer, pulled out a pack of cigarettes from beneath the dishtowels. "Wanna do something wicked?"

"I didn't know you smoked," Anna said.

"I don't. Only when I'm feeling rebellious. Mike hates it."

"Sure, I'll have one." She'd been a regular smoker in college, but hadn't had a cigarette in at least twenty years.

Anna followed Greta to the deck in back. A small fence here separated Greta's yard from Anna's. "I have to ask, Greta."

"Yeah?"

"Is everything all right? Between you and Mike?"

Greta didn't answer at first. "I don't know," she said. "He's staying away longer and longer. He sometimes leaves the house at six in the morning and doesn't get back till nine or ten. Yesterday he didn't get home until midnight."

"Well," Anna said, "well, what do you think?"

Greta exhaled, shook her head. "I don't know. I doubt he'd be that brazen if it were another woman. He'd at least have the decency to lie to me."

"Where does he say he's been?"

"Driving. Just driving around."

"He might be. I mean, that might be the truth." There had been a time in Anna's own life, as a new mother, when she felt at peace only in the car. Though she never came close to leaving her family, the possibility that each exit off the freeway held, knowing that with one turn she could take the off-ramp and head into Canada, was beguiling and thrilling. Those early years, especially, when Hugh was working a twenty-four-hour shift at the hospital, Anna sometimes felt as if her life were as precarious and flimsy as a rotten floorboard.

She'd been a scholarship student at Smith, double-majoring in chemistry and physics when she met Hugh at the freshmen mixer. Her plans were to go on to medical school—by her junior year she had been accepted early decision at Tufts—but the romance with Hugh was so intoxicating and so perfect that Anna couldn't imagine anything going awry. They married the month after graduation. Their plan was for Hugh to get through medical school and into a residency before Anna started her studies.

She completed a med tech program in nine months and worked in a lab to pay the bills. It was easy, pleasant work, a temporary stopgap while she waited for her turn to go to school. Even in her long hours alone while Hugh worked, her boredom with the repetitive lab work, she was satisfied with their life, glad to come home at the end of the day to their shabby rooms with the threadbare furniture and the smells of bad cooking from the neighboring apartments. It was the kind of marriage she'd always wanted but dared not hope for. Everything was exactly on track the first two years. Then Anna discovered she was pregnant. She and Hugh had been so careful, and Anna knew her cycle so exactly—down to the hour she ovulated—that they never worried about accidental pregnancy.

She knew when she had conceived. Hugh had gotten a rare four days in a row off and they drove up country to stay at Hugh's family summer home in Maine. Anna was the happiest she'd ever been, riding bikes and walking along the beach every afternoon, the two of them eating lobster in the burnished gold of evening light, lulled by the hiss and roil of the water and the waves.

Anna had never thought of herself as a mother and was content with a childless marriage. The idea of an infant infuriated her, made her feel panicked and trapped.

She wanted Hugh to at least consider aborting, but he wouldn't hear of it. Hugh tried to reassure her. "Nothing will change, darling. We'll simply switch jobs. I'll get into a residency program, and then you'll go to medical school. We'll get a nanny for the baby."

Except that it didn't quite work out that way. Hugh joined the orthopedic surgical staff at Boston General. Anna had Poppy—named after Hugh's grandmother—and prepared to begin her studies. But the baby left her exhausted, and there were dinner parties for Hugh's new colleagues, social events for doctors and their wives, and clubs Hugh suggested she join, including one called The Medical Wives' Society. She laughed at him. But he pleaded with her, said he knew it was a bunch of bored women, but it didn't entail much more than afternoon teas, a charitable event or two.

"How can you possibly ask me to join something like this?" she'd said to him. "It shows so little respect for who I am that I have to wonder if you know me at all."

"Anna," he said quietly, "darling Anna."

In the end he won—though she didn't think of it that way; she loved him, and she made the concession. She dressed up and lunched at the club once a month, sat through the endless chatter about shopping and decorating and suspicions about pretty, predatory nurses. Twenty-five years later, Anna still occasionally attended some of the Medical Wives' events. There was nothing like the consistency of disliking someone for nearly three decades to make one feel ageless.

Anna shook out another cigarette from Greta's pack and lit it. "I'm fifty-three, what a drag," she said. "Anyway, my insomnia is back these days, so you can call me later tonight if you want."

"What are you going to do now?"

Anna stubbed out her cigarette in the potted geranium. "Grade papers. Then practice, if I'm still cogent. I've joined the community orchestra again, and Rachmaninoff's on the program, which would have put me behind even if I hadn't missed the first two rehearsals."

"Oh," Greta said, looking past Anna to the street.

Anna hugged her. "It will be okay. Call or just stop in at any hour. Last night I was up till four."

"Okay. Thanks for hanging out."

"Thanks for calling off the surprise party." Anna went inside to get her jacket and bag.

"Oh, hey," Greta called.

Anna turned.

"You dropped this." Greta handed the hairpin to her.

"This again," she said, and felt the hole in the lining of her coat pocket.

She sat in the dark when she got home, not tired enough for bed but not sharp enough to practice or to read through two dozen quizzes on viral pathogens. She kicked off her shoes and headed to her bedroom where she saw the message light on her machine blinking. Greta, probably, it was only ever Greta these days. She pressed the PLAY button.

"Mother, it's Poppy." There was a pause. "I hope you'll call me back, it's kind of important." Anna heard a child's voice in the background, a girl who must be Flynn, the granddaughter she'd never met. Somewhere she had photographs of Flynn as an infant. She must be about ten now. Anna braced herself. Poppy gave her number, an area code of 907. What state was that? The second message was also from Poppy: "Hi, it's me again. Well, I suppose I can just ask this on the machine. If I don't hear back from you in the next few days, I'll assume the answer is no. Marvin and Flynn and I would like to visit. This summer. In a few weeks. Hope to talk to you soon."

Anna sat down on the bed, and felt all the evening's earlier dread gather into a sickness in her stomach. She hadn't seen her daughter in twelve years. There were occasional postcards, but in the past five years Anna hadn't heard anything at all from her. And after Hugh died it was as if her daughter were dead, too.

Poppy left home at eighteen, with Marvin, the nut who called in response to the newspaper ad Hugh placed to sell the old VW bus that had been languishing in their backyard for a decade. Anna recalled exactly the day Marvin Blender came into their lives. It was October, and Hugh was sick. Poppy had just come back from Europe with a heroin habit. It was the worst time in their lives. A month after Anna and Hugh returned from their summer home in Maine, they learned that his extreme fatigue and headaches—he'd been complaining all summer but insisted it was from overwork and stress—was sarcoma. Anna herself drew his blood. His white count was so high that the slide looked like something by Monet, the cells like a covering of water lilies.

It was with this news that she and Hugh went to pick up Poppy at the airport. Anna watched the passengers disembarking, but not until Poppy walked right up to her did Anna recognize her daughter; Poppy was like a torn page from a favorite book, familiar but unidentifiable without the whole. She was so thin Anna could see her kneecaps jutting up against her jeans when she walked. Her hair, shoulder-length when she left six months ago, was now so short her scalp showed through. Anna knew right away, knew from her mask-like expression, the dullness in her eyes. Hugh refused to believe it at first, saw Poppy through the eyes of a loving father rather than the physician he was.

Anna went through Poppy's things, searched every inch of her room but found nothing. It was the cleaning lady who finally solved the mystery; Poppy had hidden everything in *their* bedroom. The heroin was in one of Anna's seldom-used jewelry boxes, the syringes in the bottom bureau drawer with the gift-wrap and ribbons. There was a note from Maria on the kitchen table on top of two tiny packages. *I knocked over the Mrs jewelry case when I dusted. These bags fell out.*

Poppy was in and out of the hospital, jaundiced, and then with hepatitis so severe that it left her with only sixty per cent liver function. She was in an on-site rehab program for two months before they released her to her parents.

By Christmas she was improved, had gained weight and was attending college classes part-time. She had a new boyfriend whom Anna and Hugh liked very much. There was talk of a wedding in a year or two, but Anna and Hugh both treated Charlie as if he was already part of their family. He came to the house every night and sat with Poppy in front of the television or with Hugh and Anna on the patio after Poppy went to bed. He was good-natured and patient, one of the producers of nature shows at WGBH, and most importantly, was crazy about their daughter. He'd been as tender with her as Hugh was.

Anna poured herself a double sherry now and took it into the bathroom to run a hot bath. No. She didn't want her daughter to visit. She slipped out of her clothes, into the hot freesia-scented water, and let her mind drift.

A year after Hugh's diagnosis, his cancer had gone into and out of remission, but by autumn the chemotherapy was working. He was exhausted, but in good spirits. One Sunday the four of them, Anna and Hugh, Poppy and Charlie, sat down to an early supper. Charlie had just returned from a deer-hunting trip with his brother so dinner that night was venison chili and cornbread. It was crisply cool. Hugh and Charlie took their after-dinner Scotches outside. Hugh was bundled up in the white wool cardigan Anna kept and wore for months after he died, convinced that it still held the scents of years of fine and perfect falls: hearty dinners spiced with rosemary and garlic, the tannin and woodsmoke in the air, the faint scent of wine from a spilled glass of Merlot.

Anna put on Chopin's nocturnes and watched her husband and future son-in-law bent together in the dusky light, the leaves from the overhanging oaks casting shadows on the broad, flat stones of the patio. After Hugh died, Anna sat for hours in Hugh's chair, in the exact tone of late-afternoon light. She watched those same shadows of leaves, the delicate filigree pattern on her skin like cool, finely tatted lace. She felt Hugh everywhere, his memory wrapped around her like an invisible shawl.

That day, Anna wondering if this was Hugh's final autumn, Poppy had come up beside her, took a step toward her mother as though to put her arms around her, but stopped. Anna and Poppy did not touch, hadn't since Poppy was a girl. They'd always been wary around each other, and Poppy's rough adolescence had driven them even farther apart. "It will be all right. It'll be okay," Poppy said.

Anna nodded, blew her nose. "Well. It's getting a little tragic around here. Will you change the music? Chopin is a bit too much right now. Maybe the happy fool," she said, her pet name for Mozart.

They were just sitting down to dessert and coffee when the phone rang. Hugh answered, and from his end of the conversation Anna knew it was someone calling in response to the ad for the VW. "Sure. That would be fine," Hugh said into the phone.

"You're finally selling that old heap, eh?" Charlie said, when Hugh returned.

"Sure. There's a demand for those old buses. A whole new wave of hippies coming up. Anna and I once drove across the country in that thing. Those were the years Anna wore miniskirts. All the way up to the watermark."

"What!" Anna said. "I *never* wore miniskirts."

"My dear, I couldn't forget something like that." He said it with such conviction and wistfulness that they all laughed.

Anna remembered Hugh wanted her to wear miniskirts. Maybe he had bought her one or two, she thought now, turning on the hot water tap with her toe, but she certainly hadn't ever worn short skirts. She balanced her glass of sherry on the edge of the tub, rolled a towel behind her neck.

They had just started eating when Marvin showed up. Hugh had told him to come at seven-thirty, but he must have driven over the minute he hung up. Charlie spotted him first, a tall man in a long black coat, with straight, shoulder-length dark hair. He walked around the backyard, shielded his hand over his eyes and stared in at the house, directly in front of the dining room window. With that strange coat—Anna remembered it as a military type of thing, double-breasted, with brass buttons—and his hand over his eyes, he looked like some lost member of a battalion, unsure of the friendliness of the territory. He snapped his head this way and that, as though he heard his name in the wind.

"Who is this chucklehead?" Charlie said.

Hugh sighed, pushed his chair back and put his napkin on the table.

Charlie stood. "I'll take care of it, Dad."

They all watched as Charlie approached the man, who squared his shoulders, held out his hand. Charlie nodded, gestured toward the house, and the two of them walked to where the VW was parked.

"He must be the one who called," Hugh said, and looked at his watch. "I told him seven-thirty."

In a few minutes Charlie came back in. "He's interested but wants a test drive."

"The keys are in the junk drawer in the kitchen," Hugh said.

Anna heard him rummaging around in there, through the heap of old keys and scissors, appointment cards and coupons that Anna clipped but then forgot about. "He'll never find those keys," Anna said. "There's a whole marriage worth of junk in there."

"I'll get them. I know what they look like," Poppy said.

Anna watched the stranger standing in the yard. There was something about him that made her uneasy, a cold spot at the base of her spine and the top of her head.

She wrapped herself in a robe. Some part of her knew, understood that this man would not just walk up, drive off with their old bus, and disappear. Maybe it was that she sensed Poppy's attraction to him. For whatever else he was, he was a gorgeous man: "There's a textbook specimen," Hugh had said, looking at him through the window. "A perfect bone structure." The man turned his head just then as though he heard this, and Anna saw the right angle of his jaw, the elegant slope of his neck. His hair was dark, but with highlights the exact shade of the turning maples. Anna watched as he held his index finger and thumb the way children do when they make an imaginary gun, and tapped the side of his head. His lips moved slightly, as if he were counting. "You might want to wait until the check clears before turning over the title," Anna said.

Poppy walked into the dining room, held up the plastic daisy key ring.

"Remember these, miniskirt Mama?" She dangled the keys in front of Anna, did a sexy swing with her hips. Anna laughed.

Charlie held his hand out, smiled.

"You know what, I haven't been in that thing since I was about five. I'll take him," Poppy said.

Charlie and Anna at the same time said, "No."

Poppy looked from one to the other. "No? And why not? Do you think he's going to kidnap me?"

Charlie shrugged, sat back down. Anna said, "Let Charlie take him, Poppy."

"Why?" She gave a surprised laugh.

Anna couldn't think of a why. She glanced over at Charlie who was taking a second helping of chili. "I don't know. Do what you want."

"Don't go far," Charlie said.

"Don't speed," Hugh said.

"Be right back," Poppy said.

An hour and a half later the VW pulled into the driveway. Poppy and the man walked up to the house at a languorous, conversational pace. Even from the distance of the living room to the end of the driveway, Anna could see her daughter's flushed face open with laughter. Poppy threw her head back and crossed her arms tightly as if holding herself together. Charlie glanced over the top of his newspaper. He wasn't the jealous type, Anna knew: He gave Poppy a wide berth.

"We're back," she called, as if this man were a houseguest or a visiting cousin. The man walked in, sat next to Charlie on the loveseat. "I'm Charlie Edwards, Poppy's fiancé," he said, and held out his hand.

"Hello again, Charlie Edwards. I'm Marvin Blender." He turned to Anna. "You must be Poppy's sister." Anna smiled tightly to show that she saw right through this; he might be able to fool a young woman like Poppy, but she had his number all right. "Are you interested in the bus?"

"You bet. She's a beauty. Great body."

Anna watched his face closely, waited for his eyes to so much as flicker

in Poppy's direction before she threw him out of her house. "I'd like to negotiate an offer," he said.

Hugh was resting, probably asleep, and she wasn't about to disturb
him for the likes of this man. "We won't negotiate the price. We're selling
it as quoted in the ad," Anna said.

He shrugged. "Fair enough. Will you take a personal check?"

"We'd prefer a money order or cash."

Poppy came in with two glasses of lemonade and handed one to
Marvin, who smiled up at her.

"I can do cash. I'll need to go to the bank, of course. I'll go first thing
Monday. How's that?"

Anna did not want to see this man ever again. He could drive off with
the stupid thing for free as far as she was concerned. "You know, you seem
like a trustworthy young man. I'll take a personal check." Charlie stared at
her like she'd lost her mind. "I'll tell you what. Write me a check now. I'll
take it to the bank tomorrow morning and once everything is square, I'll
leave the keys in the newspaper box along with the title and registration."

Poppy and Charlie both looked at her curiously. Marvin said, "Fine. I
understand." He sat back, sipped his lemonade.

Monday afternoon, after Marvin Blender's check cleared, Anna left the
keys and title in the newspaper box as promised, but it was two weeks before he came back to claim the bus and when he did he took her daughter
with him. In retrospect, it wasn't hard to see the course of it: Anna was
working full-time and Hugh was at the hospital all day. Poppy was home
most of the time, going to a class or two if she felt like it. She must have
started seeing him then.

The day Anna came home from work and found the note—*Have decided to do a little traveling with Marvin. Will call from the road.*—she knew
two things: One, that this wasn't just a whimsical road trip on Poppy's
part—flaky as she was, when Poppy made a decision it was with gravity—
and two, that they'd lost Poppy in some irretrievable way.

To her astonishment, Hugh and Charlie didn't treat it as an emergency
and dismissed her suggestion to call the police.

"How can you be so cavalier?" Anna asked Charlie. "This is the woman
you're going to marry. The woman you love."

"She'll be back," Charlie said. "She needs to get some things out of her system. I accept that. Poppy knows I love her. That I'm here for her."

"He's right, Anna," Hugh said. "Her judgment's off. She's a bit erratic right now, but she's a smart woman. She loves Charlie."

"Hogwash. You're going to regret this," she said to Charlie. "Either we act now or you're going to lose her."

"Now, Anna, you don't know that. There's no need to be alarmist. She might be back home before dark, for all we know," Hugh said.

"I do know this. I'm certain of it." She strongly sensed that Hugh would never see his daughter in the flesh again.

"Anna, darling," Hugh said. "She'll be back. This is vintage Poppy," he said with a false laugh, looking from Anna to Charlie. "Even as a young girl, Poppy had her own ideas about things. One time, when she was nine, she decided she wanted to go to Disneyland. Remember that, Anna? Somehow, she managed to get to the bus station on her own. She'll be back."

It was a full year before they heard from her. For a while, Charlie still came over almost every night, sat with Hugh and Anna to the end of the evening news. He wanted to be there when or if Poppy called. Anna watched him sink into a depression, then into a kind of helpless fugue state.

Finally a letter arrived from New Mexico. Anna tore it open and photographs spilled into her lap. Poppy and Marvin and an infant. She skimmed the letter. Marvin was some sort of artist. They'd gotten married shortly after leaving and now had a baby. "I've never been happier," she wrote. "Marvin is working full-time at his art and I'm doing this and that, going to school part-time and taking care of the baby, whom we adore. Her name is Flynn."

A year after this letter was another, one every year or year and a half for five years. When Hugh had fallen out of remission for what he and Anna both knew was the last time, Anna spent months tracking Poppy down. By this time she and her family were in Seattle. "It's just a matter of months or weeks," Anna said, when she finally got her daughter on the phone. "If you want to see your father alive you better come now."

"I'll get a flight next week," Poppy said.

Except that she didn't. Didn't call or send a card or get in touch with her father in any way. Anna made the mistake of telling Hugh that Poppy was on her way. He perked up every time the phone or doorbell rang, asked for Poppy until he drew his last breath. Anna couldn't ever forgive her daughter for this.

She rinsed out the tub, hung up the wet towels, then walked back into her bedroom and replayed Poppy's message. She picked up the phone and started to dial, then put the receiver back. What would she say? Yes, you can come. No, don't bother, I never want to see you again in my life. Maybe she should just call and find out why Poppy wanted to visit. Anna picked up the phone again, but instead of dialing her daughter's number, she dialed Greta's. Her fingers found the numbers as automatically as they found F-sharp on her cello.

Greta picked up on the third ring. "Hi, it's me. Were you asleep?"

"Are you kidding?"

"Is he home yet?"

"Not yet. What's going on over there?"

Anna suddenly didn't want to talk about it. She and Greta never talked about her daughter. In fact, Anna wasn't sure she ever told Greta about Poppy. Maybe once, when she first moved into the townhouse and gave her new friend a broad autobiographical sweep. An all-inclusive statement about burying her husband, the past, starting anew as nobody's wife or mother.

"I can't sleep, either." She paused. "Anyway, one of the doctors at school today asked me to pick my most compassionate student to lead a support group."

"Uh-huh," Greta said, and Anna heard her exhale cigarette smoke.

"Isn't that a mystery?"

"Why? What do you mean?"

"How would I possibly know if someone's compassionate?"

"What do you mean? Of course you know. Someone is either open or they're closed. They can feel another person's trouble and anguish or they can't."

Anna said that made sense, but deep down she suspected that this trait, along with the maternal one, had never been activated in her. She doubted if it was possible to understand someone else's suffering. Even her beloved husband whose pain had become a private geography on which she couldn't trespass.

Anna listened to Greta's lengthy examples of what compassion was. "Well," Anna said finally. "I'll be up for another hour or so grading papers so come over for tea if you want."

"Okay," Greta said, and sighed.

"And I might be calling you back to ask your opinion on whether you think forgiveness exists outside of biblical myths."

Greta laughed. "Oh, do tell."

"Nothing. It's all crap," Anna said, and hung up.

TWO

BODY OF THE BELOVED

From the window of their Back Bay apartment, Stuart watched Jack down on the street corner talking to the tiny Italian shoemaker, Mr. Fabrizi. He seemed to have taken up residence in the coffee shop next to the Korean grocery where Stuart and Jack shopped. Fabrizi came racing out to say hello every time he spotted Jack. Stuart could usually get by the window with just a friendly wave, but Jack was a verbal hostage to the scenes and tribulations of Mr. Fabrizi's life. Who knew why.

Mr. Fabrizi was gesturing wildly, the way he did when he talked about shoddy workmanship or how he couldn't break the habit of shining his wife's shoes every day even though she'd been dead over a year. Jack was nodding continuously, shifting from one foot to the other.

Stuart went into the kitchen to check the bread. Another ten minutes. He clothed the naked David magnets on the refrigerator with red panties from Venus. Stuart had been cooking most of the day. Their friends Leila and Jane were coming tonight to discuss what Jack called the Tykes for Dykes campaign: the women hadn't actually declared their desire for a child, only that there was something they wanted to talk about. Jack insisted it had to be about conception.

"Why else does a lesbian couple want to have dinner with a couple of beat-up fags?" Jack had asked earlier.

"Maybe they simply want our company. Friendship, Jack, remember that? People who you don't necessarily work for, sleep with, or want something from."

"Right, sweetheart, what world do you live in and where can I sign on?" He'd grabbed his wallet from the hall table. The Korean grocery was just around the corner. "Saffron, a pinch. Anything else?"

"No. That should do it. If for some reason they don't have fresh saffron, don't accept a substitute herb." The last time Stuart was in there looking for fresh rosemary, he'd somehow been hoodwinked into buying chervil, by the owner, Mrs. Kim. She insisted it would do "miracles" for lamb if he beat it with egg whites and basted every half an hour. The meat had ended up with a texture like milk jugs and a taste like lawn clippings.

"Back in a flash," Jack said, holding open an imaginary coat.

At the window, Stuart saw Jack was still at the corner, talking now to a young man. Jack held a brown grocery sack on his hip, which meant it was stuffed and heavy. He could never buy small quantities of anything. But if Stuart had sent him for saffron *and* coconut milk—which he could have used—Jack would be holding *two* bags. All of their household items were family size, huge bottles of shampoo that would be replaced with another kind before they'd used even half. When Stuart cleaned the bathroom last Saturday, he'd counted six bottles of shampoo, four conditioners—two deep, one daily, and a leave-in—and seven bars of soap. The cabinets and drawers were crammed with medicines for every possible ailment, foreign and domestic, including, Stuart saw with horror, Vagisil.

"Jack, there's very little chance either one of us is going to be afflicted with minor feminine itching."

"What?" Jack had called in from the living room.

"What's this Vagisil doing in here?" The package, thank God, was un-opened.

"I bought it, what do you think?" Jack said.

"Why?"

"It was in the sale bin at Rite-Aid."

"Oh, Jesus wept."

"Crocodile tears," Jack called back. "And it's not inconceivable that we could have female guests. My sister could come to visit. Don't throw it away, Stuart."

"Really, Jack. What are the odds that your sister would visit, first of all, and second, arrive with an itchy booty?"

"Itchy booty." Jack laughed. "Your talk of itchy booties is lost on me, darling. I can't tell one Japanese car from another."

Stuart took the bread out of the oven and set the table with the good china for their guests—he knew Jane would appreciate the Wedgwood plates. Jane was the first to befriend them when they moved from San Francisco a year ago. She was in personnel at the investment firm where Jack worked. Neither Stuart nor Jack had really wanted to leave San Francisco, but the Boston office had offered to double Jack's salary and it seemed foolish not to take it. Both agreed that if either one of them didn't acclimate well to New England they would move back. So far, Stuart didn't like it much here. The general atmosphere of the city struck him as distinctly unfriendly, one of suspicion and distrust. Partly it was that he missed his studies, the routines of academia. He'd been enrolled in the Ph.D. program at San Francisco State, working on an interdisciplinary doctorate in anthropology and art—specifically, the relationship between color and design patterns in Incan pottery and the culture's rituals and habits. His preliminary thesis linked human sacrifice and geometric landscape patterns on bowls. Stuart's theory was, the greater the culture's strife, the more intricate and beautifully bright the pottery. In the Bay Area, there was a private antiquities collector who trusted Stuart enough to give him a set of keys to his loft. Stuart came and went as he pleased, sat for hours in front of ancient grain bowls and ceremonial chalices.

Stuart hadn't yet found a doctoral program in Boston that seemed like the perfect match, but B.U. offered enough courses to keep him interested until he figured out where he wanted to study. Things would work out if he was patient. Jack was thriving, and for now, that was enough.

This coming October would be their ten-year anniversary. They'd met in a twenty-four-hour Walgreens in San Francisco. Stuart had run in for nighttime cold medicine. In aisle one, an obese woman flanked by two policemen was praying to Saint Cecilia and opening packages of curlers. "You know you have to *buy* those curlers," the policemen kept saying, but the woman went on rolling up her hair and shooing them away. In the pharmacy, the pharmacist was banging on the bulletproof Plexiglas and shouting at three boys who were stuffing their pockets with vitamins. By the time he'd come around and unlocked the door the boys had run out of the store, right past the cops guarding Saint Cecelia's acolyte. Stuart hung around the medicine aisle pretending to study labels so he could see how the commotion would turn out. A man dressed in a pink bathrobe and scuffy pink slippers, hair slicked back under a scarf and a fully made-up face, wheeled his cart past Stuart. He shook his head. "This place is getting so crazy," he said, nodding at the woman with the curlers. His cart had nothing in it but cosmetics. Stuart chose a bottle of NyQuil then stood in line while the pharmacist gave a description of the boys to the cops, who had the curler thief in handcuffs. Pink Scuffy wheeled up behind him, humming, and opening his package of press-on nails. The man in front of Stuart turned around to see who was behind him, then smiled at Stuart.

They exchanged small talk. He said his name was Jack. He was the handsomest man Stuart had ever seen in his life. By the time they left the store, Jack had mentioned a relay-for-life walkathon the following Saturday, a benefit for the Bay Area AIDS association. Maybe Jack would see him there. At this point in his life, Stuart had considered himself bisexual. For the past three years, he'd been living with a Japanese woman he thought he would marry. He loved Roberta, loved their camaraderie and ordered life, but it wasn't until he met Jack that he realized how being in love truly felt. Before now, he'd scoffed at claims of passion, thought anyone who blamed desperate or extreme acts on the mania of being in love was mentally ill at worst, too dependent on Hollywood depictions at best. Certainly, he felt pangs of tenderness when he was away from Roberta. But seeing Jack again had engendered a whole new feeling, as though his skin was electrified and stretching away from his muscles and bones, his body instinctively making a space for what he didn't know, until now, was love.

The day of the relay Stuart spent most of the afternoon threading his way through the crowds looking for Jack. He finally spotted him when the group ended up in Golden Gate Park for a picnic. Stuart watched Jack from a distance, felt something like sickness rise up in him: a man like Jack would never, he thought, be interested in the likes of him—soft, doughy, the scent of a woman and a woman's ways clinging to him. Looking at Jack—God, with his shirt off now—Stuart realized how much he'd let himself go. He'd always preferred libraries to gyms, theater to sports, but his body had never felt this lumpish and thick before. He looked around at the men at the picnic, admired some of them, was indifferent to others, but no one had the magnetic power Jack had. Stuart felt an ache when he looked at Jack, deep in his gut, like the emptiness of hunger. Stuart circled closer to him, stood in the group next to Jack—the men were three deep around him. Jack didn't once look his way.

Later, the crowd thinned to just a dozen men, Jack included, all of whom seemed to know each other. One of them suggested tequila shots at a bar around the corner and Stuart, though he promised Roberta he'd be home early, went along.

At the bar—a working-class, blue-collar place where all the men looked like pipefitters or union electricians—Stuart sat between Jack and another man from the relay, a blond in his early thirties with pockmarked skin and a '70s layered haircut, who gave Stuart dirty looks for getting the seat next to Jack.

This close to Jack, Stuart felt light-headed. He was gorgeous, by anybody's standards, his eyes not quite brown, not precisely green. When Stuart was a boy, he spent hours lying on his back under the birch tree in his backyard. The late autumn light on the underside of its leaves was what Jack's eyes reminded him of.

Stuart watched him for an hour before Jack spoke to him. Expressions moved across his face slowly, elegantly, like the passing shadows of clouds over mountains.

Just as Stuart was about to give up and go home to Roberta, Jack turned to him. "I know we've met somewhere, but I can't place you at the moment. I'm Jack."

Stuart took his hand, was so flustered that he could barely speak his name. Jack asked if he was new to the Bay Area; clearly he didn't remember the night at Walgreen's. "I came here four years ago. When I graduated from college, I moved here."

"Oh? Four years?" he said, and Stuart heard the reproach in his tone: So what the hell took you so long to find us?

Jack looked him up and down. Stuart cursed himself for not being in better shape, for tucking his T-shirt into his jeans so that his love handles were clearly visible when he slouched on the stool. His stomach was none too flat, either. He caught his reflection in the mirror behind the bar. His skin and hair looked all right; he had gotten a bit of sun and his hair was going golden, the way it always did in the summer. Jack watched Stuart watching himself.

"The answer is yes," Jack said suddenly.

"Pardon?" Stuart turned to him.

"You were wondering if I found you attractive. The answer is yes." He smiled.

"How can you presume to know what I was wondering?"

Jack laughed. "Sorry." He laughed again. "No offense."

Stuart shrugged. "None taken."

That was the beginning of his new life. It was that simple. All his agonizing over how or if he should come out was answered that Saturday. They'd gone back to Jack's place that night, and it was three days before he called Roberta. When he finally did go back to tell her and to collect his things, she wasn't angry or hysterical or accusatory. When he said, "I met someone," she guessed right away that it was a man. "How could you know that?" Stuart asked, incredulous.

"*You* were the only one who didn't know. I always knew it was just a matter of time."

In the end, they'd remained friends, though Jack became increasingly hostile when, in the beginning, Stuart met her for coffee or had her over to watch a video. She stopped coming over after a while. The last Stuart had heard, Roberta had gotten married and moved to Paris.

Stuart went back to the window to see where Jack was: still in the same place, talking to the unfamiliar young man. Who the hell was he? A boy, from what Stuart could see, a young man's hips and shoulders. Lanky, with the loose-jointed posture of a runner. "Pathetic, Jack," Stuart said aloud, and turned away. He no longer allowed himself to feel jealousy; Jack would always have men around him, would always be able to charm and enchant and seduce. At thirty-eight, Jack was still young enough to get the babies if he wanted; though many of the young ones were as unbearable and conservative as straight boys. This generation frowned on promiscuity and unsafe sex, was almost schoolmarmish in their dedication to healthy food, exercise, and monogamy. A good thing, in Stuart's opinion. The option of being conventional didn't exist when he was twenty-two. Back then, it was stay in the closet or come out in the margins.

Stuart walked into the kitchen when he heard Jack's heavy footsteps on the stairs, dumped the veal in the skillet to brown.

"Saffron boy is back," Jack said.

"That's a pretty big bag for such a little spice."

"Well, I bought some rhubarb and plantains, too."

"Super."

"I thought you could make rhubarb pie."

"Oh?"

"Or, maybe not. Whatever. What time are the bush-bangers due?"

Stuart looked over at him. He hated this side of Jack, hostility splashing like a leaky battery over everything and everyone he cared about. "Cool your jets," Stuart said.

Jack laughed, mocking. "Cool my jets? Really. Twenty-first century to Stuart, hello? Cool my jets?" He pulled the vegetable oil from the cabinet overhead, took down a skillet.

Stuart looked over. "What are you going to do?"

"Fry plantains. Did I ever tell you about the time I was in Malawi and ate so many fried plantains I shit yellow and green for four days?"

In his early twenties, Jack spent two years in the Peace Corps, building bridges and teaching English. "Only about seventeen times, " Stuart said.

"Cool your jest," Jack said.

"Anyway, plantains don't fit in with what I'm making."

"So? Who says it's for *them*? I want a snack. This is for me."

"You'll ruin your appetite."

"Never. I am a man of considerable appetites. I thought you knew that about me."

Stuart ignored him. It was best to just let Jack work himself out of this kind of mood. It no doubt had something to do with the boy in front of the grocery. Jack probably wanted to sleep with him, Stuart suspected, and either the boy didn't flirt back or Jack pulled back before it got to that point. Stuart was certain Jack had cheated on him twice since they'd been together: once back in San Francisco and once with someone here in Boston. He hadn't ever asked directly, but Jack's renewed attention and immersion in their lives together made him both want to know and not want to know at the same time. In his darkest moments, Stuart wondered about Jack's business trips and drinks with business associates that sometimes lasted until late into the night. Stuart himself had cheated once with a man he picked up in a bar just after he and Jack got together. He was, he supposed, testing the depth of his feelings for Jack as much as testing Jack's reaction—of course Stuart told him, and Jack was furious at him, not for the act itself, but for reporting it. "Who do you think I am, your little Japanese pussy? Why are you telling me this? If you lapse, that's something you deal with unless you're risking my safety in some way." A few days later, though, Jack came home and presented Stuart with a baby parakeet and launched into a discussion about fidelity.

Stuart cupped the tiny bird in his hands. "Am I supposed to cook or feed this?"

The evening ended with Jack's insistence on a monogamous, exclusive relationship. He made Stuart promise faithfulness and he pledged the same. Most of the time, Stuart believed that as an honorable man Jack could override his baser instincts.

"Try some," Jack said, blotting the plantains on a paper towel. He speared three slices at once and ate them, his eyes watering from the heat. "God, that brings back memories."

Jack was baiting him, Stuart knew. When he was feeling particularly feisty or frustrated, Jack started talking about Africa, about Tutti, the boy "who was as glossy as mahogany, so polished I could see my face in his biceps." Stuart thought maybe Tutti was an invention, like many of Jack's stories, a boy, perhaps, who guided him on one of his treks up a mountain. Jack had turned it into a torrid love affair over the years, gradually embellishing the tale until the ubiquitous Tutti was the great tragic love of his life.

"Wanna do something useful?" Stuart asked.

"Not now, dear, I have a wicked headache."

"There's fresh basil and garlic in the fridge. Make the salad. I still need to cook the cappellini."

"All righty. I think I'll slip into something more comfortable, though. I've had this monkey suit on long enough today."

"Okay. But can you step up the pace a bit? I'm feeling a bit harried. I still need to do the dessert and they'll be here in half an hour."

"Cool your zest." Jack picked up a handful of plantain slices, kissed Stuart on the cheek. "Back in a Gordon."

"What?" Stuart said.

"Back in a flash."

"And while you're at it, feed Loki. There's a new bag of seed under the cage."

*

They were halfway through the meal and into their second bottle of wine when Jane and Leila exchanged a conspiratorial look. Stuart and Jack both caught it, which made Leila color deeper.

"Okay *chicas*, let me say I *know* this visit isn't just for the pleasure of our company or for Stuart's fine cooking, which, by the way, is beyond superb." He raised his wineglass in Stuart's direction. "I mean, really Jane, you see my ugly mug every day."

Jane and Leila both laughed. "Well, actually there is something we'd like to explore with you," Jane said. She was a tall redhead, with long, Pre-Raphaelite curls that hung nearly to her back. In candlelight, Stuart found her beautiful, but in less forgiving light her skin had a strange uneven texture, scaly-looking, as though she were recovering from a bad sunburn. Jane usually wore loose, drapey clothes in jewel tones, Eileen Fisher-type things for stylish overweight women, though she was in fact on the thin side of average. Tonight she was dressed in a prim, petal-pink dress that made her look like somebody's Sunday school teacher.

Stuart liked Leila less, though his opinion might have been tainted by the stories Jane told of her. She was attractive, with strong, even features, though the military-short hair, combat boots, and multiple piercings seemed to Stuart more like a self-conscious statement of her sexuality than anything else. She was twenty-something, a domestic abuse counselor for some sort of women's program. She had a confident, self-contained air, which is what Jane reportedly first found appealing. "She's so poised for someone who isn't even thirty yet," Jane told Jack and Stuart the day she'd met Leila and claimed love at first sight. Jane, in her late thirties, had been through two troubled relationships in the year Jack and Stuart had known her. Katrina, the woman before Leila, had done a real number on her. Jack and Stuart both despised Katrina, a Croatian veterinarian who had lived all over the world, but mostly in Russia and Alaska, studying the seasonal feeding habits of reindeer and their possible links, through neuropeptide-y, to eating disorders in human beings—she talked about her research ad nauseum.

Jane grew so thin and unhinged over Katrina that she had had to take a leave of absence from work. Jane was, by everyone's assessment, brilliant. A summa cum laude Stanford grad, funny and generous, but with such bad taste in lovers Stuart wondered about her sense of self-worth. What he liked best about her was that she spilled over a lot, risked looking foolish in the way many truly generous and kind people did. She thought nothing of cooking meals for former lovers who had treated her badly, or moving them in with her when they lost their jobs.

Jane had met Leila as a result of Katrina, who had begun to leave thinly veiled threats on Jane's answering machine and notes on her car. Leila was the one who intervened and helped Jane get a restraining order.

One of Jane's most curious traits was that though she had a hard time leaving relationships, she didn't get involved quickly or fall in love very readily. She had pitch-perfect intuition when it came to people, including her own lovers, until she fell in love and her clear-eyed judgment turned fuzzy and myopic.

Jack and Stuart had high hopes for Leila, trusting Jane's assessment of her. They were expecting an Audrey Hepburn look-alike with the soul of an Earhart and the heart of Mother Teresa. What they saw was a woman—a girl, really—dark-haired and dour, whose face was so tight and immobile that it seemed to absorb all the light in the room without reflecting anything back. She was low-key to the point of no-key, answered their questions with shrugs and monosyllables. She was bossy and moody. There was nothing about her that gave a clue as to why Jane was so crazy about her. Even when Jane came over without Leila, she never really relaxed; she had become a clock-watcher, worried about getting home in time so as not to upset Leila, who would begin calling all their friends two minutes after Jane was due in. It surely wouldn't last, Stuart thought—Jane was probably finishing something leftover from Katrina. From his experience, you expressed in a new relationship the part of yourself that was repressed in the last. Although Jane seemed just as submissive as she had with Katrina, Stuart suspected this time it was out of choice and not fear.

"So, what?" Jack was saying now. "What exactly do you want to explore with us? Though I'd be willing to bet it's anatomical."

Jane laughed. Leila looked stricken. "Just as I suspected," Leila said. "Gay men, straight men, it makes no difference in the end. They all assume we're interested in their penises."

"Have you ever been interested in that? It seems to me you wouldn't recognize a penis if it jumped up in your soup," Jack said.

"Hey," Stuart said, warning, "hey."

Jane draped her arm across the back of Leila's chair.

"Anyway, prove me wrong," Jack said, and raised his eyebrows.

Jane looked at Leila, took a deep breath. "Well, as you know, Leila and I are sure we'll have a lifelong partnership." She paused, took a sip of wine, then drained her glass. Stuart refilled it. They all looked at Jane nervously, even Leila, who was watching her partner as curiously as Jack and Stuart were.

"We desperately want a child. I can think of nothing finer than raising a child with Leila."

Jack smirked at Stuart. Stuart looked away.

"I'm getting toward the outer edge of my child-bearing years," Jane said. "It's now or never."

"You'd be the one to get knocked up?" Jack said. "Or, excuse me, im-pregnated?"

"Yes."

"Wouldn't it make more sense for Leila to be the biological mother?" Stuart asked.

Leila looked at him suspiciously. "Of course we considered that," she said.

"My genetic profile is stronger," Jane said. "Leila's maternal line is marred by breast cancer and alcoholism. I come from Polish peasant stock. We live forever."

"This is a serious thing," Jack said. "It wouldn't be a simple donation. We'd want shared custody. It would be our child, too." Stuart looked at Jack, confused, then shocked. He seemed to be genuinely entertaining the idea. "After all, Stuart and I are just as committed a couple as the two of you, not to mention the fact that we've been together ten times as long.... Bringing a baby into this messy mix would mean that the four of us are bound together for the rest of our lives. That's what you need to think about. Not a scrap of DNA will leave my pants until there's a custody arrangement on paper, probated, in advance."

They all stared at Jack. Clearly, the women hadn't expected this kind of response. Stuart was baffled, though thrilled with Jack's ironclad assertion of their coupledom.

No one spoke for several minutes.

"Who's ready for some dessert and a dram of Grand Marnier?" Stuart went into the kitchen and fixed the desserts and drinks on a tray.

When he returned to the dining room, only Leila was sitting there. Jack and Jane were on the balcony outside, sharing a cigarette.

"They'll be back in a minute," she said. "So, what do you think of the idea, Stuart?"

He shrugged. "Jack and I need to talk about it."

"But, separate from Jack, how do you feel about the idea of children?"

"Well, quite frankly, I can't imagine *not* having them eventually. But I'm not convinced this is the right route. I can certainly see myself adopting a child someday."

Leila fell silent. They watched Jane and Jack passing the cigarette back and forth between them like a couple of high school delinquents. Stuart felt a pang of something—not jealousy or regret, but something about seeing Jack with a woman evoked the life he always assumed he would have. As a boy, his secret shame had been how much he desired the conventional life, how envious he was of the way girls could be so forthright about their longings for motherhood and marriage. More than anything, he wanted to be in a life-long partnership and to be a father. His was a rare family: his parents had been happily married, and his three siblings were all married now with children of their own. When Stuart left Roberta and moved in with Jack, his mother knew what that meant. Anyway, she told him, she'd always suspected. "I don't have a problem with it. I think love of any kind makes the world just a little bit better, don't you?" she said.

Instead of being relieved and grateful he was a little depressed, as though everybody but him had known all along. He occasionally wondered if he made the right decision leaving Roberta: he didn't love her the way men typically loved women, but would his love for the children he would have had with her been as strong as his love for Jack?

This was silly. He was just indulging in self-pity. He was lucky. Not many people felt for someone what he felt for Jack.

"We were just debating the turkey baster method versus the time-honored way," Jack said, stepping in with Jane. She looked weary all of a sudden.

"Dessert is served," Stuart said, passing around the plates.

Jack took a big mouthful of creme brulée. "Delicious, darling. What I think is, we have a game of naked Twister first, Steppenwolf or Golden Earring on the stereo. Everybody with me so far? Then, Stuart and I go do our thing in the bedroom, mixing it together. Then *both* of you baste yourselves. That way we're leaving something to God." Jack winked at Stuart.

Leila sighed, held up her hands and turned to Jane. "What did I tell you? I knew they wouldn't take this seriously."

"We'll talk about it later."

"Well, anyway, it's something we all have to think about," Stuart said.

Leila pushed her dessert away, untouched. "Are you about ready, Jane?"

They took their brandies to the balcony after the women left. The breeze was cool, smelled like rain. Stuart felt himself relax listening to the steady hum of traffic on the street below. "I have to ask, Jack. Were you serious? Is this something you want us to think about?"

Jack lit a cigar, tipped his head back to exhale the smoke. "No. I mean, I knew those dykes were coming here to ask that and I didn't take it seriously. But then I thought, here we are. I make good money. I know how much you love children. We're stable. Certainly ten times more stable than those two. I give Leila six months before she goes truly psycho. But I know one thing: I don't want a child with Leila and Jane. I love Jane, but I can't stand the women she dates."

Stuart reached for the cigar, took a puff. "We could adopt."

He poured another half-glass of brandy. "It's not politically correct to say this, I suppose, but it's our child or no child. In my Eden, anyway. I mean, my urges to parent are not so desperate that I'll be daddy to a legless retarded Chinese orphan."

"Jack, for God's sake."

"I'm a pig, I'm sorry."

"Anyway, we don't have to talk about it now. Unlike Jane, we have nothing but time."

Jack looked over at him, then quickly away, his expression impenetrable.

"Feel okay?" Stuart asked.

"Yeah." He reached over and squeezed Stuart's hand. "I forgot to feed the bird."

"Okay. I'll do it before we go to bed. I'm about ready to turn in, how about you?"

"Pretty soon. I want to finish my cigar."

Stuart kissed him goodnight. "I'll set the alarm for seven." He went in and fed Loki, ran water in the sink to soak the saucepans and skillets, then slipped into bed after swallowing a melatonin tablet. Between the brandy and the cigar, his stomach was queasy. He grabbed a book and sat up, heard Jack puttering around the living room and the melancholy strains of Chet Baker on the stereo.

Stuart smelled cigar smoke, which meant Jack must be having another and would be up for a while. He'd thought they would make love tonight—the renewed sense of togetherness in the presence of Jane and Leila, the warm pressure of Jack's hand in his. It had been almost a month. Not that he was counting. Well, he was counting, but he was trying not to let it bother him. Jack had insomnia. He was working too hard. Trying to build a good client base and subsequently taking too much on. Stuart shouldn't take it personally, Jack told him, but how could he not? Tomorrow he would start running again for sure. No excuses. Make himself so gorgeous Jack wouldn't be able to take his eyes away, insomnia, work pressure, or not.

He tried to concentrate on his book—an anthropological study of African Bushmen called *The Harmless People*. The cigar smoke seemed to be getting stronger, aggravating his nausea, the kind that signaled a migraine. "I smell smoke," he called in.

"What, darling?" Jack yelled back.

Stuart sighed. They still hadn't gotten used to living in a townhouse this size; in San Francisco their apartment was so small they could hold conversations in normal voices while in different rooms. "You're smoking in the house!"

"It's too chilly to smoke outside."

"You're going to kill the bird."

"I'm about through."

"Please put it out, Jack, or take it outside. The smell is making me sick. Are you coming in?"

"What, dear?' He called back.

Stuart closed the bedroom door, didn't bother to answer. He made sure the alarm was set, flicked off the light and fell asleep almost immediately.

*

At two o'clock, Jack was still awake. He was so far from sleep that he didn't even bother going in to lie down. He had another brandy, read through the current issue of *Details* and Stuart's *Vanity Fair*, sliced and fried two more plantains, which he then had no appetite for. He flicked on the TV, found nothing in the sixty-four channels that interested him, turned it off, turned the stereo back on—Coltrane, this time—and when even that didn't work, he went to the last measure, the foolproof guarantee to settle and relax him, a Robert Mitchum video. *Night of the Hunter* was his favorite, and hadn't yet failed to mesmerize him even after dozens of times through it. He nuked a bag of microwave popcorn, brewed some tea, and put the movie in.

But he couldn't concentrate, even after fast-forwarding to his favorite scenes. The popcorn tasted rancid. Everything lately, come to think of it, tasted off.

Jack tiptoed to the bedroom door, heard Stuart breathing deeply, then walked back into the living room. Even the bird was asleep.

He picked up his car keys. Gillian Welch had recently come out with a new CD and Jack had been meaning to get it for a while. Now might be a good time to find a late-night music store, to have something fresh to listen to.

Jack was sweating and dizzy by the time he got to the street. He walked past his car and knew as he did that he had no intention of shopping for CDs; for three hours he'd been talking himself out of what he was now about to do. The magazines, the videos, were like trying to stop a spillway with paper plates. It was like a craving for a drug, this restlessness in him. Years ago, when he used coke, this was exactly the feeling he remembered, this hollowness nothing but the drug could fill and which refused to budge even when he distracted himself in any way possible. Everything that wasn't the drug knocked against the steel need of it.

He was just walking, just taking a walk in the direction of the Korean grocery. He was equally divided in his desire for the boy to be there and not be there.

There were times lately when he felt nothing but extreme self-hatred—like he could kill himself without a second thought—or pure nothingness, as though his brain translated the rich textures of the world into a blank. He was empty at the center, his life without edges or direction.

He slowed as he neared the grocery, then stopped. He stared in the window at the jars of tiger balm and green tea. He glanced to the left and right, saw that the streets were empty. Relieved, Jack turned to go just as the boy stepped from around the side of the building. His mouth was turned up in a sneer and he flicked his cigarette into the street in a way that was both laughable and touching, a boyish imitation of something from a movie.

"How you doing," the boy said. He stepped closer to Jack, so close that Jack could smell his skin—musky and fresh in the way only a young man can smell, a combination Jack always thought of as fresh hay and nervous sweat. "Wasn't sure you were coming," the boy said.

Jack winced. This made it sound so planned. What Jack said earlier when he met the boy in front of the grocery was, "maybe I'll see you around sometime." He certainly didn't arrange a date. Jack looked back in the shop window, not sure now about the signals: earlier the boy had been loitering at this corner, caught Jack's eye and smiled as Jack walked into the store. The boy was beautiful in his white tank shirt and gym shorts, his skin light brown, but gold, too, so smooth Jack's mouth watered with a craving so achingly intense he had to lean against Mrs. Kim's meat cases and pretend to be studying the bizarre animal parts—pig's feet, hooves, and what looked to be half of a cow's head shrink-wrapped on a Styrofoam tray, its glassy eye as dark as a child's bedtime.

The boy was Hispanic—or part Hispanic. He had the fine-boned features of northern Spain, sculpted cheekbones and a broad, high forehead. His hair was black and curly, cut just above his ears. Jack was halfway in love because of those ears—delicate and pearly as shells—and those blindingly white and even teeth. The boy's body was nearly hairless, as far as Jack could tell, except for the fine down on his legs and arms.

Back outside, he stopped Jack and asked for a light. Jack found some matches, and lit the boy's cigarette, then bummed one of the Winstons for himself. The boy's hands were perfectly manicured, his fingers long and brown. They talked about the weather, the heat, and Jack made a joke of the Dahmer-type meat case inside.

But now Jack wasn't sure. Was the kid a professional? Surely Mrs. Kim would never allow this, would have spotted him at a hundred yards and called the cops if the boy had been there longer than five minutes.

Jack turned to the boy who was watching him intently. "What's your name?"

"Hector." He put out his hand. Jack shook it.

"Would you like to walk with me?"

"Where?" Hector said.

"The park?"

"Do you have a car? A car's better."

"I do. Except that I'm walking." It was no trouble to go and get his car, of course, except that he didn't want Hector anywhere near it. The idea of Hector seeing his forty-thousand-dollar BMW embarrassed him.

Jack smiled, took Hector's hand, squeezed it, then led him to the back of the store where the dumpsters were. The air felt hot and linty back here, vented exhaust from air conditioners and clothes dryers. Jack pulled him under the small awning. He backed Hector against the building, leaned his body against the length of the boy's and kissed him. Hector's lips were soft, his mouth as cool as wet grass. Jack ran his tongue over Hector's smooth white teeth, caressed the satiny fingernails. He tilted his hips, rocked a little, encircled Hector's narrow waist and hard belly, then down, inside his pants where the hair felt like corn silk. Jack sank to his knees, took the boy in his mouth and tasted the musky salt of him, the warm pearl of fluid. Jack imagined Hector in some tropical setting, Honduras, Guatemala, some dusty side street with vendors selling melons and bright fabric. He closed his eyes, ignored the stench of cabbage and rotting fruit coming from the dumpsters, and saw Hector in a wrought-iron bed, white sheets and a red velvet coverlet. Black and gold embroidery of stylized birds on white satin pillows. Urgent Spanish from the street below. A ceiling fan with bright streamers and the scent of roses perfuming the air. The brown gold of Hector's legs wrapping around him, a carved exquisite figure against stark white sheets.

Hector pulled Jack to his feet and kissed him, a clumsy, childish kiss that told Jack at once this boy was a professional. This was a kiss learned with women, quick and careless, half-attentive.

He guided Jack toward him, stroked him harder. "Do you have a rubber?" Jack said.

Hector shook his head. "I'm clean. I've been tested."

"Still…," Jack said. He and Stuart got tested every six months at first, but since moving to Boston they'd been lax. Stuart would never cheat on him—except that one time he told Jack about—and Jack hadn't cheated on Stuart. He did backslide once, but that was just before leaving San Francisco, a two-week binge with half a dozen or so anonymous pickups. But he used protection every time. Well, with two exceptions, but those had been with men as safe as gravy, bi-curious men at bars—not bathhouses—who hailed from suburbia and Sunday services.

Nearly a year ago, just a month or so after they moved here, he'd had a scare: flu-like symptoms, night sweats, a nagging cough and a high fever. He obsessed about it for a week, knew that these could be early signs of sero-conversion. Just to be safe, he called an AIDS hotline and asked about his condition. The young woman on the other end said there was no way to be sure without being tested, but that if he was positive, was indeed sero-converting, the night sweats wouldn't abate and it was likely that he'd end up with a secondary infection—a respiratory illness, a cough that persisted. Jack had decided it was the flu, since his symptoms disappeared in four days and in the mornings the sheets were sweat-free.

Jack smoothed Hector's hair back, looked into his eyes as he pushed himself into Hector's body, tight and narrow and snug all around. He moved slowly. Hector closed his eyes; his mouth drawn thin and hands splayed against the brick wall to steady himself. "Oh," Jack said. "You are so gorgeous."

He'd felt strangely calm when he thought he might be infected. There was a little part of him that was curious, that wanted to experience the disease without actually having it. When his sister got pregnant she tried to describe to him how it was. "It's like this creature inside me is part me and part not," Susan said. "What I think about most, though, is how rooted I feel, how closely linked I feel to Mom and Grandmother, and all the way back. It's like this continuation."

That's exactly what Jack had felt when he imagined he might be infected, the lineage of all those he'd ever loved and his lovers' loved ones, through this virus, a kind of terrible, merciless child who gestated over and over.

"You are so beautiful." He kissed Hector's neck, licked the sweat at his collarbone and thought of how he could get through the next day, and the one after that, without seeing him. He rested his head on Hector's shoulder, inhaled the scent of clean laundry. Jack imagined Hector's mother washing this shirt for her son even as Hector sweated through her good intentions. It made Jack sad for a moment, thinking of this boy's innocent mother looking after her son in this way. Or perhaps Hector had a girlfriend. Jack shuddered. He kissed the cool bone of Hector's nose, traced the elegant arches of his silky eyebrows.

Hector straightened his clothes. He pulled out two cigarettes and handed one to Jack. "Maybe you could give me some cab fare," Hector said. "Maybe a little extra, too, since I got fired last week."

Jack nodded, pulled out fifty dollars from his wallet and folded it into Hector's hand. So, that was it. Jack knew this kind: not a prostitute, not a cruiser, but an opportunist, one who was no doubt propositioned at some point by a queer like him and learned to take advantage of it. "Let me ask you, Hector, did you like that?"

Hector shrugged. "Sure, I like. Whatever. I like you." He smiled.

Jack stopped himself from asking when he could see him again, if he lived at home with his mother, or with a woman.

"I gotta go, man," Hector said. "You be good."

"Right back at you." Jack flashed him his best Robert Mitchum grin, the one that had charmed men on both coasts.

Jack finished the cigarette and started home but thought better of it. It would be best to have a window of time before returning to Stuart.

He passed dark storefronts and a few college bars with unbearably loud music and shrill female laughter. A single malt Scotch would be nice, but he wasn't about to go in one of these places replete with fat, cheesy-thighed college women and their breeder boyfriends.

Normally, he wasn't this misanthropic. The baby discussion with Jane and Leila had put him in a strange mood. He was surprised, then shocked, at his own paternal longings. It was specific to Stuart, he understood now. It made sense. Stuart as a parent to his child made sense.

He walked another block. A bar at the end of the street looked promising; it was dark and relatively quiet. He peeked in the open door. Just a dozen or so people staring up at a television. A few couples here and there in booths. Two thirtyish men playing pool. He went in, ordered a double Scotch, neat, and stared up at ESPN. He drank quickly, let the alcohol smooth down the rough edges in his head, the snags his thoughts kept catching on: the beauty of Hector, his love for Stuart. It was because he loved Stuart so much that he had fucked Hector. All other men were pathways to Stuart—how could he ever explain that to anyone? That other men were a way to reclaim what he gave of himself so completely to Stuart. It was, he thought, precisely because his love for Stuart was so constant and abiding that Jack strayed. Or maybe it was just greed, pure and simple. Because Stuart had everything Jack needed, giving into temptation was, if not wrong, then wasteful, like going into a grocery store and heaping a cart with things he wouldn't use. But who didn't need this comfort? Who didn't want to believe there was plenty of everything in the world?

THREE

THE CHILD OF FAITH IS MAGIC

Anna awoke before her alarm, set for six, and got up to make coffee. In the month since her birthday she hadn't slept well or long enough. It was easier to stop fighting it, to simply get up and start her day at whatever hour she opened her eyes.

It was four-thirty now, well before even the summer dawn, plenty of time to get in a few hours of practice. The orchestra rehearsal was tomorrow, with the first performance of the summer in two weeks. Anna still hadn't mastered the Rachmaninoff, the elusive fifth, which seemed as chaotic to her as any music ever written: the piece simply refused to be herded, the notes like small animals darting in and out of the corner of her brain, sliding down her arms into her hands before screeching off again, whippet-like eighth notes skittering away in wild terror.

Just short of an hour, she put her cello down and wandered to the window. Mike's car was outside, a good sign since, this early, it probably meant he'd parked it there last night. Anna assumed he'd been coming home at decent hours, since Anna hadn't had any late night calls from Greta in a week or so. She skimmed the newspaper, washed the dishes from the night before, glanced over some student quizzes on bacterial infections, and mopped the kitchen floor. At eight o'clock, when she finally picked up her cello again, the phone rang.

"It's me," Greta said.

"How's tricks? What's the news of the hour?" Anna looked at the purple fingerprints on the sheet music, a casualty of the Wright's stain used for medical slides that never seemed to completely wash off. She checked her cello to make sure none of it had marred the wood. Anna prized this cello, a gift from Hugh when she started playing again, right around the time she turned forty. It was Austrian, and its tone was lovely and somber and full, the golden whole notes of a lake loon.

"Are you terribly busy?" Greta said.

"I'm just sitting here about to spread my legs for Sergei, the sullen S.O.B."

"Who?"

"Mr. Rachmaninoff. I'm about to start practicing."

"Oh. Okay, then. I'll let you get back to it."

"No, wait. I'm also desperate for distraction. What's up?"

"Mike needs to go into the office for a few hours, and I need to get to my rehearsal. My car is in the shop again."

Greta's group, the No-Tones, was opening the symphony's summer season. "Can I borrow your car?"

"Sure. If you have it back by two." Anna had selected one of her students to oversee the AIDS patients' extra group time, and she had an appointment with the student and Nick Mosites later in the day. "I'll tell you what, I'll drive you into the city, then come pick you up later. I have to be at the hospital for a meeting anyway."

"Are you sure?" Greta asked.

Anna said that she was.

Greta's rehearsals were in Cambridge, in an old warehouse near Harvard Square. There were probably twenty or thirty children, Anna guessed, ranging from ages six to ten. She sat in one of the folding chairs—might as well stay for part of the rehearsal—with the parents off to the side, some of whom were wearing earplugs. When the music started she understood why: the bass was turned all the way up so the children could feel the vibrations. This was for rehearsal only; during the actual performance, Greta told her, the bass would be equalized and the children would rely on counting instead of the rhythm.

"Okay, parents," Greta called across the room. "This is the first dress rehearsal, so I hope by now everyone has purchased a costume for his or her child. Also, for those in the Beethoven sequence, don't forget to tease out the gray wigs. Think big. Think bird's nest. Think half-crazy genius." Greta held up a picture of Beethoven, his hair going every which way. "This is the look we want." Greta turned back to the children who were filing in. The older ones were in costumes of giant foam-rubber ears, their faces painted black and surrounded by Spanish moss to represent the opening of the auditory canal and the cilia within. The little kids were dressed as ears of corn.

The music was in a 2/2 time signature and turned up so loud Anna's eardrums ached.

The ears of corn swayed in a line at the front like a field with wind rippling through it, albeit a kind of rap wind, Anna thought. The children in front sang loud, with a pitch that Greta taught them to feel first in their diaphragms before sending the vibrations up to recreate the sounds in their throats. Anna was amazed. The harmonics were remarkable given no child had any idea what the next child was singing.

The kids in front sang: "We are corn. We can hear. We listen to the kernels around our ears."

The older kids, the human ears, stood behind the ears of corn and sang in counterpoint to the child in front. This was the part that was especially difficult, Greta had told Anna. The human ear singers couldn't lip-read to determine where, lyrically, the ears of corn were. The vibrations the human ears felt had to be mostly ignored, since they indicated the main melody line, not the harmony they were singing. But Greta had, miraculously, managed to pull it off. The whole production, Anna understood, was about faith, each child believing the vibratory sounds he made would harmonize with the whole.

A girl representing the wind—long diaphanous streamers tied to a gauzy gown—scampered around the stage and pretended to whisper to the ears of corn. The human ears bent toward the vegetable ones then began to dance and sing, this time without music. The story line here was something about how silence was the way of animals and plants, and the manner by which wisdom was channeled from heaven to earth. The creatures who used language heard only dumb mumbling.

The finale showcased three Beethovens who entered from stage left, one with a viola and two with violins. The trio played the first movement of Beethoven's fifth. Eyes straight ahead, without sheet music, and without any mistakes that Anna could hear. The performance ended with the wind coming back and announcing: "Magic is the child of Faith."

"Okay," Greta said, and signed, clapping along the whole row of children to show her appreciation. "Very, very good. Beethovens, perfect. Let's do it one more time through."

Anna caught Greta as she was rewinding the cassette tape. "I'll be back to pick you up before five."

Greta nodded. "Nifty, huh?" she cocked her head toward the children and grinned.

"I can't tell you how wonderful it is."

Anna still had over two hours before her meeting at the hospital. Insomnia always accelerated her pace; she moved faster through the world, did things in less time than when she was fully rested. She drank a cup of coffee, then went into an enormous bookstore and wandered aimlessly through the aisles for an hour before landing in Travel/Adventure. A book of essays written by women who hunted big game caught her eye. The cover depicted a middle-aged woman beside a dead bison, holding up the animal's head as though she expected it to smile. Anna skimmed through it, put it back, then picked it up again and tucked the book under her arm. There was another about a woman who had hunted antelope in Africa. She would buy this one, too. She had never in her life been interested in hunting, very rarely even ate meat, so why she was buying these two books—three, now, as she spotted an autobiography of a woman deer hunter—or why she was picking up a flyer attached to a shelf about a women's hunting group, was a mystery to her. Something about watching Greta's children had taken her outside of herself. Those pitch-perfect Beethovens, especially.

Anna had been at her peak, musically, at twenty-three, but hadn't known it at the time. Her playing was the best it would ever be, though her technique sharpened and became more sophisticated over the years. She'd played Rachmaninoff occasionally as a young woman, along with Saint-Saëns, who used to be one of her favorites but whose music she hadn't touched in thirty years. Something to do with emotional complexity; nuances of tone and pitch had been more accessible when she was young, though that seemed counterintuitive. She'd have imagined that the somber weight of, say, late Beethoven or the measured sorrow of Bach's cello suites would become more familiar over time.

She remembered playing Saint-Saëns one late afternoon in her junior year in college, ditching her biology class in a sudden fit of melancholy. She stood by her window, watched the slant of October light shimmer over the quad. Back then, she could stand on any note and let herself sink down to the bottom.

She walked out to her car. What if she really was the kind of woman who wanted to hunt lions in Africa? A woman of independence and ferocity, not worrying about social conventions or niceties, oblivious to personal and professional failures, focused on the thrill and danger of dusk falling on the Serengeti. A version of herself she often longed for but couldn't be: the Anna who loved humanity and read books about safaris and knew how to field-dress a moose. Maybe a boyfriend for her elderly years, quiet days and drives up-country on weekends. The Anna of even emotion and even-temper, of peaceful sleeps and hearty appetite. *I am not Prince Hamlet and have never been*—stray lines of corrupted poetry from long-ago college literature classes, swirling around her head. *I am not a pair of claws scuttling along the bottom of the ocean.*

Anna spotted her student, Amy, and Nick Mosites sitting in the corner of the hospital cafeteria.

According to the criteria Nick had given Anna—a student with a good working knowledge of basic immunology, compassionate, bright—Amy had seemed the obvious choice. But here in the hospital with the smells of sickness and Betadine and formaldehyde, Anna's nose went into panicked overdrive and she second-guessed herself. Amy was young, but that wasn't it. It was that she was too eager to help. The compassion necessary for facilitating an AIDS support group probably had nothing to do with embracing alternative lifestyles or empathizing with another's suffering, and everything to do with seeing how things like support groups didn't matter a damn in the long run, then proceeding anyway.

"Anna," Nick said, and waved her over.

"Howdy," Anna said, and sat. "You're early."

Nick tapped his watch. "No, actually, you're late. We said one o'clock."

Anna rarely got meeting times mixed up, but it was possible that she had misunderstood. "Apologies," she said.

"Perfectly all right. Amy and I were just reviewing what her role will be."

Anna turned to her smiling, freshly scrubbed student. "And are you comfortable with it? Does it seem like something you can manage?" Anna asked.

Amy nodded. "I think so. I mean, yes."

Anna listened as Nick spent a half an hour reviewing the objectives of this support group, and how to recognize when it was her job, as a moderator, to steer the discussion into a different direction if necessary. "You'll do fine. Occasionally patients might ask you for medical advice, but you'll remind them that you're not a physician. The focus should be on living with AIDS, not dying from it. A chronic life-threatening illness, not an immediate death sentence."

Amy said she understood.

"This is really just an overflow meeting, remember, at the patients' request. So, your primary duty is to defuse the occasional outburst. Most of these group members have known each other for years. If there's anything you're unsure about, call one of us."

Amy nodded. Anna looked at Nick. "Us? Who's included in that pronoun?"

Nick said, "Me, Dr. Klein, the psych resident, and you."

"Me? What kind of assistance would I be?"

"Oh, just in the capacity of Amy's mentor," Nick said.

Anna felt her temper flare a little; she'd told Nick from the beginning that she had little interest or belief in support groups. But, she turned to Amy. "That's fine. I'm sure you'll be terrific, but you can always call me if you need to."

"And I was hoping you wouldn't mind just sitting in on the first meeting, which starts at three. I reserved the conference room on the third floor for today and next week. Subsequent meeting places yet to be determined. Maybe here, maybe not. I'll let you know." Nick looked at his watch. "Okay, Amy, if you want to head upstairs, Anna will join you in a few minutes."

Amy stood, gathered her papers. "Thank you, Mrs. Brinkman," she said to Anna. "For agreeing to help me the first few weeks."

Without missing a beat, Anna said, "It's my pleasure, dear. This is a good opportunity for you." She smiled, waited until Amy was gone, then turned to Nick. "You're a jackass."

"Anna—"

"I didn't agree to anything other than to provide you with a student, who by the way, from what I can tell will be nothing more than a glorified babysitter."

"Now, Anna—"

"My husband was a physician. I know how hospitals run. Risk management probably wouldn't agree to let you have the extra time unless you provided them with a coordinator. Which is in name only."

"That's not true, Anna."

"Someone from the janitorial staff would also qualify. Or one of the clerks in the gift shop."

"Anna!"

She stopped.

"I did tell you that your student's role would not be as an official mental health worker. It's true that it's hospital policy to have an appointed leader for any gathering, but it is certainly not true that I am using her as a glorified baby-sitter."

Anna took a deep breath. "And is it also true that I'm sitting in on these meetings for the *first few weeks*?"

"Well, that was unfair of me not to ask you. I'm sorry. But I told you I wouldn't be available Saturdays. I'd supervise today's meeting except that I'm filling in for a colleague on hospital rounds. For which," he said, and looked at his watch, "I'm late. Also, Anna, I do think Amy will be more likely to admit any problems or concerns to you than to me or Klein." He paused. "I'll make it up to you."

"Oh? What did you have in mind?"

"Dinner?"

Anna snorted. "Pass. But I wouldn't say no to five or six new Bausch & Lomb microscopes for my lab. Or a box of rare specimen slides of viruses from far-flung places."

"Done," Nick said.

Anna stood, turned to go.

"Oh, hey Anna." Nick held out the book she had left on the table, frowned at the title, *Women Who Roar: A Pride of Women Hunting in Africa.*

She took the book from him and headed upstairs.

The next hour was such a disaster that even Anna was tempted to walk out fifteen minutes into it the way Amy herself did.

How was she supposed to anticipate this? She'd been around medicine most of her life, had helped people, including her own husband, through sickness and dying. She'd softened the blow of bad news, and helped the convalescing, but this illness, apparently, didn't gentle and humble most people the way something like cancer did. Anna was half-expecting exhausted patients propped up in chairs and their equally exhausted caregivers. Instead, she heard them from halfway down the hall when she first walked up. The room was filled with a riot of personalities and the sugar-saturated energy of a kindergarten class.

As soon as Anna walked in, Amy brightened and introduced herself. "Hello, I'm Amy," she'd said, and the group of them, in unison, replied, "Hi, Amy," as though it were an AA meeting. Things tumbled downhill from there. They interrupted her, talked over her, and ignored her attempts to moderate the discussion. Anna remained silent; she didn't want Amy to feel undermined.

Then fifteen minutes into the meeting, Amy walked out. Anna stayed and finished out the hour, then went immediately to find Nick on his rounds.

"Hi," he said, writing in a chart. "How did it go? Where's Katie?"

"Amy. She had the good sense to leave."

"Shit," he said, and snapped the chart closed. "Was it as bad as all that?"

"Worse than all that. Those men gave her a hard time."

"I'm sorry. They're lively it's true. I thought I told Allie that."

"*Amy*. You did, but she's out of her depth here."

"Maybe I should have prepared her better." He waved over a group of residents, who were huddled together at the nurses' stations like a flock of starlings on a telephone line. "I have to finish rounds, but can we talk about this later? I'll call you tonight, okay? We'll sit down with the next student you give me for a few hours. I should have stressed one of the unique features of this illness. Assholes become complete assholes as they get sicker. This is the single most difficult thing the patient's caregiver has to deal with. Their partners were always a little demanding and obsessive, for instance, but now when they're really sick, it gets out of control. I'll call you later."

"No," Anna said. "Sorry, but I don't think any of my students are adequately trained for this. Why don't you ask one of your students to run it?"

Nick glanced over Anna's shoulder. "Dr. Lee, start the rounds without me. Room 405, sixty-year-old Caucasian male who presented with abdominal pain. Hypertensive, previous M.I." Nick waited for the group to walk past. "I told you, Anna. My residents are ridiculously overworked as it is. I can't ask them to take on extra duties. Well, I did ask, but none of them agreed to help out. If you don't want to commit another student, I'll just tell my patients that there will be no overflow Saturday group until I can find another moderator. They'll have to adjust. Sorry to have involved you in this."

"Okay," Anna said. "Good luck with finding someone. By the way, why did you come to me in the first place?"

He shrugged. "Hugh used to talk about how bright you were, how much you loved medicine and how good your instincts about people were."

Anna caught her breath. "You knew my husband?"

He nodded. "We were on-call together a lot when we were residents. He talked about you all the time. We were all envious of him. Of how lucky he was to have a wife who understood the demands of the job."

Anna leaned against the doorway of a supply closet. From inside, a panoply of odors reached her, the most prominent of which was Xylene, the chemical used to clean microscopes and slides. Hugh used to tease her about how much she loved the scent of it.

"Let me think things through. I'm not promising anything, though. But it seems to me that if I give you another student, I should give you a lion, not a lamb."

Nick looked at her over the top of his glasses. "What do you mean?"

"I mean, you don't need someone with a surplus of compassion, you need someone with an edge who can deflect all the insults. Edges, I understand. The touchy-feely-weepy instinct is one I never had."

"You might be right," he said. "Incidentally, was there one person in particular who drove Amy away?"

"Well, sort of. Two men. They were having a fight about blue socks."

"Alan and Michael. I would have guessed that. I'll speak to the two of them. They're almost always keyed up."

"Okay. Because if I agree to send in another student, I'd ask that you kick them out the minute they start with the personal insults."

"Deal," Nick said.

The two men had dominated the first fifteen minutes of the meeting. One partner accused the other of intentionally losing his lucky pair of socks, which resulted in three ensuing sleepless nights until the socks were found. The sleeplessness, he claimed, then further weakened his immune system. Anna's head reeled from trying to follow the man's logic.

"It's this kind of carelessness that got me sick in the first place," the man had said. "It's recklessness. You either keep track of what's important or you don't. You didn't, that's why we're here."

Amy had stepped in at this point. "Let's keep the discussion on one thing at a time."

"There is no one thing at a time, sister. This is everything at once. That's what you need to understand, but never will." Amy burst into tears and stood to go. "That's right, leave. Go back to your Girl Scout camp and toast marshmallows with your little flower friends. You can tell them all about your day with the big bad wolf who huffed and puffed and blew your house down."

"That's enough," Anna said. "Stop it." He was quiet then, but his words hung in the air. There was truth behind his rage. How could she or Amy— or any noninfected person, for that matter—understand how it felt to be assaulted by an illness like this? He was rude, certainly, but she thought now it might be more than that. Maybe it was the impatience that came with having a finite number of years left. Even small bits of time were weighted. Social niceties were wasteful, including the few seconds it took to introduce oneself. That was her hunch, anyway.

Anna turned to Nick now. "I need to get going. I'll get back to you early next week."

"Sounds good," he said. "Thank you."

She was halfway down the hall when Nick called her back. "You dropped these," he said, and handed over her car keys. She really needed to sew the lining of her pocket.

It was still too early to pick Greta up, so she went into her office. She enjoyed working in the deserted building on weekends. She liked the emptiness of the offices, the absence of inhabitants echoing those Bible stories her maternal grandparents pelted her with during her girlhood summers where the virtuous were taken up to heaven, the world drained of all but the wicked. Their beliefs eventually made them a little pathetic to her, but she liked the peace and solitude and beauty of the Lancaster County farmland, spent hours wandering around the neighboring Amish pastures and properties.

Anna's parents were eclectic in their religious beliefs. Her father was a Jewish convert to Buddhism, a professor of Eastern Studies at NYU. Anna's mother worshipped only her career as a physicist. Once, Anna's father had taken her to a Seder at his parents' apartment in Manhattan. She remembered a gathering of women, though surely there were also men there. She was ten or eleven and fascinated by the women in their black dresses and lace mantillas, serving the hard-boiled eggs and salt water. Her father had sneered, before and during the meal. When he donned his yarmulke, he crossed his eyes and stuck out his tongue at her. Afterward, the two of them left early to get the train back to Brooklyn. Her father tossed his yarmulke into a trash bin on top of a crumpled newspaper.

"Sorry, dear," he said. "I'm getting old and sentimental." He shrugged, smiled. "Wanted a sampling of my boyhood, I suppose." Anna had laughed with him at his mocking irony, but secretly she was enchanted. She thought the Seder was beautiful, though she wouldn't admit this to him, and part of her never got over the disappointment in her father for shielding her from such reverence, for keeping this part of her heritage secret and out of reach.

She called home to check her messages. One from Greta to tell her she was already at home and didn't need Anna to pick her up, and two more from her daughter. Anna would have to call Poppy back tonight, she knew, since unlike the first message when Poppy said she'd take Anna's silence as a no, her daughter had called three more times.

Poppy must be assuming Anna was still trying to make up her mind, which she most certainly wasn't. She never wanted to see her daughter again, period. There was no forgiveness big enough.

She turned on her microscope, slid one of the student-prepared slides underneath the lens. It was waxy and opaque with stain, as were the next five she checked—all unreadable. She would have to repeat the lesson Monday. Anna picked out the slide for AIDS from her specimen box, focused it under the light. She thought about what Nick had said earlier, that patients' unpleasant characteristics often became exaggerated. Part of her wanted to push aside the issues of psychology and empathy and all the man-made handholds and explain everything at this, the cellular level. There was something moving about retroviruses like AIDS, the fact that an individual's DNA was scooped out like half-melted ice cream to be replaced with the virus's own code. She found it inexplicably engaging, the notion that all the various personalities of the sick in that awful meeting harbored the same skewed viral coding, a bad science-fiction movie coming true, everybody slowly becoming the same person in the end. It was easier to forgive tantrums when one saw the devastation at this microscopic scale, the heroics of the battle being fought over each of the body's cells.

When Anna got home she found Greta in her apartment. Anna had given her the keys and told her to use them anytime, but it was a bit disorienting to find furniture—she'd finally gotten a decent couch and table—Jimi Hendrix on the CD player, lit candles and huge vases of flowers. There were six arrangements in the living room alone.

Greta came out of the kitchen with two glasses of wine. The scents from the kitchen were of rosemary and lime and rich autumnal spices.

Anna smiled. "Are you trying to seduce me, dear?" She nodded at the flowers on the coffee table.

"I was running out of room at home."

"He's still bringing you flowers?" Anna asked.

"He's bringing flowers home." She sat beside Anna on the couch. "He doesn't actually present them to me, they just mysteriously appear."

"So, he's been coming home, I noticed. I've been seeing the car parked out there."

Greta shrugged. "Anyway, something exciting happened." She picked up a stack of manila folders. "Today after the rehearsal, the mother of one of the Beethovens told me about an adoption agency that specializes in placing hearing-impaired children. I have five of them here. The oldest one is eight, the youngest is three." Greta opened the folder on top of the stack.

"Look at her. Her name's Lily, deaf since birth, natural parents deceased. Nearest relatives provided inconsistent care, in and out of foster homes since birth." Anna glanced down at the black and white glossy, then over at Greta, who was gazing at the photo with a kind of maternal intensity that made a heat rise in Anna. This impulsiveness was something she never understood about her friend: Greta heard about a group of deaf children in need of homes and by the end of the day had eight files, no matter that she had no idea of the burden and heartache of motherhood or that her marriage was in a precarious state.

"Well," Anna said. "You'll have to make some sober decisions."

"I have. I want a child, and who knows better than me what it's like to grow up in silence?"

"What does Mike think about this?"

"I don't care what he thinks. I'm doing it with or without him."

Anna shook her head and took a sip of wine. "You need to think about it. It's not like getting a puppy from the pound."

Greta looked at her sharply. "There's nothing I've ever wanted more than to be a mother, which I will be, one way or another."

"I'm sorry. I know." Anna looked away, a little ashamed. She thought of her own body and its prodigal fertility. It wasn't fair, Anna thought, her ovaries with their clutch of eggs falling uselessly all those years like beads from an unused evening bag. Early on in her pregnancy, the O.B. ran his fingers lightly over her abdomen and said, "Young lady, you are superlatively fertile. You have years of childbearing ahead of you." Anna had looked away, furious. And later, after she had given birth, the doctor made some smug comment—to her ears, anyway—about her elegant internal architecture that had made for such an effortless labor and delivery. "Oh, and what kind of elegant architecture will make raising this child easy?" Anna remembered asking.

Anna looked down at the folder of the little girl. Blond and curly-haired with a round, cherubic face. She flipped through the stack of the others. No boys in the bunch. "Are you set on a girl, or were there no boys available?"

"I want a daughter."

Anna nodded. The biggest disappointment after finding out she was pregnant was delivering a female. If she'd had a son her life would have been more open somehow, richer and finer, she was sure of this. Daughters were doomed in a way sons were not. A girl would never get everything she wanted. Girls were born divided—part of them would always be in thrall to family or nurturing in some way or another. How could a mother look at a newborn daughter and not relive the disappointment of her own life? Although perhaps that wasn't quite the way to think of it. Maybe it was just a matter of personal preference, whether one liked the traces of things or the things themselves: sons came through you and left to pursue their own lives, which was what made loving them as children—she guessed—poignant. Girls, well, most daughters, never really left. Daughters were dazzleflauge, a herd of zebras in which one was indistinguishable from the next. She'd heard other mothers say that they didn't know where the mother ended and the daughter began. As for Poppy, Anna had never felt her daughter to be fully present or foregrounded; she was merely part of the landscape of Anna's life. Here for a while, then gone, a presence indistinguishable, an absence unnoticed.

"Do you think I should consider a boy?"

"Yes," Anna said. "I mean, I wouldn't rule against any child based on gender alone."

Anna felt an uncomfortable silence rise up and she knew Greta was waiting for her to offer information about Poppy. She'd glossed over that part of her life so quickly when they first met that Anna didn't know for sure what—or if—Greta remembered. But Anna saw from her friend's expression, the hard defensive set of her jaw, that she certainly had.

"I wanted a son, quite frankly. My daughter and I were estranged almost from the beginning."

Greta looked up.

Anna shrugged, poured herself another glass of wine. "Some women aren't meant to be mothers. I'm one of them."

"But you love her, right?"

"Of course," Anna said, and wondered if this was true. She searched through the stack of folders until she found the one she spotted earlier and liked the best. A little girl who looked to be of mixed race, whose intelligence was apparent even in the poor quality photograph and strange department store studio smile; to look at the faces with their forced ear-to-ear grins one would think the whole lot of them had just been pulled from

Santa's lap. "I like this one," Anna said, "Rashida McNeil. She's smart, you can see it in her eyes."

"I know. I was looking at her. Kind of a rough history, though, might have some behavior problems."

"Anyway, there's a lot to think about." Anna wanted to be done with the subject. She hoped Greta would reconsider the whole idea of adoption. It was stressful enough when you had nine months to work yourself into being somebody's mother; Anna couldn't imagine anyone intentionally saddling herself with this role overnight. And what if the kid turned out to be defective? What kind of trauma would Greta be in for if she'd have to return the child? But of course, Greta wouldn't ever do that. Anna picked up the vase of hyacinths on the end table and inhaled their sweet and heady perfume. There was no scent she liked better than this, no fragrance in the world that carried her back in time more than this. The languid days of her youth when everything was possible and still ahead and richly promising. She put the flowers down when she saw Greta watching her. Anna hadn't meant her attention to the flowers to be a reproach, but she saw that was how Greta was taking it. The mysterious bouquets from an absent husband, the faces of the orphaned children blooming on the couch between them.

"You're welcome to stay here tonight," Anna said quietly. "As long as you need to."

"Thank you. I just might do that."

Anna sighed, grateful for Greta's willingness to let things go. "I remember what it was like to wait for my husband to come home so I could finish fighting with him." She laughed. "We'd have a little tiff in the morning, he'd go off to work, and I'd fume all day. He wouldn't take my calls, which only made it worse. By the time he did come home I would be homicidal. Mild annoyance turning into murderous rage over nothing." She paused. "I'd trade everything to have him back."

Greta's eyes filled. "What am I going to do? What am I doing wrong?"

"Nothing. Nothing is my guess. I suspect he's going through something that has nothing to do with you."

"How do you know that?"

"I don't. It's just a hunch." She remembered driving up country with Hugh, of the utter peace she felt with him, even early in their marriage. He used to hold her hand as he drove. The memory of the light of the north and the way his skin looked in it still had the power to stop her in her tracks. There was nothing more exquisite than that kind of happiness. Their fights were infrequent, but when they did happen Anna was frantic, terrified that this was the fight that would drive him away for good.

"I feel for you," Anna said. "Marriage is a kind of wonderful hell. I think I'd trade all my remaining years to relive just one of the ones I shared with Hugh. One of the good ones."

Greta nodded. "Let's eat. This is getting morbid. Mike's driving around. Until I can prove otherwise, I'm taking him at his word."

"A fine plan," Anna said, and moved into the kitchen.

After dinner Anna sat in the back room with her cello, too sleepy from the food and wine to really practice, but too restless to be good company either. She put the vase of hyacinths beside her and played a Brandenburg concerto from memory with her eyes closed, let herself relax under the mathematical logic of Bach and the scent of the flowers. She drifted back to the summers on her grandparents' farm, heard again the sound of the nighthawks and cicadas, smelled the cooling pies on the windowsill and the damp night air.

She forced herself back into the present, back into the knotty coils of Rachmaninoff. Why didn't orchestras play Bach anymore? She found her sheet music and jumped to the middle of the third movement, the one giving her the most trouble. Her hands simply weren't big enough to span the chords. She felt every note physically, an ache in the webs of skin between her fingers, the pressure of holding the strings tight when she bowed through the D chords.

The phone rang when she was a few measures into it. She hesitated, unsure whether to pick up or let the machine take it.

"Do you want me to get it?" Greta yelled from the living room.

"Well," Anna said, and put her cello aside. Greta was on the phone when Anna walked in. "Oh, hello. One second." She held out the receiver to Anna. "It's Poppy."

"What? Who?" Anna said.

"Your daughter."

What could she do? She certainly didn't want to talk to Poppy, but wanted even less to have to discuss the reasons with Greta. Anna took a deep breath. "Hello," she said.

"It's Poppy."

"Yes." Anna heard the crackle of long-distance static, an echo in the line. "It sounds like you're on Jupiter."

"Close. I'm in Alaska."

"Oh," Anna said. Greta was sitting on the couch in front of some epic war film she'd rented. Anna knew Greta was only pretending to watch the movie; the real drama was on Anna's end of the couch. There was a cordless phone in the bedroom, but before Anna could ask her daughter to wait while she switched phones, Poppy rushed in.

"I'm guessing since you didn't return my call that you don't want us to come. But I wanted to make sure."

"Well," Anna said. "No. I hadn't decided anything. What is it you wanted?" Greta looked up, raised an eyebrow. "I mean, what is it you wanted to discuss?"

"I really don't want to get into it over the phone. I was hoping you would say yes to a visit. Even a short one."

Anna heard a child's voice in the background. Her granddaughter. "Do you need money?" There was a trust fund, money in escrow from Hugh, that Poppy had never touched.

"No, it's nothing that simple."

Anna paused, listened to her daughter's breathing over the line, glanced at the television, where a battlefield scene shot from a great distance made the soldiers tiny, a teeming zoo of microbes. "Okay."

"It's okay if we come?"

Anna cursed herself for not taking the call in her bedroom. That way she could have insisted that Poppy at least tell her the general category of the question and let a little of her anger spill out. This would not be a visit about Anna welcoming her back. There would be no forgiveness.

"Mother?"

"When?"

"Two weeks? In two weeks?"

"That will be all right. So, it's possible to drive down from Alaska in about two weeks?"

"Oh, yes," Poppy said. "We plan to hurry. I'll call you when we get close, how's that?"

Anna said fine, and hung up. The men in the film were supposed to be gladiators, Anna determined. "Well, that's that."

Greta looked over. "Is everything all right?"

"No. No, it's not. Poppy wants to come and visit."

"That's not good?"

She shook her head. "No. Something's wrong. I feel it." She poured a glass of water. Her head was light, spinning, a panicked fluttering of adrenaline rushing through her.

Since childhood, a kind of knowledge, a prescience, welled up like it was now, with just these physical sensations of a racing heart and ringing ears, shaky legs and tingling scalp. But with her intellectual parents on one side and her devout grandparents on the other, she'd shut it out, disturbed by any knowledge that didn't come empirically or through one of her five senses. Occasionally, though, her intuition burst through anyhow: the time when five-year-old Poppy went to a pool party at the neighbor's house and Anna, two doors down, heard her daughter calling her. This was what she told herself, anyway, that she heard Poppy's voice, though over the drone of the TV—it was on continuously in those days—and the neighborhood traffic, it would have been impossible.

In a flash she saw her daughter face down in the water. She ran over, saw the group of children at the picnic table about fifty feet away from the pool watching some insipid discount clown with a black greasepaint cross on his forehead—Jokers for Jesus, she was horrified to learn later. The clown had two puppets, a headless John the Baptist on one hand, and a fierce, Old Testament God with a warty face and wild hair on the other. She scanned the dirty, fat faces of the children, and, not finding Poppy among them went straight for the pool where her daughter was already unconscious. She didn't know how she knew, but the knowledge, not where it came from, was what mattered. She'd always been suspicious of the Jesus-ridden Millers with their slow ways and absurd belief that Christ was some giant babysitter who wouldn't let anything bad happen to their precious flock.

"Anna?" Greta said.

Anna looked over.

"Is Poppy okay?"

Anna shrugged. "Time will tell." She sipped her wine. "She wants to come visit."

"Oh?"

Anna turned her eyes back to the television. "What is this movie anyway?"

"That's it? That's all I get? 'Time will tell'?"

"I don't know what to say. My daughter and I have never been friends. Contrary to what Hollywood and Hallmark want you to believe, mothers don't love unconditionally. No human relationship is without conditions." She reached for the bottle of wine on the coffee table.

"But she's your daughter."

"Yes, she is. A daughter who did unforgivable things."

"She's your child, Anna. Nothing is unforgivable, right?"

Anna looked at Greta evenly. And how would you know, she wanted to say, not having a child of your own, but instead, keeping her voice calm said, "I think some things are. Unforgivable is a promise to a dying parent you simply don't keep. To a father who adored her and called for her with his last breath. Unforgivable is making someone suffer because they're waiting for you. That look in the eye, that look of hope every time the phone rings. Unforgivable is not getting on a plane."

Greta squeezed her hand finally. "I hope you can work it out."

In the morning Anna awoke to the smell of frying bacon and Greta's voice on the phone in the living room. Greta had spent the night on the couch. The clock read eight-thirty. Anna was going to miss her nine-o'-clock orchestra rehearsal. Her insomnia was catching up with her and playing Rachmaninoff right now seemed as impossible as running a marathon. She stretched beneath the sheets, let herself drift, knowing from the pitch and intensity of Greta's voice that she was talking to her husband. She thought about Poppy, tried to imagine what could be so critical that she was willing to drive thousands of miles to see her. Something awful was going to happen, she was sure of it.

Greta came in with two mugs of coffee. Anna sat up. "What's the good word?"

"I was just talking to Mike."

"Where is he?"

"Home now." She sat on the edge of the bed.

Anna sipped her coffee, didn't speak. Greta's face was soft and Anna saw that something had been worked out between Greta and Mike. She would be a mother, Anna knew now, and would be heartbroken in ways she couldn't begin to fathom. In her mind, she saw Greta wearing a schleppy frock, her hair in pigtails. Saw her take her braids in each hand and tug, then watched as the braids became two children. Daughters. Greta would have two little girls. She looked at Greta now, her lovely hair and skin, her dreamy eyes. She would give anything to have a little of Greta's wide generosity, to have even a fraction of her impulse to believe in the goodness of people.

Anna flicked on CNN to shake the dreams and daydreams from her head. Greta turned at the sound of the television. "I made bacon and eggs and French toast."

"I'm getting fat," Anna said. "Your food is turning me into a bus."

"Yeah, right. Like that could ever happen. As a matter of fact, I've been thinking you might be too thin."

Anna shrugged. "Are you going to see Mike?"

"Later. I told him he can take me to dinner."

"You can come back here if things get too much. If you don't want to stay there with him. You know that."

"Are you sure?"

"Consider it your vacation home. Your exotic adventure land."

Greta gathered her hair into a loose ponytail. "Come and eat. You need to eat this breakfast I made. I'm feeling queasy."

Anna stared at the TV with its litany of hijackings and bombings and now a story of a cloister of nuns in southern France whose order was being disbanded—disordered would be a better word, she thought—because of the scarcity of new novitiates. She'd had a dream last night. Two dreams. One was of her granddaughter. The child didn't have any skin. Or, she did have skin, except it was black and baggy with decay. When Anna took her hand it stretched all the way across the street and still the child didn't move. Anna walked frantically, tried to pull Flynn—who looked nothing like a girl at all, but had a horrible, malicious face—but she walked for miles and miles, tangling people in the grainy translucency of her granddaughter's hand, the lines on her palm sticky as spider's silk.

"I had the strangest dream last night," Anna said, flicking the channel to local news to get the weather. She thought back to her first dream, a direct result, she was sure, of having read a P. D. James novel the night before about the human race dying out. "I dreamed I was the last person left on Earth and God was speaking to me and I refused to speak back. I was mad as hell about something."

Greta rose. "Come and eat this giant breakfast."

"Okay. On my way."

Anna tucked into the breakfast without much appetite. There was no room, she decided, for anything other than the dread that was already filling her.

FOUR

STUART'S COAT

Jack and Stuart, two Marilyns in a sea of Monroes, were riding down Beacon Street on a rose-covered float behind the Elks and just in front of a high school marching band. It was the Fourth of July parade, and PFLAG—Parents and Friends of Gays and Lesbians—had sponsored the float to raise public awareness of "gays in the mainstream, being civic leaders and holding jobs as lawyers and bankers and teachers."

Except that gays didn't, of course, go into surgery or onto the trading floor dressed as a fifties sex goddess; this campy image was exactly what PFLAG was trying to overcome. The men were supposed to ride in the parade dressed in their typical work clothes, but there were no volunteers until somebody suggested dressing up, something like "fags in drag, and dykes on bikes."

The president of the Boston chapter of PFLAG, a woman whose son had died of AIDS two years before, was incensed when she learned of the costumes. "You're promoting a stereotype. All gay men love fashion and movie stars. All lesbians are butch and wear leather jackets."

In the end the Marilyns had won out. "After all, if we're going to be ridiculed," someone said at the meeting, "we might as well be ridiculed as someone else."

The lesbians were divided—more agreed with the president of PLAG than not, but still, many of them, having heard of all the Marilyns, planned to come as John F. Kennedy. As it turned out though, not one JFK had shown up, and all fifty men sang Happy Birthday, Mr. President, to no one in particular.

"It's just like those bitches to bail," Jack said, adjusting his breast, which had slipped out of his halter-top. At a prosthetic supply store, he had found shelf after shelf of breasts in all shapes, sizes, and colors. He had no idea women would need this many options. He shopped for two hours, finally buying five pairs, two of which were for Stuart, C cups in Ecru and Bisque. The first pair was a standard young shape, round and high, very Heidi of the Alps, the other clearly for an older woman: National Geographic low-riders, the profile like change purses sagging with quarters. He bought the same size for himself only in slightly darker tints: Barely Beige and Born to be Beige, manly colors, Robert Mitchum shades. Just for good measure, he bought the pair of Rose of Sharon DDs he couldn't decide about in the store.

Stuart was mad, of course, when Jack walked in with the bag of boobs.

"So what?" Jack said. "Don't you think women buy them this way? The average consumer of these things must try a hundred and fifty pairs before she finds the right ones. It must be twice as hard as finding jeans that fit."

Stuart pursed his lips. "They're not socks, Jack. You don't buy a pair and a spare." He threw up his hands. "I give up. I'll just put the extras next to the vaginal cream in case your sister visits."

From the front of the float Jack scanned the crowd. Hector was supposed to be somewhere along the parade route, had promised he would show up, if not for the parade, then for the party afterwards at Jack's friend Craig's house in Beacon Hill. Jack had seen Hector a handful of times since that first night, though lately he went out of his way to avoid him. He was starting to feel too much, found himself wondering about Hector's home life, fantasizing about him during the day and when he was with Stuart, which made him more ashamed than the actual cheating. Jack never fantasized about other partners when he was with a lover. And especially not with Stuart.

He glanced over at Stuart, slumped against the side of the float, his blond wig awry, his lipstick smeared halfway up his cheek. He looked so unhappy lately—no surprise, Jack thought, since though he'd been careful about where and when he met Hector, at some level Stuart must know.

Jack walked over to him. "You look like Marilyn during the DiMaggio years, darling."

Stuart looked away. "I guess I'm about ready for this to be over. My feet are killing me. And I've heard enough shouts of 'pervert' and 'fag' to last a lifetime."

Jack cupped his hands over Stuart's breasts, kissed his waxy, Cherries-in-the-Snow lips. "How about that? Are we now lesbians?"

Stuart laughed half-heartedly. He wasn't in the kind of mood Jack could jolly him out of. Jack knew it was best to just leave him alone. He sighed, patted Stuart's augmented ass, and joined the Marilyns at the front of the float. The men were throwing chorus-line kisses to the spectators, taking turns standing in front of a small fan that blew their skirts up.

Jack scrutinized the faces in the crowd—sparser now, since they were nearing the end of the parade route. Hector wasn't here, probably had no intention of showing up. The stupid, worthless boy. Who did he think he was? He was getting a little cocky, Jack thought, knew the rich fabric of Jack's attraction to him and played it down to the threads. He was getting bolder about asking Jack for money, had come to expect it, even. Jack always met Hector behind the Korean grocery, but never at a pre-arranged time. With one exception, whenever Jack wanted him, Hector was there. "Let's go to your place," Jack said the second to last time he'd seen Hector.

"Sorry, man. Can't do it."

Jack raised his eyebrows, but didn't ask. Hector hadn't offered any information either, which infuriated Jack so much that the next night, he adopted his best steely-nerved Robert Mitchum posture, left the house after Stuart was asleep, and drove by Hector's corner in his BMW. He slowed down and waved. Hector walked hesitatingly toward him.

"Just wanted to say hello. I'm on my way somewhere." Jack noted with pleasure, and not the shame he thought he'd feel, Hector's slow glance at the car, the look of envy and hostility as he took in Jack's Armani suit and Ascot Chang shirt. Just to be sure Hector saw the suit Jack flipped on the dome light, pretended to read a map, then waved and drove on.

Well, so what. It was pure physicality with Hector, that was all. Not love. Stuart was love. Sex with Hector was white-hot fire and ice mixing together and snaking up his spine in bright swirling colors. Being with Stuart was to be deliciously buried in a pile of leaves, Stuart's love for him falling down piece by piece to cover him. Anyway, his libido the past few weeks wasn't so strong. Something felt a little wrong, an edge of panic and desperation just beneath the surface of his days. It was partly physical—he was plagued by headaches, and his sleep dropped him off the steep cliff of horrible dreams—and in part just a garden-variety free-floating anxiety.

Jack tugged at the waistband of his pantyhose. The nylons were stuck to his skin, which only exacerbated the irritation and itch that had returned a couple of days ago. Last month, he and Stuart posed for a photographer friend who was putting together a book he was calling *The Redneck's Handbook*. The photographer, Avery, provided costumes from Am Vets—Jack's was a pair of Wrangler jeans and a black Megadeth T-shirt with the sleeves cut off. Stuart's look was Saturday-night-on-the-town: too-blue jeans with a Harley Davidson belt buckle and a Hawaiian shirt opened three buttons down. There were individual shots, and one of the whole group of rednecks, enjoying a redneck barbecue surrounded by crushed cans of Coors and tarty, trailer-trash girlfriends with crayonish eyeliner and hair that looked like it was sprayed out of a can. The shoot was great fun, and they actually did drink all those cans of cheap beer. He and Stuart had a grand time.

Two days later, though, there was a message from Avery on the machine. "This is terrible, but don't panic. When I was collecting the clothes after the shoot, I found a louse in a pair of pants. I'm not sure it's anything, or if it infected all the costumes, but just to be safe I'm bringing over a bottle of Qwell."

They checked themselves and everything was fine, but used the lice shampoo just in case. A few days later Jack had had some kind of allergic reaction. His crotch felt like it was crawling with fire ants, and the rash on his upper thighs and genitals had scabbed over and simply refused to heal. Stuart's reaction was similar, though his rash faded in a day or two. Jack bought some anti-inflammatory cream, a drying talc, but so far, it wasn't helping. In fact, he thought it might be getting worse.

"Jack!" one of the Marilyns called to him. "Somebody is trying to get your attention." Jack walked over to where the man was pointing, scanned the faces of the crowd lining the sidewalk, his heart leaping and ready to forgive Hector his surliness, his secrecy, anything. But it was just Jane and Leila.

"Hi, darlings," he said, blowing a Marilyn kiss, and standing in front of the fan so his skirt blew up to his waist. He'd found gorgeous black lace panties in the fat women's store. Jane and Leila screamed with laughter.

"Are you up for Craig's party, darling?" Jack asked, linking his arm through Stuart's. The parade was over and the men were scattering. Jack smiled as he watched five identically dressed Marilyns walk into O'-Malley's, a blue-collar bar.

"Sure," Stuart said. "A nice stiff drink is just what I want. Besides getting out of this absurd dress."

He looked so sad, so dreamy and abstracted that Jack felt a wave of sickness rising from his gut, self-loathing and regret. Why was it that it was easy to forgive the people who surely didn't deserve it, and so hard not to take the right ones for granted? Jack was making Stuart miserable, he knew, rejecting his sexual advances and ignoring his hints.

Stuart's face was lovely, even through the cheap makeup and streaked rouge that looked welted, as though someone had slapped him. He didn't know why being naked with Stuart right now seemed wrong. It had nothing to do with Hector, and Jack was as attracted to Stuart as ever—perhaps more than ever. If Stuart only knew how often Jack thought of him during the day, how many expressions of Stuart's he found endearing to the point of heartsickness—the way he raised his shoulders slightly, tipped his chin down to his chest when he laughed, for instance—he would be astounded.

"Do you feel all right?" Jack asked. "You've been so quiet all day."

"I'm fine. Just a little weary."

"Should we maybe go home and have a quiet evening?"

Stuart glanced over, looked meaningfully into Jack's eyes but saw at once that Jack's idea of a quiet evening didn't necessarily mean an intimate one. "No, let's go to the party. I need to shake these blues."

The party was so crowded that it took Jack nearly an hour to determine that Hector wasn't in any of the rooms. Curtis's house was amazing: a three-story Arts and Crafts-style design, with spiral steps that wound up three floors. The upper rooms all had open views to the downstairs. Jack saw people on every balcony. The living room was circular, with parquet flooring and exposed brick walls and antique furniture. Over the fireplace was a painting that looked like an original Andrew Wyeth. Jack wasn't in the mood, suddenly, for this high-pitched hilarity, the Twister game going on in the corner with the men in Marilyn lingerie, the loud shrieking music of the B-52s.

"I'll go get some drinks. What do you want?" Jack asked.

"Vodka tonic."

Jack wandered into the dining room, stopped at the spread of food—caviar, smoked salmon, prosciutto and three kinds of melons. He loaded up a plate, then loaded another for Stuart. Red Sturgeon caviar, it tasted like. This, too, was an awe-inspiring room: a Gustav Stickley breakfront and dining table, and, turning the corner of the carpet over with his toe, a real Oriental, he saw. His father would die if he saw this place, Jack thought, the dentil molding along the ceiling, the wide plank floors that looked like quarter sawn oak, the solid mahogany of the mantels. That was the one thing, the only thing, he had in common with his old man: like him, Jack loved beautiful carpentry and well-crafted furniture.

Jack took two highball glasses from the breakfront, mixed a vodka tonic for Stuart, and a vodka martini for himself.

"Any more people in this room and we're going to need a lubricant," a voice beside him said.

Jack turned. The man looked vaguely familiar. "It's quite a spread." Jack took a bite of the salmon. "This tastes like Scottish Spey," he said.

"It most certainly is. At forty dollars a pound."

"Jesus!" Jack said. "This is all so extravagant."

"You said it. Mr. Spare-no-Expense, Mr. Opulent, Mr. Dickhead."

"Oh, yeah? So he's your ex, I take it?"

"Darling, he's the X-files. There's a history to fill volumes. I'm Gary," he said.

"Jack." He offered his hand.

"So, Jack, are you involved?"

Jack smiled. "Sorry, yes." Gary was cute; a little too blond for Jack's taste, a little short, but he had a solid athletic build and a flat stomach. Stuart's stomach remained disappointingly poochy regardless of how much he worked out. "Excuse me a second."

Jack walked back into the living room and found Stuart deep in conversation with a woman. "Hi, darling," Jack said. "Vodka tonic, and a sampler plate."

"Thank you," Stuart said. "This is Pamela. She's a grad student in art history. We're discussing the Incans."

"Don't let me stop you. I'll be circulating."

Jack wandered in and out of conversations, circled through every room, finally ending up in the kitchen where there was a lesbian couple clearly in the middle of an argument. Jack pretended to look for something in the refrigerator. The women were silent behind him. He grabbed a handful of Greek olives, then went back into the dining room to make himself another martini. The stool where Gary had been sitting was empty. Jack went back through the kitchen—the women were now in an embrace—then outside to the backyard. Votive candles burned on low tables. He squinted at the shadowy outlines, looked for Hector's shape among the figures grouped in twos and threes. People were speaking in soft voices, almost whispers—but perhaps it only seemed that way after the screeching music inside. There was something a little spooky out here, an odor of compost and closed-up rooms. No, that wasn't it: it was a kind of graveyard smell. When Jack was eight, he and his brother, Ben, found an open crypt in a cemetery, and this was the smell he remembered, damp stones with the humid musk of decay.

A voice behind him spoke. "Hello, Jack."

He squinted. Gary. Just Gary, goddamnit. Where was that arrogant cocksucker Hispanic? "Hey. What's going on?"

"Just inhaling the luscious smells," Gary said.

Jack startled. So he noticed the strange scent, too. "What the hell is that?" He walked over, sat beside Gary on the chaise.

"I believe the technical name is Balm of Gilead." He swigged from a fifth of something.

"It's what? What's that?" Jack thought of embalming fluid.

"It's the scent of cottonwood trees. Isn't it wonderful?"

"Oh. That's not what I smell." He finished off the last of his drink, took the bottle from Gary and took a long swig. Tequila.

"Ho there, tiger!" Gary said. "What's troubling your Eden, sweetheart? What's bunching your Bradys?"

"What?" Jack said. "What's bunching my Bradys?"

"Who's the nasty Marsha making you feel like Jan?"

"Oh, nothing. It's nothing."

"Okay, sweetheart. Whatever you say. You just let Uncle Gary make you feel better. We'll get you launched on tequila for a start, how's that?"

Jack laughed. "And then what?"

Gary leaned forward, nibbled Jack's earlobe.

Between them, they finished off the bottle. Jack took the last swallow and got the worm, a nasty thing textured like a stale potato chip. He bit it, swallowed. He'd heard somewhere that the tequila worm gave you visions. Probably of the inside of a toilet bowl.

Gary's hand moved up Jack's leg, stopped just short of his crotch.

"Where can we be alone?" Jack whispered.

"Follow me."

Jack ducked around Stuart in the living room, followed Gary up the stairs.

The hallway up here was dark, with four or five doors, all closed. Gary took Jack's hand and led him inside a tiny room not much bigger than a closet. Inside, to their surprise, a man who looked to be in his fifties was lying on the narrow bed. The portable television blared "Baywatch," Pamela Anderson running around in that dental floss she called a bikini. On the bed were two or three magazines, and two James Michener novels.

"Oh," Gary said. "Sorry." He looked confused a moment, then said, "Who are you?"

"I'm Walt Eisenberg. I sell insurance," he said, in such a way that Jack thought for a moment that he wanted to write up a policy right then and there. "I'm Craig's uncle. Uncle Walt. I'm with Mutual Life of Omaha."

"Okay, whatever."

"I'm in town for an insurance convention. How's the party?"

"Swinging. How's the Baywatching?"

"Don't I love it," he said, and turned back to the set.

Gary closed the door, pointed to the staircase leading to the third floor.

The entire third floor was one open space that functioned as a library and study. Jack sat beside Gary on the leather sofa in the greenish light cast from Craig's computer. Jack looked down at Stuart in the living room. He was talking to a man Jack didn't recognize.

"Can they see us up here?" Jack asked, feeling like he was eight years old and ambushing girls from a tree house.

"Only if they look up."

"Maybe it's not such a good idea," Jack said. His head was pulsing from the tequila, his crotch with its colony of fire ants burning and painful. He'd have to see somebody about this rash. Except for cursory glances when he was soaping up in the shower, he hadn't really looked at it, but he thought it might be spreading.

"What is this?" Gary said, touching the inflamed area, which Jack, now partly undressed, felt on his belly.

"An allergy to a soap. Just a little contact dermatitis," Jack said.

"Is it contagious?"

"Are you an idiot? Can you catch an allergy?"

"Well, now, such an outburst," Gary said.

He was in no mood for this. All he wanted right now was to be home. He stood up, rearranged his clothing.

"Where are you going?" Gary said, petulant.

"Home."

"You bitch. You're not that good-looking, anyway."

"Sure, whatever."

"You old fags are all the same. Can't keep the promise in promiscuity."

By the time he and Stuart got home, Jack felt miserable. He was sure he had a fever. He was chilled and overheated, shivering then sweating. His throat felt thick. Stuart looked worried, though Jack didn't tell him the extent of how lousy he felt.

He took a long shower, first hot, then cold, then hot again—he couldn't seem to regulate his body temperature. The rash was spreading, and there were places where it had become infected—a sore on his inner thigh that he'd scratched open. He stood in front of the mirror, and was shocked. No wonder that boy called him old—he looked positively haggard, at least ten years older than he was. The scabs and bumps appeared much worse in the glass than they had when he'd looked down the length of his body. And when had he lost weight? His skin was the color of old ivory, looser somehow, a thin covering over the sprung trap of his ribs.

He toweled off, wrapped himself in a thick chenille robe and slipped into bed beside Stuart, who was still awake. Jack could almost feel him thinking.

"I'm fine," Jack said. "It's just a touch of flu. It's strange. I felt fine this morning. I felt okay as recently as a few hours ago."

"I want you to go to the doctor tomorrow," Stuart said. "Call first thing in the morning."

"I will." Jack kissed him. "I promise."

All night long he woke and dozed, never falling into a deep sleep. At one point, he got up and took his temperature. It was 103, but in the morning he would remember it as being 99. His dreams were strange: railroad stations, train tracks. The whistle of steam engines in the distance. A feeling of absolute grief and despair.

When he awoke Stuart was gone. In the kitchen, there was a note taped to a pan of freshly baked bran muffins. *Sweetie, I called in sick for you. Also, here's Dr. Mosites's number so you don't have to look it up. Call him! Stay in and lounge today. I'll call at noon to see if I need to stop at the pharmacy for any Rx. Love, S.*

Jack called the doctor's office and the receptionist took his name and number for the doctor to get back to him. He thought of just going in, but the idea of sitting around the waiting room with a bunch of prissy suburban mothers in their Benetton knit ensembles and their coughing, baby-Gap-clad toddlers filled him with anxiety and fury.

He turned on the TV, waited for the phone to ring. His fever felt as if it had broken. He watched a series of talk shows—white-trash tubbies who shot their husbands; cross-dressing men and the women who loved them. All better than any sitcom. That fake Hispanic, Geraldo, was the worst: he had a barely disguised sadistic streak, a way of ferreting out the truth to make all parties involved look foolish.

Jack changed the channel to Oprah, the bomb, the real wood to the veneers and cheap varnishes that tried to be her. The goddess and wise old woman. She needed to gain a little weight back, though; she was a better interviewer as a size twelve than she was as a six or an eight.

By the time the doctor called, at eleven, he was feeling much better. Exhilarated, even, as though he had won something.

"How are we doing, Jack?" Dr. Mosites said over the phone. Jack liked him, a middle-aged Greek man who was at once both no-nonsense and warm.

"I'm fine, actually. Stuart insisted that I call. I think it's just a touch of flu."

"Fever?"

"Last night, yeah. But I think it's broken now."

"How high?"

"Ninety-nine."

"Okay. Any nausea or vomiting? Diarrhea?"

"No."

"Anything else out of the ordinary?"

"I had an allergic reaction to Qwell, that medicine for lice. And I think I may have gotten an infection from scratching."

"On your scalp?"

"No. The pubic area."

"You said your fever was 99?"

"Yeah."

"Okay. It sounds like a low-grade infection. But I want you to come in before I prescribe anything. How about three-thirty. All right?"

"Yes. Thanks, Nick. Anyway, have you seen this kind of thing before? Allergic reactions that get out of control?"

"Sure. Look, Jack, it sounds as if there's nothing to be alarmed about. But all the same, we need to be sure."

"Okay. See you this afternoon."

Stuart called at noon, as promised.

"I'm feeling much better. Mosites seems to think it's a low-grade infection from the Qwell reaction. But I'm going in later for him to look."

"Oh, good. Good. I'll go with you. I can ditch my Anthro class."

"No, don't. It's nothing. I'll just see you tonight. Maybe if my appetite holds we can go get some dinner."

In the waiting room, Jack thumbed through old issues of the *New Yorker*, but his attention was clipped; he couldn't concentrate on anything much beyond the cartoons. His heart was racing, palms sweaty.

Finally, after an endless half an hour, the receptionist took him back to an examining room. Jack knew the second he saw the look on the doctor's face. Mosites untied the gown, swept a flat hand slowly and lightly along Jack's arms and trunk, legs and back, knees and toes. Jack felt the rash everywhere Mosites touched, the raised bumps like a Braille text, the body writing its illness on the parchment of skin. Mosites's expression changed from friendly casual pleasantness to professional alarm. Jack wanted to laugh it was so obvious, Mosites's face with its wide, plump planes drawing into knots. He took Jack's vital signs.

"Your temperature is a hundred and two."

"It is?"

Mosites wouldn't meet Jack's eyes. "I want to take a white count. Fortunately for us, I have a friend who is gifted at reading differentials. White blood cells, that is. We won't have to send it off to a lab. I'll draw your blood, and then Anna can take a peek. Her lab is just a few blocks from me. Shouldn't be any trouble to ask her. Okay?"

Jack looked away when the needle went in. He felt his heartbeat thrumming against his eardrum.

"All done. Come into my office when you're dressed."

On the other side of the door, Jack could hear Mosites on the phone. "Anna, it's Nick. Is this your cell number?" He paused. "Are you anywhere in my vicinity?" Another pause. "Right. Right, I know. But I need to ask a favor. I have a patient in my office and I need a CBC and an HIV test. Probably should do a mono spot, too."

Everything went black before Jack's eyes when he bent to tie his shoes. He sat. Waited for his vision to clear. Stood, shaky and weak-kneed, and walked into Nick's office.

"Have a seat, Jack. Anna will be here in just a few minutes. She was nearby when I talked to her."

"You're bothering the poor woman for my little allergic reaction and fever?" He tried for levity, angled around to get back to the breezy, casual side of Mosites, but it didn't work.

"Try to relax," Nick said.

Jack took a deep breath. Nick's office was cool and shadowy, the blinds drawn against the late sun. Jack sat on the leather sofa beside an antique sexton. The room smelled of lemon oil and buttery pastries, old books and humid soil from the English ivies hanging at the windows. Mosites looked at him with his great black eyes, beautiful soft eyes that seemed to caress everything they fell on.

"You don't think this is just a skin allergy, do you?" Jack asked.

"Jack, I'm not going to do a duck and cover here. I'm concerned. This looks to me like a systemic bacterial infection. Probably staph."

Jack sat back in his chair, let out his breath. Thank God! Just a stupid skin infection. He probably needed to be more vigilant about changing out of his exercise clothes after a workout, use some real soap instead of that goat's milk organic crap he couldn't resist buying at the health food store. "Thank God," Jack said. "From the look on your face I was beginning to think I was about to die."

Mosites's look didn't change. "When was the last time you had an HIV test?"

"About a year ago, I guess. I was negative."

"And since that time, have you or Stuart engaged in any high-risk behavior?"

Adrenaline flooded through him. His vision started to tunnel. Not this. Anything but this. "What are you implying?"

"That I think this looks like an immune-deficiency-related problem. A staph bacterium doesn't rage this out of control except in rare cases. The elderly, those with compromised immune systems." He picked up Jack's chart. "Also, are you aware you've lost fifteen pounds since you were in here six months ago?"

"Are you saying you think I'm positive?"

"What I'm seeing is not inconsistent with HIV patients. I'd like to test you for the virus. Anna can check your status when she does your white count."

"No," Jack said.

"Pardon?"

"No. I don't want an AIDS test. There's no reason to think I'm at risk."

"Okay. You might be sure of that from your end, but are you a hundred per cent sure about Stuart?"

"Stuart would never cheat on me."

"I can't insist, but you should do the right thing and get tested," Mosites said.

Jack nodded, his eyes filling. Anyway, it was too late. The seed of possibility had been planted. If he didn't learn his status now, every little head cold or sniffle would have a question mark after it.

By the time Mosites came back with his results, Jack had worked himself into a state where he no longer cared. He had prepared himself for the worst—or thought he had until Mosites came back in after an eternity with the news on his face. He sat down next to Jack on the sofa, took him in his arms. Mosites started in about his T-cell count and viral loads, about protease inhibitors and AZT cocktails.

"Don't. Don't talk to me yet." He buried his face in the snowy shoulder of Mosites's lab coat, breathed in the clean smell of laundry soap and after-shave. He wanted his father here, but not as a son wanted a father, exactly. He didn't want to be anyone's son at the moment, anyone's lover or boyfriend or brother. What he wanted was the tenderness distilled out of all these relationships, the pure unconditional love of a father, a child, a priest.

"The new drugs are good, Jack. More and more this disease is be-coming a chronic, long-term illness the way diabetes is. You need to take care of yourself, and there's no reason not to hope you can't live fifteen or more years with this."

He drove around for hours after leaving Mosites's office, drove by Hector's corner—he was there, but Jack didn't stop—pounded three shots of tequila and two vodka tonics at two different bars, then drove down to the Charles River. It was dark now, getting late, the city lights silvered on the water. How was he going to tell Stuart? And what about Hector? Maybe it was possible that the test was wrong. Maybe a bacterial infection could look a lot like AIDS. And testing positive didn't mean it would become full-blown.

He lit a cigarette, shivered. He didn't want to be awake. He wanted to be anywhere but inside his own skin. He toed the dirt beneath his feet. It was soft from a recent rain, smelled sharply of algae and brine. He put his hand down, pulled away clumps of dirt. It was pliable as potter's clay. He dug deeper, as though looking for something, felt the panic he'd been wrestling with the past few weeks rise up again, this time with the force of certainty behind it: some part of him had known, of course. He sank to the ground, cleared away the dirt with the heel of his hand, scraped deeper down with a nearby beer bottle. He lay down in the space he made, out of the way of the dog walkers and runners. A calmness washed over him. He worked his hand down into the coolness of the clayey mud, starfished his fingers wide apart until he felt the wetness between them. If he could re-make himself he would. Start anew and keep goodness intact. In a little while he would rise and go home to Stuart, would confess his indiscretions in San Francisco. He would leave off the sin of Hector for now. It would only be more for Stuart to deal with. It was highly improbable—or impossible?—that Hector had given it to him since he had never penetrated Jack's body. He didn't want to know, didn't want to dissolve the mystery. Finding out who and when and how would only make it more unbearable. Mysteries and miracles, miracles and destinations, weren't that far apart, in his view. The stricken and the blessed both followed the same path, faith the common point of origin. In the end, there was no difference between Bethlehem and the bathhouses.

Now he had practical things to consider, like how to live through one day at a time—that horrible maxim of the sick and afflicted everywhere. He didn't want to wake up each day and take an inventory of his health, work his way past this terrible fact each morning, and God forbid, be grateful for feeling good and getting through another day. It would be too much like waiting, like waiting for the virus to quicken in him until it carried him off in pieces. He'd seen friends die, they all had. Suffering was one thing, but subtraction was another. Every day something was taken away. Dignity, of course, was first. Memory, sometimes. Thinking back to those who had died from this plague, Jack couldn't think of a single person whose death wasn't met with thankfulness and utter relief. Not that the dead one's suffering was over, but the suffering of those who had cared for him had finally ended.

When Stuart got in from school Jack wasn't home yet. All the Robert Mitchum tapes were out and scattered around the living room, magazines and the remains of at least two meals on the coffee table. He'd eaten, which must mean he was feeling better. Stuart had been so worried these past few weeks. Jack was completely worn-out looking, edgy and irritable. It had been months since they'd made love, even longer since Jack slept through the night. Jack thought he didn't know, thought he didn't hear him get out of bed and leave the house, but Stuart was aware of every second ticking by, every moment Jack wasn't beside him.

Jack was cheating, he was sure of it. With whom, he didn't know, and he couldn't have said if it was one time with one person or a hundred with fifty different people. He hadn't yet made up his mind what to do. Confront him, ignore it and hope it went away, or leave Jack altogether, which was what he was considering after last night. As much as the thought of being without Jack made him feel hopeless and lost, he couldn't stand the alternative, either, which was loving someone as much as he loved Jack and having his heart break over and over. Jack's behavior at the party last night had tipped the scales toward exodus.

Stuart had gone to the backyard to look for Jack and saw him sitting on the chaise with the boyish-looking man who was Craig's ex-partner. Stuart watched long enough to see them hand a bottle of booze back and forth, and to see the man pawing at Jack. He had felt so sick then, his stomach turning to hot needles. Later, he couldn't stop shaking with grief and fury. It was getting too painful to be with him. Infidelity aside, Jack's moods and flippancy, excesses and bluster were corrosive. Jack had the energy and spirit of two men.

After finding Jack with Gary, Stuart talked to his friend Pamela on the phone about what was going on. Pamela offered him her place if and when he decided to leave Jack. Stuart felt hives popping up just thinking about packing his things.

He took the dirty plates to the kitchen, then cleaned up Jack's sick bay area: a used handkerchief, a half-completed grocery list, doodles on the note pad by the phone, a heap of pistachio nut shells and a sour-smelling sweatshirt. He took the nutshells and handkerchief and notepaper with Jack's handwriting into the bedroom. The doodles were all of trains and ladders—or maybe they were supposed to be railroad tracks.

Hidden behind the blankets in the spare bedroom's closet was Stuart's special coat. On the outside, it was just an ordinary trench coat, but on the lining he had sewn various mementos of Jack over the years. Race numbers from marathons; a square of denim from an old pair of Levi's Jack wore a lot when they'd first started dating; bits of hay from a farm in Idaho they stopped at while driving across the country. Jack had first told him he loved him at that farm, and everything Jack touched that day, from the foil his sandwich was wrapped in to the guitar pick he'd found on the street then snipped in the center with fingernail clippers to form a heart, was sewn into this coat. It would seem fetishistic to some, Stuart knew, and Jack himself would make fun of it, but whatever else happened, Stuart would always have these traces of Jack.

Near the hem, he glued the notepaper with Jack's doodles and grocery list, right up against the maple leaves and acorns from their trip to Maine last year. They'd stayed in a bed and breakfast on the coast, spent long mornings in bed and afternoons walking on the beach, evenings around the enormous fireplace in the nearby ski lodge.

Maybe they should travel together, go back to that quaint B&B to try to reconnect. How could he give up Jack? At the shoulder were the liner notes to Steely Dan's "Dirty Work," the first CD they bought together, and beside it, ticket stubs from *The Magic Flute* around which he pasted the pistachio shells that had been heaped in Jack's soup bowl earlier this afternoon.

Stuart refolded the coat and took it back to its hiding place. He'd start an appetizer plate. Foccacia with herbed chèvre and Greek olives. It was seven o'clock. Where the hell was Jack? Stuart expected him hours ago. Things were going to be fine, Stuart told himself. Jack's rash was just an extreme reaction to that medicine. Nothing to be overly concerned about; the doctor told him as much. He decanted a bottle of port, poured half a glass, and before he realized what he was doing, he'd opened a bottle of sixty-dollar champagne they'd been saving for two years. He set the table with candles and their best china and loaded up Dave Brubeck and Lightnin' Hopkins on the CD changer. Was Stuart celebrating? It looked like celebration. It was a sign, he decided, an omen that Jack was all right.

By the time Jack walked in at eleven, Stuart was drunk, the candles burned down to stubs, and the food cold and congealing on the plates. Jack just stood in the doorway, looked at Stuart from there as though waiting to be invited in. He was filthy, covered in mud, unsteady and droopy-eyed.

Brubeck was playing "Take Five" for the third time. He stared at Jack, tried to make sense of the mud, the sticks in his hair. "Is it raining?"

Jack shook his head.

Stuart got up, walked closer to him, but Jack didn't move. "What's wrong with you? Why do you look like that?" Stuart asked.

Jack opened his mouth as if to speak. He met Stuart's eyes then looked down.

"Did you see the doctor today?"

Jack nodded. "Darling," he started.

What was coming next, he wasn't ready to hear. "Stop," Stuart said. "Don't speak. I want five minutes." He sank back down into the sofa.

"Stuart—"

"Shut up, Jack. These are the last few minutes before my life changes forever. And they're mine." How could this be? Though even as he formed the question he knew.

"I'm standing in the doorway, Stuart."

"I see that."

"I'm waiting for you to ask me in."

"Why?"

"Because if you tell me not to come any farther, I'll disappear from your life forever. I understand if you hate me. I'm an evil man. I've lied to you. I've betrayed you. I'm the worst kind of evil."

Stuart didn't respond.

A few minutes went by. Jack said again, "I am standing in the doorway."

"What do you want me to do about it?"

"I want you to tell me which way to go."

He looked up. "Tell me first. Do I need to be tested?"

"Yes."

"How could you do this?" Stuart turned off the stereo, began to clear the table. Ordinary things, one ordinary thing at a time. Two forks, two plates. Dishwater and sponge. He turned on the tap and added soap. Scraped the dishes into the trash.

Fifteen minutes later when he went back into the living room, Jack was still there. He walked to the birdcage with fresh newspaper.

"I stand here in the doorway."

"Go through it," Stuart said, as he opened the birdcage and spread seed, "and don't come back."

"Before I go," Jack said quietly, "I want to ask you something. I have no right to ask this. But, even if you have to lie, tell me you love me just one last time."

Stuart wheeled around. "I won't say that. I will never say those words to you again. How could you ask that? It's the same as asking me for my forgiveness."

"No," Jack said.

"There is no forgiveness that will change this. In five months, in five years, this will be as devastating as it is right now. There is no past tense with this."

Immediately after Jack left Stuart picked up the phone, started to dial Jane and Leila's number, then stopped. He looked up Pamela's number, but he didn't want to talk to her, either. He sat for a minute, then before he thought about it, he was calling home. His father answered.

"Dad? It's Stuart." He heard a sportscaster droning in the background and instantly he was transported to the damp basement with its conditioned air, big-screen TV and brown furnishings. Stuart could almost smell the mildewy pool chalk in the air, the dust coming off the 1972 *Encyclopedia Britannica*s that no one ever opened.

"Hey, hey. How are you, son?"

"I'm doing well." Stuart said. "It's just been a while so I thought I'd call."

"Good. It's good to hear from you. How's school?"

"I still haven't officially transferred to one of the Boston schools yet, but that will happen soon. I'm taking a few classes."

"How's Jack? How are you two enjoying Boston?"

"We like Boston a whole lot."

"Good. You just missed your mother. She's at her girls' night out thing. She's become a gallivanter, that woman. I suspect she's been to some male strip clubs."

Stuart laughed. "What? My mother? The church deaconess?"

"She's running with a rough crowd. She and her high school friends are getting together twice a month. They stay out late, and I don't ask. But your mother comes home with alcohol and cigarette smoke on her breath."

"Well, good for her."

"Yeah, that's what I think, too. Though I pretend to be shocked."

Stuart asked after his brothers and his sister. "How are Kevin and James? Did Carol decide to take the job in Maryland?"

Stuart listened to his father run through the litany of what his siblings and their kids had been doing. He envisioned his aging father in front of the football game, his mild, farsighted eyes blinking behind his glasses, his hands becoming arthritic. His father hoped for modest things—health, a little travel, children and grandchildren who visited. Stuart felt a lump in his throat. He'd gone so far outside of his father's realm, had at various times pitied and scorned his parents for what he believed was a cowardly, limited life—work, church, family. No hobbies, no real interests.

"Is everything all right, son?"

"I think so. I hope so."

His father paused. "Your mother and I love and miss you. You know you and Jack are welcome here anytime."

Stuart's throat got tighter. "I'll come and visit soon. Give my love to Mom," he said, and hung up after his father's goodbye. His father was a kind man, a good and generous man; for so long he'd underestimated the value of that.

He remembered the fall day when he was with four or five of his friends in the backyard. They were boys from his class, two of them the most popular in school. Stuart had gotten their attention for his irreverence one day in art class when he drew a nasty portrait of their teacher, Miss McCarthy, naked with strategically placed chopsticks and the caption, "Two sticks are better than one!" The trip to the principal's office, the stern lectures and the call to his parents were well worth the reward of getting the attention of these popular boys. And now here they were, in his backyard, throwing a football around with him while his father cooked hot dogs on the grill. He was only a little ashamed of his father, much less than other boys. His father had played football in high school and was still in decent shape, although the way he acted that day was like a telegram announcing that Stuart rarely had anyone over. Parents who were used to their children's friends didn't tell so many corny jokes or hang around and smile so much. His father had the same ridiculous grin he wore while watching Stuart's sister in the junior high production of *My Fair Lady*.

That day was the first time Stuart knew something was different about him. When Tim Eberhardt caught a pass and Stuart went in to tackle him, he was aware of the boy's body in ways too particular not to be disturbing, even at nine. The silky hair on his legs, the musky boy sweat at his hairline and armpits. Stuart's legs were entangled with Tim's, his pelvis tipped in so he felt the boy's small penis against his own. This felt so right, the boy beneath him with the smell of fall leaves and the amber light through the canopy of maples, that he had to will his body not to move, stop himself from burying his face in the hollow of the boy's neck.

"Get off me, Carpenter," was all Tim said, but his expression was as astonished as if Stuart had kissed him. Much later, Stuart thought the boy probably felt his half-hard penis against his leg. Luckily, Tim had never said anything—maybe, like Stuart, he was too young to understand what it all meant.

By the end of that day, he was miserable. He took a cool bath, lathered his hair with Breck shampoo, his body with Ivory soap.

He turned down his bed and opened the windows. Outside, the air already had the ashy smell of autumn. The nighthawks and crickets made him feel a little less lonely. His brothers were away on a Scout trip that weekend so he had the room to himself.

He combed his hair with a blue plastic comb, then took out his Superman comics. He felt as if he had lost something, or, crestfallen, like the time his grandfather promised to take him on a fishing trip then canceled at the last minute. Stuart had been preparing and daydreaming about the trip for three weeks.

He slid his hand inside his pajama bottoms, cupped his scrotum. There were magnets in here. Here was where the magnets in him attracted the magnets in the body of a lady. When he kissed a girl, this part of him stuck to that part of her until a baby grew inside her. A special water was formed in him, and came up through his penis then flowed into a girl's space. But it must be that his magnets were turned around somehow, shaped like a girl's, in a horseshoe. Nothing had ever happened when he spied on the girls with his friends. His penis didn't get hard; he didn't want to touch himself through his Speedo at the pool like his friends did when they watched the girls. This was the problem: His magnet was facing the wrong way, attracted another boy instead of a girl.

His father knocked on the door, and then waited for Stuart to invite him in—he was always so good about that, never barged in or snooped. "It's me, son."

"Come in."

His father had changed into his pajamas and slippers. He walked in and sat on the edge of the bed, smiled over at the Humpty Dumpty lamp on the night table. "We really need to get you boys some new furnishings. I think you're getting a little too old for Humpty Dumpty lights and Bugs Bunny blankets."

Stuart shrugged.

"I just wanted to come in and congratulate you on having such a good day. I enjoyed your friends. You positively shone."

Stuart looked away, ashamed, though he couldn't say why. Once, at a family reunion, Stuart took his cousin's Kennedy half-dollar collection. Stuart's aunt called the next day, and he heard his father say, "My sons don't steal. I will walk through fire defending that belief." He felt like that now, as though he had lied to his father.

"What's the matter?" his father said.

"I don't know." He couldn't hold back any longer and he started to cry, his breath coming in jagged waves. "There's something wrong with me."

"No," his father said firmly, "there isn't." He pulled Stuart onto his lap, as though he were a very young child. The comfort he felt soon erased any awkwardness. His father didn't say anything further, but he must have known, must have felt the odd tension that had sprung up between his son and the boys he tackled. His father let him cry, and after a little while bade him good night.

The next morning, when he and his father were driving across town to the hardware store, his father broke the unbearable tension. "I was thinking this morning about the Fourth of July parade last year." Stuart looked over at his father's profile. "I had to help you find a place where you could see, remember? The man with the hat, those tall teenagers."

Stuart nodded.

"The world's a big place. You have to find yourself a clear view. You need to move to the place where you can see best. The place where you're most comfortable. Do you understand this? There will be a place for you. It just might take you a little bit longer to find it."

Stuart brewed a pot of tea now, then went in to take a cool shower. He slid into his freshly changed bed. Outside the street sounds lulled him to sleep, the voices of teenagers, the blaring of radios. Normally he would have been irritated. But now, he found the noise rather poignant, their innocence about what the world was yet to deliver to them, the myriad ways it would tell them no.

FIVE

WONDERING WHERE THE LIONS ARE

Nearly a month after Poppy and her family were due in, the phone rang just as Anna was heading out the door. The machine picked up and gave her Marvin's voice, the hesitating baritone that even after all these years made the hair at the back of her neck stand up. There were no gradations of emotion where her son-in-law was concerned; fury was what it always boiled down to, unadulterated anger like a chalky residue left in a test tube after some weird experiment.

She slipped the T-shirt emblazoned with the words "Mood Team" over her head and slammed the front door. It was still early, but Mike and Greta were out already working in the garden.

"Mood Team, doing a random house-to-house check," Anna called over, flashing an imaginary badge.

"Halfway between good and great," Greta called back, and smiled. "Are you going to be home later?"

"Oh yeah, oh hell yeah. My daughter is coming in tonight. Just got a call."

Greta's eyes widened. "Finally."

Anna nodded like it was no big deal, though already her heart was pounding with anticipation. "But come over. I haven't seen you in days. Poppy has never in her life, including the first day of her life, been on time. My guess is they'll be in around midnight."

Greta's eyes swept over Anna's shirt, took in the thermal undershirt she had beneath the T-shirt.

"We're playing hockey. I mean, they are, so I'll be in an ice rink," Anna said.

Mike chuckled. When was the last time Anna saw this? In fact, both he and Greta seemed unusually upbeat. Under the best of circumstances, Mike had a sullen, melancholy air about him. "C'mon Anna, I want pictures of you with a goalie mask on. I would pay money to have that." He laughed, clipped a row of daises and delphiniums and added it to a voluminous pile of flowers between him and Greta.

"Jeez," Anna said. "You have enough for a fleet of July Fourth floats."

He flushed and laughed again—was Anna hallucinating? Was this tall, secretive, lugubrious man actually laughing? She looked over at Greta, incredulous, but Greta's expression wasn't giving anything away.

"Anyway, keep up the good moods. I'll be at the ice rink with the sick and dying if anyone needs me."

Anna got into her car and checked the directions to the ice rink. After the fiasco with Amy, Anna was convinced that none of her current students was really qualified, regardless of Nick's claim otherwise. At the same time, Boston General's administrators determined that even a Saturday overflow group was still under the auspices of the hospital and they sent down a strict policy about staffing. Facilitators had to be psychiatrists, psychiatric residents, or psychologists. A licensed clinical social worker was acceptable, but only in "conjunction with a co-leader trained in the medical field."

"I'm off the hook!" Anna said, when Nick called three weeks ago to tell her the new rules. "Though I guess now I won't get my new microscopes."

Nick began, "Actually, Anna..." and ended with not only a guarantee of new lab equipment, but also a promise to endow a scholarship—pending her college's approval. Nick wanted Anna to agree to sit in on the meetings as the co-leader just until he could get someone else. He found a young social worker who was eager—"thrilled, in fact"—for the opportunity to get field experience. Anna's status had been cleared through the appropriate channels. According to the language of the policy, Anna's instruction of technicians, along with her phlebotomy work, meant that she worked in the medical field.

"The hospital said you would be fine until I can find a medical resident or intern," Nick had said. "Oh, and I have to change the name, since my group is technically the official support group. You and Christine, the social worker, will be running the Mood Team."

"Charming," Anna said. "Though, personally, I'd like to call us the Mood Rings. I like the secret underground echo of that."

Nick wasn't amused. "So, please, Anna? New equipment and rare specimen slides are on their way to you."

"How rare?"

"It's a surprise. But don't be surprised if you find yourself in possession of the Hantavirus and Nipah Virus Encephalitis."

"Nice!" Anna said. "Can you find me histology samples from The Elephant Man? I'd also like rabies, slides from both the dumb and furious stages."

"Now, Anna...."

"Oh, Christ. All right," she said, which was how she found herself now, weeks later, on yet another outing with the exuberant Christine.

Anna admired Christine's energy and high spirits, though she was a bit overzealous in planning special events. In the six weeks Anna had been co-leading, the group met at the hospital just twice. With Nick's approval (delight, in fact), Christine had organized two picnics, a Sadie Hawkins dance (half the men dressed as women), and participation in the Fourth of July PFLAG float where she rode with about a hundred Marilyn Monroes. She and Christine were the only two not in costume other than big dark glasses and headscarves, twin Jackie O's.

Today's outing was to be a hockey game between the men in Anna and Christine's group, and the residents of an assisted-living senior citizen home, many of whom suffered from Alzheimer's. "The Gay Moods vs. The Forgetful Dudes" was the name somebody had come up with.

The game was already underway—and unraveling—when Anna got there. She counted six elderly men and four men from The Mood Team actually on the ice; there were ten or eleven cheering in the bleachers. Anna watched as Christine, on skates, was trying to talk to the group of senior men at one end of the rink. They were teetering, rolling this way and that like a handful of stray pennies. Some of them were eating hot dogs. The goalie was reading the newspaper. Each time the puck hit the net he looked up and said, "It's in." The two senior men who were actively playing seemed so aggressive that Anna was sure there were going to be some broken bones by the end of the day.

Anna walked out on the ice in her street shoes. "How's it going?" she asked Christine.

"Isn't it reasonable to assume that in a group of men, at least a few know the basic rules? I can't teach them. I've never been to a hockey game in my life."

"Somehow, I don't think it matters. We just need to make sure nobody gets hurt," Anna said, as one of the "Forgetful Dudes" went full bore toward a "Gay Mood" who was hobbling away on the tips of his skates, using his hockey stick for balance.

"Whoa, there. Whoa big fella, chill," he said, then toppled to the ice. He picked up the puck and tucked it into his jacket. "You don't have to be so nasty, Brutus." He tiptoed toward the goal box, slid the puck in, then did a little victory dance. "Money Shot!" he yelled, and the men in the bleachers cheered.

The goalie looked up from his newspaper. "It's in. The cows have all come home to Montana."

"Uh, well," Anna said. "Maybe we should stick to picnics in the future."

Someone beside her spoke. "The thing is, gay men don't play hockey, and senile straight men can get the puck, but they don't always remember why they want it."

Anna turned, took in the short blond man with the Truman Capote voice. He was wearing a tuxedo and, Anna thought, eyeliner and lipstick.

"I'm Gary," he said. "Ex-partner to Craig, who's in the support group. I'm coordinating the half-time show."

"Half-time show?" Anna asked.

Christine said, "I told them they could stage an ice capades."

"Sweetheart, it's *gaycapades*," Gary said.

An hour later, Gary, as emcee, announced the ten men in the half-time show. Though all had elaborate costumes, not one of them wore skates. Five Peggy Flemings, a Katerina Witt, two Dorothy Hamills, one Nancy Kerrigan, and a lone Tonya Harding slid around in street shoes to the music of *Carmina Burana*.

Anna sat beside Christine, felt herself relax for the first time all day. There was something enviable in the playful affection among many of the men; even those who were at war during the meetings seemed to be genuinely delighted with one another—the resentments and accusations put aside for now. In the bleachers, Anna spotted the man who had instigated the blue sock fight that first session. He was beaming down at the Tonya Harding, who looked up every time he heard his partner's laughter and grinned.

When the half-time show was over she watched Tonya Harding thread his way over to the bleachers. The couple had such a look of peace and contentment that Anna couldn't take her eyes away. Love was a river full of submerged rocks. Over time, it was how you diverted the flow around the boulders that mattered. She ached for her husband, his tender solidity and companionship.

The men from both teams were out of energy by the end of the half-time show. A few of the healthier members were going out for pizza and beer, and invited Anna and Christine to come along.

"I can't," Christine said. "I have to drive a van to help get the other team home. Mrs. Brinkman might want to join you. Otherwise, I'd love to."

"No, I'm afraid I can't either," Anna said. "I'll tell you what, though." She turned to Christine. "If you want to go out with them, I'll take the seniors home. You can take my car. We'll switch later."

"That is so nice of you, Anna!"

"Well, you deserve to have a little fun."

Anna loaded the men and their gear into the van and drove them the ten or so miles back to the Golden Years Assisted Living Community. Most of them slept the whole way back.

"Might you turn the heat on?" one of the men said. "I have a chill."

"Sure," Anna said, and despite the summer heat cranked it up as far as it would go. But it seemed to be broken, blasting heat one minute and cold, accompanied by a loud staccato rapping, the next.

"Come in," one of the men said.

Anna looked back in her mirror and saw it was the man who played goalie earlier. "It's just the heater making that sound," she said.

"Yes," he said. "Come in."

The man dozed and woke with each knocking. "Come in, I say. I say, come in ye wildebeests, come in. Come in and lie beside me. There are no lions here."

At home, Anna sat on her bed and massaged her right temple where a hot, egg-sized lump was forming. She'd cracked her head against the edge of the Plexiglas at the ice rink and now she had a killer headache that wasn't responding to ice or aspirin. She looked at her watch. Six o'clock, and no sign or message from her daughter, which could mean anything. Anna didn't expect Poppy much before nine or ten o'clock, but had left a note on the door with instructions about where to find the spare key, just in case. Anna was suddenly ravenous. She hadn't eaten yet today. She'd been off her feed for a few weeks. Most days, she relied on the clock, rather than her nonexistent appetite, to tell her when it was time for a meal.

She stepped on the scale and was shocked to see she weighed a hundred and nine, sixteen pounds lighter than her usual weight. Still, she was in the normal range for someone of her height and frame. In fact, she liked the way her body felt light and lean. She was perfectly healthy, routinely offered her blood sample for every class she taught on venipuncture, and so knew what her hematocrit or monocytes were up to in any given week. The class lesson on CBCs had been just two weeks ago, at which time her white count was perfect, her red cells round and ripe as July tomatoes.

She turned this way and that in front of the mirror, squinted. She'd been this slight as a young woman, and it was almost as if she could see the outline of her girlish body once again. The straight angularity of her shape before womanhood stuffed her full, threatened to burst through her overburdened skin. The melon-breasted months of pregnancy. The striations on her belly and thighs—every cramped inch of her staked out as someone's territory, the claims that her husband and baby put on her flesh. It was wonderful to feel the fluid, loose boundaries of her skin again.

She lay down for what she thought would be a short nap, but slept for over two hours.

When she awoke, her temple was hot and throbbing. She'd had a dream in which the lump had become an egg case for baby spiders.

Anna then heard someone moving around the apartment. Her heart pounded as she worked her swollen feet into her shoes. Surely Poppy would have awakened her the minute she and her family arrived.

But it was Greta, Anna saw, as she walked into the living room.

"Hey," Greta said. "I was just coming in to wake you. I peeked in a couple of hours ago and you were dead to the world."

"I can't believe I slept so long."

"You probably needed it."

"Any phone calls? Any word from my wayward daughter?" She picked up the newspaper. The season's program for the community orchestra was already printed in the Events section. She hadn't practiced in days and the first concert was in less than a month. Rachmaninoff would never come to her now. She tossed the paper aside, looked up at Greta. "What's new, my friend?"

"Nothing much. Just back from a rehearsal with the kids."

"How's it coming?"

"Good," Greta said, and looked away.

Anna raised her eyebrows. "And?"

"And what?"

"Since when do you give a one-word answer to a question like that? Normally I get pages."

"Oh, well." She looked down, flushed. She put her feet on the edge of Anna's chair, cracked open a bottle of water. Anna pulled out a cigarette, poured a glass of wine. "Vice, anyone?"

"No, thanks," Greta said.

"Pardon me?" Anna said.

Greta laughed, shrugged.

Anna didn't take her eyes off her friend. "What's wrong? What's different?" And then she knew. "You're pregnant," Anna said.

Greta's eyes widened. "How do you know that?"

"Are you?"

"I don't know. I might be. I'm a little late."

"Well, you are," Anna said, because it was immediately obvious. Anna had seen so many pregnant women over the years she could tell after a while just by their posture: even very early a woman's body seemed to pull in toward the middle, the hands never very far from the belly, the head and chin tipped down slightly, the shoulders rolled inward. In a room full of women to be tested, Anna could usually pick out the pregnant ones just by the way the women were spaced; the gestational woman always sat a little apart from the group. It was pure biology, pure instinct, the expectant mother giving herself a wide space to thwart any unexpected assaults.

"Have you done a pregnancy test?"

"Not yet," Greta said. "I'm afraid to. I'm afraid to find out. I can't stand the idea of so much happiness so early. Things can go wrong, you know, and I've miscarried once before. Mike's little swimmers, anyway, are not altogether all right."

"Oh?" Anna said.

Greta nodded. "We found out last week. Motility? Is that the right word?"

"Yes. But apparently one made it to the finish line." Anna smiled. "I'm really happy for you, dear."

"Not yet. Don't say that yet. It might jinx me. But thank you."

After Greta left, Anna sat in the chair by the window with a book. She was just about to give up and go to bed—it was twelve-thirty—when she heard that unmistakable sound of the past, the rattle and hum and sputter of the VW bus. Surely it couldn't be the same VW Marvin bought from them all those years before.

Anna stood, lightheaded, not sure what to do: rush out and greet them? Wait until they rang the bell? She heard car doors slam, a man's voice: "Take that off right now, Flynn."

"No," the child said.

"Get the cat," he said. "And I told you to take those goggles off."

The doorbell rang. Anna walked down the hall stairs, turned on the lights. Marvin's big frame filled the doorway. "You made it," she said, and stepped aside. "I was getting a little worried."

"Sorry," he said. "We got a bit behind schedule. We had, uh, a slight problem along the way."

"Oh?" She peeked around him for Poppy.

Marvin cupped Anna's elbow lightly, led her away from the door. "Flynn?" he called over his shoulder.

"I'm getting the cat," she called back. "I'll be right in."

"Where's Poppy?"

Marvin sank down on the couch, sighed, and ran his hands through his hair—still shoulder-length, the way it was when Anna first laid eyes on him. He smoothed it back and secured it in a ponytail. She'd forgotten how beautiful he was.

"We had a little problem in Pennsylvania." He took off his jacket, loosened his shoelaces. "Poppy disappeared."

"What? What do you mean, disappeared?" Anna stood, turned toward the door as if some part of her believed he was lying.

"Anna, please," he said, and led her back to the couch. "Let me say this before my girl comes in, okay?"

Anna couldn't catch her breath and her head was pounding. "How could you do this to me? Call me and disrupt my life, get my hopes up again of seeing Poppy and not bring her back?"

"I tried. I did. We've been having problems. This visit was her idea. She was actually looking forward to it. But she has this mood thing. The closer we got to you the more she got cold feet. In Pennsylvania, we stopped for breakfast. The next thing I knew, there was a note on the windshield saying she'd changed her mind. That Flynnie and I should go on without her. She said she'd check in from the road. She'll be here later. That's what her note said, anyway."

"How could you do this? Why didn't you go and find her? Disappeared where?"

"Poppy has problems. She's always been moody. I can live with that. But things have intensified in the past few years."

Anna started to speak, then heard Flynn's footsteps on the stairs.

"We'll talk about it later," Marvin said softly. "Flynn?"

"I am here," Flynn called from the stairwell.

"Come in and meet your grandmother."

"I'll be in shortly."

"I'll go get the rest of our luggage," Marvin said.

Anna was astonished: he'd already brought in enough stuff for two months. And not the ordinary things for a short stay, either. There was a carton of coffee mugs, one filled with pots and pans. Dishtowels. Both summer and winter clothes. They weren't visiting at all; they were moving in. She felt strained to her bitter limits.

When Anna looked up, Flynn was standing in the doorway holding a giant cat. She had on a pair of ancient optometrist's goggles—the old-style optimeter doctors once used to test vision—and a carrot stick in each nostril.

"You must be Flynn," Anna said.

"I am the walrus." She walked into the room.

Marvin walked in and dumped an armload of things on the floor. He looked over at his daughter. "I told you to put those goggles away, Flynn.

Do you want a time-out?"

Flynn removed the goggles and the carrot sticks, frowned, and slumped cross-armed on the couch beside Anna. "Do you know that in a former lifetime I was married to Marvin, who is now my father, and that Poppy, my mother, was a blind cowherd who used to beg for grain. We were Hindu then. Marvin beat me."

"What?" Anna instinctively scanned the girl's body for bruises.

"He didn't want children, and he beat me to make them disappear. In the tummy."

"Oh," Anna said, still a little stunned by the notion of being a grand-mother, awed by the presence of this lovely child. Anna put her hand up to her head. Her headache was starting to shake free, but the knots in her head had somehow coiled in her chest. Anna hadn't given much thought to the girl really; mostly she tried to imagine what she would say to Poppy after all these years.

Flynn was gorgeous, Anna noted, seeing a little bit of Hugh in the curve of her lips and jaw line, but mostly Flynn looked like the women on Anna's father's side: there was a spectacular resemblance to Anna's second cousin Ella. Ella was the seventh and favorite daughter of the baker in a little village outside Warsaw. Sixteen in 1939, she had picked up her father's new oven peel and was on her way to the shop that September morning when the blitzkrieg started. Ella rushed into burning homes and helped people to safety. Legend had it that she hit a German soldier over the head with the oven peel as he was getting ready to shoot a kneeling line of vil-lagers who then escaped. Ella later died in the camps.

"My mother is mentally ill," Flynn said, clutching the cat tighter as he struggled to get down.

"No," Anna said, angry with Marvin for his apparent careless language. "She's not." But then before she could stop herself she asked, "Has she left you before?"

"Certainly," Flynn said. "But this time she's not coming back."

"Only God knows such things," Anna said in a voice that was so much her grandmother's it made her head ache all over again.

"We've barely met," Flynn said, though Anna didn't know if it was a reference to herself, Poppy, or, given the peculiarity of this child, to God.

"What's the kitty's name?" Anna said.

"My parents are divorcing. They think I don't know this, but of course I do."

"Does the kitty have a name?"

"His name is Hoover McPaws. He just happens to be Irish."

"Oh, yes? I can see a certain Irish cast to his features."

Flynn looked back at her grandmother, smiled nervously. Something frightened her here. Her grandmother's look pierced through her like the prickly spines of a cactus. "I think you and I were gladiators together under the rule of Caesar Augustus."

"How old are you now, Flynn?"

"Ten. And you?"

"Fifty-three."

"My mother is thirty. Have you met her?"

"Yes. She's my daughter, the way you're her daughter."

"Oh, right." She shifted the cat, which was yowling now, pinned belly up against her knees. "Did she seem mentally ill to you?" Flynn let the cat had go with a gasp, sucked her finger where the cat had scratched her. "Because she was always a good mother until she left. She took very good care of me."

Anna heard her husband's tone in the girl's words, the bewilderment without a trace of anger at Poppy's behavior. "She said she would come," were his last words. "I hope nothing has happened." She couldn't have this girl here. Her very existence was a kind of reproach, the flaws in Poppy that led her to abandon her child were, really, Anna's failing as a parent. She'd buried the guilt long ago, and the last thing she needed was to have all the pain of attachment resurface.

Marvin came back in, straining under the weight of a huge trunk. "I hope you don't mind, Anna," he said. "I, uh, brought a little work with me."

"And just what sort of work do you do? Large-game taxidermy?" Already her house looked like a yard sale. Which she didn't care about, except there was something underhanded going on here, something neither he nor Poppy had respected her enough to tell her.

"Are those the heads?" Flynn asked.

"Go get ready for bed, Flynn," Marvin said, breathing hard.

"Heads? What?" Anna said.

"Clay heads. Busts. I'm two-thirds of the way though casting. I'm not sure about the humidity levels in the bus, so I didn't want to leave them in there. Too much moisture and I lose the correct slip."

"Yeah, okay whatever," Anna said. She looked over at Flynn. "I have a bed all set up for you in the guest room."

"Go brush your teeth, Flynn," Marvin said.

Anna waited until she heard the water running in the bathroom then said, "What the hell is going on? What is all this?"

Marvin sighed, then pulled a bottle of vodka from his pocket, the same oversized trench coat she remembered him wearing all those years ago. "Let's have a drink."

"No thank you," she said. "Look, I don't know what kind of game you're playing, mister, but I won't have it. You tell me straight out what you're doing here, or you can leave right now. I'm too old for this kind of crap."

He nodded. "It's late. Can we talk in the morning? I've been driving for sixteen straight days, mostly in circles looking for my wife. Okay?"

Anna didn't answer. Flynn reappeared in the living room.

"Bedtime, young lady," Marvin said.

"I have to feed Hoover," she said.

"I'll feed him," Marvin said.

"But I need to. He has a delicate stomach. He needs consistency."

Anna and Marvin both watched as Flynn took a pouch of cat food and a small bowl from her backpack, then watched, along with Flynn, the cat eating his dinner as though they'd never seen anything quite like it before.

All night long Anna lay awake. Flynn was in the guest bedroom, and Marvin had the foldout couch in the living room. Anna heard him get up numerous times, the front door opening and closing, the slam of the bus door outside.

Already it felt to her as if they'd been here years instead of hours.

At seven-thirty the next morning Anna stumbled bleary-eyed toward the kitchen to make coffee. She'd forgotten to ask what time they usually got up—late sleepers, she'd bet on it.

Marvin was snoring when Anna walked by him. His feet hung over the end of the mattress. He was uncovered, wearing only a pair of paisley boxer shorts that looked like silk. His hair, loose from its ponytail, fanned out over the white pillow as though it had been arranged like that: geisha-girl hair on the body of a Roman soldier. He was thin but perfectly muscled. His thighs and shoulders and calves were lovely. A perfect specimen, as Hugh once said. She looked away, a little guilty.

But this was Marvin after all. He had draped his clothing over her cello like it was a cheap chair. She tossed his shirt and pants on the floor so he'd get the hint.

There were tracks all around the living room, chalky white footprints that stopped in front of the antique table she'd recently gotten out of storage—Duncan Phyffe, over a hundred years old—on which Anna saw one of the most gruesome sights she'd ever seen: twisted, grimacing busts of what looked like Nixon, Ronald Reagan, and Gerald Ford. The Reagan was the worst, a face full of angry confusion, deep lines etched around the blank eyes and slack mouth, but which, drawing nearer, she saw was another face in profile. This one was unmistakably Jeffrey Dahmer. The clay was dyed reddish brown, Dahmer's face smooth and peaceful-looking. The expression—beatific half-smile, eyes gazing upward in the classic manner of Catholic saints—was provocative in the manner of gruesome car wrecks. She tried to look away, but couldn't.

"Horrible!" she said. And her table: smeared with clay, the finish no doubt ruined. She glanced at Nixon. The face of John Wayne Gacy—labeled on an index card—was superimposed on Nixon's, a snake coiling out of Gacy's mouth wrapped around the substantial jowls of Nixon. "Horrible, horrible," Anna said, and stormed back to the couch. "I need to speak to you!"

Marvin opened one eye. "Good morning, Anna." He yawned, sat up and looked around him as though not remembering where he was. Anna registered this, and it gave her a strange pang. The slow to wake look of a child, which led her in a flash back to Poppy and her husband. All the Saturday mornings when Poppy awakened so slowly that she and Hugh had time for breakfast and uninterrupted lovemaking before Poppy in her Scooby-Doo pajamas stumbled in with her scent of baby shampoo and Dreft laundry soap.

She yanked her attention back, pulled this image behind her memory's vision like a kite string.

"What's the meaning of these clay heads?"

"Well, it's a conceptual study linking presidents with serial killers. The idea is the slaughtering of Americans, either individually, as in the case of the killers' victims, or as ordinary citizens—"

"I don't mean that," Anna said, forcing herself to keep her voice low and level. "I don't give a damn about your artistic vision."

"Oh," he said, visibly disappointed. "What do you mean?"

"I mean, what the hell is it doing on my table like that? You've ruined the finish, do you realize that? That table has been lovingly taken care of for over a hundred years and you destroyed it in one day."

He stood, reached for his pants. "I'm sorry, Anna. I didn't know where else to set up. I'm at a critical moment in my work. I'm just rabid with creativity and I sometimes don't sweat the details. I'm sorry. I'll pay to have it refinished."

He did look sorry, Anna thought, and she felt like a fool, like a petty, shrill matron. If anyone else had done this to her table she would have been irritated, maybe a little angry, but nothing like the rage she was shaking with now.

"I'll go take a look at it, and if it needs a professional I'll get one," Marvin said.

She looked back at him. "I have to go to work. And then I have orchestra rehearsal till seven." She hadn't planned on going back to the rehearsals, but something in her now wanted to attempt Rachmaninoff. And she needed a little more time away from Marvin and Flynn to think about why this broken family had washed up here. *Why don't you meet me for dinner at Davidé's.* She wrote down the directions on the back of a sheet of a Brandenburg concerto, the one she liked least and never played.

Anna gathered up her cello, put it in the back of the Volvo and jostled through the rush-hour traffic. She never left this early. But the place seemed airless with Marvin and Flynn and all of their junk. She didn't feel well. She dodged in and out of lanes, sped ahead, slowed down. Calm down, she told herself. Had she had too much coffee? Her hands were shaking, her heart beating against her ribcage like a trapped bird. Food. Maybe she hadn't had enough to eat. She sped toward an exit when it felt as though she might black out, pulled into the nearest gas station. Was she having a heart attack? Her breath was short. It felt like her heart was missing every third beat. A curtain of dread fell down. She went into the convenience store, wandered through the cool aisles, knowing if she collapsed someone would call the paramedics. She bought a package of black licorice and a box of Sudafed.

*

The alarm went off at eight-thirty in the room where Flynn slept. In the middle of her dream about Oscar de la Hoya—a good dream where Oscar scored a seventh-round knockout—the music from the clock radio seeped into the space between waking and sleeping. A retro music weekend, the DJ said, featuring music from the '70s by those underground, where-are-they-now artists. The Bay City Rollers sang "Saturday Night."

In her dream, Oscar smiled at her as she peered into the ring. He sang about Jeremiah being a bullfrog as he sent his opponent down for the count. Oscar held the other boxer against the mat, looked up, and blew her kisses that turned into yellow feathers.

One Pip Is Worth a Thousand Knights

Anna waited for Marvin and Flynn in the corner booth of Davidé's. The shakiness of the morning was still with her but the martini she'd just gotten was helping. She'd finished up some things at school, then went to orchestra rehearsal where she did better with the Rachmaninoff, but struggled with a timing problem. The principal cellist noticed, then the conductor. Anna was coming in too early, midway through the downbeat. She excused herself after the first run-through, said she felt ill.

The violinist next to her, a humorless woman who taught second grade and was self-consciously married to a garage mechanic, had never liked Anna. Anna never liked her, either, but now there was true animosity. "Some of us take this very seriously, Anna, and don't look kindly on missed rehearsals or poor preparation."

"Sorry," Anna said, deciding she was done for the day. She waited until the conductor cued the woodwind section, then slipped out and drove straight to the restaurant.

Anna ordered a martini right away, and an appetizer plate to have something in her stomach. Other than a few strands of licorice earlier, she hadn't eaten all day. Even the fragrant bouquet of garlic and sweet basil marinara didn't seduce her. Maybe she had some sort of eating disorder. Well, it would pass. Perhaps not until Marvin and her granddaughter left, but it would eventually subside.

Marvin walked in just as Anna got out her phone to call him.

"Sorry I'm late," Marvin said, and sat down. He had on a white shirt and a red tie. His hair was pulled back, sleek as onyx, his face freshly shaven.

"I suppose I'm used to it," she said, then felt a little sorry for being so bitchy. She downed the last of the martini, chewed the olive. She would have to try harder to get along with this man. He was her son-in-law, after all, the father of her only granddaughter. In that way, family. "Where's Flynn?"

"She's with your neighbor, Greta." He picked up the menu.

"What? You asked her to baby-sit?"

"She wanted to. We were on our way out and she came over and introduced herself. Offered to watch Flynn. She and Flynnie hit it off right away. It was uncanny. Like they'd known each other for years." He looked around the dining room. "Where the hell is the waiter? I need a drink."

Anna looked over at him, was ready to say something sharp, like, where did he think he was, The Olive Garden? But he smiled at her so sweetly that she backed down.

"What are you going to have?" Marvin said, looking at the menu.

"Probably the lobster ravioli."

Marvin fiddled with the candle on the table. "I can't ever go into a restaurant without thinking about Poppy. I always have to order for her, if you can believe that. She's the most indecisive person I've ever known. She'll read the whole menu twice, pick something, then the minute the food comes she looks at my plate and says, 'I should have ordered that.'"

Anna smiled. "She was always like that. Her father used to call it entrée envy and tell her she was neurotic."

"Really? I was going to ask you, Anna, if you have any pictures of Poppy as a girl. I've put images together in my mind of what I think she must have been like, but I would love to see photos."

Anna nodded. "I'll look for some."

His eyes sparkled. "I would really appreciate that. Was Poppy shy as a child? What did she really love? I mean, activities, toys." He leaned toward Anna, his eyes wide.

"Well, I wouldn't have called her shy so much as wary. She was quiet, watchful. Sensitive." Anna laughed, embarrassed by these generic descriptions. She could have been talking about anybody's child. Marvin was still looking at her, hanging on her every word. "Poppy was strong-willed. And she had definite ideas about things. She used to insist that we take her to Sunday school, though Hugh and I never could figure out where she got that notion. We were not church-goers ourselves."

"Was she imaginative?" Marvin asked.

"Sure, I guess. Aren't all children?"

"Yeah, well, I'm just thinking of Flynn. Flynn is off the charts. Her imagination is positively frightening." He paused. "She draws things in too deep. Last year when she took ballet, her teacher was trying to get them to use the entire floor when they danced. She told them to be space hogs. Flynnie was convinced there were pigs in the sky and refused to go outside after dark because she was afraid they'd fall on her head."

Anna chuckled. A silence fell between them. Anna glanced around, looked at the overdressed women at the table next to theirs—mid-management types, women-taking-control-of-their-own-social needs-post-divorce type thing—and felt a sudden fearful anxiety mixed with distaste. Their exaggerated hilarity, forced gaiety, was apparent even from here. It was bad enough pretending to be cheerful, but being dressed up like that somehow made it even worse. After Hugh died, she met a group of women once a month for dinner or drinks. Anna liked a few of them a great deal, but she grew tired of the formality. The pleasure of female company was in part the freedom from artifice, from spangles and beads and lipstick. Sitting around with coffee or lemonade watching a video, drinking wine and listening to music.

She looked back to Marvin, who was watching her in return. Anna's heart started to pound, despite the alcohol she'd thought would be soporific. He began to fidget. Moved the salt shaker and sugar bowl and breadbasket as though they were materials for a sculpture.

The waiter came to take their dinner order. "And a bottle of the house red," Anna added.

"I should call and check on Flynnie," Marvin said, pushing back his chair.

"I'm sure she's fine," Anna said, and patted his arm. "Greta has my cell number if anything comes up."

Marvin nodded. "Is this the smoking section?"

"I don't know," Anna said, and looked around. One of the women at the next table was smoking. "It must be."

Marvin reached into his pocket and took out a package of Drum tobacco. He rolled a cigarette, then one for Anna when she couldn't do it herself.

"So," she said. "I have to tell you how surprised I was to hear from you and Poppy after all these years." She took a deep drag of the cigarette, let the smoke drift in her head. The tight bands in her chest began loosening a little. "I'd made up my mind years ago that my daughter and her family were gone forever."

"Well," Marvin said. "We thought it was time you got to know Flynn. She's never known a grandparent. Do you think you'll enjoy spending time with her? I mean, just the two of you?"

Anna said she would. "Sure. Maybe I'll take her to the zoo. Does she like zoos?"

"No. Probably not. That would upset her, I suspect. Flynn has only seen animals wild, in their natural habitat. She would enjoy a boxing match, though. If you told her you were taking her to the fights she'd melt like cheap chocolate in your hands."

"Okay. I'll see what I can do," Anna said, and turned to the waiter who brought the wine for her to taste. She nodded. "It's fine."

"What I have in mind is more than, uh, day trips and outings."

Anna looked up. "Pardon?"

"I said it's more than taking Flynn to boxing matches. It's more than that."

"What is? All right, why don't we stop tap-dancing here? What is it that brought you five thousand miles across the country in a van that shouldn't have been driven farther than the grocery store?"

Marvin swirled the wine in his glass, took a long sip. "I'm at my wit's end, Anna. Poppy has been disappearing like this for years. I can handle it, I've always handled it, but I can see now that it's having a profound effect on Flynn. I'm worried that she thinks it's her fault. I guess I'm asking for your help." He searched Anna's face, smoothed his hair back.

"What kind of help? What can I do?" Her head was swimming, her concentration filmy.

"This was all Poppy's idea. It was Poppy's idea that we come to visit you," Marvin said.

Anna shrugged. "Fine."

"And when she disappeared in Pennsylvania, that's when I formulated a plan. Of course, I thought about turning around and going home. But I'm thinking of my daughter, of what Flynnie needs. She needs a mother. She needs *her* mother, but that's not going to happen with Poppy. So, naturally I thought of you. Of you being the stable maternal influence in her life. Of the possibility of me and Flynnie settling here permanently." Marvin emptied his wineglass, twirled it by the stem. He unfastened his hair so it was a cool, dark waterfall around his shoulders, ran his fingers through its silky length. Anna watched the women at the next table noticing him. In one smooth motion, he had it back in its ponytail again.

"I've never been a stable maternal influence, Marvin. I'm no good at nurturing little creatures."

The waiter brought the food, refilled their water glasses. Anna leaned back in her chair.

Marvin nodded. "I know. I mean, I've heard Poppy's side of things." He paused. "But I thought maybe once you got to know Flynn...well. I had these great fantasies of the two of us moving to Boston. I know it's unrealistic to expect that we can all live under one roof."

"Yeah," Anna said.

"Poppy has been extraordinarily unstable for about three years. We've moved from place to place, but nothing makes her happy. She is the great love of my life. But I don't know what to do anymore."

"You're divorcing," Anna said.

He shook his head. "No. I will never divorce her. I will take her back anytime she comes back. I mean, I've been taking her back almost from the time I took her away." He smiled a little. "I gave her choices. I gave her ultimatums: me or the drugs. Me and the child or the drugs. In the end, Flynn and I always lost. She'd get clean for a while, then backslide. Even our daughter wasn't enough. And then I realized nothing would ever be enough."

Anna saw Poppy in some seamy back alley with crusted hypodermic needles, the stench of sick bodies and sweaty need, of unwashed flesh and clothing. The bright sick yellow of heroin suns rising behind her eyes. "I don't really understand," she said. She pushed her food away, untouched. "I don't understand how you can just disown your child. How Poppy can simply turn her back on her own daughter. What kind of drug can do that? What kind of substance takes precedence over your own child?" Anna glared at the table of women; they were getting louder and shriller. One of them in particular was driving Anna crazy, the heavyset brassy blonde whose laugh was like a donkey's braying. She was the most unattractive of the group. Her tight silk dress printed with tropical birds and flowers rippled over layers of fat. The woman was looking at Marvin too intensely and too often. Anna stared her down.

"I'm trying, you see, to think only of Flynn. Her mother will never kick the habit. Poppy's been using since she was fifteen years old. And now that Flynn is getting older, what she needs most is stability. My parents are dead. You and I are her only living relatives. You are the closest she can get to a true mother."

Anna's attention snapped back. "She's been using since she was fifteen?" Anna recalled the long summer drives to cheerleading camp, Poppy with her mouth full of braces and her sulky adolescent silences. She was in cheerleading camp at fifteen. Marvin must be mistaken. But what did it matter now? "No. I will have none of this, Marvin. But what about you? What prevents you from successfully raising her alone? Many men do."

"I am successfully raising her. Flynn is everything to me. But she needs more than just me. I realized this on the drive out here. On that long-ass hellish ride from Alaska, when I had a feeling Poppy was going to do what she did. Poppy's idea was that we give you temporary custody. That you could be Flynn's legal guardian until Poppy and I worked out what we needed to work out. Our marriage. Her drug habit. But it's all an illusion. Things aren't going to work out with Poppy, and Flynn is my daughter. It's ludicrous to think I could leave my daughter for any length of time. And a child like Flynn...." He looked away, picked up his tobacco and rolled another cigarette.

Anna caught the waiter's eye. She handed him a ten-dollar bill when he walked over. "Please bring me some cigarettes. Anything nonmenthol. Keep the change."

"Certainly," he said. "And may I ask if there's a problem with the food?"

Neither she nor Marvin had touched their dinners. "No. No problem. We're just slow."

"Look, I'm an artist, which is more stable than being a drug addict, but not by much. I've traveled a lot, I've switched jobs. Flynn has no sense of stability or constancy. A child like Flynn needs a CPA for a father and a kindergarten teacher for a mother."

"You keep using that phrase. 'A child like Flynn.' What does that mean? You make her sound like an alien."

Marvin paused. "She's imaginative."

"Well," Anna said, "that's hardly the worst problem she could have. It's not as if having an imagination is a lethal condition."

"I'm not sure," he said quietly. "Everybody says, 'sure, my child is imaginative.' But they have no idea. Imaginative to them means their kids make up conversation for their dolls. Or pretend they're puppies. Flynn thinks she talks to dead people. She believes in reincarnation. She sees things that aren't there. Hears things that nobody else can and is convinced they're true."

"Well, that doesn't seem so out of bounds."

"Trust me, Anna. She can be frightening. And being around me...around the way I work and the creativity I need to work...this can't be good for her. I have been awake for three straight days thinking about this. About what's best for my daughter. And I'm leaving the two of us at your mercy. I don't want to move to Boston, but I will. If it means that you'll be in our lives, I'll do anything."

"Of course I don't have a problem with you living in Boston. And I certainly don't have any problem with getting to know my granddaughter. But I guess I don't fully know what you have in mind. I can't be her mother."

"I am asking for your help," he said.

"Do you need money?"

"No," he said sharply. "I need your presence."

"You need me to love the girl like a mother would. I can't do that. I'll be her grandparent, but I don't want to raise her. I can't. I don't want her to live with me. You and she are welcome to visit, but if you move here, you need to find your own place." He looked surprised, Anna thought, as if he'd expected she would be thrilled at having Flynn live with her.

"You can think about things. We can see how comfortable you and Flynn are together. How much involvement you want with her, ultimately."

She didn't need to think about it. She didn't want them here. Why should she? After so many years, what she thought she had lain to rest was coming back like an awful reprise. She'd gotten through motherhood, cobbled together a way to deal with Poppy as best as she could, and closed off that part of her life when Poppy disappeared. And now, this nut bar, Marvin, who both took away her daughter then failed to deliver her as promised, wanted her to reopen everything, take on that heartbreak all over again.

"Did you expect that I would welcome you all with open arms?"

He sighed, poured the last of the wine between their two glasses. "I imagined the years might have softened you a little bit. I hoped for maybe just a bit of forgiveness toward Poppy and me."

She shook her head. "No. No forgiveness. I'm not capable of that charitable quality."

He shrugged. "Fair enough. At least I know where I stand. But don't take it out on my girl. Flynn had nothing to do with the choices her mother and I made."

"That," Anna said, and reached for the check, "I of course know." She took out her wallet, put some bills on the little tray. Neither one of them had eaten. "And incidentally, even if I did agree to become Flynn's temporary guardian, what makes you think I'd be a more stable adult for her than, say, you? I was a terrible mother."

"Yes," Marvin said. "I know."

Flynn had been listening to the radio all day, the '70s weekend of underground stars, first in her grandmother's house, then with Greta in her kitchen. Greta fed Flynn an early dinner of couscous—which Flynn knew to be Italian for excuse me, please—with chopped-up vegetables and currants—as in events—and some black dots that Greta said were capons. Or did she say they were capers? Flynn couldn't remember now, but she thought there might be a secret message in this strange food: couscous; currants; capon; capers. She translated it to possibly mean, Excuse me, I know no current events, and must put my cape on to do my capers. There could be an Italian superman around here somewhere.

"I'll eat with you," Greta said. "I'm starving these days."

"Are you, dear?" Flynn said, and smiled.

Greta smiled back. "Tell me what it's like living in Alaska."

Flynn swirled her couscous in the bowl, looked up at this woman who made her long to start her life over again. Start over as a tiny baby with this woman as her mother. On the drive out here, her father said that she would be getting a new mother. Or, someone who could act more like a mother to her. She didn't quite understand the difference. Maybe this was the woman he'd picked out for her. Someone who would treat her as an adopted daughter.

"Do you believe in hell?" Flynn asked.

"Pardon?" Greta said, and Flynn smelled her fear. Greta was probably afraid to die; in her last lifetime, Greta was a Cuban drug dealer. Somebody shot her—though in that lifetime she was a man—and dumped her body in the ocean. When people died like that, it took hundreds of years before violence was erased from the spirit.

Flynn shrugged. "Alaska is hell. It's cold as hell. It's dark as hell. Hoover McPaws frostbit the end of his tail and his ears. That's why he looks so hip-hop." Hip-hop was something the DJ said this morning. A kind of music. A song called "The Midnight Train to Georgia" was playing in her head.

"It's too cold for kitties to be out, probably." Greta took a large helping of couscous and ate very fast. Flynn wondered about the baby inside Greta. If it died would it go to heaven or hell? It wasn't true, as her mother told her, that all babies go to heaven. Some were punished and then forced to come back as new souls on earth. Her mother was one of them. Flynn knew Poppy had been to hell and back, and Flynn had followed her. And Flynn's father had followed *her*. The heart was a wheel. And here she was again.

"Do you believe in reincarnation?" Flynn asked.

"No," Greta said. "Do you?"

"You and I were great friends in the Second World War. We were Japanese. You were small then. I was a general, and I played the bassoon. When I died, you held my head. You wrote a letter to my wife and daughters." Flynn's heart was pounding. Her palms got sweaty just thinking about the pain of this.

"Interesting." Greta took a sip of her coffee. "Do you think that means we'll be good friends now?"

Flynn said that she did think so, and poured herself a glass of Tang, a drink she didn't like so much, but, as the jar said, it was the drink of the astronauts. Flynn thought she might want to be an astronaut someday, if she lived that long. "Have you considered adoption? Of a girl?"

"What?" Greta said. "How did you know that?"

"It's true, then?" So, her father hadn't been lying. Greta was to be her new mother while her old mother got better and Anna would be around to love them both. Her grandmother, Flynn knew, was someone who would listen. Anna would believe her. She wouldn't get mad or make her change the subject when Flynn talked about building the Great Wall of China and what it was like to work in such heat with cut-up feet and hands.

"Yes," Greta said, and smiled. "We're adopting a special little girl. As a matter of fact, we're going to have *two* children. I have a baby growing inside me. Did your grandma tell you?"

"No, not yet. My mother is ill. She's mentally ill. Did she seem mentally ill to you?" Flynn reached for the optometrist's goggles and set the meter to 20/20. This helped her stay in the ordinary world. If she was feeling just a little visionary, she adjusted the lenses to 20/40. Right now, Flynn didn't want to know too much. Just to be safe, she turned the settings to 20/200, the numbers of blindness.

"I never met your mother, dear. But she's probably fine. Do you think you and your father will visit with your grandma for a while?"

"I believe they're discussing that topic even as we speak," Flynn said, cocking her head to one side as though she could hear them. A radio somewhere played "The Ink Is Black."

"So, tell me what you like to do for fun, Flynn. What you and your friends do in Alaska."

"Oh, I don't have friends. I'm a freak show. I'm freaky Flynnie, the mental case. Freaky Flynn with the head of a pin, that's me."

"You must have *some* friends."

Flynn shrugged. "Spirit friends. I'm well-known and greatly admired in the spirit world."

Greta sipped her coffee, but didn't look mad the way Flynn's mother got mad when she spoke of these things. Greta was going to be an ideal adopted mother and her grandma, Anna, was going to help her make sense of the spirit world. Her grandmother knew things, Flynn believed, because there was light all around her. Spirit light, the light of six angels, maybe more.

"But you must have at least *one* friend who isn't imaginary."

"I do," Flynn said.

Greta smiled. "See? I thought so. What's her name?"

Flynn cleared the setting on the heavy glasses and looked at Greta with normal sight. "Greta. Her name is Greta."

Greta filled Flynn's glass with milk and didn't speak for so long that Flynn began to worry. She knew she confused people. Made people afraid. Not scary-movie afraid, but the way you drive around a cardboard box on the highway because it might have glass or sharp things inside. "Well, you have a good imagination. Maybe you'll be an artist."

Flynn shrugged. "My father's an artist. I've been an artist in other lifetimes. In my next life, I'm scheduled to be an artist who makes things in blue glass." She took a sip of the milk and asked if she could have more Tang.

Greta mixed up a new batch and Flynn watched as the orange crystals swirled around in the cloudy water like tiny astronauts trying to get to the moon. "My father is probably also mentally ill. My mother is definitely mentally ill."

Greta said softly, "Do you think you are?"

Flynn smiled but didn't answer. How could she answer? She explained to Greta about how in a previous life she and Marvin were husband and wife, and Poppy, her mother in this life, had been a blind cowherd named Ahmed who Marvin got jealous of. "He killed both of us in that life." Flynn stopped. This was what people didn't like to hear. This was why they called her freak show and mental case. She saw things. She knew things. But it wasn't her fault. Just before her mother disappeared from the International House of Pancakes in Pennsylvania, she got mad at Flynn because her father asked her to tell him a story to pass the time and Flynn told him about when he was Sarti, her husband. Poppy had turned around then and said, "Why can't you just pretend you were once Cleopatra or Queen Elizabeth? If you're going to believe in other lifetimes why do you invent such poor and unhappy ones? Huh? Why do you turn me into a blind cowherd?" Flynn remembered her mother asking.

"I don't make them up. I see them. I see things," Flynn had told Poppy.

"No, Flynn, you don't. You invent. Do you understand the difference between imagination and fact?" Poppy had asked.

"Yes, I do. And the fact is I've been Japanese and I've been Hindu. I've been rich and I've been poor. I was a famous horse veterinarian in England

and a witch in America. Right now, I'm not even a person. I'm not even human. I am distance."

"What?" her father had said. "What, sweetheart?"

"I am not a person. I am the distance between New York and California. I am every one of those miles."

"That's interesting," Marvin had said, taking a little notebook from his shirt pocket and writing something down.

"Christ," Poppy said. "Don't encourage her, Marvin. It's not interesting. It's not normal. Why can't we be normal?"

"Because you're a drug addict," Flynn had said. "The next time around I'm not coming back to help you. You have done wrong."

"Okay, Flynn, that's enough," Marvin had said.

Her mother was crying and wouldn't stop and that was the last thing Flynn remembered before Poppy had disappeared for good.

"May I be excused?" Flynn asked Greta. She put the goggles back on.

"Sure," Greta said. "What would you like to do now? There might be some cartoons on."

"No, thank you. I don't like cartoons. Can I go to my grandmother's backyard? I told her I would dig her yard." Flynn was lying, which she didn't like to do, but she had a project she needed to start.

"Well, I guess that would be all right, if you promise to stay just in the yard. It'll be dark soon."

"I promise. Can I borrow your radio?"

"You sure can." Greta unplugged it—at least that's what Flynn thought she was doing; she'd moved down to 20/600, the setting that made the world easy: everything was just a shape that was either moving or not moving.

In her grandmother's yard, Flynn put the radio on the picnic table and got a shovel from the shed. She began to dig. Hopefully her grandmother wouldn't be too upset. According to the DJ this morning, there were underground musical stars who had been there for over thirty years. It would make her grandmother's yard ugly, but if she could find the Bay City Rollers it would be worth it.

After an hour of steady digging she pressed her ear against the hole. She thought she heard something very, very faintly way down in there. The kind of muffled noise Hoover McPaws made when he purred from beneath layers of clothes in a laundry basket. She couldn't be sure, though. It might be something or it might not. She would be happy to find anything. Really, she didn't care all that much about finding the Bay City Rollers or Gladys Knight; what Flynn wanted was a pip. One pip would be worth a thousand knights.

"Where's your car?" Anna asked, as they walked out of Davidé's.

"I took the bus in. So I'll have to ride with you if you let me."

Anna drove through Boston then headed north on the highway. She had no destination in mind, but it felt comforting to be pointed toward Maine. How many times did she and Hugh make this drive in the course of their marriage? Fifty? A hundred? An image of the house was forever lodged in her mind. The living room blazing with firelight, the sharp scent of birch and the dormant scents reawakened from the heat: dusty old carpets, the lemon and pine polish on the furniture and brass, and, Anna's favorite, a faint beachy smell that seemed to rise up from every nook and tucked-away blanket.

"Where are we going?" Marvin asked.

"I don't know. I don't have the foggiest idea." Anna took the next exit, drove down a side road and pulled into a closed Texaco station. She rolled down the window, reached for her cigarettes and stared into the fading twilight. The tree frogs and crickets called.

"Just like high school. Hello, 1983." He laughed.

"What?" Anna said.

"Every empty parking lot is a potential lover's lane."

Anna snorted. "You're drunk."

"I am, it's true." He rolled down the passenger window, reached for one of her cigarettes when he couldn't get the hand-rolled tobacco to hold its shape.

"I guess I need to say that I don't want you here. I'd like to get to know Flynn, but I want only limited contact with her if you do decide to move to Boston. I mean, I'll be the kind of grandma who goes to the school plays, but not the kind who makes the costumes. Do you know what I'm saying? I can't relive all this again, Marvin. I'm sorry."

"Relive it?"

"Motherhood, grief, all of it. I don't want to be attached to anything anymore. I mean, it's like you're all back from the dead. All those years. All those years without a word. Who can live with that kind of worry forever? You have no idea. You have no idea how after a while absence turns into grief. And this sounds terrible, but it was just easier to imagine my daughter, that all of you, were dead. Mourning is easier than worry. Or any of those emotions you feel for the living." She remembered now how sweet Poppy was as a young girl, so loving and obedient, a near-perfect child. But it was as if Poppy had been the daughter of a close friend instead of her own. Like any mother she was haunted by the idea of losing her child—to death, to strangers, to terrible, irreversible accidents—but that was simply maternal instinct. Motherhood was a different state entirely, one that she never really inhabited. Poppy seemed part of her, certainly, but Anna suspected her attachment differed from other mothers. The child who had been joined to her body once continued to seem like one of the most expendable parts of herself. A growth, a tumor. Well, not that exactly. Nothing so malignant. An extra finger or toe that got in the way and was not useful or needed.

"I'm sorry, Anna," Marvin said. "I'm sorry for everything." He covered her hand with his own.

"Well," she said, and drew away. "That's that. I wish you well. I'd like updates and calls now and then." She lit another cigarette, stared at the old soda vending machine against the side of the gas station. It was one of the styles from the '50s or '60s that dispensed Coke in bottles. Anna remembered how satisfying it was to drink sodas from a bottle, the icy slush cooling her palm, the cold glass against her lips. What an odd thing to still have around.

She put the car in gear, but stopped. "Actually, before we go, I need to see." She nodded to the old Coke machine, dug around for some change. "I have to see if it works."

"No way," Marvin said. "That thing looks like it's been there since the Johnson administration." He took the change from Anna. "I'll go." Anna watched him walk away. Marvin did have admirable qualities. He seemed extraordinarily patient—with his unusual daughter, with his flighty wife, and even, Anna had to admit, with her. In all of her tirades against him, he never once lost his temper or yelled back. And most men would have written off the likes of Poppy years ago. There was a real nobility in the way he loved his wife and daughter. Ironclad and without conditions. Even now when he talked about Poppy, there wasn't any trace of bitterness or resentment in his voice. Still, there was something about him that made her stop short every time. A darkness, an incomplete telling of the truth, she didn't know.

Marvin turned back, held up a cold bottle.

Anna got out of the car and walked over. "Amazing," she said, oddly elated. She found the opener along the side of the machine. The icy sweetness was how she remembered it. The smell of the bottle was the same, too. She passed it to Marvin, who passed it back after a sip, and they finished it this way, taking turns until it was gone.

Flynn was waiting inside her grandmother's house, watching from the living room window. She could hardly wait to start their new life together. Ever since Greta had let it slip earlier about the adoption, Flynn's excitement had grown over the afternoon until now, nearing eight o'clock and her bedtime, she was shaking with anticipation. Maybe she and Anna would buy new clothes so she wouldn't have to always wear things from the second-hand store. She figured that they would move into a big house—Flynn saw it in her head. A huge place with many rooms, but also many spirit people. Flynn didn't mind living with the dead. She'd always seen them, and they her. There was a murdered woman here in her grandma's house. She once lived here, but somebody killed her in another country. Flynn had seen her in the bathroom a few times, and occasionally sitting beside her grandmother, especially when Anna did her doctor things. The woman liked Anna's microscope. Once, the woman touched Flynn awake with cold air. She was sitting right on Flynn's bed! Flynn held her breath. She didn't blink.

The woman said, *Can you tell me what time the football game starts? Will you direct me to the train that will take me downtown?* Flynn told the woman she could see her, but not help her, and after that the woman left her alone.

People got a free house from the government when they adopted a child, Flynn knew. Her father and Greta might get married, though Greta said she already had a husband. Flynn thought she was probably lying, since her house was too neat and kitchen table didn't have any mail or newspapers on it. This new life was going to be perfect. Every morning when she thought about Poppy she cried a little. Every night of her life she was sad. Each time her mother disappeared, Flynn felt so terrible she was sure she would die. This time, though, when Poppy got back everything would be different. It would be better. Poppy would live in the adopted house, and have her own room to do her drugs. She wouldn't have to feel guilty about not taking care of Flynn because other people could do that. Her mother's room would have two lights on the door: yellow and red. When the yellow was lit up, Flynn would go in and visit. Yellow meant high and happy. The red light would tell her to stay away. That was the color of angry cravings that made Poppy say things to Flynn she didn't mean.

Anna walked in just as "Can't Take My Eyes Off of You" was playing on the radio.

"Hi, Flynn," Anna said, then turned the volume down a notch.

"I've been waiting for you all day. I'm so glad you're home. I was getting worried."

"Oh?" Anna said. The girl looked drawn and ashy. "Are you feeling okay?"

"Where do you want this?" Marvin said, from beneath the twin-size mattress that Anna bought earlier. The lumpy mattress that Flynn was sleeping on was old and worn. There was no reason for the girl not to be comfortable during her stay.

"In Flynn's room," Anna said.

Flynn felt her heart beat wild with joy: already her grandmother had bought her a new bed. She had never had anything new in her life, except maybe for Christmas, and now here was something of her very own in *her room*. She hugged Anna around the waist, buried her face in her grandmother's sweater that smelled of lavender and smoke and garlic. "Is this going to be the adopted house?" Flynn imagined something bigger, but maybe people had to sign papers before the government gave you the big house.

"What, dear? Is it going to be what?" Anna looked down at her granddaughter. Her face was like a flower, open and radiating light. Every young girl was lovely, but this one even more so: she had her mother's deeply pigmented lips and cheeks, Marvin's dark curly hair. Her eyes were the deepest brown, almost black, and sparkling. Anna wondered how long it had been since she had touched a child. In ways like this, out of affection rather than clinical necessities. She remembered Poppy hugging her once or twice the way Flynn was now, her sharp head just under Anna's breast-bone. So long ago.

"Greta told me," Flynn said softly.

"Told you what," Anna said, and touched the girl's warm cheeks.

"That I'm going to live here. With you. And her."

"What? No, I'm—"

"I've been waiting for you my whole life."

Something about the way she said it, or the events of the evening, or the touch of the child herself, made Anna melt a little. This, after all, was her blood. But more than that: she was the grandchild of her husband. Part of him. His genetic material coded in her DNA. Anna was surprised by how long it had taken her to remember such a self-evident fact. Any little bit of Hugh that shone through in the girl—a tilt of her head, an arch of an eyebrow, a preference for fruit at room temperature—any minuscule resemblance would be a little like having him back.

She sat down next to Flynn. In the car, Anna had told Marvin in no uncertain terms that he was to be out of her house in two weeks. A short visit was fine. No harm in that. It would give Anna and Flynn a chance to get to know each other, but it wasn't so long that she or the girl would form deep bonds.

Anna turned the radio back up. What was with the songs from the '70s she'd been hearing all day?

From the other room she heard Marvin singing along, and she joined him, the two of them sharing the song the way they had the bottle of Coke earlier.

By the end of the evening, something felt as if it had shifted—as though something had been decided that she had no say in. It was hard to put her finger on what had changed. Except that when she looked up at the clock, three hours had flown by as she and Flynn rifled through Anna's closet and jewelry box, sifted through boxes that Anna had left unopened since moving.

"I love cooking," Flynn said, paging through an old Betty Crocker. She had put on an old dress that Anna had saved for sentimental reasons, one from the year when she and Hugh started dating. Flynn liked girlish things, to Anna's delight; Poppy never bothered with jewelry or perfume, both of which Flynn now had on abundantly.

"See this diamond ring?" Anna picked up the two-carat solitaire that had been Hugh's mother's. "This was your great-grandmother's. Someday it will be yours. Some day you'll have all this jewelry."

"Which day?" Flynn said, adding another bracelet to the stack already around her wrist.

"Tell me something, Flynn," Anna said, remembering how Hugh liked his fruit and beverages at room temperature. "If I told you I had a bowl of grapes for you in the kitchen, where would you look for them, on the counter or in the refrigerator?"

Flynn looked at her with an expression of amused disbelief. "The counter. Why would you keep grapes in the refrigerator?"

SEVEN

The Ninth Order of Angels

Nobody at work, with the possible exception of Jane, knew Jack was sick. His health status was his business, and he planned to keep it that way. Jane, of late, had begun putting odd stresses in the middle of her sentences—"How *are* you?"—which led him to suspect that she'd talked to Stuart. Jack wasn't worried about indiscretion from Jane; in this conservative office, right-wingers and old New England stock, she had as much to hide as he did.

It had only been one month and eight days since he had left Stuart. Or more accurately, was shown to the door. Kicked to the curb, tossed away like a used Kleenex. One month, eight days, and twelve hours since Jack was forced to rely on self-pity rather than Stuart's ministrations to get him through the night.

From his open office door, Jack watched the partners file in. He surreptitiously observed any unusual reactions or expressions from those who passed by as he pretended to study stock quotes. Nothing had changed. The same people who always ignored him, ignored him still, the friendly ones waved, same as ever.

At ten o'clock he picked up the phone to call Stuart, then changed his mind. Jack had called him a few times—well, fifteen to be precise—in the first week, but Stuart hung up the instant he heard Jack's voice. Two days ago, Jack left a message on the machine asking Stuart to call him at work if he wanted to talk for any reason. That was probably a mistake, he thought now, as he sorted through the stack of files on his desk, bleary-eyed from too much vodka the night before. Stuart might assume that the absence of a home number meant that he was with someone else and didn't want to give out his home number. "I'm such an idiot!" he said, and banged his hand down hard on his desk. Why didn't he just indicate in his message that he didn't yet have a home phone number? Jack knew how Stuart's suspicious mind worked. "I am such an incompetent moron."

Molly, his secretary, appeared in the doorway to his office. She sat on the other side of the thin wall. "Did you need something? I had headphones on. Sorry."

"No. Just talking to myself." He waved her away. "Carry on."

After leaving Stuart, Jack spent two days in a hotel, which he thought might do as a makeshift apartment; it was cheaper than rent, and he had maid service, access to workout rooms, and a fully stocked wet bar. The lounge had a bartender called Ace, and Jack wanted to stay there if for no other reason than that; it was a name right out of Hollywood. Robert Mitchum himself couldn't do better than be served old-fashioneds by a guy who was almost typecast—he had everything except the Guinea tee and the wife named Maria. But in the end, the hotel made him lonelier. The common areas were full of budget-minded honeymooners too broke to afford Cancun, overweight, balding businessmen, newly divorced middle-aged women already hopelessly thick around the middle. Society's downtrodden. One night while walking off his insomnia, he came upon a boarding house with a sign advertising rooms rented by the week. The next day, he leased the entire third floor—six rooms in all. It was squalid, but by renting all the rooms he'd have privacy and space; it was one thing to live in squalor, another to be cramped in a tiny room while doing so. Jack asked the landlord to paint the rooms. "Preferably off-white, in a Sherwin-Williams semigloss."

"Huh? Paint?" The landlord said. "What?"

"Paint. The liquid substance one applies to walls."

"Paint?" he repeated again.

"Can you come and get the junk out of all these rooms?" Jack said finally.

"Yeah, yeah, all that stuff'll be gone by when you come."

Of course the pile of cast-off possessions remained. Jack was both depressed and intrigued by the remnants of these other lives. There were the requisite broken hot plates and chipped mugs, torn shirts and stained, sprung mattresses, but there was also a room full of toys, all with something broken or flawed. He found six See 'n Says and not one had all the animals making the correct sounds. On one, the pigs mooed, on another, they brayed. The one Jack especially liked had the elephants chattering like Cheetahs and the monkeys roaring like lions. Few of the Lego blocks snapped flush, and all the Monopoly games were deficient in money or property. Jack called Stuart that first evening, wanting to tell him about the hard-luck toy salesman who had apparently inhabited this room, but he chickened out. Jack had ached for his partner at that moment. It was ridiculous, but he never could have imagined it would come to this, the enormity of his loss driven home by the pull-cord of a cheap, flawed toy.

Anyway, Jack had gotten what he wanted in the boarding house. There was a special kind of privacy that could come only from the transient zoned-out tenants he lived among. Nobody noticed him or cared who he was. He didn't have to make small talk with the neighbors on the elevator. He wasn't even expected to make eye contact. An air mattress and some camping goods made things on the Zen side of comfortable. Early on, Stuart had sent some of Jack's clothes to his office, so Jack had his Armani suit and his five best Ascot Chang and Thomas Pink shirts. He had one pair of jeans, and a single sweater that still smelled of Stuart's careful laundering.

Jack turned back to the paperwork on his desk. One of these days he would have to go buy some more clothes; he'd worn the Armani suit to work every day for a month, and the pants, he saw now, were dusty at the cuffs, stained faintly with the red wine he had last night after he trailed Hector home to a shabby apartment house on the south end of Back Bay. The building had a locked front door. Jack waited over an hour before one of the tenants left so he could get in. There were fifteen mailboxes, and Jack guessed that H. Ramiriz & R. Elsasser, apartment nine, would be Hector's; the other mailbox with an H. had the last name of Johnson, so it was likely that apartment nine—third floor, he saw with dismay—was his boy's.

Since leaving Stuart, Jack drove by the Korean grocery every day at the same time. Last night was the first he'd caught Hector there. He parked across the street, watched as Hector chatted up some aging queen, flashed the smile that convinced you it was only for you that he showed it, some private store of sunlight he bestowed on you and only you. He wore a yellow shirt—he almost always wore yellow—and was even more hand-some than Jack remembered, though it could be that the derelicts Jack lived among with their nicotine faces and boozy eyes made everyone look better by comparison. Hector was a little heavier, which suited him.

Luckily, Hector hadn't left with the man he'd been talking to and it was easy enough in the slow, congested rush-hour traffic to follow him. Jack needed to talk to him, needed to tell Hector he was sick, but it would be best, he'd decided, if he could do it on Hector's home ground and not some public street corner. After finding out Hector's street address and apartment number, Jack had driven home. He would talk to Hector the following night, or the night after, preferably after he learned who the R. was on Hector's mailbox.

Over the past few weeks Jack had determined that he must be in love with Hector. There was no other explanation for the heartsickness he felt for the boy. It was, though, a different kind of love from what he and Stuart shared: he felt Stuart's presence everywhere, in every thought, but Hector was all about absence, the blank space where Jack could spill over, bleed past the careful outline he maintained with Stuart.

There would be no easy way to tell Hector the news. But he was pre-pared to do anything. He would take Hector in and the two of them would be able to live in fine style on Jack's income. Hector could have anything he wanted, do anything, work or not. What mattered was that Jack be able to care for him. There were things Jack wanted to teach him—Hector was still a boy after all, with a boy's childish ways and habits. Jack doubted that Hector had much exposure to museums and operas, or had ever been abroad. He could imagine nothing finer than watching as Hector's sensi-bility expanded, to be able to lead him over the final threshold of his boy-hood. This fantasy, anyway, was the only way he could sleep at night.

Stuart, he'd learned through Dr. Mosites, had tested negative.

It was close to eleven before he actually started working. He picked up the stack of files from the IN basket. Sixteen, he counted, which should have been dealt with last week. His deadlines for these accounts had prob-ably come and gone.

He picked up the Kobayashi account, his most demanding client, the company's top money-maker he'd been given a year ago when he was at the height of his confidence and success; everything he touched then turned to gold. The president of the firm, a crusty old Bostonian with a pedigree longer than God's, had said to him at the last Christmas party, loud enough for everyone to hear, "Jack, my wife's been bugging me to let you go shopping with her."

"Oh?" Jack said, bracing himself for what might come next. He wasn't out at the office of course. As far as he knew, only Jane knew anything of his private life. He smiled tightly, prepared himself for a barb about gay men and their instinct for glamour and accessorizing.

"Yeah, she says if you can get nearly a hundred per cent returns on sixty per cent of our flagship clients, what could you do at the return counter at Saks?"

People laughed heartily, Jack among them.

"She claims she's going to buy a mink coat and have you go with her to get double her money back."

Jack floated all evening; that was the closest he'd come—that anyone had ever come—to warmth from Hank Sherman.

He glanced down at the client information sheet stapled to the outside of the folder. This account was his baby, the one he never, until the past few weeks, let slide. He was aggressive and assiduous and meticulous with this one—Kobayashi was persnickety, had already been through three investment houses before landing on Jack's desk. Showing losses in more than two quarters, Jack knew, would be the end. If there was one thing Jack had learned about Japanese corporations it was that you came in through the side door, so to speak, with the humility of a pizza deliveryman. You exchanged pleasantries, you asked about the weather, their wives, how their kids were doing in cram school and *then* you got down to business, but only as if you happened to be there by sheer coincidence: It appears I have a pizza for sale, would you like it? Seller and buyer both pretending the exchange of money was a low, but necessary thing.

He picked up the phone, dialed his secretary's extension. "I need you to ring Tokyo for me, Molly," he said.

"Again?" she said, her nasal Brooklyn accent grating on Jack's ear.

"What do you mean, again?"

"You asked me to do that yesterday morning. I already typed up the information from the conference call."

"Conference call?"

Jack could almost read Molly's expression through the wall as she said, "Yes, sir." His heart raced. He didn't remember anything other than in a kind of distant, dreamy way. He'd been so stressed that his memory was shot, his brain a sieve. Was this dementia of some kind? No doubt the alcohol and the late nights had something to do with it.

"Where is the report?"

"In your IN basket," she said, incredulous. "Typed, proofread, copied and distributed for the two o'clock meeting."

"All right then," Jack said. "And did I know about this meeting?"

Molly paused, took in her breath sharply. "It's on your calendar."

Jack thanked her, and hung up. Christ! He checked his schedule. A meeting with the senior partners and Hank himself penciled in Molly's neat handwriting. Did he schedule this meeting? And what was the agenda? Why couldn't he remember a goddamn thing from the previous two days?

Jack inhaled and exhaled slowly. Okay. This whirlwind. He'd been drinking too much, for starters, and spending too much time checking Hector's corner or driving by his old place to see if the lights were on, if Stuart was still awake. He took a few too many of the Percodan Mosites had prescribed to manage the pain of the shingles he'd recently developed. Swallowed them with vodka, no less. Still, for the life of him he couldn't remember if he called this meeting, or if Hank or one of the other senior partners had. He picked up the notes Molly had made of the conference call with Mr. Kobayashi. Apparently, Jack had suggested a larger, riskier stock portfolio, moving from steady growth to aggressive, questionable investments. The report was sixteen pages long, and half of Molly's transcription from Jack's dictation was followed by question marks, which meant he was mumbling. The gist of it was that Jack had recommended the company invest in the purchase of art and memorabilia; specifically, to authorize him or an agent of the firm to attend a Sotheby's auction of Jackie O's estate. He was horrified. Had he really convinced a state-of-the-art electronics firm to bid on pearl chokers and cigarette lighters? The only thing to do at this point was not back down, to make the case that estate investments would perform as well, and maybe outperform, blue-chip corporations in the long run. When in doubt, bluff your way into swaggering confidence.

Molly called him at two-ten to tell him that they were all waiting. "The meeting has already started, Jack. Hank wanted me to ring you."

"Okay. Thanks," Jack said, and grabbed the top four files on his desk. He smoothed down his hair, brushed away the dust on his clothes.

Molly looked at him suspiciously. He turned right, then left. "Conference room, third floor," she said.

"Right."

"Good of you to join us, Jack," Hank said, when Jack walked in. The six senior partners—Jack was the seventh—turned to look at him.

"Apologies for being late," he said, taking the seat across from Hank.

"Okay, then. As you all are aware, Jack has proposed estate and art investments for our top-shelf clients. I'll let him present the particulars of splits and returns and ratios of probable risk to gains." Hank nodded in his direction. Jack poured a glass of water from the carafe, glanced through the window behind Hank at the maples and oaks just beginning to turn.

"Ready, Jack?"

"All set," he said, squaring the folders in front of him.

Hank stood, cut the lights, and one of the partners slid a laptop computer in front of Jack, pulled down a screen in the front of the room.

"Oh, well actually, this presentation will not be with PowerPoint. I thought I would just give you all an overview, get general feedback and input before I proceed."

"Didn't we agree to give this the green light?" somebody beside him asked.

"Just proceeding with caution," Jack said. "This is the Kobayashi account, after all. I'm covering all my bases."

"Jack, no visuals?" Hank said, his hand poised on the light switch.

"Not for this meeting," he said, and spotted an old-fashioned easel with drawing paper and markers in the corner. "Okay, then," he said feeling the sweat bead under his collar and run down the length of his back. He picked up the folder on the top of his stack, stood and dragged the easel to the front of the room. Pie charts would give him time to think on his feet. "All right. The idea is to do a fifty-fifty split in high-performing stocks, and the rest in art. Now—"

"Wait a second," one of the partners said. Jack looked over. Evan, the youngest and the newest senior partner, a gorgeous boy who looked like Greg Louganis. Jack often wondered if he was family. He'd come from Baton Rouge, originally, and Jack had never heard him mention a wife or a girlfriend. "In your report, Jack, you talked about a 70-30 split. Are you now proposing 50-50s?"

"Well, yes. This is what I wanted to put out at this meeting. If we can convince Kobayashi to put fifty per cent of his investments in art, we can manage the other percentage in blue-chip stocks, diversified in four areas of industry: pharmaceuticals, telecommunications, electronics, and services, for instance."

"I have my doubts about this," someone else said.

"Think big, people," Jack said. He drew a large circle in green marker on the paper, divided it into four parts, each representing four of their richest clients. He had no idea what he was doing. If someone else had proposed this asinine plan he would have voted it down immediately. It was absurd. Popular culture, especially, had no documented consistent performance: Jackie's pearls today were Warhol's soup cans tomorrow. He drew percentages and ratios in red and purple markers, started to relax—this was it, certainly. Hank would come in for a private meeting this afternoon and inform him in that chilly, old-stock New England way that what the firm needed was solid teamwork and proven investment strategies, not wild cards like him.

He rambled on, made up numbers and statistics as though he had spent hours researching this topic. He didn't dare turn around and face his colleagues. He addressed his remarks to the window. "As we know from John F. Kennedy and Marilyn Monroe memorabilia, investments in pop culture are far less risky than certain stocks. Without question, the value is immune from the buffeting and volatility of, say, technology. We may lose interest in telecommunications, may change our brand of footwear and soft drinks, but we never give up our goddesses and heroes."

Jack capped the marker, turned. To his surprise, nobody was smirking or exchanging hooded glances. He felt so ill suddenly. Dizzy and scattered. He sat, poured a glass of water.

"Jack, this is most interesting," Hank said. "I've already tentatively green-lighted this, so if anyone has other ideas, now's the time to put them on the table."

No one spoke for a few agonizing minutes. "I know it's a bit radical, and hasn't been part of the firm's strategy in the past, but it's a new world," Jack said.

"I agree in part with Jack," Evan said. "I like the idea of diversification. A fifty-fifty split, though, might be taking it too far, in my opinion."

Hank looked from Evan to the rest of the group. "Other input, positive or otherwise?"

Jack was astonished at their indifference; losing the Kobayshi account, which undoubtedly he was about to do, would affect all of them.

The meeting went on for another half hour, with minor debates about the percentages, memorabilia versus fine art. Jack's stomach was pure acid, his mind wandering to Stuart, to Hector. His ears had been ringing half the day.

"Well, Jack, your instincts about this account have been sterling in the past. It's one of the most well managed portfolios in the firm. So, I'm leaving it in your capable hands to do as you think best. I haven't heard any strong oppositions." Hank looked around again. "Attend the Sotheby's auction, see what Christie's is hacking. I'm giving this project six months to fail or succeed, before we either present this to other clients as a new investment strategy, or we kill it." He smiled coldly at Jack. "Don't make any mistakes."

Jack smiled back. Christ! He would have preferred to be let go on the spot, rather than six months from now, after he had bought Judy Garland's shoes and Marilyn's *Seven-Year Itch* dress.

What he needed to do was work twelve and thirteen hours a day to get even the rudimentary structure of this new plan in place. Starting early next week, he would put in long hours. Weekend hours, too. For now, though, he was going to have to call it a day. He still wasn't feeling up to par. There was a ringing in his ear, an ache that felt as though somebody was leaning against his temple with a pointy elbow. He stuffed the file folders in his briefcase, turned off his computer and picked up his Palm Pilot to give to Molly on the way out.

"Please call and schedule a phone meeting with Tokyo at Kobayashi's earliest convenience," he said to Molly. "Also, get me a list of all upcoming auctions at Sotheby's and Christie's. That is, please." He turned.

"Jack?" Molly said.

"Yes?"

Molly stood, walked over to him. "Is everything all right?" She looked at him, frowned, and picked at something on his tie. Green Silly String.

"Everything is fine, *mia cara*," he said, and smiled. "I'm a bit under the weather, is all. A bit of a low front, high-pressure zone moving in. I'm going home to rest."

She nodded, brushed at his overcoat. "What is this?" she said.

"I believe it's Silly String." He noticed strands at the hem of his trousers. "I believe I went into a corporate meeting clad in Armani and Silly String. Super. I suppose you couldn't have noticed before I went in there, eh, before I went in there looking like I'd just been at a birthday party for a five-year-old."

She laughed. "See you Monday. I'll call you at home soon as I have the times set up, since it will probably have to be scheduled for an ungodly hour."

"Ungodly hours are all I know lately. Actually, I'll have to call you. My home phone is out of commission."

"Oh, I have your cell number," she said, flipping through the Rolodex.

The cell phone was one he and Stuart had shared. Stuart had it now. "No, that's not working, either. I'll have to call you."

Molly unlaced a thread of green string from around the button on his sleeve, dropped it in the trash. She saluted. "Whatever you say, Captain Kangaroo."

"Aren't you a sketch," Jack said, and headed toward the elevator.

He stretched out on his mattress when he got home, poured a double Scotch and swallowed a Percodan, watched the rain sheet against the windows. His fever was only 100, he was relieved to see. Just a touch of a cold. He took off his tie and untucked his shirt. He should have shopped on his way home. He had no food in the place, and he had nothing comfortable to change into. Outside, the rush-hour traffic roared below in the street, people going home to their dinners and wives and evening sitcoms. He missed Stuart horribly, missed all the little things he'd taken for granted, like clean sheets and the sweet-smelling, fleecy clothes Stuart laid out on the bed for him to put on when he came home, sweatshirts that always seemed to be warm from the dryer. Now, for instance, if he'd been at home, Stuart would be babying him because he didn't feel well, would run one of those magical, curative baths with fragrant salts and oils.

What he should really do was rest for a while, he knew, but late afternoon and early evening always made him think of Hector and Jack's desire to see him now was overwhelming. He refreshed his drink, downed it quickly, and went out into the rain.

At the back of the building the fire escapes traversed every apartment above the ground level. He narrowed Hector's apartment down to two possibilities. One was dark. He climbed the steps in the direction of the other, thankful that the rain would drown out any noise his shoes made on the metal stairs.

He sank down on the step slowly, watched the light from within. After fifteen minutes he decided that either the tenants weren't home or were in another room; he didn't see any shadows flickering on the glass or hear any voices. Jack raised his head carefully until his eyes were just barely above the sash. The furniture had plastic slipcovers, and there were doilies on the end and coffee tables. There was a miniature poodle sleeping under a dinette table, a picture of four or five very blond—striking even from this distance—children on the wall. An old man tottered into view. Not Hector's apartment. He tiptoed to the other window, the dark one, and peeked inside. Lights coming in through the opposite window suggested that this wasn't Hector's apartment, either: this living room featured a playpen and a clutter of toys. Just as he was turning to climb back down a light came on. He slid carefully to one side of the window, peeked around only when he heard the sound of a television. A woman holding an infant stood with her back to him. The baby with its milky monkey eyes seemed to look right at him. He shuddered. How could this be? There were five apartments to each floor. Hector had to be on this floor unless he was H. Johnson in apartment two. Of course, that old man could have been Hector's father, or this woman could be his mother. He looked back in at the woman. She was young, not more than twenty-five. She was petite and plump, dark-haired like Hector. Maybe his sister. His newly divorced sister, perhaps? The R. Elsasser on the mailbox? She hadn't gotten Hector's genes, that much was clear even from this angle: she would be fat in five years, her figure lacking the exquisite sculpture and long limbs of her brother. Oh, Hector's legs! Jack could still feel Hector's legs, firmly muscled and strong, as cool and smooth as palm leaves.

He went down one step, sat. Poor Hector, living here with an ugly sister and a whiny kid. Surely someone with Hector's exquisite looks could find a man to put him up. There was no reason he had to live like this, though Hispanics were family loyal, Jack knew, took care of their own in the way WASPs like him never dreamed of.

He saw another shadow come into the room. He stepped back up. It was Hector himself. Jack's heart started to beat faster. He was wearing a creamy silk shirt, expensive-looking and gorgeous against his dark hair and eyes. He smiled at the woman, reached for the baby, kissed it, and tossed it playfully in the air. Jack looked around at the cheap furnishings, plastic flowers, and brass-framed prints that undoubtedly came from a discount store and were chosen to pick up the colors in the sofa. Behind Hector, Jack caught a glimpse of the dingy kitchen, saw even from here the cockroaches scuttling about on the grimy linoleum and hood over the range top.

Hector put the baby in the playpen, turned to the woman, and took her in his arms. Jack felt his stomach threaten to empty, shock bolt through him and settle like a cold piece of animal fat in his throat. Of all the things he could have witnessed this was the scene he dreaded most. He shivered. Hector was kissing the woman now. Jack's mind started to race. His face burned. His lungs felt like they were full of broken glass. Every breath hurt. Inexplicably, his mind wandered to his crew coach in prep school. Hal Davis was a wheezing fat man who stank of cigars and garlic and who drove Jack to the limits of endurance. Never in his life had he been so focused and single-minded, up at dawn every day to row on the Charles, rain or shine. His stamina increased the longer he trained, and in those disciplined years everything in his life was immaculate: a perfect grade point average, every assignment and task completed on time, monkish weekend nights where he was in bed by eight-thirty. The first keg party he'd been to was also his last: the night before graduation. It was no real hardship to stay away from parties or coeds—contrary to what he led Stuart to believe, he was a virgin with undeclared sexual preferences until he was nineteen; he simply didn't think about sex until he had given up rowing for good. On holiday breaks, when he didn't have to worry about classes, he read novels as soon as his practice was over. Stuart would die laughing, picturing Jack in all his athletic glory hiding out in his bedroom reading *Pride and Prejudice*. Those were the Stendhal years. He went through *The Red and the Black* at least a dozen times.

Jack was Olympic-class, everybody said so, and he had scholarship offers to four Ivy League schools by the time he was a junior. He missed a spot on the National team by eight-tenths of a second.

When Coach Davis suffered a heart attack in Jack's last year and had to retire, something went out of Jack's competitive drive. He still rowed as hard, trained as rigorously, but the mysterious force that had pushed him was gone. His pace slackened, his time slowed. It wasn't that Jack didn't like the new coach, a young guy not long out of Brown, but rowing had always meant Coach Davis; as much as Jack resented him, as much as he thought he hated the man, and dreaded his inevitable harassment day after day, he simply didn't perform as well without the obnoxious presence of Davis. Physical conditioning was easy to achieve, a rower could learn the skills of the catch, slide, and return, and improve his speed, but great rowers were fueled by passion of some kind—misdirected passion maybe. Davis was as unforgiving as Jack's father, and like his father, doled out just enough praise to keep him frustrated and unsatisfied. Anger pushed the oars away; the snap return toward his chest was forgiveness. Some rowers purposefully fought with their girlfriends or parents to keep the mental edge. Davis used to say, "Great rowers are either rowing toward, or rowing away. It's up to you to figure out which you are." Jack thought himself as starting from a point of emptiness, racing toward an unknown thing on the opposite shore. Answers to questions still in their nascent state, not yet even formed in his mind.

One day, shortly after Davis died, Jack was sculling one afternoon and broke his own personal record, a time that would have qualified him as third on the National Team. But when he dragged the shell ashore, he walked away, and never went back to it.

He looked at Hector now with the woman, and he felt exactly as he had that afternoon, like he'd gotten to some distant shore after a long journey to find that he didn't know himself at all. He'd deluded himself about Hector, had ignored all the signs of what was now irrefutable. He expected Hector had other men, but what he didn't expect was this lie. In his darker moments he considered the possibility of a woman with Hector, but it wasn't the same as seeing it before his eyes. Jack was a man who loved men; this was the one thing he could say about himself that was virtuous. When his homosexuality surged to the fore after he stopped rowing, he didn't try to fight or deny it. His will to achieve, to win, to get on the Olympic team, was not really what had gotten him up before the sun every day. It was the life of training itself he needed, his sixteen-hour days that precluded having to think about dating and girls. To be able to roll his eyes and say, "Coach Davis, water Nazi," as a ready-made explanation to anyone—his father, his family—who asked about a girlfriend. What Jack discovered was that, after all, he had been an athlete who was rowing away.

He had to resist the urge to bang on the glass, smash Hector's face in, the lying piece of shit. He was the lowest of the low, a whore, a lying slut. Hector didn't care about Jack, didn't feel the things he pretended to. The hell with him, then. The hell with the unhappy news Jack had for him. He was under no moral obligation to tell Hector he was sick, not with the immorality of the life Hector was living. This is what women did to men, turned them into liars and thieves and whores.

He climbed down the fire escape and started home. The rain was cold, and he shivered in his thin suit jacket. His head was throbbing. By the time he got back to the boarding house he could scarcely breathe, his lungs watery and thick, the air rattling horribly in his chest. It took nearly forty-five minutes to get to his floor. The steps seemed to have doubled in number. The lights were off in all the hallways. He pulled out the key ring—absurdly large, since each room was individually keyed—and fumbled around until one of the doors opened. This space was unfamiliar. He lay down on a very lumpy mattress, pulled a chenille bedspread—actually, a garbage bag, he noticed—up to his chin. A light from a neon sign across the street shone in. He stared at it, little blue bubbles coming out of a martini glass. He hadn't ever been to that bar. He closed his eyes and drifted off.

He was rowing, though not on the Charles. He was sculling on what appeared to be the ocean, black high waves that clipped over the front of the shell and hissed along the bottom. The oarlocks groaned like footsteps on a wooden floor when the oars snapped back in return. He rowed and rowed. The waves got higher, fiercer. Soon he was swallowing water. His lungs were filling and he was drowning, sinking all the way to the bottom of the ocean. In the dream, he opened his eyes and found himself on a beach where the Italian shoemaker, Mr. Fabrizi, held out a pair of shoes. *Put these on. I polished them. A lifelong habit doesn't die so easy. Put them on and follow me.* Jack walked through nine doors, one after another, held open for him by striking young men wearing white gloves and blue hats. They were all blond and pale, blue-eyed and tall. They didn't smile. The ninth door opened out onto the sky itself. *You can walk through it or not. The shoes won't wear out. Will you come?* Jack looked at the sky, which had never seemed so bright before. It started to shimmer and break apart.

Something pulled at him from behind, a tug and a shaking. Mr. Fabrizi smiled sadly at him. *It's okay. I have the last,* he said, and Jack realized he meant a shoe last, the shape of his feet molded in cedar. *I have your last. I can make you a pair anytime.*

When Jack awoke, someone was calling his name. There was a mask over his mouth, a woman telling him to breathe naturally. "You're going to be okay. Do you remember what happened?"

He shook his head.

"You passed out on the street. Your lungs collapsed. But you're going to be all right."

He was in an ambulance. The paramedics were hooking him up to wires, tubes. The siren was shrilling. His skin felt like it was loosening, falling away from the bone, shaking him out, trying to peel away from the muscle. He imagined he was sitting atop his own chest, his skin like a huge pair of pants that stayed in place only because he was holding them up; if he moved even a little, he'd slip right out of his body.

"Can you find Stuart? Can you call Stuart Carpenter?" Jack wasn't sure he'd actually spoken; nobody seemed to be paying any attention to him. He strained to open his eyes. The woman who had spoken to him earlier was replaced by one of the tall blue-eyed doormen in his dream. He tried again to make himself heard. "Can you help me? Will you get Stuart?"

The man didn't speak or smile, just took Jack's hand and watched as the EMTs did their work. He was right there as they lifted Jack onto the gurney in the hospital, running alongside it with the medical personnel, red shoes squeaking on the linoleum.

EIGHT

Three Pips in Search of a Gladys

Anna awoke Saturday morning to Flynn wearing the optometrist's goggles, peering down at her. Even from the warmth of her bed Anna felt how cold it was outside, saw the gunmetal gray of the sky and sparsely leafed trees like vain, underdressed women.

"Good morning," Anna said to her granddaughter. "How did you sleep?"

"I dreamed about Oscar de la Hoya again. Also, that my mother joined a cult and quit using drugs."

Anna flipped back the covers. "Shimmy in."

Flynn smiled, the tops of her cheeks squeezed against the frame of the heavy goggles. She folded her body against Anna's and stared at the flowers on her grandmother's nightgown. Through the 20/100 lenses they looked like little pink oceans. Flynn turned on the radio. "This song is called 'Strawberry Letter 22'. They played it yesterday."

"You're right." Anna sang along to the words she remembered. She'd found this station a couple of months ago, shortly after Flynn and Marvin showed up. It played All Seventies All The Time, and she woke to it every morning. It sent her back to a happier time in her life. For a few brief moments every morning, she could hover on the edge of wakefulness listening to The Fifth Dimension and Roberta Flack and recapture the feelings of those times, the days in her early married life when she and Hugh were so busy that an hour in the evening on the porch with a nightcap was their

only shared time in the day. Those were the days of abundance, the uninterrupted sixty minutes with Hugh a haven she couldn't wait to enter.

She turned to Flynn, chuckled at the way her granddaughter's eyes were
slivered behind the thick lenses like some terrible tiny fish. Anna drew Flynn
closer and breathed in the sweet, sleepy girl smell of her—baby shampoo
and floral soap layered over something vaguely sharp and clay-like.

"Who sings this song?" Flynn asked, when the music changed.

Anna listened. "Bill Withers."

"Is it called 'Ain't No Sunshine'?"

Anna said yes, loving the irony of Flynn's taste in '70s music. Anna
thought of it as retribution for all those long car trips when Poppy and Hugh
made her listen to country. Poppy hated this music. It was delicious to see
her granddaughter's face light up when Anna walked in with Jim Croce and
Gladys Knight digitally remastered on disc.

"Are we going to go shopping today?" Flynn said.

"Wasn't planning on it. Why? Is there something you want?"

"It's Saturday," Flynn said. "And there's a sale on chicken."

Anna laughed. The first few weeks that Flynn and Marvin were here,
Anna had gone to The Warehouse Club frequently to stock up on things
she wasn't used to running out of so often, living alone as she did. Flynn
had a genuine bunker mentality, keeping Anna informed when they were
down to their last six rolls of toilet paper from the case of twenty-four.
"You remind me of my grandmother," Anna said. "Anybody listening to
you would think you've been through the Great Depression."

"Well, I have. You and I both have. We were neighbor wives in Montana. You kept cows and chickens. I baked pies and took in laundry. Between us we had eleven children. One of them was Poppy, who was my
daughter. She was unhappy then, too. Even then she was mentally ill. She
was a deaf-mute, I think. She could see spirits and the next world the way
you and I can."

Anna stopped. She'd learned to ignore a lot of Flynn's flights of fancy.
Despite what Marvin said, she didn't see anything so alarming about the
girl imagining other lifetimes. Millions of people worldwide believed in
reincarnation. It didn't seem so farfetched. Anna wasn't sure *she* didn't believe in it. What was most troubling was Flynn's fascination with death and
dying. This is what stopped Anna short and gave her a chill of doom. Her

solution for now was to ignore anything unusual in Flynn's speech or behavior. Though it wasn't always easy.

A few days ago, Anna had come home from work and tripped over her granddaughter, who was lying in the middle of the floor, wrapped completely and tightly in a bed sheet. Only her eyes peeked out, over which there were two shiny pennies. Anna kept her voice level. "What are you doing, Flynn?"

"Trying to remember what it was like when I was a pharaoh. Dying for so long, taking forever to return to dust." Anna kept the alarm out of her voice as best she could. "Get up and wash your face before dinner."

She looked over at Flynn now, still going on about other lifetimes. In a minute Flynn would circle the conversation back to Poppy, Anna knew. This was what she was learning about the way Flynn's mind worked. Reincarnation, followed by worry about her mother, followed by fear of abandonment.

"Which would you rather," Anna began, starting the game she'd invented to short-circuit Flynn's imaginative embroideries. "Would you rather be a chicken or a superhero?"

Flynn eased herself up onto one elbow. "What are the conditions?"

"You're in a chicken coop in Wisconsin. But you have a secret destiny and a secret map to a distant galaxy. If you can make it, you turn into a talented woman who can rule the universe. As a superhero, you can have the power now. The power is to be invisible anywhere."

"Easy. I'd try to get to the galaxy."

There were little pockets of mysteries in Flynn, things Anna didn't yet know like this one; the girl was probably brave. Maybe very brave, who knew.

"Which would you rather: would you rather be a fig tree or a whale?"

"What are the conditions?"

"As a fig tree you are beautiful and have millions of yummy figs all over you. But you can't eat them, and you can't move. You have to wait for someone to come by. As a whale, you have the whole ocean. Your whale family is all over the world and you spend most of your day lonely and having to look for food. But you are the boss and are huge and can do whatever you want, including killing fishermen in boats."

"Fig tree. I would always prefer to bear fruit."

"Even if no one sees you? If you're a forgotten fig tree in the middle of the desert?"

"Especially," Anna said, surprising herself.

"Would you rather speak the truth and have no one believe you, or tell a bunch of lies that you know aren't true, but which make people like you?" Flynn asked.

"Speak the truth."

"Always? Even if people told you that you were a freak and you had no friends and you would maybe die because you were honest?"

"That's a tough one. I'll have to get back to you on that."

Anna heard Marvin's heavy footsteps in the hallway just outside the bedroom. "Flynnie?"

"Yesie?" Flynn called back.

"Your bath is ready. Let's get moving."

"Where are we going?"

Anna sighed, exasperated. "Why can't you and your father hold a conversation in the same room? It would mean you wouldn't have to shout like this."

Marvin knocked and came in when Anna said it was all right. "Let's go, sweet beet."

"Where are we going?"

"First we're going to take the bus into the garage. When and if it's done in time, we have an appointment to look at an apartment."

"You do?" Anna asked. Marvin being who he was, Anna hadn't anticipated that the question of living arrangements would come up again unless she said something.

"Why?" Flynn asked. "Isn't this our home?"

Anna rushed in. "Tell you what. Forget all that for now. Why don't you and Flynnie take a break? I have to be at the hospital to help run a group, but you can drop me off and use my car for the day."

She couldn't read Marvin's look. Some mixture of curiosity, triumph, and suspicion. "*The Little Mermaid* is playing at a theater near where I have to be."

"Oh, far out! Groovy and wavy gravy, baby," Flynn said. She adjusted her goggles and navigated to the bathroom with 20/400 vision. There was an invisible Seeing Eye dog that went with this setting. His name was

Jumbo. He wagged and huffed in front of her, always stepping out of the way just in time.

Marvin looked back at Anna, who shrugged. "Why not?" Anna said. "Stay a few more weeks. I'm just getting to know Flynn."

"Are you sure? Because that would be fabulous. I have two job interviews this week. In a month my finances will be much better."

"Job interviews? Really?" She sat up, ran a comb through her hair.

"Just adjunct teaching gigs at community colleges, but they'll pay the bills."

"Groovy," Anna said, and flashed a peace sign. "Wavy gravy, baby."

Marvin laughed. "Isn't she something?"

Anna said, "Indeed." She looked through her closet for something to wear. Nothing seemed right today. She wanted to dress a little nicer than she usually did, since this Saturday was her last as the official co-leader of the group. Nick had found an intern to step in. Finally. And as promised, her lab was outfitted with not only state-of-the-art microscopes, but also a new centrifuge, and rare specimen slides of the Hantavirus, monkey pox, and both stages of rabies. She wasn't sorry that her duties were over, but she would miss the perks that went along with Nick's gratitude.

She searched for something bright. Color helped to keep her alert when she hadn't slept well. The red Missoni jacket was elegant, but red was always wrong for meetings like this. Too inflammatory, too bloody and gladiatorial. She finally opted for her long-stored pink suit. Only in the car, when it was too late to change, did it occur to her that she was overdressed. She'd been thinking only of color.

There were conditions, and the two of them were not a couple, Stuart had insisted to Jack and to himself. It was strictly out of human charity that Stuart agreed to let Jack move back in after being released from the hospital. He had very nearly died, pneumonia compromising his respiratory system to the point where his lungs had collapsed three times. Jack's stay was temporary, just until he stabilized. In the meantime, one of the conditions was that he attend a support group. "I don't need a support group," Jack had said.

"Well, I do," Stuart said. In truth, the support group *was* for Jack, for the time when he needed friends and people to care for him.

The two of them walked into the meeting fifteen minutes late, into a group of dying fags and pathetic, afflicted breeders, by Jack's lights. Jesus in Japan, this was going to be without end. They were in the dayroom of the psychiatric wing, a strange space filled with scraggly geraniums and stained furniture. The walls were dingy, yellowish from the good old days when they let the loonies light up. The upholstery and carpets smelled faintly of stale tobacco. Jack wished smoking were still permitted, not because he wanted to, but because at least here, in a room full of the dying, they should all be allowed to abandon the absurd illusion of health.

Because Jack and Stuart were late, the only empty chairs faced into the circle. He would have much preferred to face the window so the sun was in his eyes and everyone around him was in varying degrees of shadow. If not for the obvious hell of dying alone in substandard housing—well, anything less than Egyptian cotton bedding and cut-pile Saxony carpets was substandard, wasn't it?—Jack would have refused this condition, the absurd weepy woe-is-me gut-spilling collection of sorry asses. He'd have probably won on this one, since it was the Hector issue that was the biggie. At the time he'd been so sick that he gave into everything on Stuart's list, the main three items being to cease all contact with other men; to respect Stuart's home by cleaning up after himself; and to attend a support group meeting. There were two meetings, Stuart had told him, one more informal than the other, which did Jack prefer? He chose Saturday.

He'd have to make a deal with Stuart, because he would not come here again. The fag hags were bad enough, the single women in their thirties who worked in hip professions like advertising or internet consulting and came with their Best Gay Friend Who Was Like A Brother! But the place was being overrun by breeders, like the pair coming in now, a fiftyish woman in a pink Chanel-type suit and a drop-dead gorgeous man, probably her son. He wore a wedding band, though these days that didn't mean much. She was a tough broad, he saw right away. Her eyes made no apologies as she scanned the room for chairs, her power suit and jewelry like a banner of her wealth and superiority. At least the fag hags dressed the part of liberal free spirits in long gypsy skirts and loose-fitting blouses of unbleached cotton. To look at the group, Jack thought now, you'd think the whole sorry lot of them aspired to tour with Fleetwood Mac. But this bitch, the mother of Mr. Beautiful—the thought that she might be his wife was too horrific to consider; if it turned out to be true, Jack would bloody her nose in the parking lot—moved around the room and rearranged chairs like she owned the place. Jack was aware of Stuart's eyes on him as he checked out the new gorgeous man—beautiful bone structure, bright dark eyes and silky ponytailed hair that he knew must smell of something wonderful like sandalwood or bay rum. Jack tried to keep his expression neutral. He cut his eyes away.

"Sorry I'm late, gang," Anna said.

Ballsy, Jack thought. He glared at the pink-suited woman. What arrogance. The diamond ring on her finger could light planes to the runway.

The young group facilitator, a social worker who looked fresh out of someplace like Emerson College was calling the meeting to order. She meant well, Jack knew, but nevertheless with her fresh-scrubbed farmgirl face looked as if she'd never put her lips around anything stronger than cherry popsicles. "I count four new faces today. So let me welcome you to the Mood Team," she started. "I'm Christine, and I've been working with AIDS patients and their families for ten years."

Jack snorted. "Ten years? Did you start in junior high school?"

Christine ignored him. "And I'd like to introduce our co-leader, Anna Brinkman, who has worked in the health care industry for thirty years."

"Now *that* I believe," Jack said.

Anna turned to look at the man who had spoken. He was handsome, with bright greenish-brown eyes that looked a little glazed with fever. His partner—at least that's who Anna assumed the cherubic-faced man was— looked sad and defeated. Nick had told her and Christine that because the virus often attacked the brain first, dramatic changes in mood or personality could be one of the earliest symptoms of AIDS. Anna suspected that wasn't the case with this man; the lines around his mouth and forehead were too deeply set for displeasure and fury to be something new.

He returned Anna's gaze with a look of such pure hatred that her heart skipped a beat. His eyes took in her suit, her shoes. She looked away. She wished she'd dressed differently. What had she been thinking? She looked like somebody's Francophile grandma. She was even wearing Chanel No.5, for God's sake.

"Just a few things before we start," Christine said. "I've planned a dance for next Saturday, ballroom and swing. The Mood Swings, which I'm hoping to make a regular bi-monthly event. So, come even if you don't know how to do swing or ballroom. Especially if you don't. I'm hoping somebody in the group will volunteer to teach the basic steps, so if someone has expertise in any area of formal dance, please see me after class."

"I can foxtrot and tango."

Jack turned. It was the gorgeous newcomer, sitting just two seats away from him now. Jack had never seen such perfect cheekbones, smooth and high and sculpted, without the shadowy hollows beneath or the under-slung lower jaw that often went with such a face. Jack thought about a trip to Florence, the first time he laid eyes on Michelangelo's *David*. His initial impression was the artist must have executed his masterpiece from some imaginary ideal, that no ordinary mortal could have such perfectly sym-metrical features. This man could have served as Michelangelo's model. Or was it just his fever making the man into such delicious delirium? Jack felt the stirrings of desire, despite the sharp pains in his lungs, his weakness and aching muscles.

Anna turned to Marvin, glared at him. What was he doing? He was sup-posed to be a silent presence. When she caught his eye he smiled and shrugged. At the last minute, Flynn had changed her mind about seeing a movie and asked to spend the day with Greta instead. Marvin said he'd like to accompany her to the hospital to watch her work. She said yes, but only if he made himself invisible, which he hadn't, which he clearly could never be.

"That's great," Christine said, and nodded to Marvin. "See me after the meeting. Also, as I mentioned last week, this is Anna's last official meeting with us. We have an intern from Boston General coming aboard. So, I'd like to take this opportunity to thank her."

The group applauded. Anna nodded, then motioned for Christine to carry on. "Okay, since we have some newcomers here, why don't we start by introducing ourselves and saying a little bit about why we're here."

Anna let her attention wander during the introductions—now from Edward, a man in his fifties whose disease was full-blown with Karposi's sarcoma covering his face and arms. He reminded Anna a little of Nathan Lane, and he'd become one of her favorites; he was always in good spirits despite being recently dumped by his partner of twenty-five years. There was something almost epic in the equanimity with which he was facing this disease. Edward had worked as a civil rights attorney, and now had

live-in help. Some days, the men's illness penetrated more deeply into her
psyche than others. Most times, she could look at it philosophically, believe
that her contribution to the whole process was to listen. But other times
Anna felt like she couldn't bear it, wanted to stay a few steps behind those
who walked shoulder-to-shoulder with their own mortality every day. Then
there were days, and today was threatening to become one of them, where
she couldn't get her mind around how horrible this all was. Not the disease
so much, but the pariahs it made people into, the hate groups who targeted
AIDS sufferers. On the windshield of her car two Saturdays ago was a pink
handbill proclaiming "Jesus Hates Fags." She could usually dismiss this kind
of small-minded ignorance but only if she didn't remember particular
people like Edward. As long as she lived, she would never understand hate
in the name of religion. Human beings were the only animals that judged
other members of their species by qualities other than behavior or contribution. Elephants ostracized rogue cows. Chimps kicked out violent males.
Wolves that didn't adhere to the order and follow the pack leader were
killed. Only the human animal killed or enslaved its own for the color of
skin, sexual preference, or how it experienced the idea of a god.

It was one of those days. She thought of her granddaughter and Greta,
wondered what they were doing now. Greta and Mike had been approved
as adoptive parents and their new daughter would be living with them as
soon as the social worker's assessment was complete—just about the time
Greta's baby was due. It was feast or famine, and Greta's plate was loaded.
Anna was thrilled for her friend, had already bought Greta a crib and a
youth bed for the two children coming into her life. Handmade blankets
from Greece, two entire wardrobes from Lilly Pulitzer, and a crib that was
fit for royalty. Anna tried to remember the name of Greta's new daughter.
She was one of the children in the stack of folders that day, a four-year-old.
Rashida? No, that was the girl of mixed race. This one was the pale, ash-
blond child. Anyway, except for Flynn, all little girls were pretty much the
same in Anna's eyes.

Anna made herself listen. The partner of the man who had stared at
her so hatefully was speaking now. "I'm Stuart, partner of Jack, who has
the virus. I'm negative."

"Just to clarify," Anna said. "It's not necessary to disclose HIV status
unless you want to. It's a state law, and hospital policy, that one's status is

to remain private unless an individual chooses to reveal it."

Michael, partner of the man with the blue sock obsession, said, "That's stupid. Why can't we ask questions that would help us understand someone? Can't we just assume that everyone here is positive or with someone who is positive?"

"No," Anna said, "you can't." She turned back to Mr. Bitter, partner of Stuart.

"I'm Jack. I'm sick. I'm here because Stuart made it a condition of taking me back in. I don't believe in this sort of thing. I don't think it's anybody's goddamn business how I feel or how I got sick."

"Jack," Christine said, "do you want to explore your feelings of anger?"

"Fuck no."

Christine colored and nodded. "Okay."

Anna tried to keep her eyes off the man—Jack—who had spoken. She felt pure nastiness coming from him, aimed at her more than Christine.

A man Anna didn't recognize spoke now. His advanced sickness made his age impossible to guess, but she knew he wasn't as old as the disease made him look. The ties from his hospital gown stuck out from the neck of his sweater, and beneath the lap blanket his legs were purple with sores. She averted her eyes, took deep breaths, compassion a flimsy rotten board that gave way the instant she ventured out to him. Anna wondered why he was at this meeting. The chairs on either side of him were empty. He must be a bed patient here, someone brought in from the hospice wing. Maybe Christine herself had brought him over. The man was clearly suffering from dementia, muttering something incomprehensible.

By the time the introductions circled around to Anna—was she supposed to introduce herself again, even after being identified as the group's co-leader?—her head pounded, every scent and sound heightened and excruciating. The smell of old clothes, of Betadine and bleach, the roar of traffic outside and the raspy breath of the man next to her. She was one impulse away from going to find him a bronchiodilator.

Christine looked at her expectantly so she said, "I'm Anna, as noted earlier. I've been the co-leader of the Mood Team for the past couple of months." She nodded and smiled to show she was finished.

"And?" Jack said.

"And?" Anna repeated.

"That's it? What is your personal relationship to this illness? What do you know of it from the inside-out?"

"I'm a medical professional," Anna said.

"Oh, I see," Jack said. "And your son?" His eyes flickered toward Marvin, whose own eyes were settled on the tender face of Christine. "Is there a reason he's here? Or is this Take Your Son to Support Group Day?"

Anna snapped her head in Christine's direction, but Christine seemed to be having a moment with Marvin, Anna saw to her astonishment and fury. "Now, look," Anna said. "I want to change the tenor of this meeting." Christine's eyes slid from Marvin's face to hers, a sleepy sated look. "Let's redefine our objectives."

"Yee-ha!" Jack said, twirling an imaginary lasso.

Anna ignored him. She directed her attention to Christine, who was blatantly flirting with her daughter's husband instead of doing her job. "Christine, maybe you want to explain for the benefit of our new members, how this meeting aims to foster the skills and support necessary to live with this disease, and to help others in the way they manage it?"

Christine looked at her and blinked slowly. "Could you repeat that?"

There was laughter all around, loudest from Jack.

"Anna, do you want to explore your feelings of anger?" Jack said.

She looked at him levelly and smiled as sweetly as she could. "Fuck no."

More laughter.

"Yes, amen sister," Jack said.

"So then." Anna raised an eyebrow at Christine, who looked back at her as if she'd lost her mind. "So, let's redefine the goals of this gathering."

A woman in the corner spoke. Anna turned. Elizabeth, who had gotten the disease from her female lover's ex-partner, a bi-sexual male, whom the women had asked to father their child. Elizabeth ended up losing her baby, losing her partner, and getting AIDS. She was angry, as was to be expected, but had a way of contradicting or challenging everything Anna said. Not at every meeting, but enough so that Anna had come to expect it. Elizabeth changed her look a lot. One week she wore flowered Sunday-go-to-meeting dresses, the next, tank tops that displayed her tattoos of Chinese characters. Her hair was so short you could scrub pots with it. Today, she wore ordinary Levi's, a white T-shirt, and a lavender velvet hat. "Anna, with all due respect, I'm feeling some hostility from you that I never have before," Elizabeth said. "I respectfully request that you excuse yourself from the meeting."

"Anna is the co-leader," Jack said.

"Oh, like I don't know that," Elizabeth said. "Excuse me, but I've been here from the beginning, and I think you're causing the problems, mister."

"Hold it!" Anna said. "No accusations, Elizabeth. But, yes, you're right, I lost my temper and I shouldn't have. Let's try to move on." Anna glanced over at Jack.

"Perhaps this should be worked out in a different setting," Elizabeth said, both to Anna and Jack. "Negativity, even in small doses, is injurious to everyone."

Anna felt her temper flare, as though she might lose control, something that hadn't happened in years. What was wrong with Elizabeth today? And what had happened to Christine? The girl was usually as solid as a brick.

"Let's move on," Anna said. "Unless you want to add something else, Elizabeth." Out of the corner of her eye, Anna saw Marvin's hands moving like caged birds. He was spreading his fingers out, then together, out, then together in the way her grandmother used to open a hairnet.

"This is a support group. We are here to share," Elizabeth said.

"Yes," Anna said, "you're right. Except we don't do that by letting accusations fly."

"Yes. Amen, again, sister," Jack said. He was beginning to like this broad.

"But if one member of the group makes us uncomfortable, shouldn't we be able to ask him to leave?"

"No," Anna said, "That's not for you to decide."

Michael, partner of Alan, who had had the blue sock fight with his partner at the very first meeting said, "And is it your decision?" He looked at Anna.

"Yes, it is. Mine and Christine's."

At the mention of her name, Christine said, "Yes. Anna and I are here to keep the lines of communication open and flowing."

Jack snorted. "It looks like your communication is flowing, all right. Right to Anna's son."

"You're hateful!" Elizabeth said. "I'm sick to death of your sarcasm."

"Sweetheart, you're sick to death anyway."

"Why don't you and Anna go and have a drink next door? The two of you can trade vitriol to your heart's content."

"My heart's content," Jack repeated, laughing. "My heart is not content. The contents of my heart are incontinent. The *in*valid was found to be in*valid*."

"All right," Christine said. "Can we at least get back to introductions? After that, we can take the meeting in whatever direction you all want, but I'd at least like to know everyone's name."

"Fuck it," Jack said. "Fuck it all to hell."

"Jack, stop!" Stuart said. "Be quiet."

Jack threw up his hands. "Fine. I'm done sharing."

The group fell silent. Christine turned to Marvin, who was seated next to Anna. He spoke now. "I'm Marvin Blender, Anna's son-in-law. I'm a sculptor in three mediums. I have a daughter, Flynn. We're visiting Anna from Alaska, hoping to mend all broken fences and share quality time. I love to tango."

"It takes two," Jack said, and smiled. "How did you get the goods?"

"What?" Marvin said.

"How did you contract the virus?"

"Oh, I don't have—"

Stuart spoke up. "No fair, Jack. You don't want to share anything about how you got it, so you can't in good conscience ask someone else this."

"Nothing's good about my conscience, darling, which is why we're here, isn't it?" He patted Stuart's knee.

"Uh, well, anyway I don't—"

"Don't answer," Anna said. She turned to Jack. "I thought I made it clear that asking about someone's health history was unacceptable."

Jack leveled his look at Anna and fell silent. He shrugged.

Anna resolved to keep quiet for the rest of the meeting. This was terrible. All of it. The illusion that this meeting supported or helped anything. The indignity of the deaths most of them faced. Nick told her early on to emphasize living with AIDS, not dying from it, but that was absurd. The war was over the second the virus entered the body. There was no exhausted surrender after a valiant fight; this was immediate occupation after an unfair siege. Anna thought back to the last days of Hugh's death, the extended trips to the house in Maine because he wanted to die there, soothed by the crash of the surf against rocks, the sea breeze wafting in at night. He'd died well, she supposed, which was to say quickly and without undue suffering. This, she thought, looking around now and smelling something sharply intestinal, was not how it was supposed to be. She turned to glance at the man in the wheelchair who was hiding his face in his hands. Others had smelled it, too. The nasty man, Jack, caught her eye and looked away.

Stuart caught Jack's eye then bent toward Robert, rested his elbow on the arm of the wheelchair. "Do you want me to take you to the bathroom?" Stuart asked. Robert's breath was a panicked staccato. Stuart knew who he was—anyone who followed gay rights in Boston had at least heard of him. Robert was in his fifties, a political activist who lobbied for antidiscrimination policies. He was tenured at Yale at thirty, a brilliant astrophysicist whose book, *An Amateur's Guide to the Stars,* had been on the *New York Times* best sellers list for a few months. When he and Jack first walked in, Stuart was sure he recognized Robert from somewhere, but it hadn't clicked until he excused himself to go to the restroom, and glanced at the bookshelves in the back. The noisy chaos in the room had intensified by the time Stuart returned, so he took Robert's book back to his seat.

"Look," Stuart had said quietly, putting the book in Robert's hand. There were at least three conversations happening at once, including a heated discussion between Anna and the woman in the lavender hat. "Look at what I found in the back."

Robert had turned the dog-eared copy over. The photograph was taken about ten years ago. He was beautiful then, a young Cary Grant. It was unmistakably the same man, but Robert looked thirty years older than he did in the photograph.

"Oh, yes. I've heard of this guy. I think I built a house for him once." Robert went on to tell Stuart about a life he remembered as a carpenter. He rambled on about dovetail joints and masonry anchors, how to recognize a fine body of wood grain at such length that Stuart would have assumed he'd been mistaken had he not checked Robert's last name and date of birth on Robert's hospital bracelet against the information on the book's Library of Congress page. The same.

All eyes were now on Stuart and Robert.

"I'm sorry," Robert said. "My dreams nudge everything out of the way. If I pay attention to what's in my head, I lose track of what's happening with my bowels. What a rotten cage."

"It's all right, Robert. Don't worry. Everything is okay," Christine said.

Stuart stood and got behind Robert's chair. Christine mouthed, "Room 219."

Stuart nodded.

"It's fine," someone said. "Accidents happen. It's okay."

Before Anna could censor herself, she stood, angled her chair out of the circle to get out. "No," she said. "It is not fine. *Nothing* about this is okay." She walked out of the dayroom, paced the hallways. Her outburst was inexcusable. She'd have to go back in there and apologize. Or show up for fifteen minutes next week to do it. If she thought the group would accept a simple apology without insisting that they *explore her anger,* Anna would do it now. Anger was anger. Did one need to look at the roots of a tree to identify it? Outrage, like a maple, shed its leaves in season.

At the break, Jack went in search of the Chanel grandma. He followed the scent of her perfume—his sense of smell was razor sharp these days—to the waiting room at the end of the hall, where she was sitting in the corner and shredding the leaves on a potted palm. She looked up as he walked in, then back to the television. "Now what," she said, so softly that he wasn't sure he heard correctly.

"I'm Jack," he said, and sat beside her.

"I know."

"I want to apologize."

"For what?"

"For assuming things I shouldn't have."

She tipped her chin up, though he couldn't tell if the gesture was dismissive or accepting.

"I'm a bitter man," he said. "I'm good-looking enough to get away with things the less endowed couldn't."

She laughed then in a way that gave her whole face a girlish radiance. The silly pink suit now seemed touching instead of aggressive. He felt something in him give way, the sharp geometry of anger and pain blunted a little in her presence.

"You're not that good-looking," she said. "Thank you, anyway, for your apology. Was that an apology?"

"Yes," he said. "And add to that a salute to your bravery."

He saw her reach for something in her purse, and was astounded when she pulled out a pack of Marlboro Lights and lit up as confidently and easily as if they were sitting in a bar. "Bravery? Is this the nasty Jack coming back?"

"No, I mean it," he said, and reached for one of the cigarettes. The smoke curling through his lungs felt somehow therapeutic. "It takes guts to say something like that. To cut away the pretty wrapping and see the crap inside."

Anna raised an eyebrow. "So to speak." She took a deep drag off the cigarette. "I suppose I should go back in there and tell them I'm sorry. But I don't want to say more than that. Never ruin a perfectly good apology with a cheap excuse. Even if there is a cheap excuse. My motto, anyway."

"You should absolutely not apologize," Jack said. "It was good to shake them up. You're right. There's nothing about this illness that's okay." He paused. "Except maybe one thing." He held out his cigarette. "Being terminally ill means that nothing else can lead to my premature death."

A nurse walked in, her nose wrinkled in a rabbit-like way. "There is absolutely no smoking in here!"

"Yep," Anna said. "We're on our way out."

Jack followed Anna outside. "Let me buy you a drink," she said, and nodded to what looked like a sedate little fern bar across the street.

"Sure, I'll let you. But only if you let me buy *you* a drink next, and I get to choose the next bar."

"Deal," Anna said. They walked in and Anna ordered them a round of tequila shots with martini chasers.

"You go, girl. There will be no beating around the white-wine spritzer bushes here," he said.

"That's right. Either you're drinking, or you're drinking lemonade." She clinked her glass against his and downed the shot in one smooth gulp. "And by the way, to you I *will* apologize."

"Oh?" Jack said, and worked the Cuervo down in three sips. He glanced over and saw the bartender smirking. Just to spite him, he shot the martini, slammed the glass on the counter, and nodded for another.

"I lied before. You *are* that good-looking." His eyes were remarkable, Anna thought. Green with flecks of gold and blue and brown, mottled as river stones.

"Ha," Jack said, cupping his chin in his hand. "A face that launched a thousand quips." He reached for a bowl of pretzels on the bar. "You should see the man I'm in love with. I am pond scum next to him."

"I did see him."

His heart clenched, and he almost whirled around on his stool looking for Hector when he realized she assumed he meant Stuart. He nodded, and let it go. "Do you suppose our loved ones are done sharing?"

She gulped the rest of her drink. "We should probably get back. I didn't tell my son-in-law where I was going."

Jack's mood sank a little at the phrase son-in-law. Still, that man was either closeted or bi, he was sure of it. "But you and I are bar-hopping."

Anna put some money on the counter. "I'll have to take a raincheck, I'm afraid." He looked so dispirited that Anna was taken off-guard. She wouldn't have guessed he had this in him.

She stood, walked toward the door. Jack followed. "Was this really your last meeting?"

"It was. I was just filling in, anyway, doing a favor for a friend."

They stood at Anna's car. He took a business card out of his pocket. "All my phone numbers. If you don't let me take you for drinks, I'll be very upset. Call me."

Anna put the card in her purse. "I will," she said, knowing the instant she said it that she never would. She saw in his expression that Jack knew, too.

"Well, maybe you'll change your mind and come back next week." He drew a martini glass in the dust on Anna's car.

"I won't change my mind. You can't imagine how glad I am to be done with this." She paused. "Listen, I'm not much into bars, but I would love it if you would stop by for drinks. Your partner too, of course." What was she doing? The last thing she wanted right now was company, especially this man, whose nastiness was probably too close to the surface to make the occasion comfortable. She was too tired and edgy lately to cater to anybody's sensitivities. Besides, she couldn't believe he had any real interest in socializing with her.

Jack, for whom even the smallest goodbye these days was painful, said,

"Yes, we'd love to," understanding Anna's invitation was only partly in earnest, and understanding his acceptance of it was composed in equal parts of curiosity about her gorgeous son-in-law, guilt for being so nasty earlier, and some inexplicable spark he felt between them.

Anna gave him directions to her townhouse though he didn't write them down. From the faraway look in his eyes she doubted whether he'd remember.

"Oh, here come our loved ones now," Jack said. "Looking ever so stricken, empty, and bereft. Ain't life grand?"

Marvin and Stuart walked up to Anna and Jack.

"We've been invited for drinks, sweetie," Jack said, linking his arm through Stuart's. Stuart smiled warily. Marvin looked at Anna then cut his eyes away to study the ground.

"How nice," Stuart said. "But I think we should be heading home."

"Why?" Jack said. There was nothing at home.

"Just one drink somewhere," Anna said. "Or, come to my place."

Jack checked Marvin's response, but he was unreadable. Marvin's arms were crossed, his hands balled into deliberate fists, as though he didn't trust what they might do. His attention was on the hospital's entrance, glancing over every time the door opened or closed.

"Maybe next week," Stuart said.

"Except that there is no next week," Jack said petulantly.

"Some other time then," Anna said.

At home, Anna heard the television blaring before she opened the door, some awful MTV screeching of an amped guitar and heart-stopping bass. Marvin trailed in behind her.

"Flynn?" Anna called. She walked into the TV room and found a teenaged boy slumped on the couch. He looked vaguely familiar. "Oh. Who are you?"

"Jeremy. I deliver your newspapers." He sat up, put on his sweatshirt. "Your neighbor asked me to watch Flynn until you got home."

"Where is she?"

"Flynn? I think she went in to take a nap."

"Where's Greta?" But instead of waiting to hear his answer, she walked into her bedroom to check her answering machine. The light was blinking.

"I think I'm in labor," Greta's voice said. "Jeremy said he would watch Flynn until you got home. Can you call Mike? I mean, can you keep trying? I don't know where he is."

Anna dialed the number for Boston General—Greta didn't say which hospital she was going to—she wasn't there, or at the next two. "Drive that boy out of here, will you?" Anna said, as Marvin headed toward Flynn's room. "I mean, will you drive him home? Pay him. Here," she said, and handed him her wallet. "And can you turn that music off?"

Marvin blinked at her with a blank expression, as if he was new to the language. "What's going on?"

"Greta's in labor."

"Already?" he said. "I thought she was just in her fifth month."

Anna nodded, and when someone in the ER at Brigham and Women's picked up her call, and after Anna lied and said she was next of kin, the operator said yes, they'd admitted Greta. "Can you patch me through to her room?"

Anna handed Marvin her car keys, and pointed at the babysitter boy.

"Okay. Is Greta all right?" Marvin asked.

Anna shook her head, walked away from him and peeked in Flynn's room. The bed was empty, still neatly made. She stepped in, spotted Flynn, asleep in some sort of good-witch or angel costume—an angel, she saw now, from the wings—on the windowseat. Flynn had plugged in Christmas candles. On the steamer trunk where Flynn kept her clothes, she had set up a crèche that had been Hugh's mother's. Where had she found that old thing? Anna didn't recall moving in any holiday decorations when she rented this place.

Greta finally answered her phone.

"It's me," Anna said quietly. She went back into the hallway, closed Flynn's door.

"I had the baby," Greta said. "It was a little girl. She was too small. They couldn't do anything to save her. They're saying she's dead."

"Oh, Greta," Anna said. "Is Mike with you?"

"No. I can't find him. Nobody can find him. He's not answering his cell."

"I'll keep trying his numbers," Anna said, and sat on the floor, her back against Flynn's door.

Greta was crying. "She looks perfect. Tiny, but perfect. Do they ever make a mistake?"

"What do you mean, dear?"

"I mean, is it possible that she'll come back to life? You hear all those stories about children being under water for half an hour, then end up being fine. Children are much more resilient than adults. I named her Stella. She's a bright little star."

Greta sounded heavily medicated. "I'm sure the doctors did everything they could," Anna said. "It might help if you hold her. Did they let you hold her?"

"I'm holding her now. I'm re-warming her. It hasn't been that long, she could still wake up."

"Is there a nurse in the room with you now?"

"Christ, they won't leave me alone. They want me to give her to them. But she's mine."

"Do you think I could speak to one of the doctors in the room?" Anna said.

Greta began sobbing. "Not you, too. I thought you were my friend. I know what they do with babies. I know they're going to cut her open and experiment. She's getting warmer. Why can't everybody just be patient?"

Anna waited for Greta's crying to subside then said calmly, "As soon as Marvin comes back with my car, I'll come over."

"No. Don't. I want to be alone."

"Let me help you," Anna said. "Let me be with you."

"You can't help me. You can't possibly understand."

"I'm a mother, too."

"You're a mother who never wanted her child. I want my child. Dead or alive, she's my daughter." Greta hung up.

Anna took a deep breath. She was so ready for this day to be over. She dialed Greta's home number and left an updated message for Mike on their machine. The bastard. Greta would be better off without him.

She crept back into Flynn's room. The girl hadn't stirred. Anna sat and watched her as she slept, the soft light of the Christmas candles spilling over Flynn's gorgeous face. Anna imagined that Flynn must have been a beautiful baby, a Botticelli angel with her dark curls, round, dimpled face, and deeply pigmented bow lips. Only Poppy had those lips; probably a recessive gene. Every now and then Anna caught a glimpse of her father's family arranging themselves in Flynn's expressions. A certain intensity in her look, a pursed half-smile that Anna was sure belonged to her great-grandfather, a tailor in Poland, though she had never seen more than a blurry photo of the man. One of these days she'd go through her things—assuming she still had all those old boxes—and kick up the dust on the family relics, talk to Flynn about her Jewish heritage, her Ashkenazi blood-lines. Though what did she know of it? Her father, the Jewish Buddhist, had responded to Anna's adolescent questioning: "We are of the Ashkenazi strain, the tribe of rabbis and scholars. The Sephardic Jews are rug sellers and general nose-pickers. That's all I know, that's all you need to know." Maybe she would enroll Flynn in Hebrew classes at a synagogue. The dear doomed child, Anna thought, then alarmed herself by wondering why that phrase popped in her head.

Flynn's costume had dirt all along the hem. Her shoes were caked with mud, as were her fingernails, Anna saw now. She'd wake her when Marvin got back, fix dinner and run her a hot bath. She bent down to look at the old crèche. Flynn had put one of her CDs under the kneeling figures of Mary and Joseph, the wise men behind them. Anna stared at the scene. There was a calf in the manger where the baby Jesus was supposed to be. The light hit the wise men in a peculiar way, making their faces look black, their teeth too white. Then Anna saw that the wise men *were* black and they were grinning from ear to ear. She picked one of them up. Flynn had cut out the faces of the Pips from the liner notes on the Gladys Knight CD and taped them onto the faces of the magi. Gladys Knight's face, also grin-ning, shone down on the holy family, recast as the Angel of the Lord.

Anna touched Flynn's back. She stirred and turned over but didn't wake. Anna would let her sleep until dinner, though it was already nearing eight o'clock. She should have asked Marvin to pick up a pizza on his way back.

Anna poured herself a brandy, walked into her bedroom and flipped on the Bose radio she and Flynn had bought together last week, along with two dozen or more CDs from the '70s. Norman Greenbaum's "Spirit in the Sky" played quietly now. Anna didn't much care for Greenbaum, didn't like his heavily synthesized sound, but it was one of Flynn's favorites, and because Flynn slept with Anna most nights, this was the song that awoke them in the morning. Anna hit the skip button, loaded up the compilation CD, the one with Frankie Vallee's "You're Just Too Good to be True," her own favorite, the one she sang to Flynn sometimes to lull her to sleep. She turned back the bedcovers, saw something centered on her pillow. A clod of dirt and a tiny shoe, the silver shoe from the Monopoly game—where in the world did Flynn find that? Anna hadn't played the game in twenty years or more. The last time was in Maine, where she and Hugh used to play occasionally with the radiologist and his wife who came up for weekends. Hugh had always chosen the shoe as his piece. But it wasn't the Monopoly shoe at all, she saw now, peering closer. It was a wadded-up gum wrapper. And the clods of dirt were twigs arranged as stick figures. Anna's scalp began to crawl. She picked up one of the little sticks, knotty, peeled, cold as a kneecap, and before she knew why or what drove her to it, she was downstairs and in the backyard, moving across the lawn with a flashlight. The same shallow holes Flynn had been digging for nearly two months. But there was something eerily unnatural out here. Feverish chills moved through her, a heat pouring in from the top, a cold pressing in from the sides. She shone the light on the bistro table. The beam caught Flynn's optometrist's goggles and glinted off the lenses. Underneath the table was a blue tarp, covered by branches. Anna moved everything aside and nearly fell in what was surely a hole deep enough for a coffin. She sat at the edge of it, pointed her light at the depths. There was a CD case all the way at the bottom. This was one of those moments when she needed her husband, needed him to tell her what to do, to help her figure all this out. What was wrong with this girl? What was Anna supposed to do with a child like this?

Anna went back in the house and shook Flynn gently until she opened her eyes.

"Gladys?" Flynn said, then more alertly, "Oh, it's you. My cherished grandma."

Anna cut her eyes to the crèche beside Flynn, saw dirt all over the figures that she hadn't noticed before. "I have an answer for you. From the which-would-you-rather game."

"Okay," Flynn said, wide-awake now.

"It is always better to tell the truth. Regardless of how it appears to anyone else or worrying about what they'll think of you. You should never hide. Never hide the things that make you who you are."

"Okay," Flynn said.

"Promise me, Flynn," Anna said, but the minute Flynn said the words

Anna's sense of dread grew stronger instead of dissipating and she wondered if it was a mistake, a terrible error to extract such a promise from a child like Flynn. She had overreacted, only wanted her granddaughter to tell her why she was digging a hiding place for herself in the backyard. The truth—whatever Anna meant by it, and she didn't quite know now—was likely to deliver her granddaughter into the hands of the enemy.

"Did Greta's baby die?" Flynn said, looking off into space.

"Yes," Anna said.

"Was it a girl?"

"Yes."

Flynn nodded, watched the fear move like a storm across her grandmother's face and didn't say anything else. She watched Anna walk out of the room then looked at the Pips in the little house barn beside her. They had been singing to her sweetly all day, in the sad echoes of Pips without their Gladys. Deep down in the hole, just a minute or two it seemed after she left Greta, who was on the couch eating Lu's Little Schoolboy cookies and watching reruns of "Unsolved Mysteries," the awful boy Jeremy with his greasy boy-madness and corn chip smell was telling her to get out of there, come inside because he was supposed to babysit her. Greta was having her baby too soon, did she understand that? Of course she understood. She climbed out, the Pips' voices in her head, telling her to help Greta's baby, help herself, to look in her grandmother's hall closet. That was where she found Joseph and Mary and the others, and the Pips told her to put them in the holy place of the house barn. Her grandmother woke her up from a dream of them, where they no longer had to be poor Pips, always singing backup, but now sang right along with Gladys, all of them singing every word to "Battle Hymn of the Republic." In Flynn's dream they were life-size, and growing, no longer miniature underground creatures lost since the 1970s, but big happy men with beautiful robes. Now, they told her, grinning, we're Pips and we're Wise Men. Do you know how special that makes us? Flynn said she didn't. Do you know what you get when you cross a Pip with a Wise Man? They lifted her up to sit in one of their giant palms. Their eyes were the size of Alaska lakes. "We, young lady, are Whips. We three thank you. We three praise you." Then they looked up at the sky and said, "We together are three. Together three are ye. Lord have mercy. Christ have mercy. Gladys have mercy."

Flynn put her shoes on and went out to Anna in the living room. "My mother called," Flynn said.

"What?" Anna said.

"My mother. Poppy. She called me."

Anna put her cello down. "You're sure you weren't just dreaming?"

"No. She called from Nevada. She won't be coming here." Flynn stared straight ahead.

"Did she leave a number?"

Flynn shook her head. Anna checked the caller ID printout on the phone. There was a number with a 702 prefix, possibly Nevada. She hit the DIAL/SEND button and was connected to the Rippling Sands Hotel. "Does your mother use her maiden name or her married one?"

Flynn frowned. "She was never a maid. The awfulest job she had was working at Kmart."

Anna asked for Poppy Blender's room. Anna's heart leapt in her throat when her daughter picked up. "What are you doing in Nevada?" Anna said.

"Mother?" Poppy said.

"Yes," Anna said. "Are you planning to come to Boston anytime soon?"

"I miss Flynn."

Anna looked at Flynn, who stared straight ahead, with her arms crossed. "Do you want to talk to her?" Anna said to Poppy.

"She won't talk to me. I tried earlier."

"Flynn, do you want to speak to your mother?"

"No, thank you," the girl said, and walked back to her room.

"She's sleepy, I guess. I woke her when I got home." Anna listened to Poppy's heavy breathing, a labored asthmatic wheeze. "Well, then. What are your plans? For reclaiming your family, I mean."

Anna positioned her cello, cradled the phone between her chin and neck, and fingered the first two bars of Haydn's D Major Concerto, as physically strenuous as the Rachmaninoff.

"I'm still trying to get my head straight."

Anna snorted. "In the meantime, everything else is spinning and up in the air."

"As far as what?"

"As far as what. Your daughter is obsessed with death. Marvin walks around here like he's in a fugue state." She picked up her bow and began playing softly to give herself something to listen to besides Poppy's crying. She always did know how to turn on the waterworks. It had worked with her father, but never with Anna; genuine emotion rarely traveled through the tear ducts, in Anna's estimation. "You should call again after Flynn has settled in fully. She and Marvin will probably be here for a few more weeks. And, meanwhile, if Flynn wants to talk to you, how can she get hold of you?"

Poppy gave her a cell phone number. Anna scribbled it at the top of the Haydn.

Anna hung up, went to Flynn, who was face down on her bed, still in her costume. The dress was too small; the wings met at the center of her back and were straining inward with the pull of the seams. She untied Flynn's red hightops and eased them off, thought about carrying Flynn into her bedroom for the night, but decided not to disturb her. She'd wake and drift in sometime during the night on her own. Anna rubbed Flynn's back gently. Maybe she did want to wake her. Maybe she wanted Flynn in bed beside her, as was becoming their custom, especially after this hellish day. As soon as Marvin came home she'd have him carry Flynn in to her.

In the living room, Anna sat in the dark and played Brahms' lullaby from memory. The soothing coil of eighth-notes was like a silk robe that barely skimmed the body. The feeling of being wrapped and enclosed without tactile pressure. An amniotic floating.

She stopped when she heard a car slow outside. She looked. Her car, Marvin finally pulling into the driveway. Anna turned on the lights.

"Where did that boy live, Rhode Island?" Anna said, when Marvin walked in. She meant it to be light and teasing, but her voice sounded even to her own ears shrill and schoolmarmish.

He sighed, then, perhaps in response to something in her face or as an acknowledgment of her difficult day, bent down and kissed her on the forehead.

"Thank you. I probably needed that."

"How's Greta?" He sat on the couch opposite her.

"She's devastated. The baby died." Anna rosined her bow. "Your wife called."

He looked over at her, then away, down at the covers of the magazines on the coffee table.

"Poppy called."

He picked up one of the magazines. "I heard you."

She positioned her cello, pretended to study the Rachmaninoff in front of her. "She was pretty upset."

"Anna," he said, then let out a nervous laugh.

She looked up.

"Don't be mad at me."

Anna began to bow through the opening bars of the fifth symphony in earnest. "I'm not mad. But I also had a lot to deal with here while you disappeared for three hours."

"You asked me to. You asked me to drive the boy home."

Anna let the bow drop, her cello collapse against her. "I happen to know Jeremy lives on West Canton. A five-minute drive. I know where you were. I know what you were doing."

"Oh, you think?"

"You were flirting with that girl all through the meeting. Which would have been inappropriate even if you weren't still married, since she was distracted from what she was supposed to be doing."

"Anna," he said quietly. "There's nothing going on. I met her for coffee. That's all."

"That's your business, I suppose. Anyway, I've had enough confrontation for one day."

"I know. I'm sorry your day was so rough." He pulled an envelope out of his jacket and handed it to her.

"What's this?"

"A gift certificate to a day spa. I figured you could use a little pampering."

"Marvin, sometimes you leave me dumbstruck," Anna said, and paused. "This is unexpected and lovely. Thank you."

"My pleasure."

Out of the corner of her eye Anna saw Flynn leave her room and stumble sleepily toward Anna's bedroom. Anna's world righted itself once again. Her muscles unclenched, loosened their tight bands of tension.

"Anna, I just wanted to say, Christine and I just went to Starbucks and talked, that's all."

"Okay."

"There's nothing going on."

"I heard you," she said, and squared her sheet music. "I heard you twice the first time."

NINE

HEAVENLY BODIES

Anna awoke early on Thanksgiving morning to the first snowfall of the season. Flynn, in bed beside her, had had a nightmare that kept the two of them up for hours. Marvin had slept through the 3:00 A.M. chaos, of course. Flynn never asked for him anyway when she woke up screaming and terrified. Anna felt partly responsible for Flynn's haunted nights, which had intensified since Anna, a month ago, insisted that her granddaughter attend school.

Marvin and Poppy had home-schooled their daughter in Alaska, but it was apparent that neither one of them paid much attention to whether or not the child was actually learning anything. When Anna discovered Flynn's bizarre sense of distance and geography—she knew Mars was a planet, for instance, but thought it was part of Minneapolis—she was furious at Marvin for his negligence.

When Anna had asked Flynn to name the nine planets, Flynn said, "Earth. India. Asia. Indiana, Mars, Venus. California, the moon, and the space shuttle." Anna had taken Flynn to the elementary school the next day for a meeting with the principal and to talk about grade placement. At ten, Flynn should have been in the fifth grade, but given Flynn's lack of formal schooling, Anna hoped for a remedial fourth-grade placement. To Anna's astonishment, the test results that came back from the Educational Testing Services ten days later showed that Flynn was indeed lacking in basic knowledge, but she read at the ninth-grade level, and had an advanced grasp of mathematics, "consistent with what a bright high-schooler would know."

"I've never seen anything quite like this," the young female principal had said going over Flynn's results with Anna. "Total population of the United States, according to Flynn, is two thousand." She chuckled. "But she's in the ninety-ninth percentile for math and reading comprehension, and she appears to be gifted musically."

"Oh," Anna had said. "Really?"

The principal nodded. "On a hunch, I had the music teacher talk to her and test her musical aptitude. What instrument does Flynn play?"

Anna shook her head. "I don't think she plays anything."

"Well, she should. She has perfect pitch."

All this had baffled Anna. Neither Poppy nor Marvin had ever given her music lessons.

"How do you know all this, Flynn?" Anna asked, when they went out for Belgian waffles after Anna's meeting. "Who taught you to read?"

"What do you mean?" Flynn heaped her waffle with berries and chocolate and signaled the waiter who was standing at the ready with the can of whipped cream.

Anna was tickled by this. Flynn took her food seriously, in ways that Poppy—and Anna herself—never had. "How do you know the things you know? How do you know about music?"

"I was born with it. I just remembered from other times. Other places I've been before I was here."

Anna dismissed Flynn's chatter. She was delighted that Flynn tested into her age-appropriate grade, with weekly, remedial classes in geography and American history. Inexplicably, her knowledge of world history was at a very high level.

Yet, she didn't like school, she told Anna right from the start. Didn't like being told what to do and when to do it, and the other kids teased her. She hadn't made any friends in the month she'd been enrolled.

A few nights earlier, when Anna was getting ready for bed she found a note on her bathroom mirror in what was clearly an intentional childish scrawl: "No buddy likes me." Anna took it down and wrote at the bottom: "Some buddy does" and tucked it into Flynn's lunch bag the next day.

Anna looked over at Flynn now, finally asleep at four in the morning after being up most of the night. She left the bedroom and tiptoed out into the hallway. There were noises coming from Marvin's room, low murmuring voices, the unmistakable sounds of lovers trying to be quiet. Her heart started to pound. For a minute she believed it was Poppy. Wanted to believe, anyway, that her daughter had sneaked home in the middle of the night to surprise her. But she saw the jacket on the back of the chair and she knew whose it was. Marvin claimed not to have seen Christine since the night they'd met for coffee, but she'd overheard him on the phone a time or two, caught snippets of conversation that indicated he was seeing her. And Anna had specifically requested that Marvin not invite overnight female guests.

Just last week, after Marvin had stumbled in at 1:00 A.M. for the second night in a row, Anna said, "We need to talk."

He sighed. "Let me guess. We need to talk about Christine."

She shook her head. "That's your business, Marvin. I certainly don't hold it against you that you're dating."

"You don't?" He seemed genuinely surprised.

"Of course not. What's happening between you and Poppy is your business. In fact, if I had to side with someone, it would be you."

"You would?"

"Flynn, however, *is* my concern. That night just after you got here, when you and I had dinner at Davidé's and you asked me about taking Flynn. Poppy's idea of me having custody of her. Or guardianship. At the time it seemed ludicrous. Now it doesn't. I want something official."

"What? What do you mean?"

"I mean, I didn't see it then, but I see it now. I can give her more than you can. She'll have the best of everything. The best education, the best schools. But it's more than that. I can give her stability. You were right. That night we talked about it, you were right."

"You want me to give you my daughter?"

"Wasn't that why you came all this way? Isn't that what you were really asking me to do?"

He looked straight ahead, rubbed his fingertips together lightly. "Okay," he said.

"Okay what?"

"Let's discuss it. But I'm not ready to decide anything, and I'm not ready to make anything official."

"That's fine," she said. "And it's fine for Flynn to live here with me. You're also welcome in my home, but I think we should decide on some basic ground rules. I won't have my house turned into Peyton Place. I won't ask where you've been, or whom you've been with, but I won't tolerate sleepovers. Keep it out of my house. And, at the risk of sounding like I'm giving you a curfew, I'd really like it if you could be home to put Flynn to bed. She gets anxious when you're not here when she goes to bed."

"I feel like I'm seventeen again."

"Marvin, you need to think of your daughter. She's had a hard time. Her mother left her, and you're in and out at all hours, it's not easy for her. It's not good for her. Especially for someone like her."

"You're right. You're absolutely right. You have a bead on Flynnie."

"On the other hand, you have your life to live. You're young. There's no reason why you shouldn't try to find someone to share it with."

He nodded, but didn't speak. She saw the indecision in his face, saw his thoughts surface and rearrange his expression, the contradictory impulses of freedom from all responsibility and the string that tied his heart to Flynn's. "We'll talk about it. I need to think. I'm probably in denial about my marriage. I need to give Poppy what she wants."

"Which is?"

"A divorce."

Over the course of a few days, they came to a kind of agreement. For now, things would remain as they had been, with definitive plans in place by the New Year. It was too risky, was what she was seeing. Marvin could just disappear, take her granddaughter the way he took her daughter all those years ago. To lose Flynn like that, to spend her remaining years worried and wondering and waiting for the phone to ring, was something Anna would never get past. In just this short time she was already hopelessly in love with the girl, though that wasn't totally unexpected. What she hadn't anticipated was how essential Flynn would become to her. Elemental, maybe. The dark heart of the nucleus in the cell of Anna's life.

After putting the turkey in the oven, Anna sat quietly by the window with her coffee. She planned on a late afternoon dinner. Greta and Mike and their new adopted daughter, Lily, were coming, as were Jack and Stuart. Jack was not an insignificant presence in Anna's thoughts, despite the brevity of their meeting.

On Monday, she'd dialed Jack's number on a whim, not sure he would even remember her. But when Jack answered with, "Anna!" it was as if he'd been waiting by the phone for her call. He and Stuart would, he said, love to come to Thanksgiving dinner.

This might be the last gathering she had here. Shortly after the night she discovered Flynn's backyard project she began toying with the idea of selling the townhouse, and moving permanently to the house in Maine. Anna suspected Flynn might do better in a small town, in the slow-paced northern community not unlike what she was used to in Alaska. The house was over five thousand square feet, which would mean privacy for all concerned. Assuming he would want to move in, Marvin could use the attic as a studio. It was probably overkill, Anna knew, but last week she had her attorney probate the papers for legal guardianship, effective as soon as Marvin signed, or at any point where parental care was compromised. Anna was making her peace with Marvin, and his presence in her home was comfortable, even, at times, enjoyably companionable. But he did have a Houdini history, and she needed to be careful. Anna wanted loose legal terms, a little wiggle room in how to define compromised care; a good attorney (hers) could have a field day if Marvin got a notion to run off with some woman, Flynn in tow. One could argue, for instance, that a father whose schedule was erratic enough that his daughter didn't have regular mealtimes, or exposed his daughter to the horrific sculptures he left around the house, was providing inferior parental care.

She began chopping the celery for the dressing, turned on the radio under the counter to drown out the sounds of the lovers down the hall. It had been going on for over an hour, for God's sake. What if Flynn awoke and heard them? The child was already insecure enough, her fragile world held together by paper clips and prayers, not to mention the fact that Marvin promised he wouldn't bring women into the house.

Anna opened the pantry door. She dropped the mixing bowl she'd been holding. There, where last night nestled innocent cans of cranberries, were Marvin's sculptures, all of them busts depicting the face of Ronald Reagan and various serial killers. She went out into the hallway and yelled to her son-in-law.

"What's wrong?" he said, coming into the kitchen a minute later.

"What's wrong? You've turned my pantry into Heart of Darkness, is what's wrong, mister. Where are my damn cranberries?"

Marvin, clothed ridiculously in a silk kimono robe that barely grazed the tops of his thighs, opened the cabinet above the sink. "Cranberries are here. I moved them."

Anna looked at him. He stepped over the shards of glass on the floor, peered into the depths of the closet. "This pantry has the lowest humidity levels in the house. Eight per cent. I just put them in here to dry overnight."

"Out. I want these gruesome things out of my house right now."

"What would you have me do with them? The college is closed for the holiday. The buildings are locked."

"Out," she said again. "And I don't mean hidden or put away, I mean out."

"Do you have any idea how much work went into this?"

She turned to look at him, but couldn't hold his gaze. "Do you have any idea that this is my house?"

He did a curious thing then, one that Anna would puzzle over for months. He stepped behind her as she stood in front of the cutting board, leaned in close, and put his hands over her wrists. He stood there like that for what seemed like minutes. "I know you, Anna. I know what you're about, don't think I don't." She wheeled around, but he had already moved on, was already carefully lifting the busts off the shelf to carry them out. She knew she was right, any rational person would say as much. There was absolutely no good reason for those things to be in the house; Marvin had studio space at the community college where he was teaching. Even given his middle of the night "art attacks," as he called them, it was only a ten-minute drive to the college. There was no justification for her house being turned into the Little Shop of Horrors.

Though for now Jack was still beside him, Stuart was already sick with Jack's upcoming departure next week. It was at his insistence that Jack was moving out, to the tiny efficiency in Jamaica Plain that Stuart helped him find. His health had stabilized, though both his viral load and white count were extremely high, putting him at increased risk of opportunistic infection. Daily, Stuart had to force himself to stick to his decision and insist that Jack leave. They'd had an agreement and Jack broke part of it—the most important part—by seeing other men. Well, at least one man.

Stuart hadn't wanted to know, of course, not really. It was David, the director of the library where Stuart now worked part-time, who pushed Stuart toward the truth. "It sounds to me like the man hasn't changed an iota. He's living La Vida Loca again, if you ask me, which you haven't." Stuart had done a little detective work, which was a mistake. Hector was the most beautiful man Stuart had ever seen, more beautiful than what even Hollywood offered.

The day Stuart came home early from work and found Jack gone, he knew. At six o'clock, a half hour before Stuart typically came home, Jack walked in, disheveled and untucked and with another man's scent clearly on him. "Don't try to lie to me," Stuart said.

"Okay."

"It's Hector again."

Jack sat, ran his fingers through his tussled hair. "It's Hector still."

Because he didn't try to rationalize or promise it wouldn't happen again, didn't beg for forgiveness or declare his commitment to change, it took Stuart two days to ask him to leave instead of the five minutes it should have.

This Thanksgiving at Anna's would be their last holiday together, the closure they needed before they went their separate ways. Stuart thought it strange that Anna had invited them, and even stranger that Jack's enthusiastic acceptance seemed so genuine. It might be a blessing though, spending the holiday with a virtual stranger instead of their friends; the idea of going to Jane and Leila's or to the feast at Curtis's was unbearable.

Stuart reached over to touch Jack's shoulder to wake him, but Jack was already awake. Jack took Stuart's hand and pulled him close. They watched the snow come down through the parted red drapes.

"What time do we have to be at Anna's?" Jack said.

"Four, isn't it? You talked to her."

Jack murmured, took Stuart's hand and held it tighter. If this weren't the last major thing they were doing together, he would most certainly cancel and stay in bed all day. The cruelest aspect of this disease so far was the fatigue. He could battle infections, put up with fevers and aches, but being so tired that the thought of getting showered, dressed, and doing nothing more strenuous than sitting in front of the television or in the coffee shop half a block away made him want to weep from exhaustion. Nothing would ever be the same again. Monday was his moving day, to the horrible apartment in Jamaica Plain with its mildewy carpet and embedded smell of cooking grease. He and Stuart had cleaned for six hours, then hired Merry Maids to do it all over again, but the bad odors remained. It was choice rather than financial exigency that made him lease the apartment. As he knew it would, the Kobayashi account pulled the plug, then Hank Sherman pulled him. Sherman, Beck and Associates had been more than generous with their severance package, and Jack certainly could have afforded a decent apartment, but he found the idea of decency was more depressing than living in a shithole. There was luxury and fine things, and there was poverty and ugliness. He was never very good at middle distance, moderation.

Most of the time, Jack was relieved to no longer be working at the investment firm. Losing the Kobayashi account started the ball rolling downhill. The heart went out of him after the Japanese corporation left the firm. Nothing seemed high stakes enough; nothing held his attention in the way he needed to be challenged. Besides, his focus was so fuzzy that he couldn't concentrate for more than forty minutes at a stretch, often much less than that. He started to make glaring errors that led to expensive mistakes. Hank—who knew but never spoke of Jack's illness—let him work part-time from home, but even this seemed too much.

Stuart had tried to show him how to make the severance money last, detailed a careful budget for him, but then just rolled his eyes. "Who am I kidding? You've juggled millions but you've never even balanced your checkbook." He didn't have a plan if his money ran out, which, given the state of the stock market, it might. He hoped he wouldn't be alive when or if that day came, peeing in his diapers and drooling puréed apricots down his chin in some substandard nursing home. When he left Monday it would be with two small suitcases. He had given away or sold or bequeathed to Stuart everything else, including his collection of African war masks.

"Do you want breakfast?" Stuart said softly.

"No. Everything I want right now is right here with me."

Stuart squeezed Jack's shoulder. "If only you could believe that."

Later, on their way to Anna's, Jack said, "Maybe we should stop and get a bottle of wine." He pointed to the liquor store across the street from Mrs. Kim's. Hector, he already saw, wasn't near the Korean grocery—she was of course closed for the holiday, and Hector was undoubtedly with his little wife having dinner with the extended family.

Stuart pulled over. Jack cruised through the small store and quickly paid for a bottle of expensive white wine.

Next to the liquor store was a working-class bar where Hector often hung out. He had to check, just had to see. He caught Stuart's eye, held up a finger and pointed to the bar next door. Inside, he dug in his pockets for change at the cigarette machine while looking around the dimly lit interior. Hector wasn't here, either. He pushed one of the buttons on the cigarette machine—some extra long menthol girly smokes, he saw now, and went back out to Stuart.

"Just in the mood," Jack said, and unwrapped the cellophane on the Virginia Slims.

Stuart glanced over. "Your boy must be having a private celebration somewhere."

Jack lit the cigarette. "Yes," he said, angry that Stuart knew what he was up to, and angrier still that it was so clear that Hector wasn't available. "He must be."

Stuart snorted. "You amaze me."

Jack exhaled, waved the girly smoke around with a Marlene Dietrich flourish. "I amaze myself."

Close to noon, Anna went in to check on Flynn, who was still in bed, the cat curled on the pillow beside her. She called Flynn's name softly, but Flynn didn't stir.

Everything was ready, the house clean except for the vacuuming, which Anna didn't want to start until Flynn was up. Marvin and Christine were loading the clay heads into the VW van. Anna watched from the kitchen window as Marvin—wearing just a jacket over his light kimono—placed the gruesome busts in a semicircle in the back. "In the back of the moving love shack," he said to Christine, as she struggled under the weight of Ronald Reagan and Ed Gein, the cannibal killer. Anna watched the snow swirl around them. Marvin's legs were bare, just the hem of his flowered shorty robe visible from beneath his bomber jacket. She felt a wave of nostalgia, an unidentifiable pang—of missing her daughter, her husband, the youth she once had that would have made her stand half-naked in the snow, numbed by the bliss of new love. She opened the window wider; the kitchen was heating up fast. Christine giggled as Marvin pulled something from his pocket. Anna squinted. A pipe. He handed it to Christine. Anna thought she heard him say, "Put a bit in a bowl and hit it, then wait for the bell to ring," he said.

Anna sent a few saucepan lids clattering to the floor. Marvin looked up, just as Anna wanted him to.

"Anna?" he said, coming into the kitchhen a minute later, breathless.

"Yeah," she said.

"It's not what you think."

"I think it's pot. Am I wrong?"

"No. Are you mad?" he asked.

"No. I'm assuming, of course, that you don't smoke in front of Flynn. I might be a little concerned if she saw you smoking, or you were under the influence when she's in your care."

He waved this away. "Certainly not."

Anna began peeling potatoes. "Then I don't have a problem with it. Will Christine be joining us for dinner?"

"No," he said. "She has other plans."

Anna opened the oven and basted the turkey, rearranged the dressing around the bird. When she turned, Marvin was still standing there. "Yes?" she said.

He ran his hands through his hair. "You might be a little mad at me when I tell you this, but I swear to God I honestly forgot until this morning, until, uh, ten minutes ago when I realized Flynn was still in bed."

"What?" Anna said, alarmed.

"Today's Thanksgiving, which is when we have always celebrated Flynnie's birthday."

"I thought her birthday was the second week in December?"

"It was. Is. But we changed it. Too close to Christmas. Anyway, Flynn's always depressed on her birthday, and this year, uh, without Poppy it's probably going to be worse."

"I wish you would have told me. I have nothing for her. I don't know what she wants."

"Well, I do. And it can be from both of us. And I actually, uh, Christine that is, has it at her house. I need to run over and pick it up."

"What is it?"

"A dog. A puppy. Flynn's been asking for a dog since she could talk. The cat was just a compromise. What do you think?"

Anna sighed, poured a cup of coffee and sat. She looked over at him. As a matter of fact, she had dreamed of a dog last night or the night before. A dog running around the house in Maine. They had acreage there, plenty of room for a dog. Why not? If it would make her granddaughter happy and give her yet another reason to move out of Boston, why not? She looked over at Marvin. She wished he would put some clothes on. "What kind of dog is it?"

"I think it's a Border collie mix."

"Yeah, okay. Why not. Border collies aren't too big."

Except that by the time Marvin got back with it, just as Flynn was stumbling out of her bedroom, Anna saw that this puppy, forty pounds if he was an ounce, was a Newfoundland.

"Oh! I knew it!" Flynn said, and got down on her hands and knees. "I knew he would come to me."

"Happy Birthday, sweetheart. He's from your grandma and me."

Flynn smiled up at Anna, the first genuine smile she had seen in days. "Thank you," she said, and hugged Anna tight.

"You're welcome, dear. You might want to take him outside to pee. Puppies have to pee a lot. Take him out back so he's safe inside the fence." Anna watched Flynn go out. She turned to Marvin. "That's one damn big Border collie."

"He is?" Marvin turned to her, with a dreamy look.

"Who told you that was a Border collie, Marvin? That's a Newfoundland. I'd say a purebred."

"Oh. Are they good with kids?"

"That dog is going to be enormous. I'd say a hundred and fifty pounds at least."

"Oh! I had no idea. I don't know dog breeds. I got him at the animal shelter. What do you want me to do? Should I take him back and get something smaller?"

She raised an eyebrow. "And why would you assume that Flynn hasn't already named him and planned his future? Too late."

"I'm sorry, Anna."

"Oh, well, we'll make the best of it, I suppose. I'm not crazy about big dogs, but if it makes Flynn happy, I'll adjust. Anyway, I've heard that Newfies are one of the best breeds to have around children."

Marvin put his arm around her and kissed her on the forehead. "Thank you," he said softly.

Flynn played with the dog under the table. He liked to chew on shoelaces, and every few minutes a voice—Greta's, her grandma's—came down from above telling Flynn to move the puppy away. The Wise Men were in the body of the dog. Flynn knew they would find a way to be with her, to live someplace besides her dreams. A big dog, with plenty of room for the men who were sometimes wise men, sometimes tiny pips, and when they couldn't decide, were whips. They weren't so nice when they turned into whips, was what she was learning. They were huge and angry, talked about how Gladys Knight had deserted them and left them underground. They wanted revenge. Plus, as the whips they bossed Flynn around. They sat on her chest this morning so she couldn't leave the bed when she wanted to, but only lie there in the morning sun while they told her things like her mother never loved her and she was never coming back. They told her it was her fault Greta's baby died because Flynn selfishly wanted Greta for herself. Greta wouldn't be Flynn's new mother; she had already adopted a girl in Flynn's place. Even her grandma, the whips told her, didn't love her so much. She only tolerated Flynn because Anna wanted Marvin around. Flynn thought this was probably true; her father and her grandmother were in true love, though she thought the whips were lying when they told her Anna and Marvin had hired kidnapers to take her away in the middle of the night.

"Flynnie, get the dog out of there," her father said from above. "Take him into the living room."

Flynn picked up the puppy and did as she was told. Greta's new deaf daughter, Lily, tried to catch him. Lily was only three, but Flynn knew the whips were making Lily do things. Pull the puppy's tail, they told her, and laughed when she did. Flynn heard the noise inside Lily, a continuous

screaming and crying and begging for help, angry sounds of not being noticed or loved enough. Being deaf meant you had the power to hear what
people said inside their heads, but not aloud. Flynn understood about not
being heard. About people not hearing her. In this way, Flynn could see inside Lily. Deaf people were usually saints in other lifetimes. Flynn thought
Lily was probably Joan of Arc. She was surrounded with the blue-white
light of angels. All the anger of that man sitting across from her grandma,
Jack, was in Lily's head. Then Flynn, through Lily, felt his anger, too: it was
like someone had held two spoons over two candles, then pressed them
onto her temples. There was a buzzing of bees. Her grandma's fear was a
cold spot behind her eyes, and made the sound of an owl. Only heaven was
silent.

The whips now rose from the dog's body, filled the room with their
awful light and their stench of sickness—the same smell she remembered
when a squirrel got into the eaves of the house in Alaska and died. The
whips' hair grew to six feet in six seconds then twisted into snaky coils and
sucked up every bit of dirt in the house. Her father used to say the '80s
stank, and this must be what she smelled now. The stench of a decade over
her grandma's delicious cooking. The whips turned into huge balls of light
and flew around the holiday table.

We're fireflies! We'll take no crap, we'll sing to you in our wise-guy rap!

Flynn covered her ears. They were so loud. But the man called Jack was
speaking to her. "What?" Flynn said.

"I said, what's the puppy's name?"

Flynn picked him up. "His name is Baby Jesus," Flynn said. She decided that this must be his name, since she couldn't find the little figure
that went with Mary and Joseph in the house barn. She assumed Baby
Jesus was with Gladys Knight somewhere, underground where the Pips
used to be.

"What?" Anna said. "What are you naming him?"

"Baby Jesus."

Everybody at the table laughed at her.

"You can't call a dog that, sweetheart," Anna said.

"Why?" Flynn said.

"Why don't you call him Buddha?" Jack said. "He's fat like a Buddha."

"He's fat like a Buddha now, but he's going to be big as all outdoors,"

Anna said. "He's from a far-flung kennel specializing in large Border collies." She winked at Marvin, who laughed.

Flynn fed turkey to the dog, who was already helping himself to her plate as they sat together on the couch. "May we be excused?"

Anna nodded to her, uncorked the sixth bottle of wine for the evening. The heavy drinking didn't feel entirely celebratory. Jack and Stuart, unlike the energetic pair she remembered meeting, seemed strained and tense; Mike had left as soon as the plates were cleared. Greta didn't even look up when he said goodbye. Even Marvin, normally the one Anna counted on for his gift of small talk, was dreamy and abstracted. Only Greta seemed happy—radiant, in fact, in the presence of the little girl she was planning to rename Agnes, after her mother, but who was Lily for now.

"You can put her in my room for a nap," Anna said, when she saw Lily was getting sleepy. Greta nodded and stood.

"This was a lovely evening, Anna," Jack said, and smiled at her.

Anna took his hand and squeezed it. "I hope I'm not hearing 'but we really have to go' next. Because there's pie and coffee. And leftovers for the midnight snack after the movie."

"Oh? There's a movie?" Jack said, leaning forward.

Marvin turned to look at her. She hadn't planned on any movie; it just came out of her mouth the minute it popped into her head. "Yep. A Thanksgiving tradition around here. *Fiddler on the Roof.*" Anna didn't especially like this movie—one of several videos left in the hall closet by the previous tenant—but she didn't want the evening to end.

As the day wore on, the idea of moving, of selling this townhouse grew from a possibility to a certainty. This wasn't the right environment for Flynn. Anna had been worried about her all day, concerned about the look in Flynn's eyes, a wild-eyed look, as though she was buried under the weight of sorrow or fear—Anna couldn't say which.

Anna started the movie, then went to check on Flynn. She was sitting up in bed, the puppy in her lap, and reading the Bible aloud. Anna smiled. The dog was pretty cute. It wore an expression of worried concentration, as if he was truly concerned with the message of the book of Revelation.

Back in the living room, Anna gathered up the dessert plates and coffee cups and took them into the kitchen. Greta followed her, grabbed a dishtowel. "Oh, don't do that," Anna said. "There's not a lot."

"Why not? Lily's asleep. And I'm not into musicals much. Sorry."

"Neither am I. But isn't it great? No obnoxiously loud football game."

Greta took a plate from Anna's hand, and it slipped to the floor and shattered. She burst into tears.

"It's fine. It wasn't even mine. It was here when I got here. It couldn't have been uglier."

"Sorry."

"Leave it. I'll clean it up later." Anna dunked her hands in the hot, lemony water. "What's the matter, dear?" Just then, she heard Flynn laugh—laugh! How long had it been?—and Jack's teasing voice. She wanted to rush in to see the pink flush that was surely on her granddaughter's face. She had Poppy's laugh, Anna decided, looked like her mother when she giggled, which she was doing now. Anna smiled, felt a flutter of happiness.

She looked over at Greta, knew what Greta was going to say before she said it.

"I'm leaving him. As soon as Lily's adoption papers are final. I had him followed." Greta's face was ashen.

"Where's he been?"

Greta laughed bitterly. "It's humiliating. All along I'd been preparing myself for some hot young thing, some whiplash blonde or buxom brunette, but *this*. It seems I'm competing with flowers for my husband's attention."

Anna turned the water off. "What?"

"All those times he's been gone. Hours and hours, claiming he's just driving around...."

"Yeah. Where was he?"

"The botanical gardens. Sitting for hours among the gerbera daisies and Eleanor roses."

Anna laughed in surprise.

"Yeah, that's what I did when the investigator told me. The P.I. said, 'Is your husband a religious man, Mrs. Allen? Because I watched him and his lips were moving like he was talking to the flowers, then I realized he must be praying.'"

"I've never heard of anything like this before," Anna said. "Well, but it's not entirely bad, is it?"

"How can it be in any way good? My husband would rather stare at a bunch of plants than at me. He should be home helping me paint Lily's nursery. Sometimes I think the only reason he agreed to adopt Lily was that she was named after a flower. 'Stargazer Lily' he calls her. Christ."

"Wow," Anna said. "Wow. You mean to tell me all those hours, all those missing hours, he's been hanging around gardens and parks?"

"Yes. There were two weekend trips. Business trips, Mike said. That's where the investigator thought he would nail him. He followed him to a cabin near the border of Maine. But no other woman, just more botany. Two days he spent bundled up in parkas staring at the vegetation." She took the saucepan from Anna's hand.

"My God," Anna said. "Did you confront him?"

"Partially. I feel like a fool. What do you say? 'I know you've been seeing the birches. I know about Daisy and Rose'? I did tell him that a friend saw him at the botanical gardens when he claimed to be at a business lunch."

"What did he say?" Anna emptied the water carafe into the fern on the windowsill.

"He said it made him less lonely to sit among beautiful things. I don't even want to consider the implications of that statement."

They fell silent. "Mysteries," Anna said finally. "What little mysteries people are."

Flynn came into the kitchen just as they were finishing up the cleaning. "Baby Jesus had an accident."

"Okay," Anna said. "I'll be right in. Go take him outside. He needs to go out every hour."

Anna found all three men on the couch engrossed in the movie. It was the scene of the eldest daughter on her wedding day, the father bemoaning the passage of time with the melancholic "Sunrise, Sunset."

"How's the movie?" Anna asked, but all three of them were so engrossed in it that they didn't look away, which Anna found comforting. The best kind of answer, she always thought, had no sound.

Five days before Christmas, Jack still didn't have plans for the holidays. Most days he stayed in, baffled and amazed at how few friends he had; all of his friendships in the past, the ones he and Stuart shared as a couple, were nurtured and sustained by Stuart. Jack hadn't appreciated Stuart's gracious elegance until now, how making guests comfortable was an art unto itself. He had one friend, two, if he counted Anna, whom he had talked to a handful of times since Thanksgiving and who promised to visit just as soon as she could. Jane came over every week, every Wednesday, with a briefcase full of work for Jack from the firm. Sick as he felt most times, he couldn't bear idleness, so he arranged with Hank Sherman to be hired on as a consultant. It was easy work and Jack could determine the pace. He had only to study the portfolios of the accounts handled by the new young hires and offer his assessment of their investment strategies.

He was working on the accounts when Jane came over at six o'clock. He invited her in, hoped the scent of vanilla he had simmering in a saucepan would mask the odor that had gotten progressively worse. The drains in the kitchen and bath were perpetually blocked, and the tenants all around him seemed to be cooking with heavier and heavier spices. Even his bath towels smelled of curry.

He turned off the overhead fluorescent light and lit some candles. "How's the weather out there?" he asked, as Jane walked in.

"Snowy. We're supposed to get a storm tonight."

"Have a seat." Jack picked up the stack of manila folders from the couch, moved them to the coffee table. "What can I get you to drink?"

"Nothing, thanks. I actually can't stay too long. Leila and I have plans tonight."

"How is Leila?" he asked from the kitchenette area where he decanted a bottle of wine and took down two glasses.

"She's good. We're good. She sends her regards to you. As does Stuart."

Every week Jack resisted the temptation to ask about him. They hadn't spoken since the day Jack moved in—almost a month ago now.

"He's doing well. We had dinner with them last night, as a matter of fact."

Jack froze for a second. He handed the wineglass to Jane who took one polite sip and put it down. "Them?" Jane hesitated, but Jack rushed in. "That's all. No more. I'm glad he's seeing someone. He deserves to be happy."

Jane nodded. "I'll tell him you send your best."

"Who is he?" Jack said, before he could stop himself. The ironic thing was that he hadn't seen Hector since he'd moved out. He told himself that it was because he felt too sick, but lying awake at night, free to desire anyone, Stuart was all he wanted.

"Do you really want me to answer that?" Jane said.

"No. I think I know anyway. It's that librarian. That guy Stuart works with." He picked up his wineglass, drained it. "Well, anyway. That's his business now. Look, I'm having a party Christmas Eve. You and Leila are invited." He hadn't thought about having a party until just this instant, but why not? He could probably get four or five people to commit, which would be enough to make his tiny place look packed.

"I'd love to come, but we already have plans unfortunately," Jane said, and stood to go. She reached for her coat, kissed Jack on the cheek. "Call if you need anything." She picked up the stack of folders.

"I will," he said. He poured the rest of the wine into his glass when she was gone. He should have been more interested in people. Should have bothered a little more with the things that sustained friendships. Was this how he would spend the rest of his days? He was going to have to force himself to do things, despite how sick he felt most of the time; otherwise he'd never have any human contact. Doctors' appointments and trips to the grocery store were not enough.

He lay back on the sofa, balanced his glass on his chest and listened to the Indian couple fighting next door, their nightly row that half the time sent the husband out till the wee hours of the morning. Jack preferred the loud arguing to the wife's solitary weeping, which, he heard now, was beginning. He sat up, blew out the candles and reached for his shoes.

He drove into Boston with no destination in mind. All the stores were fully decorated for Christmas. He stopped in front of the Gap where every year he bought Stuart a red sweater. He went in and chose one. He'd mail it after the holidays so Stuart wouldn't feel obligated to reciprocate. Maybe he should shop for Jane and Leila. Stuart got them something every year—Stuart gave presents to everyone—but he didn't have a clue as to the kinds of things they might want or need.

He wandered over to Cambridge, drifted toward some folk music festival under a giant tent in Harvard Yard. He wasn't much into this kind of music, but he was tired of walking. Gypsy-intellectual types buzzed around him. Cheryl Wheeler was singing now about fall coming to New

England, though he couldn't make out many of the words over the street noise and the food vendors behind him.

He heard Anna before he saw her, heard her voice in line at one of the concessions: "Holy God, man, how long does it take to cook a hot dog? I've been in line long enough to break a habit, backslide, and recommit."

Jack called to her three times as she was moving slowly through the crowd, looking up at the musicians and hesitating, as though unsure about whether to stay.

His voice finally carried to her and her eyes looked in his direction and found his face. "Well, Jack! You have no idea how often I've thought of you. I've been meaning to call."

He embraced her, inhaled the fresh-air scent of her clothes, and a heady perfume of exotic florals. "How have you been? Where are you going? Have you been in the city awhile, or can you get a drink?" He laughed with her at his barrage of questions. "What I meant to say is, don't walk away from me, Anna, I couldn't bear it." He laughed again, but couldn't get the cavalier self-mocking tone that he wanted. "Don't tell me you're on your way somewhere."

"Well, isn't everybody on their way somewhere?" She took a bite of the hot dog. "I've been Christmas shopping like a madwoman, since we're leaving for Maine in the morning, that is, Flynn and I. Marvin will come later."

"Oh? Did you finally sell the townhouse?" Jack had seen the listing in the Sunday classifieds last week. He tried to match strides with her, panting to keep up; she was the fastest walker he'd ever known, bar none.

She shook her head. "Marvin is going to live there till it sells. He'll come up to Maine on the weekends to visit."

"Good, that sounds good."

"I hope so." She stopped in front of a classy-looking bar with polished brass railings and suited businessmen within. "Want a brandy?"

He nodded, followed her into a booth by the window.

"I'm so glad I ran into you. It's been so hectic I haven't had time to call anyone," Anna said.

"It's all right. I haven't called anyone either."

She raised her glass to his. "*Cent anno.* To the next hundred years, as the Italians say." She sipped. "I drink Grand Marnier only at the holidays.

I love Christmas, don't you?"

He nodded, felt his throat get tight.

"Is everything all right?"

"Oh, hey, you know. Heartbreak, AIDS, joblessness, angry Indian neighbors, the usual."

He drank his brandy down, signaled to the waiter. He looked back to Anna and saw that she was watching him with the intensity Jack had seen in Flynn's expression. He thought of Flynn frequently, which surprised him because he didn't like children as a rule. But something about the girl and her worried look, her intelligent strangeness, reminded him of himself as a child, of feeling like he was guarding a secret without knowing what it was.

Anna lit a cigarette, looked at him through the coils of smoke. "I know you're probably as overextended as the rest of us, but I would love it if you would come to Maine for part of the holiday. My husband and I used to have an annual Christmas Eve party at our house in Maine, and I've decided to start it up again, though scaled way, way back. It'll be pretty sedate, but I'm getting caterers from Boston. Greta and her daughter will be there. Marvin, too."

"Really?" Jack said. "You're inviting me?"

"Will you come?"

"I would love to." He could have wept with gratitude.

"Great. You can get as drunk as you want. The house is huge and the guest bedrooms are ready and waiting for the heavy revelers."

"How Gatsby-ish."

She laughed. "Yeah, right. Anyway, we're leaving tomorrow, Flynn and I. I'll give you directions and you can come anytime and stay as long as you want." She took a long sip of her drink, looked him in the eye. "I mean that."

When they parted, Jack watched Anna until she rounded the corner. Something about the way she turned her head from side to side, looking at this and that, made him think of Thanksgiving night when he and Stuart were leaving Anna's. Flynn was in the backyard making snow angels, her puppy balanced on her chest. "What do you know of heavenly bodies?" she said to Jack. "How many do you know?"

"Not enough, and too many at once," he'd said.

At home, he packed a suitcase, then another. Before he knew it, he had gathered together all that he'd brought. Nobody should be expected to live here. He would find a new place after the holidays. Maybe Anna wouldn't mind if he spent a week or two, long enough for him to find a decent apartment that didn't speak so loudly of punishment.

That night, he slept peacefully for the first time in months. Anna was so gracious, even the thought of her like a warm shelter. He had never put much stock in kindness, never felt, until now, how small gestures of good will could bring such happiness. Things suddenly seemed bearable. He would call Stuart in the morning to wish him well.

PART TWO

THE LIVING AND THE DEAD

TEN

THE THIRD SUZANNE

It felt to her like all she'd done for the past few days was soothe somebody. First Flynn with her nightmares, then Jack with his pneumonia, and now Marvin, on the phone, for the third time today. Ostensibly, the calls were about real estate—her townhouse was still on the market after sixteen months, and the realtor was urging Anna to lower her price, which she didn't want to do. Why should she? She was in no hurry to sell. Marvin was still living there, coming to Maine on weekends—though his visits had become more infrequent over the past month or two. She and Jack and Flynn were humming along up here quite nicely. Most of the time.

"Flynn is outside with the dog," Anna said. "Do you want me to get her, or do you want me to have her call you later?"

"She doesn't want to come to visit me anymore. She barely acknowledges me when I'm there. Did I do something to make her mad? What did I do wrong?"

"It has nothing to do with you, Marvin. She's at that age." Anna cringed, hearing her mother's voice in her own. "She's just twelve and weird. All girls go through these stages. They start to develop their adult characteristics, but haven't yet worked them into the weave."

"The what?"

"She's changing, is all. It's not that she doesn't want to see you. She's just strange and solitary these days. Come up this weekend. Take her to the movies. She'll be all right." The truth was, Anna was a little concerned. To say Flynn was solitary was an understatement; whole days went by with Anna barely seeing her. She'd grown taller in the past year, and was beginning to develop, which Anna saw as a hopeful sign—Flynn's moodiness was mostly due to surging hormones and not mental imbalance. Anna couldn't remember much about Poppy's adolescence, except that it was unbearable.

"I thought girls were supposed to adore their fathers. Shouldn't she being going through some Ophelia complex?"

"Oh," Anna said. "I can't remember what that is."

"It means I can do no wrong. That I'm a kind of demigod in her eyes."

Anna sighed into the phone.

"I'll try to make it up Friday." He paused. "I heard from Poppy last week," Marvin said.

"Oh? Where is she? How is she?"

"She's in England. Trying to get into some interior design school. She's dating someone." Marvin made a wounded noise. "I might have to go over there and kill him."

"Well, you're dating, too. You started seeing someone almost immediately."

"That's different. Poppy is my home, Christine is my home away from home."

"Something tells me Christine doesn't know that. Anyway, I have to go. I'll have Flynn call you soon."

Anna hung up and went into the sunroom where Jack had been for four straight hours, listening to every recorded version of Leonard Cohen's "Suzanne." He had lucid days, and not-so-lucid days, but this one was a mysterious blend of both. He debated with Anna, with Flynn, and on the phone with Stuart, about which version of the song was the best. She didn't know what to do with him today. His emotions were all over the place, which was partly a result of his medication. His physician had recombined the AZT cocktail when the original meds seemed to be failing. For a stretch of a few weeks he seemed so sick that Anna was afraid he was going to die. His white count was now slowly on the rise. His fortieth birthday was in three weeks. Assuming he remained stabilized, Anna planned to throw a party, the size and style of which to be determined later.

Joan Baez's rendition of the song was back on. "Anna!" Jack called, with the urgency of someone having a stroke.

"What?" She wheeled around. "What's the matter?"

"Nothing. I just wanted you to hear that Baez has varied the song in key places." He stopped the CD then started the track anew. "Listen. The original line as Cohen wrote it was 'and she's touched your perfect body with her mind.' Here comes Baez." Anna stopped to listen, dust rag in hand.

"Do you hear how she changed the line? Baez replaced 'perfect body' and 'mind' with 'being kind.'" Did Anna think the song was diminished in any way? She didn't, she said. She dusted the end tables, ran a damp cloth over the wicker chairs. The cushions needed to be washed.

"But which is better?" Jack said.

"Which do you like better?" The windows, too, were filthy. Flynn's dog had pressed its nose all along the glass.

"That's not what I mean. Is Baez's version better than Cohen's and Judy Collins's? Is kindness better than perfection and beauty?"

"Yes," she said, "it is always preferable. Perfection can be achieved through gentle kindness. Unkind beauty can only go so far."

She said it off-handedly, but he started to weep. "Oh, Anna, you are such a reproach to me."

"Jack," she said, and turned off the CD player. "I think it might be time for something else. How about something classical? It's getting a little tragic around here."

He blew his nose, agreed she was right, said that after one more time through the Judy Collins's he would find something else to listen to.

She tucked the blankets around his legs, kissed him on the forehead, and went to answer the phone, which was ringing again. This time it was Violet, the neighbor down the road, a widow who grew more eccentric by the year. She'd lived in the same house for decades. Anna and Hugh used to invite Violet and her husband, Floyd, to their annual Christmas party. Anna saw Violet in the grocery store last week wearing what looked like three pairs of pants.

"Anna?" she said.

"Hi, Violet, how are you?"

"Have you been by Thibbidoux's drugstore lately?" No small talk with

Violet. She was the heart-of-the-matter kind of woman. "I ask because I was in there last week for Flonase and there were condoms in full display, not too far from the Almond Joys." Anna stifled a laugh. "I thought you'd want to know, with the girl there and all." Anna let her go on for a while about neighborhood transgressions major and minor, grateful for this distraction. She half-listened to Violet, but her attention was drawn to Jack. He was singing now in such a way that made her freeze, hold her breath. He had Joan Baez's "Suzanne" on yet again and something about the singer's honeyed alto and slow, measured lyrics made Jack's baritone shine forth. The acoustics in the sunroom were grand, thanks to Hugh, who had hired the best architect in the East so Anna could have a place to practice her cello. The stereo was a good one, too. A Bang & Olufsen system that was, to her ears, the auditory equivalent of pointillism: each note a bridesmaid coming forth, dressed alike but distinct, part of the music's unified pageantry. Jack's voice fit alongside Baez's so perfectly it was almost as if they were in the same space.

"Anna?" Violet said.

"Yes, I'm listening."

"Does the man not know that candy and prophylactics aren't first cousins? I've written a letter to the editor I want to read to you. It's titled 'Looking for Mr. Goodbar in a Trojan War.'"

Anna laughed. "Clever." She picked up the ammonia spray and began cleaning the big bowl of glass doorknobs on the hall table. Her mother-in-law had changed them all back in the '60s or '70s when tacky ruled. A thrifty New Englander, who used wrapping paper three times, Anna knew her mother-in-law wouldn't have thrown out the doorknobs. Anna had searched on and off for twenty-five years, and finally found them in a storage closet under the hall steps.

Jack was going at it with gusto now. Anna had never cared for that maudlin song, but Jack's phrasing and tone were lovely. She listened. Something about Jesus being lonely, watching sailors from a wooden tower. It was lovely. Over two decades since Hugh had built that room for her. Who could have imagined she'd end up like this, completely estranged from the daughter she never wanted, sharing the house with a gay man she inexplicably loved, and a granddaughter whom she loved with an intensity that sometimes bordered on anguish. *The soul selects its own society*. Who was that? Dickinson? One of those reclusive female poets at any rate. The strange thing was, she was happier than she'd been for years, even despite leaving her teaching position, which she thought she would miss, but didn't, not even a little. Her days had a rhythm and urgency, things that fell to her to do: keep the household running, keep Flynn on track, and keep Jack healthy. Money was plentiful—Hugh had left her well off, Jack's contribution was abundant—but nonetheless Anna worked four hours every day for the town's sole internist. It got her out of the house long enough to be away from all the worry for a while, but not so long that it made her anxious about what might be happening in her absence.

The changes in the past year had taken their toll on Flynn, though she seemed, overall, to be healthier here than in Boston. Flynn still had trouble making friends and refused to take part in after-school activities, but Anna thought that would come in time. Flynn walked for hours every day with that giant dog—the vet weighed him in at one-seventy-eight—who never left her side. Like Jack, Flynn had good days and bad, days when she focused on her schoolwork and wanted to go to the mall, and days when she insisted she talked to the dead. Yesterday, Flynn had refused to go to school on the grounds that she didn't need earthly knowledge, that the wisdom of heaven was enough. "Oh yeah?" Anna said. "You have ten minutes to get your heavenly wisdom onto the school bus, missy."

The granddaughter holding a one-sided conversation in her bedroom this morning with the ghost of Anna's mother-in-law, and the man who played the same song about a crazy woman and Jesus a hundred times in a row. That's what had been on her docket since the start of the weekend. And now the highly verbal three-trousered widow in her ear. Anna thanked Violet for calling, and hung up.

She walked back into the sunroom, flipped off the stereo, and picked up all three discs. "Jack, I'm sorry sweetheart. I love you, but if I have to listen to this song one more minute, I'm going to commit a violence."

"Fair enough." He leaned back in the rocking chair, tipped his head up to the path of the late November sun.

"What else can I put on?" Anna flipped through the stack of CDs, named fifteen or sixteen, none of which elicited any interest.

"Nothing. I relish the silence," he said, exasperated, as though it hadn't been he who chose the music in the first place.

"Okay. I'm going to start dinner. Can I get you anything?"

He shook his head.

She was chopping carrots for soup when she heard version number four of "Suzanne," Jack's a cappella rendition. She sighed, flipped on the radio above the sink to get the evening news. It wasn't until she heard Noah Adams identify the program as "Weekend All Things Considered" that she remembered this was Saturday and she hadn't seen Flynn since the morning. She dumped the carrots in the soup pot and went upstairs to check the rooms. "Flynn?" Anna called. Not anywhere on the first floor, either.

Jack interrupted his song long enough to tell her that he hadn't seen Flynn all day. This wasn't entirely unusual, though she often stayed close by on weekends. On school days, Flynn almost never came straight home. Anna might not have noticed, busy as she was, getting home after six each evening—she agreed to help out the local pediatrician with sports physicals this semester—if not for the observant Violet.

A week or so ago, Violet called just after seven one morning. "Is everything all right?" she'd asked.

Anna said that it was. "Well, I just saw your girl not get on the school bus. The bus stopped, but she did not." Anna pieced together from Violet and Flynn's teacher that Flynn sometimes got to school late—between ten and twenty minutes—and back to the house, according to Violet or Jack, about five or five-thirty. Anna confronted her granddaughter gently, without accusation. After all, how many of her classmates had mothers who just disappeared at a pancake house and never called? There would be an adjustment period, Anna knew, so as long as she was safe Anna wasn't going to punish her for cutting classes. School could always be repeated.

"Where do you go?" Anna asked, when Flynn had finally gotten home that day Violet called her.

Flynn shrugged. "Nowhere. Just walking around."

"Violet said she saw you down by the train."

"Sometimes. Sometimes I like to walk along the tracks."

The next day at work, vacutainer and patient's arm in her hand, Anna had a flash that something was wrong, a panicked certainty that Flynn was in danger. It was what Anna had felt, years ago, the afternoon she'd found Poppy in the neighbor's swimming pool.

She left Dr. Naylor and the patient alone in the examination room and went out to call home. Jack answered, said, No, Flynnie isn't back yet. A quick call to school confirmed her half-day absence. Anna left, got in her car and raced down to the railroad tracks. She was just about to chastise herself for overreacting—something she'd been doing a lot of in the past year, it seemed—when she saw her. Anna couldn't believe her eyes. Flynn was standing on the tracks; right in the path of the 5:35 whose mournful whistle was already audible in the distance. All at once the train thundered into sight, and still Flynn didn't move. Anna ran as fast she could, yelling as loud as she could, but the thundering engine drowned her calls before they could reach even her own ears. The whistle sounded again, louder and drawn-out. Flynn jumped off the track just as Anna reached her, the train at about a hundred yards. Anna grabbed Flynn and slapped her hard across the face in the sheer shock of terror.

"Why were you doing that? What's the matter with you? You are all I have left." She folded Flynn into her arms and waited for her pounding heart to quiet.

Flynn rubbed her cheek. "Please do not strike me ever again."

"You scared me to death," Anna said. "I'm sorry. What were you doing standing there like that? Didn't you hear the train coming?"

"Of course I saw it. I was just watching, that's all. There's nothing wrong with watching a train closely. I know what I'm doing."

In the car, Flynn turned to her and said, "You worry too much. You worry when you shouldn't. You shouldn't ever be afraid. There is nothing whatsoever to fear."

"Maybe. But all the same, I don't mind if you watch the train, just stay off the tracks. If I catch you doing that again, I'll lock you in your room and handcuff you to your bed."

Flynn snorted exactly the way Poppy did when she was a young teenager. This time around, though, Anna found it less infuriating; the turmoil of adolescence was a mental illness all its own.

Anna walked to the back of the house, down the steps that led to the shoreline. She saw Flynn from a distance, sitting at the edge of the water and digging in the sand with a piece of driftwood. The horizon was pink and gray, the November light draining out of the sky. As she got closer, she saw Flynn's lips moving.

Flynn looked up as Anna edged toward her.

"Hey," Anna said.

"Hi there."

Anna wrapped herself tighter in her sweater, sat. "I'm cooking dinner. Got the oven way too hot, and thought I'd come out for air." She had to be careful these days not to give the impression that she was checking up; Flynn got angry when she thought Anna was tracking her.

"How has your day been?" Anna asked.

"Good. I hiked up to the blueberry patch." Flynn stretched out against the dog who was napping, filthy and covered with burrs. Were there nettles up in the blueberry patch? Anna couldn't remember.

"How are the blues?" Anna said.

Flynn looked at her suspiciously, until she realized Anna was talking about the berries. "Blues are way finished. Low-bush cranberries are still hanging on. I might go get us some tomorrow."

"Good," Anna said, and stood. "Dinner's almost ready. Are you coming in?"

"Pretty soon. Start without me."

"It'll be dark soon."

"That, I know." She looked at Anna, then away, as if there was something she wanted to say.

Anna bent down to the dog. "And what about you, Baby Jesus?" The dog thumped his tail at the sound of his name. "Are you ready for a nibble of kibble?" Anna patted him, looked out at the water, waiting.

"Your husband sends his regards."

"What?" Anna said, trying to keep the alarm out of her voice.

"He tells me I should plant pink rosebushes for you. That it's been too long since you've had the pleasure of your favorite flower."

Anna froze in place, caught between exhilaration and fear. Poppy must have talked to Flynn about Hugh at some point. Flynn's memory and power of observation were phenomenal, so it wasn't totally unexpected that Flynn would know this. The girl never forgot a thing.

"Yes, that's true," Anna said. "Don't stay out too long. I'll keep your dinner warm."

Anna carried two bowls of soup into the sunroom, where Jack still sat, though without the morbid music, thank God. "Navy bean and ham," she said, and cleared a space for him on the ottoman.

"He's not coming is he?" Jack said.

"What? Who?" He did this a lot lately, resumed conversations that had taken place hours or days before.

"Corduroy man." He slurped his soup, some of which traveled in thick rivulets down the front of his sweater.

"Oh, no," Anna said. This was Jack's new name for Marvin. Marvin commented to Anna during one phone call that Flynn needed a hobby. Perhaps sewing, he said, and the next day UPS delivered fifteen bolts of blue corduroy, enough to sew uniforms for an entire grade of British schoolchildren.

"It might be time for a medieval Icelandic saga, what do you think?" Anna said, and held up volume two of *Kristin Lavransdatter*. Television gave Jack migraines so Anna had started bringing home books on tape. For such a small town, the library had a surprisingly good collection. Both she and Jack were captivated by this trilogy. "Do you remember where we left off?" she said, rewinding a little back into volume two.

He nodded. "With Suzanne."

"In *Kristin Lavransdatter*. Kristin and Erland have decided to marry, and her father is heartsick and ashamed at the poor match."

"Yes, okay," Jack said, though Anna saw that not much would get through to him tonight. She'd have to replay this part for him when he was feeling better. She listened for a little while, but her own focus was getting fuzzy. She went outside to check on Flynn.

Jack watched her go out. His head was a fevered waterfall: hot and rushing and loud. And how long he'd waited for Hector, the shining bird, love surrounding him in plumes, the kiwi smell of his hair and his cool brown fingers scented with sandalwood. Hector and his warm umbrella of aroma. Sometimes he could draw Hector to him in this way, sing about the lady of the harbor and Hector would appear, the gold cross gleaming against his yellow shirt and he would smile his white-toothed smile, though his appearances were just wishes made into visions, because the instant he would look directly at Hector, try to speak to him, he vanished. Walking up the stairs, he would see Hector rounding the corner, and if Anna, supporting him, heard him say "hurry" it was to the bathroom she took him when all he wanted was to touch Hector, tangle his fingers in the silky curls once more, press his face into the hollow of the collarbone. Hector was always just far enough away that Jack knew with part of himself it was a kind of delusion, but real enough, too, like a waking dream. The second he felt Hector's presence and turned to look—a movement out of the corner of his eye, a shadow falling over his right shoulder—he wouldn't be there.

Jack closed his eyes, felt the viscous cold soup begin to soak through his sweater, but he didn't have the energy to take it off and find another one. He listened to the drone of the tape, to the crash of the tide against the rocks outside. It sounded a little like it might be sleeting, the icy hiss of weather that made him cold just thinking about it, his bones frozen wax, every rib a cold taper. Dying didn't scare him. What scared him was the possibility of something beyond, something continuing. Spirit without body was repugnant, desire no longer limited by the boundary of skin, expanding to fill the universe, love like sound waves going on forever, not stopped by the density of flesh. How could he ever keep track of himself when his margins were infinite? He concentrated, tried to conjure a god to pray to: if there was just someone who would listen, he could make a good case. All he wanted was for an exception to be made, that if there was an after-ife or continuance of some kind, he be permitted to opt out. What he wanted after death was death, not life. He was tired, but it wasn't that, not really. It was the idea of an eternity of not getting things quite right.

But now wasn't the time to think like this. Right now what he wanted was exactly what he had, the mohair blanket on his lap, the thick navy-blue fisherman sweater, the raw New England autumn out there and, inside, the thick fiesta of Anna's soup. If he had only known this before, humbled himself to the dignity of small pleasures, how happy he would have been. Now that he was leaving, what he loved most were the feelings things evoked, not the things themselves. The cozy house with its rough-hewn wood and wide-planked floors, the way his thick-socked feet glided over the lemony varnish. The slabs of quarter-sawn oak that made up the cabinets and counters. How could he have known these things would matter? He felt a little cheated. If he knew happiness—or what could it be? Peace? —was so near he wouldn't be sick now, wouldn't have left the solid shelter of Stuart for the transitory pleasure of other men. Flynn's company brought him such comfort every evening. The two of them sat before bed listening to The Tokens or Johnny Nash or The Fifth Dimension. Sometimes he revisited his boyhood, a happy one from this distance. Flynn would play "A Horse with No Name" and he was back in 1973, a ten-year-old on Christmas morning, inhaling the scent of frozen car seats, mad with excitement about the Risk game balanced on his lap as they drove to the house with the dozens of cousins. If he had known the pleasure of nostalgia, of remembering, his life wouldn't have been all about racing forward with a desperate need to erase everything that predated the version of himself he considered most true.

He saw little-girl Flynn out of the corner of his eye, just outside the French doors. When he turned, he saw that she was talking with someone out there, though through the dripping windows and shadowy dark he couldn't see who it was. Maybe their mail carrier who often stopped to chat. It wasn't Anna—he heard her clanging around in the kitchen. He squinted. Flynn looked somber, unhappy maybe, the way she looked when Anna asked her to do something she didn't want to do. Jack waved his arms, but neither Flynn nor the man she was with paid any attention. He stood, his head dizzy and swimming. He placed one hot hand on the cold glass, pressed his face against it, but there was no one out there now. From somewhere, geese were calling out their coordinates, and layered over that sound, the whistle of a train from a quarter mile away. He sank carefully to the floor, dizzy with sharp pains coming from odd places—it felt to him as if his entire nervous system had been rewired. The skin under his fingernails was raw and tender, his knees were so cold they were numb. He took a deep breath, concentrated on the five things he found most exquisite:

One. Flynn coming in with the fresh sea air clinging to her hair and clothes. Every evening, this was their ritual, Flynn pressing her face to his face, touching his neck with her cold hands that smelled of seaweed and brine. Flynn could entertain herself for hours with driftwood and seaweed. The mermaid girl, the little changeling.

Two. The warm bath Anna drew for him every night. Usually she had fresh pajamas on his bed when he came out, like Stuart used to. Sometimes a pot of mint tea and Pilot bread biscuits with blueberry jam.

Three. What was three again? He bent his head to his knees, tried to get lower than the curtain of dark sweeping over his vision. The bed itself was three, a huge walnut sleigh bed with sideboards wider than most bookshelves. It had a feather bed under the bottom sheet and a thick down comforter encased in a duvet of Egyptian cotton, sweetly laundered with French lavender.

All was right with the world when he climbed into this bed, and everything—number four—was as perfect as the world could get when Flynn climbed in beside him. Anna let her play outdoors for the hour while Jack was bathing, and he'd taken to flickering the bathroom light when he stepped out of the tub to let her know that he was ready for her.

In she would come then—five—and lie beside him until he fell asleep, chattering away about her previous lifetimes or conversations with the spirit world. She left a trail of sand in his sheets, a whole little beach at the bottom of the bed.

How was it he had lived all these years without having known the pleasure of children? He should have taken the idea of fatherhood more seriously, should have considered having a baby with Jane and Leila. He and Stuart could have shared custody. Jack hoped Stuart would come to the birthday party Anna was throwing for his fortieth. He'd seen Stuart a few times since moving to Maine. Last Memorial Day Stuart and his partner, David—whom Jack despised for his wheedling insincerity—came for Anna's annual barbecue. There was another time, too, though the circumstances of his visit were fuzzy now—sometime during a summer month, but he didn't know for sure what he remembered and what he had conjured. Like the yellow bird, the riotous plume that was Hector.

Jack had tried to tell Hector, tried to make Hector see the danger of physical love. A few weeks after he discovered Hector's secret married life, Jack started up with him again. As simple as that. He'd been at Stuart's recovering from pneumonia, his long idle days besieged with exhaustion, too weak to work but with an overwhelming restlessness that drove him out of the house. Hector was where Hector always was, the whole delicious feast of the boy filling the circle of his skull, Hector's skin shedding its own honey-colored light in the shadowy late afternoon.

Jack had talked his way into Hector's apartment and for four months he went there every morning after Hector's wife, Rosaria, was at work. He stayed sometimes until Stuart was due home. Hector was falling in love with him—he never said as much, but Jack could see it in the way Hector became more himself in Jack's presence. He stopped asking for money, stopped the swaggering pretenses, and became more boyish and lovable than ever in his New York Yankees sweatshirts and old jeans. There were days when Jack didn't even have to ring the doorbell; Hector sometimes waited and watched for him from the window that overlooked the streets. Sometimes they just lay in bed, side by side, silent.

Jack insisted on being safe, persisted in precautions. One day, though, Hector rolled off the condom Jack had just rolled on himself. "Hey, man, I'm clean, all right? I know you are, too. I hate these things."

"We have to. We need to," Jack said, but then Hector's mouth was traveling everywhere, his skin and hair and hands like cool cream on Jack's fevered body and it was just that once, or just a few times, and he told himself nothing bad could come out of something that was tilted so exactly to perfection; the afternoon, the exquisite body of a boy who loved him, blue pieces of sky opening like wings.

By Thanksgiving, though, Hector was nowhere. The apartment was vacated, as if overnight. He wasn't on the street corner or in the nearby bar where they sometimes stole away in the after-dinner hours for a quick beer. Jack never saw him again and, if he hadn't called Stuart one last time, December twenty-first, the day he left his little shithole efficiency after meeting up with Anna, he would have never known.

"I'm calling to wish you a Happy Holiday, and to tell you goodbye. I'm moving in with Anna until after Christmas," Jack said.

"You are?" Stuart sounded baffled.

"I am. I'll be in Maine."

Stuart was silent. "Listen, I needed to talk to you anyway."

"What's up?"

He paused. "Hector is looking for you. He came by here the other day."

Jack's heart started to pound. "What did he want?"

"He wanted you. He was angry. Really angry."

"Well, Hector's an unpredictable boy." Jack heard the table being set on Stuart's end, the unmistakable heavy clank of the good silver on the bone china. They were having a dinner party, Jack heard with a pang. How could he stand this?

"Jack, this is no longer my lookout, but I still need to ask. Is Hector sick?"

"How the hell should I know that?"

"Does he know you're sick?"

"Again, how should I know? Hector is, shall we say, socially gifted. I am not the only name on his dance card."

A year after moving in with Anna, Hector came to him in a dream. He was wearing his signature yellow shirt and wingtip shoes as shiny as a beetle. He wanted money for cab fare. Jack peeled off bill after bill but still Hector didn't take his hand away. *More*, he kept saying, *I need more, It's going to take a lot to get me there, I'm going far.*

Flynn was hovering above him suddenly as he sat on the floor. She was wearing a beret and Irish dancing shoes. "My grandma wanted me to ask you if she should run your bath now." She bent down until her face was inches from his. "Are you feeling all right?"

"Yes," he said. "I'm just resting." She put out her hand to help him up. He stood, his balance unsteady. His bath. Flynn-girl with her sea scent. His freshly made-up bed. "Sweetheart, who were you talking to out there?"

She snapped her head around. "What do you mean?"

"I saw you through the window here. I saw you talking with a man."

"You could see him?"

"Certainly."

"What did he look like?" Flynn said.

Jack saw Hector as he was in the early months. The yellow silk shirt, the smooth perfect ovals of his fingernails. "What did he look like?" Jack asked. "He was beautiful. Spanish eyes and skin. He liked yellow." Jack chuckled. "Every now and then he used to talk about getting a dog. Hector loved dogs. I don't think he ever got one, though." He turned his head and saw Flynn's dog beside him. "Oh, he would have loved Baby Jesus." The dog wagged his approval, cleared the coffee table with his tail.

Flynn looked down at Jack, who didn't seem to be looking back at her. The newspaper boy had been out there, a boy from her class who liked her because she was the only one who didn't make fun of him. But the boy had red hair and thick glasses, so that wasn't who Jack saw. Flynn hadn't seen anyone but Erroll, her classmate. But when Jack started talking about the man in the yellow shirt, there he was, standing right beside Jack as vivid to her as Jack himself was. Outside, she'd felt something behind Erroll. This must be whom Jack saw. Someone had been talking to her about birds. A Spanish man in a yellow shirt. Hector. The man's name was Hector; he was the spirit she sensed, yes. He needed her to understand something about the Canada geese, the real story, and not the one she was taught in school last week. *Listen: This is the truth about heaven and earth.*

"Who was the man?" Jack said now, looking straight at her.

"He was Spanish. He wanted to tell me things. He wanted me to go with him to play soccer. He says you'll play, too."

"No," Jack said, inexplicably relieved. "I have never played soccer. I don't know how. Did you bring in the newspaper?"

"But you will," Flynn said. "You will play soccer one day. He said you would."

"Now stop this nonsense, Flynn. Stop inventing stories that upset everybody."

She frowned, anger flashing across her face. "You asked. I was telling you only because you asked."

Later, Flynn moved close to Jack as they lay in bed. Things were about to change. Down by the train today, she saw three geese. She understood what it meant. Her teacher explained how far the geese had to travel and how tired they got. Three together meant that one was sick or dying, and was being led to the ground by the other two who would stay with the sick goose until it died or got better. The goose in the middle of the formation would die. Flynn knew she probably didn't have magical powers, but sometimes, she slipped out of herself. Sometimes she became whatever she looked at long and intently. The bird in the middle was falling more than flying, the wind rushing around the pinfeathers was as loud as thunder when the sick bird tried to beat its wings against the air. The world through its eyes was milky and shadowed, and Flynn smelled the rain in the cold wind, felt the bird's breathing in her own chest and how it couldn't get deep enough into her lungs. The other two geese honked, the hinges that worked their jaws clicking as they opened and closed their beaks. There was a smell of rotten meat coming from the sick bird; something spoiled in the flattened oily feathers. The birds were looking for a landing place, a place where two would fly away after one died. Until now, she didn't understand why she was being shown this.

Listen: This is the truth about heaven and earth. Sometimes things turn upside-down. The birds see you. To them, you are a faraway star. You are in their heaven, walking in their heaven, just as they fly in yours. And, listen,

listen: sometimes we are like the birds, too. We come from there to here, to help fly you home.

"Jack," Flynn said, though she saw he was almost asleep.

"Yes, love," he said.

"Listen, this is the truth about heaven and earth: When the geese die, they fly down. When we die, we fly up. We live in their heaven, and they live in ours."

"Hmm," he said.

There was more she was supposed to tell him, but he was snoring now. She needed to let him know that his time was near, and that the man in the yellow shirt, Hector, was here to help him. He would wait with Jack, just the way the birds waited. Hector was sitting on the bed, touching Jack's hair. Flynn kissed Jack goodnight, and stood to go. She turned around at the door. Hector was right behind her. She looked at Hector, then back at Jack, confused. Maybe this was just his way of thanking her, or of telling her to leave him alone with Jack. But when she walked out into the hallway, Hector followed. When she put her hand on the banister to go downstairs, Hector put his hand on her shoulder, wrapped her in a soft and suffocating embrace, and she began to weep with fear, with what she thought she now understood. Hector hadn't come for Jack. He had come for her.

ELEVEN

Venus in Pieces

Stuart was halfway to Anna's before he realized he hadn't gotten Jack anything for his birthday. Even after all this time, after all that had happened, he couldn't just let it slip by—he'd never let a birthday go by unacknowledged. This year was the big one, his fortieth, and Anna was planning a party.

Of course, more generous ex-lovers would say that Stuart's presence was enough, that risking a stable relationship with a partner of nearly a year was more gift than Jack deserved. Jack, of course, wouldn't see it that way. The one birthday Jack would never forget was his own. Stuart had resigned himself to it long ago—shopping for his own birthday and Christmas gifts, dragging Jack along as punishment while he went into every kitchen store, every clothing boutique, intentionally not buying what he'd picked out weeks before until he saw the suburban-husband glaze in Jack's eyes.

David had thrown a fit when Stuart mentioned his plans. Anna had called one Saturday afternoon, asked if he would come to Jack's party which might be a full-blown celebration or just an intimate gathering, she hadn't decided. But either way. Sure, we'll be there, Stuart said. David was so easy-going, so good-natured and trustworthy that Stuart took for granted that he would come along or not care that Stuart wanted to go. But one night, not long ago, Stuart had gone too far. David listened, thin-lipped and pale, as Stuart detailed the anguish of loving Jack, the way it felt as if every cell in his body had been infused with the man. It felt, he said, as though his very DNA had spiraled with Jack's; to fully disentangle himself would take years of careful unraveling. David shook his head and looked away.

Stuart and David had a great place in Worcester, a rambling—once genteel, and now shabby-genteel—three-bedroom Victorian with rococo accents and innumerable gothic archways. David was director of libraries for B.U. and there were dinner parties nearly every weekend for one group of David's colleagues or another. Stuart, having finally finished his Ph.D., was teaching as an adjunct while he searched for a tenure-track position.

He and David had been painting the living room when Anna called, were trying to find just the right tone of yellow. They had fourteen samples from the paint store, and had narrowed it down to nine. "I think Buttercream," Stuart said, "Buttercream with the trim in Winter Sunlight."

"You're kidding? Winter sunlight is not a submissive shade. I think Buttercream with plain old eggshell would be friendlier." They stepped back and stared, then laughed. "We're such fags," Stuart said, and rolled the lightly coated sponge down the front of David's sweatshirt. He answered the phone, talked to Anna for five minutes, and then went back into the living room.

"Who was it?" David said.

"Anna. We're invited up to Maine next weekend. Jack's fortieth." He rearranged the plastic drop cloth so it covered the skirt of the sofa.

"I don't think so," David said.

Stuart shrugged. "Whatever. I'll be back Sunday night." He walked over to the fireplace, not sure that the mantel should be anything but white. Maybe off-white.

"I mean, Stuart, I don't think it's a good idea for you, either."

He turned. "Why?"

"I think it's perpetuating your relationship with Jack. In the long run, your way is more painful." Stuart just looked at him. "The relationship is over. You've already grieved for the man once, do you need to do it all over again?"

"What's it to you? It has nothing to do with you. With us." He gave David a quick, light kiss before turning back to the problem of the yellows. One of the things he loved most about David was that he could speak so freely; insults and sarcasm had always been the price of being candid with Jack.

"I really don't want you to go. I'm asking you not to go."

"You're being silly. Insecure and silly."

But David hadn't backed down. "If you leave, I might or might not be here when you come home."

Stuart had looked at him evenly. "Is that some sort of threat?"

"No. It's just that I have to think about what it means to have a partner who doesn't respect me when I feel strongly about something."

"Okay," Stuart said. "I understand." David didn't mean it. Or, if he did, they would deal with it when he got back. All those years with Jack had squashed his panic response. Stuart no longer felt unhinged and desperate every time his lover slammed out in anger or wasn't precisely where he said he would be. Still, David hadn't ever come down so strongly before. Was he serious?

Stuart would talk to him later from Anna's, he decided, speeding through the tunnel in the forest green Jeep Cherokee he and David had bought just last week. The seats were leather and the car even smelled rich. He loaded Thelonius Monk and Coltrane on the CD player, hit shuffle, and picked up his phone. No. Not now. Why stir it all up now?

He stopped in Portland to browse the shops. What the hell could Jack need or want? Clothes? Books? DVDs were always a safe bet. At a Block-buster, he found a digitally remastered boxed set of Robert Mitchum's lesser-known movies, as well as every one of Ben Affleck's movies—Jack's other schoolboy crush. For Flynn, whom Anna had said was into Irish dancing, he found *Riverdance* in addition to the god-awful sequel.

It had been snowing lightly when he left Worcester, but it was seriously winter up here. The pines and spruce were bent under the weight of ice and snow.

He stopped at an inn just an hour away from Anna's for a cup of tea, and to get out of the weather for a bit. In the back dining room, the one with windows on all sides, a huge stone fireplace was fat with birch logs. He'd been here twice before—once with David, on their way to a New Year's Eve party at Anna's, the second time alone, when he left on a whim to visit Jack but got control of himself in the end.

Stuart asked for a corner table, far from the madding crowd of tourists. It was always a good idea to sit quietly, to gather himself in, before seeing Jack. Occasionally, he felt nostalgic for the life they'd had, but not often; mostly he felt lucky to have what he had now, a man who was stable and loyal and who loved him unreservedly.

The dining room was full of families and noisy children. He ordered a brandy. Outside, the mountains were already fully sheathed in white. Stuart wondered about the rooms here, if they were as nice as the B&Bs where he and Jack used to stay. David had not a trace of sentimentality. The times when Stuart suggested driving up north to look at the leaves, he at first thought Stuart meant rare archived manuscripts—as in the leaves of the frontispieces of old books. "And what's wrong with looking at the leaves in Massachusetts?" David said, when Stuart clarified what he meant. Stuart just rolled his eyes. In his darker moments he wondered if they were too different to make it for the long haul. But there was something to be said for pragmatic love as sturdy as a handrail.

Maybe there would be significant snow accumulation tonight. Anna would have a pot of her amazing soup going, probably a fire, too. It was a little like going home, the clean warmth and gentle lighting, the mouth-watering food smells. He was grateful for Anna, felt blessed to be invited to her parties and for all her invitations—even if he didn't accept most of them. If not for the problem of Jack living there, he and David might visit more often. Both of his parents were gone, dead within fourteen months of each other to the day. His father had died painfully, of pancreatic cancer. One by one the adult children had filed in to their father's hospital room to say goodbye. Stuart's brothers and sister had eight kids between them. Stuart studied his father in the bed, propped up by the inadequate pillows, and it seemed improbable that this was the man who knew his boyhood, the arms that held him as a child. It seemed an odd thing to be thinking, that this man would be taking the knowledge of his childhood away for-ever. That was the worst thing, Stuart supposed, the way in which his family history just disappeared when his parents died. He supposed it was the same for his siblings, though not exactly. They had their children, their own families, for holidays. Both of his brothers lived in Massachusetts, his sister in New Hampshire. Stuart had never been invited to their homes. He hadn't realized how estranged he was from them—he didn't *feel* es-tranged—until his parents were gone and he and David ended up either celebrating holidays alone or tried to forget Christmas altogether. It wasn't that his siblings shunned him, it was just that he didn't occur to them. He wasn't resentful for not being included, but he was hurt by their forgetfulness—intentional exclusion, he sometimes suspected—in leaving him out of family gatherings.

He sipped his brandy, turned his body away from the two families who had come into the dining room. Two terrible women in their thirties, fat suburban mothers wearing Land's End khakis and some poly-cotton turtlenecks they probably picked up at Kmart. He wanted to lean over and tell them if they wanted to sneak a cheap turtleneck into their wardrobes, the secret was to buy black, and black only. Nothing advertised price better than the dye lot of those rainbow colors. Fat women with soft asses and softer brains, sprayed hair and inferior children. Repulsive, these stupid cow families from the boroughs and provinces, with their conservative politics, mini-vans and self-righteous certainties.

What was wrong with him today? He rarely felt so hateful. Maybe it was the run-in with David, who seemed increasingly manipulative. David was subtle in how he applied pressure, Stuart had to give him that; often, not until a foul mood overcame him did he realize David was its source. Though it didn't quite feel like that now.

He turned back to the window. Outside there were two men with Russian-looking hats carving a block of ice with chisels and what looked to Stuart liked sanders. They had lights set up all around their work area as though they planned to be there a while. Stuart watched absently as the men worked. He started to relax a bit with the heat coming from the fire and the warm flush of brandy moving through him.

Someone at one of the big tables saw what was happening outside and before he knew it Stuart had four children crammed between his table and the window, craning their necks to see. Two of them actually stood in his sightline. A couple of bulldozers, knocking into his table and nearly upsetting his teapot. He looked over at the mountainous mother who smiled at him, self-confidence creasing her doughy face, as though it was only natural that they use the entire room.

"Excuse you," Stuart said, and with his foot pushed the chair opposite him when one of the boys knocked it with his thick body. How could a mother let her son get this way? Thighs as thick as spruce trunks, face pale from bad food and too much television. Stuart pushed the chair back, eased it into the space the boy was occupying, but the kid was oblivious. He shoved hard a second time so the chair caught the boy in the middle and knocked him off balance. The kid stumbled and toppled. There.

Instead of getting the hint, though, to Stuart's horror, the boy started to cry. Conversation stopped at the tables, and one of the women, presumably his mother, called over, "What's the matter, Gerald?" The kid looked at Stuart, who returned his look with a hostile arch of his eyebrow. There. The world isn't moving out of the way for you, sonny. The boy's mother came over. "What happened?"

"He shoved that chair into me!" the kid said between sobs.

The mother looked at Stuart, her little mouth with its shimmery pink lipstick—pink lipstick against a red turtleneck!—shaped exactly like those old-fashioned bottle-openers. Apparently, the woman was waiting for him to deny it. Stuart downed the last of his Hennessey. "You need to teach your son some manners," he said quietly.

"Pardon? What did he do to you?" She looked at Stuart with a mixture of surprise and defensiveness, mostly surprise, which infuriated him.

"Ask him," Stuart said. "But kindly ask him at your own table and leave me to mine."

The woman's face darkened, and Stuart could see her retreating, ready to let it go. "He's eight years old. It wouldn't kill you to have a little tolerance." She wrapped a protective arm around the boy.

"Oh? Actually, you may want to take your own advice," he said. "About the tolerance part, I mean."

The whole noisy table of them departed, and Stuart was left in peace, though ashamed. He truly hadn't meant to get so angry. All-consuming fury wasn't his style.

He left money on the table and went out. The air smelled of bayberry and pine from the wreaths hanging on the porch, the perimeter of which was lit up with white Christmas lights. He sat in the car and just stared awhile at the white Georgian columns and felt the ache Christmas always brought up in him. He found his phone, dialed home, but didn't let the call go through. Too near Anna's now, too close to the whirlwind of Jack.

Stuart had brought his coat, the one with the mementos of Jack, and put it on when he got to Anna's. He didn't especially want to bring it, but he suspected that David had been going through his things and he didn't want this under his eyes. It hadn't fit in his suitcase and he didn't want to leave it in the car—some of the pressed flowers might be sensitive to cold. He juggled his armful of luggage and bags, knuckled the doorbell. Maybe he wanted to show it to Jack, maybe that's why he'd brought it along.

Through the glass blocks alongside the door, he saw Anna backlit by the yellow light of the hallway, blurring toward him. "Hi, dear," she said, opening the door. "I was just about to call the state troopers." She took his packages and hugged him. "We just finished dinner. We waited as long as we could."

"That's okay. I'm good." He followed her into the living room. "Where's our boy?"

"He's in the bathroom. Flynn is doing the dishes." Anna held up a decanter of Scotch, and he nodded. "Flynnie?" she called in the direction of the kitchen.

"Yesie?" she yelled back.

"Uncle Stuart is here."

"Lord a mercy!" she called, "All the blackbirds is flyin' outta my pies."

Anna set her mouth, shook her head at the look on Stuart's face. "It's a new thing, speaking in what she thinks of as rural Southern dialect. We're trying to ignore it." She glanced down at his coat. "Do you want me to hang that for you?"

"Oh, I can do it." He went out to the hallway closet.

"Uncle Stuart?" Jack called from the bathroom, and laughed. "Did I hear the name Uncle Stuart?"

"The same. Get your rumpus out here." He walked back in to join Anna.

"He might be just a little while." Anna poured herself another Scotch, poked at the fire and added another log. "He's having a little trouble. How to put this delicately? The breakfast cuisine around here is stewed prunes. It's all the medications he's taking. His system is going into revolt. Forty-eight pills a day, all carefully timed." She sat back in the chair, propped her feet up on the table in front of her. Stuart saw the fatigue in her drooping shoulders, the slackness of her jaw line. She was thinner than ever, she who hadn't anything extra on her to begin with. "I meant to tell you on the phone, Jack has developed a dowager's hump. It's a fairly common side effect of the medication, along with a thickening of his neck. But the drugs are working. He has more lucid days than not, and his viral load is down by about forty per cent, which is a gift."

"That's good," Stuart said.

Anna nodded. "That's very good."

Flynn came into the living room, walked over to Stuart smiling. She was huge! Inches taller than when he saw her last, her little-girl figure starting to soften and curve somewhat, though she hadn't added the pubescent fat around the middle. Everything on her was going to form; she wouldn't have to wait three years for her figure to emerge, clarified, through the baby padding. "My God, you're gorgeous." She returned his kiss, embraced him warmly. "Shucks, Rhett, you make a lady blush."

He laughed. "Have you been reading *Gone with the Wind*?"

She shook her head. "No, suh, I don't know nothin' about it. I'se in the kitchen, keepin' my nose in business entirely my own."

Anna spoke sharply. "Flynn! Stop that talk. Do you realize that you're being offensive? That someone might think you're making fun of a culture?"

"Yes'm," Flynn said. "But, Miz Anna, there ain't be no Southern crackers roun' heah." She nuzzled closer to Stuart. "Suh, do you know the plantation heah is crawlin' with the spirits of the long-dead?"

Stuart felt Anna's irritation toward Flynn. "Tell me about school. How do you like your new school?"

Her face fell. "It's okay. I don't do well with kids my own age, which is how it's always been. I'm a freak."

"Are you playing any sports?"

"No. I'm a Celtic dancer now."

"Are you? Well, it just so happens that I have something that you might like." He pulled the video of *Riverdance* out of the shopping bag.

"Oh! I haven't seen this one! Thank you." She was about to put it in the machine when Anna stopped her.

"Not now, Flynn. Or watch it upstairs."

"Okay. I'll wait for Jack."

"Jack is going to visit with Stuart. Watch it alone, or with Jack later."

"But I was going to keep it on low. Stuart won't mind. It's background music." She moved toward the television.

"Flynn—"

"Just five minutes. Let me just watch until Jack comes out, then I'll turn it off. It's eight o'clock. This is when Jack and I always do something together."

"No, Flynn," Anna said, as patiently as she could. Flynn's defiance was something new. Her moods changed from one minute to the next. It was only to be expected at her age.

Flynn flounced off in a huff. Anna heard her start up the stairs, then come back down. "Jack? Please hurry up in there. You're upsetting everybody's schedule."

Anna stood. "Excuse me," she said to Stuart. She went into the hallway and took Flynn by the elbow, pointed her toward the stairs. She could abide Flynn's mocking her, could withstand her defiance and rebellion, but she would not stand for this. "The healthy do not dictate the schedule of someone's illness. What's the matter with you, Flynn?" Anna felt both Jack and Stuart listening to her. "What's gotten into you?"

Flynn looked at her grandmother's bony bare feet. She didn't know what to answer. Except that she wanted to be anyone but herself, and couldn't bear the interruption of routine, even for Stuart, Jack's special friend. It panicked her to the point of tears not to be able to watch TV or a movie with Jack like they did every night after their musical tour of the '70s. The world was ending.

"Go feed Hoover McPaws and change his litter. And has Baby Jesus been walked for the night?"

Flynn nodded, her eyes teary. "I want my mother," she said.

This, too, was something new. Anytime Anna corrected her, Flynn brought up Poppy. "Why don't you go take a bath? Get into bed, and then Jack and I will be up to kiss you goodnight."

Instead of moving, Flynn stared off into space, entranced.

"Flynn," Anna said.

She fell against Anna, sobbing. "Something is wrong with me. Something is really, really wrong. Why can't I be normal?"

Anna took her upstairs and calmed her down. She ran a hot bath, turned down the sheets on Flynn's bed, then gave her the option to either come back downstairs when she felt calmer, or go to sleep. "Okay. Okay, Flynn?"

Flynn nodded, and Anna went out.

"Sorry," Anna called as she came back down the stairs. She went into the kitchen to fix some food for Stuart. She ladled out the soup, cut slices of bread and cheese, decanted a new bottle of burgundy. She needed help with Flynn, another healthy adult to help deal with Flynn's prodigious energy. Maybe Marvin was right—maybe Flynn needed a hobby. The dance classes didn't occupy that much of her time, and her attendance was intermittent—since Anna was the only driver and the classes started at seven, it meant racing home from work, whisking Flynn to class, and waiting the interminable hour and half for the class to end. She salted the soup, polished the goblet on the tray. Maybe she would teach Flynn to knit, though that wasn't much better than Marvin's insisting that Flynn learn to sew. She needed something, some activity that could absorb her. Flynn didn't have enough to do with her evenings. Her homework was finished perfectly—Anna checked—in under an hour each night.

She carried the tray back into the living room where Jack was sitting on the sofa with his arm loosely around Stuart.

"Well, well. I was getting ready to send in a rescue team," she said, and set the tray in front of Stuart. "Did you...did your bowels move?"

Jack laughed. "Sweetheart, not only did my bowels move, they moved and left no forwarding address."

Stuart laughed, snorted wine up his nose. "That's my boy," he said, Jack's quick sharpness piercing right to the heart of him. Hopeless. There was no way not to bleed right into Jack in his presence. It would always be so. Jack's appearance was shocking, his neck thicker by far than his thighs, and his back had that old lady's hump, but the rest of him was thin. His color was pale, but not ashen. Not healthy, but not knocking on death's door, either. He wore a cabled navy sweater and a loosely knitted cap of fine, light wool through which Stuart saw his thinning hair. Nothing, though—illness, weight loss, humps and bruises—could make Jack anything less than completely beautiful. There was something new in his expression, actually, that Stuart thought made Jack even more handsome, a depth, a glitter in his eyes, as though he was storing his dreams there, instead of in his faulty brain.

"So, tell me what's new in your world, my boy," Jack said, patting Stuart's knee. His eyes took in the length of Stuart's body. "How's your love life?"

Stuart pretended shock. "Not in front of Anna's delicate sensibilities."

"Oh, please. The iron butterfly? The roller coaster Madonna? The goddess with whom I had a three-hour discussion of the joys of gay sex? The woman knows all our secrets, darling."

"Not the secrets between the two of you," Anna said.

"Naturally," Jack said. "Anna, would you mind sitting on the other side of me?" he patted the sofa. "It makes me anxious to be so far away from you. And where did my girl go?"

Anna walked over to the couch, sat. "I sent her upstairs. She was in one of her moods."

Jack pulled Anna close to him. "If there's one thing I can tell the two of you about dying...no, two things I can tell you: the first is that it's not as bad as advertised. It's like the nostalgia you feel for a house you're about to move out of." He sipped the burgundy, reached for the bottle, which Anna nudged out of the way with her foot. "Careful. You shouldn't, you know," she said softly.

"Yes," he said. "I know it. But I'm about to turn forty, and we're celebrating Stuart home." Anna shrugged, watched as he poured a quarter glass and held it up to her for approval. "It's your liver," she said, and turned to watch the fire. She, too, was a little drunk, but pleasantly so, warm and content.

"What's the second thing?" Stuart said.

"What, baby?" Jack said.

"What's the second thing you wanted to tell us?"

Jack stared straight ahead, as though trying to remember something from long ago. "Oh! The second thing is that it's important to have people as physically close to you as possible. The flesh is precious."

"That," Stuart said, rubbing his hand along Jack's shoulder and meeting Anna's hand there by accident, "has been a long-held belief."

"I should go and check on Flynn. Let the two of you visit." Stuart smiled up at Anna, but Jack pulled her back down. "No, Flynnie's fine. Stay for a while. Please."

"Jack, you see my ugly mug every day. I'm sure you and Stuart would like private time."

"Anna, please, I cherish you."

"Jack." She laughed. "No more of that wine. You're starting to act like a breeder in a bar near closing time."

Stuart felt the disappointment sink all through him. He never expected Jack to meet him with heart-fluttering joy and open arms, but it was always a surprise to him how casually Jack regarded him, as if he were merely another houseguest.

Even now, there was so much that he wanted to let float up on calm waters, just the two of them. Anna and Jack talked about Flynn for over an hour, discussed whether or not she needed to be evaluated or treated by a therapist. They moved on to real estate prices in the area, and the question of whom to invite to Anna's annual Christmas party. "I'm pretty sure I offended half the population last year by not doing it as an open house," Anna said.

"There are five hundred people in this town. Nobody expects that," Jack said. "Besides, do you really want every greasy Billy and Bob showing up with Wonder Bread casseroles? Why not be elitist? Who cares about the other side of the tracks?"

"I do. Well, kind of," Anna said.

"I don't. Those Yankees? No way. I would have no compunction whatsoever leaving the 'Fags are going to hell' side of town off the list."

Stuart stared at the fire, wondering if it was a mistake to be here. Jack had come back; he was very near to being his old self, the man who lived squarely inside his own heart where there was no room for anyone else. He wished for a little of the heat, the edge, he'd had earlier in the day.

"Well, you're probably right," Anna said. "I am a snob. Why pretend otherwise? Still, it might be nice to feel a part of this town. Flynn and I are going to live here a while."

"As opposed to the rest of us, who are just passing through or dying," Jack said, and reached for the wine decanter on the table in front of him.

"Jack, you're making me tired. You and Flynn both are like two fat asses on an overstuffed suitcase."

Jack laughed. "What the hell does that mean, Anna?"

She was caught between exasperation and amusement. "I don't know. Just that I'm short on patience today. I am stuffed to the brim and don't want any more pressure. I'm just not in the mood for your word salads. Your stupid verbal puns or whatever."

Jack put his arms around her, kissed her neck. "I'm sorry, darling. I'm sorry. I'm thoughtless sometimes. You know I love you."

Stuart felt a darkness well up inside him. Jack had rarely said words like that to him, almost never showed that kind of tenderness when his feelings were hurt. There was no reason to be envious of Anna. He knew that. It was just that Anna was the one person right now Jack couldn't afford to offend, to lose. Stuart would not come here again. This was the goodbye visit, the door he would close and lock behind him. He would go home to David and their uncomplicated life, worry about things that didn't really matter, and be happy for the small things, the daily evenness that made life easy, predictable, and safe.

Later, Stuart lay in bed in the guestroom, listening to Jack talking to Flynn in the room next door. He stared at the rind of frost on the old-fashioned window, shuttered and four-paned, heard the crash of waves at the shoreline, the hiss as they broke against rocks. He hadn't felt this miserable since he actually lived with Jack, when he would lie in bed and wait for Jack to join him. Stuart heard Flynn's girlish giggles. She was such an engaging child. Though not really a child any longer. Not yet a young woman, either. The bewitching netherworld where boys and girls were the same, but on the cusp where everything was about to change.

He picked up the phone on the bedside table but then thought better of it. David would probably be awake, worrying about why Stuart hadn't called, feeling anxious and lonely, and second-guessing his threats of desertion. It didn't matter. It didn't matter to him, not really, if David threw his things out on the street. What mattered to him, still, was Jack. It was that simple. Why did he think it would be otherwise? Stuart felt this to a lesser degree the other time he'd seen Jack here, but it was mild enough to ignore or identify as something else. Stuart didn't especially believe in God, but sometimes, like now, he thought he might believe in this way: God wasn't a remote omniscient being, but the power of the least pursued. The tug of unrequited love. Nothing in the world, not even outright cruelty or rejection, was more powerful than confirming someone's notion that he was almost, but not quite, good enough.

A little while later Stuart heard Jack outside his room. The door opened softly, with a slow creak and Jack stood framed in the light from the hall, a dark ghost with a medicinal smell and a wool-encased skull. "Baby?" he said, as though he'd been looking for Stuart for a long time, in every darkened corner and night-black room.

"I'm here," Stuart said. "Come in." He turned down the bed sheets, eased Jack into his arms and held him, surprised by the intact strength of Jack's body, the muscle tone that didn't seem to be diminished at all by his illness. Stuart held Jack tighter, entwined his legs around Jack's and wished time would stop right here so the moment was big enough to live in for a while. He didn't want to feel the next minute, and the one after that, pressing in with its sadness and tedium and longing. He kissed Jack, swept his fingertips lightly over Jack's tissue-thin eyelids, as delicate and soft as moth wings.

"What if I asked you to stay? What would you say?"

"Stay for how long?" Stuart asked.

"Forever," Jack said. "Just stay here with me and Anna and her family. Our family. You can't imagine how happy I am here. Who would have thought. Everything is simple here. Slowed and clarified. I'm hardly ever lonely."

"Don't be stupid, Jack. You know I can't stay here. Besides, you don't want me here. You didn't want me when you had me."

Jack fell silent then said quietly, "You have no idea, Stuart. No idea what you have meant to me. It's always been you. You brought me to the best part of myself. I was a fool not to believe that sooner." It was too late now, he knew, too late for Stuart to believe him. Jack pulled Stuart close to him again, inhaled his milky-white clean smell, the garden of his hair, and his rain-scented skin. He wanted just once more, just one more time with Stuart.

"Anyway, it's no good talking of these things now," Stuart said. "It's all philosophical at this point. I'm with someone."

"Well," Jack said. "Not really."

"What do you mean by that?"

"You heard me. Can you really be with him if you're here?"

"I don't want to talk about this, Jack." He closed his eyes. The sheets under him were so nice, the softest cotton imaginable. Anna, despite his initial impression of her as an idiosyncratic decorator, was in fact as much of a voluptuary when it came to luxury and fine things as Jack was. Her townhouse in Boston had been an anomaly; surrounded by her own things here in Maine, her taste was expensive and impeccable. He listened to Jack breathing beside him and for a moment was cast back to Boston, back to their apartment in Back Bay where he waited in bed for Jack, waited for Jack's body to slide against his. The scent of fried plantains, the gravelly complaint of some Robert Mitchum movie.

Jack watched as Stuart drifted off. Stuart looked so sweet when he slept, noiselessly and deeply as a child, a stone that had been dropped to the bottom of a well and had to be retrieved every morning. Like a child, nothing woke him up. Jack kissed Stuart's forehead, kissed the full lips and felt weepy. Loving him was a little like spotting an Empire bureau at a garage sale: there was the thrill of the find, the solidity and rarity of it amidst the junk, the timing of being there to get it, then the discovery that it wouldn't fit through the door when it was delivered. Jack's love for Stuart had been forever doomed to the hall, kept outside the place he lived. He'd been so stingy and small with his life, so narrow in what he allowed in.

Out of pure habit, Stuart wrapped his body around Jack's when he felt the pressure of Jack's hand over his skin. He opened his eyes when he felt Jack's lips. "Am I dreaming?" Stuart said.

"No," Jack said.

Stuart reached out to him, but then pulled away.

"Let me," Jack said, and kissed him. He followed the familiar pathway, his mouth finding Stuart's rhythm, the pressure and speed he liked best.

"We shouldn't do this," Stuart said, but already he was responding instinctively, making the automatic adjustments and movements of a body that has done something a thousand times.

Sometime later Stuart awoke to the sound of the alarm on Jack's wristwatch and heard him shuffling off to the bathroom. He moved to Jack's side, let his body sink into the warm impression there.

Stuart reached for the phone. This time, he let the call go through. David, naturally, had been asleep, but awoke fully at Stuart's voice. "I've been so worried about you," David said. "Are you at Anna's?"

"Yes." He sat up. He felt David waiting on the other end. "I just wanted to check in, that's all."

David paused. "I'm not angry, if that's what you think. Come home. I shouldn't have threatened. Just come home, okay?"

"Okay," Stuart said.

"I love you," David said.

Stuart said, "I know." It was all he could manage.

"Is everything all right, then?"

"What do you mean?"

"What do you think I mean? Is everything all right with us?"

"I don't know," Stuart said. "I hope so. I do." He promised to call David the next day, then hung up. He listened to Jack running water in the bathroom, the clink of the water glass against the tap. How could he possibly do this? He wouldn't walk on eggshells the rest of his life, wouldn't censor every word before it left his mouth in fear of Jack's reaction. He'd seen those pamphlets and fact sheets about safe sex, about how the healthy partner of an AIDS patient could stay that way, but all of it seemed absurdly simplistic now. Sex was only one factor in this equation. Sometimes when he imagined being with Jack again he had to stop himself from believing that Jack's having a terminal illness would change him in any way, that it would make him gentler and grateful for the presence of Stuart in his life. Jack was who he always was, and this was what was hard to get his mind around when he fantasized about being with Jack again. Being with Jack, with anyone who had AIDS, meant you lived in two columns: every sneer, insult, and selfishness, one side; tenderness, thoughtfulness, and loving acts, the other. Even the most minor of squabbles would have him tallying. The risks to his health weighed against Jack's behavior. Feeling inadequately loved or insecure, balanced against the months or years of Jack's failing health and eventual death. This is what he found most troubling. It was sentimental nonsense to think that a disease like AIDS ennobled someone. It caused suffering for all those connected to it. Jack would be who he always was, only sicker. And if was true what the doctors said about personality traits sometimes becoming more pronounced as the disease progressed, God help them both. Jack would, no doubt, out-Jack himself. Stuart smiled, thought of giant grocery bags, drawers stuffed with beautiful and useless things, a hundred bottles of shampoo, ninety-dollar magnums of champagne, and feverish lust that spilled over everywhere.

Flynn heard Jack go into the bathroom. She'd been lying awake for hours, disturbed equally by the aches and cramps in her head and belly, the absence of her nightly ritual with Jack, and the shadowy figures walking past her door and milling around the foot of her bed. It was better when she could dig, could see worlds underground and not have to worry about the topside. Now, every time she turned her head she saw faces, forms of people she didn't know, mostly men, and none of them very old; she'd always believed ghosts were supposed to be old, unhappy, mean. But if these were ghosts, they were happy ones. An hour or so ago, when she finally closed her eyes and thought she might sleep, she was awakened by Baby Jesus growling from his bed on the floor and the sound of clinking of glasses, laughter. In the hallway, she counted ten men having some kind of party. There was music playing, something with a disco beat, a buffet table with food, and two men kissing each other. She knew all of this wasn't real, or wasn't real enough that she could talk to anyone about it. Even to her grandma, who pretended not to believe or know these things. There was a man who followed Anna around, for instance, who stood right up against her when she was making dinner and touched her hair, or sat beside her on the sofa when she read the paper. Flynn saw him, but she knew he didn't know she could see him, until she made the mistake of staring at him as he was whispering something in Anna's ear that she of course couldn't hear. Flynn couldn't either, because it wasn't intended for her ears, but the minute he caught Flynn's eye, it was as if some barrier had broken. *Tell Anna not to worry,* he said. *Everything is fine.* Flynn looked away; down at the math homework she was supposed to be doing. She never relayed the message, except once, when Anna came in and asked who she was talking to. "An old man," Flynn said, "who loves you a lot, now, still, and forever." Those were the words in her head. But Flynn mistook the look on her grandma's face and she kept talking. Told Anna that the old man said he was waiting for them all, described how beautiful it was where he lived and that nothing was lonely or alone. Even the raindrops came down in pairs. But Anna had been so upset by it all that Flynn never spoke of it again, and the old man disappeared from her view.

Flynn felt really sick now, a dragging tightness in her belly, sweaty and achy all over. She called to Jack quietly, not wanting to walk through the wall of spirits in the hallway. "Jack?" she said louder. And then louder again.

Finally he heard. He stood in the doorway of her bedroom, framed by faces who looked in at her curiously, as if noticing her for the first time, and the Spanish man in the yellow shirt was here now, too, grinning at her in a mean way and holding a knife with blood on it. Flynn wished Jack hadn't told her about him. If Jack hadn't described him so well, he wouldn't now be so vivid. "What are you doing up, baby girl?"

"I don't feel well."

"Oh?" he sat down on the edge of her bed, flicked on the light. "What's the matter?"

"My stomach."

"I'll lie with you a little while, how's that?" He turned back the covers. There was blood on the sheets. "Oh," he said. "Are you having your period?"

She felt herself waver between terror and calm familiarity. She knew what this was, had been waiting for it in fact, but still she felt her head go light with shock. "I don't know. I never have before."

"Oh. Did your mother tell you...do you know what to do?"

Flynn started to cry. She wasn't ready for this, wasn't ready for this nipping pain along the inside of her thighs, the dragging heaviness of her breasts. She was used to her body being small and quick and light.

Jack drew her close, kissed her sweaty brow. "Don't cry, darling. This is a good thing. Anyway, your mother and grandmother would tell you about how wonderful this moment is because you're officially a woman. I'm telling you, what's wonderful and what you want to remember for later, is that for five days every month, you can rant and rave and bitch, eat all the chocolate you want and blame it on that little bit of blood flowing out of you."

"How long will this last?"

"Four, five days."

"No, I mean, how many years will I have periods?"

"How many do you think?"

"Twelve?"

"A bit longer than that." He reached his hand out, helped her up, and the two of them walked into the bathroom. In the back of the linen closet, he found a box of tampons, size super, which surprised him, since Anna was such a small woman. Christ. What was wrong with American culture? It wasn't enough that fast food restaurants kept increasing the size of their portions. Now you could even get your tampons supersized. "I don't suppose you know how to use these?" Jack said.

Flynn shook her head, her eyes wide, her face white.

He went through all the cabinets again; didn't most women use pads in addition to tampons? "These are all I can find. Did your grandmother ever use Kotex?"

Flynn frowned, looked down at the toilet. "She uses Ajax."

Jack sighed. "I'm going to go wake Anna. She'll know what to do."

"No, don't," Flynn said. She wrapped her arms around Jack's waist. "Don't wake my grandmother."

"Flynn, darling. I'm a gay man, which is about as far away from a twelve-year-old girl as it gets. The only periods I understand are at the end of sentences."

"Please don't wake my grandma. I want you to help me."

"Why? Oh, all right. What's the point of arguing." He turned on the light above the sink, perched on the edge of the tub to read the instructions in the box. He skimmed past the warnings about toxic shock, blah blah blah, and looked for the schematic: just three parts, the applicator in two parts, and the pad inside. Simple. "Okay. Here you go," he said and handed her one from the box. Flynn looked at it as if were an explosive, or a living thing about to hatch. "Flynn, I'm going to walk you through this, step by step, but I am not, understand me, under any circumstances, under threat of death, going to insert it for you. Okay?"

"Okay."

"All right. I'll be right outside." He closed the door. "Step one is to remove outer wrapping."

"Check," Flynn said.

"Step two...oh," he said. A drawing of a woman, hollow and faceless except for the internal reproductive organs. How terrible! He was glad Flynn didn't have to see it—what kind of message was this? The shape of a woman, curvy with long hair, but no internal organs other than the vagina and uterus. "Step two is to find the position that's most comfortable for insertion." He felt dizzy. "You can either stand with one foot on the toilet seat, or sit, with both legs spread wide. The sitting position puts the vagina in a more horizontal position." Jesus! He sat on the floor.

"Is this whole thing supposed to fit inside me?" Flynn called.

He looked down at the directions. "No. Just insert to where the little ridges are." He looked for the next step. "When you've inserted it as far as the ridges, gently push in the plunger." He couldn't leave Flynn with the instructions, couldn't let her see the awful faceless woman with the uterus and vagina and labia taking up fully one-third of the otherwise blank body. At least they could have given the woman a heart. Tomorrow he was going to write to the manufacturers, write and tell them that they needed to either make this drawing a woman with a face and features or eliminate all but a close-up of the parts necessary for comprehension. "How are you doing in there?"

"I can't do this. It's not working."

"Which part isn't working?"

"Can you come in here?"

"I'm sending the directions under the door, okay?" He started to tear the part with the drawing away, but saw that if he did that he'd be ripping off part three. Normally, a mother or another woman would be in there with her, guiding her through, and she wouldn't have to see this blank woman. He couldn't let her see this. No twelve-year-old should be made to feel there was something unnatural about his or her body. This drawing more than suggested that.

"Jack?"

"I'm here. Just hang on one second. Keep practicing." He went to the little antique desk in the hallway, found a pen in the drawer, and sat down. He gave the woman eyes and lashes and brows, drew in a smile that was supposed to represent a calm self-confidence, but which made the figure look like the cartoon character, Sally Forth. Long hair, wispy bangs and a ring on the right hand. That was better. He slid the directions under the bathroom door then went in to wake Stuart.

He shook him, called his name three times before he stirred.

"What? What's the matter?" Stuart said.

"You have a sister," Jack said.

"Another one?" he said, then coming a little more awake, "what's wrong?"

"What do you know about tampons?"

The two of them walked to the bathroom door. "Slide the directions back out here, Flynn," Jack said. "Here's the schematic," Jack said to Stuart. "We're on step three, gently insert."

Stuart glanced at the drawing and read the instructions. "Flynn?"

"Yeah?"

"Are you sitting?"

"Yeah."

"Okay." He read through the steps that accompanied this position. "All right, if you're seated, what you want to do is aim back and down, toward your tailbone. Take your time."

"Can you send Baby Jesus in?"

"Why?" Jack said.

"For company."

Jack didn't want to open the door, didn't want to risk a glimpse of anything. "He's a boy. It's not a good idea to have boys in there. Even boy dogs."

Flynn sighed. "But why?"

"Boys aren't as strong as girls. He might have a heart attack."

Stuart shot Jack a look. "Take your time, Flynn."

They waited through the silence on Flynn's side of the door. In a few minutes she said, "Okay."

"Okay?" Jack said. "Okay means you did it?"

"Yes," she said.

The men applauded.

Flynn came out of the bathroom and sidled up to Jack.

"Good work, Flynn," Stuart said, smiling.

"Yes. We should celebrate. I'll go see if Anna has any champagne," Jack said.

"Jack," Stuart said, and shook his head.

"What? Oh, no? Maybe hot chocolate, then."

"Where does Anna keep the sheets? I'll change your bed," Stuart said.

Flynn pointed to the hall closet. "Can we watch *Riverdance*?" Flynn asked.

"Not now," Jack said. "Tomorrow. It's late. How about some hot chocolate?"

"No. Can you sleep in my room tonight?"

"I need to be with Stuart. But if you need me, come get me." He kissed her goodnight. "Okay?"

"Can I sleep in your room? I'll sleep on the floor."

Jack considered. It would be all right with him, but Stuart might not be comfortable with it. "I think you need to sleep in your own room tonight. But the minute you need me, I'll be there. That's a promise," Jack said. "Okay?"

She nodded. She kissed Stuart goodnight and then Jack again. Back in her room she felt like her body was closing in around her like those heavy drapes her grandma used to block out the light in her bedroom. It was dark both inside and outside herself and she was trapped in some terrible basement that she couldn't tunnel her way out of. Her belly was a boxing ring, two big powers fighting against each other. Flynn was a TKO. The cheerful cocktail party of men was gone, and there was nothing around her but the twin scents of wishes and dreams—lemon and lavender—and the deep-down dread that everything was about to change again.

ON THE WAY TO SANTIAGO

Anna, vaccinating for the flu at Dr. Naylor's office, guessed she was on her twentieth patient and it wasn't even lunchtime. Naylor was offering a reduced price for adults and free vaccinations for the elderly and children. Just before nine, a whole busload of senior citizens from the nursing home poured in like it was bingo night at the church social hall.

"What was my rationale, again?" Naylor said, as he peered out into the waiting room beside Anna.

"That's what I was wondering. My skills are wasted on the healthy trying to stay that way. What ever happened to the local jaundiced? The great unwashed? I was hoping for a white count raging out of control," Anna said.

He chuckled. "Sorry. But I appreciate your coming in."

"Next," he and Anna said in unison.

A young mother and her toddler went with Anna, the town librarian headed toward Naylor—for some reason she didn't like Anna, would barely speak to her when Anna went in for her weekly stash of books on tape.

"How are we today?" Anna asked, leading the mother and boy into the examining room. Anna had examined both of them before. The woman was about twenty-three or twenty-five, the toddler about three. The last time they'd been in, Naylor treated the woman for pelvic inflammatory disease and her son for head lice and an ear infection. Anna had looked at her chart, the intake care worker's rounded script that described the woman's welfare status and her activities thusly: "Pt. spends her days watching television." To the question, "Are you sexually active?" the woman had declared, "Not really. I just lay there."

"I can't sleep. Can you give me medicine?" the woman asked.

"No," Anna said, and positioned the syringe against the woman's skinny arm. "Only the doctor can prescribe. Make an appointment at the front desk."

She didn't especially like working here, didn't care for Naylor's laid-back country doctor ways, but Naylor had privileges in the lab at the local college, where he sent Anna to read patient slides. She could check Jack's blood samples while she was there.

"Next," Anna called, and called for the subsequent two hours.

At lunchtime, Anna walked over to the Shimmer Deli—terrible food, but she could never resist the alluring name. She sat in a booth by the window and picked at her food; not hungry, but not ready to go back to work, either. It was a near record-breaking warm day—the clock on the bank said sixty-two degrees. Thanksgiving was just around the corner, and it felt like Indian summer. She and Flynn checked the forecast daily. Flynn loved snow as much as she did, and like Anna, preferred the cold to the heat. Last summer she and Flynn swam every day at the quarry or the public pool, muted and fuzzyheaded and somber; Flynn was the only other person Anna knew who reacted to heat the way she did.

Anna used her cell phone to call Flynn's school. Flynn had been having more trouble than usual in her classes. Her classmates' teasing had inten-sified after her teacher assigned the students how-to reports, oral presen-tations to demonstrate some special skill or talent.

"I'm really worried about her, Mrs. Brinkman," Flynn's teacher had said at the first conference of the school year. "Most children brought in blenders and knitting needles and basketballs." Miss Jamison paused. "Most of the students showed us how to make fruit smoothies or knit scarves. Flynn brought in some glasses from the eye doctor's office and told us how to communicate with the spirit world. The kids are picking on her without mercy." Anna said she knew this; Flynn had been telling her all along. *It is always better to tell the truth.* Anna remembered that long-ago game she and Flynn played, and was haunted by her words. It would have been better if she had taught Flynn to tell healthy lies.

The phone rang and rang; they were probably all in the cafeteria. Anna left money on the table and drove straight to the middle school. The children were eating lunch outside at picnic tables set around the playground. She scanned the crowd, saw the bright yellow hair of Flynn's teacher, and then the group in her charge, who flocked around her in twittery energy. She spotted Flynn sitting alone, her lunch spread out over the entire table. Anna was pulled back through every sadness she'd felt in her own life. She caught Flynn's eye and smiled, and Flynn's smile in return was the most genuine Anna had seen in nearly a year—*this,* then, was why she had come, for this bit of happiness she saw now in her granddaughter.

"Hi," Flynn said. "I had a feeling you'd be here."

"Did you?" Anna glanced down at Flynn's uneaten lunch. "Wanna ditch school and go to the quarry? I don't know if it's actually warm enough to swim, but we can sit by the water at least."

And then the second smile, one of surprised delight that filled Anna with relief at the thought that everything might be okay after all. Anna called Naylor's office from the car and told him that something had come up and she wouldn't be back in until tomorrow.

It was warm enough in the sun, the day windless, so she and Flynn did swim. They floated on their backs in water so smooth and perfect the trees and rocks and clouds were mirrored in its glassy dark surface. Anna tasted the granite in the water at the back of her throat.

"Do you believe in heaven and hell?" Flynn asked.

Anna turned. Flynn was watching her intently. She was going to be beautiful, Anna saw; why hadn't she noticed that until now? Her eyes had changed—or maybe it was just the light—from a dark brown to a deeper shade, nearly black. Her features were chiseled yet lush, her lips full and curvy and deeply red. One day, Anna thought, some man was going to fall in love with her for that mouth. Flynn's hair was thick and dark and to her shoulders. She had recently had her bangs cut, and she swept them off to the side, which gave her a look of grave sophistication. She probably wouldn't be tall, Anna thought, but she was perfectly proportioned with the long, lean legs of a runner. She was going to be more beautiful than Poppy, if that were possible.

Anna turned away, watched as the shadows of birds, disturbed from the stand of trees rimming the quarry, moved over the water. What kind of woman would Flynn be, Anna wondered. Not like her mother, certainly, at least Anna hoped Flynn hadn't inherited her mother's streak of weakness and self-indulgence. She would be a handful, artistic like Marvin, if her highly developed imagination were any indication, her fanciful visions channeled into a creative outlet. Anna tried to visualize her granddaughter as a woman of thirty, of twenty-five, but she couldn't get past the girl she was now. Perhaps there would always be something girlish about Flynn, something ageless and childlike.

When Flynn repeated her question, Anna said, "You shouldn't be thinking of such things as heaven and hell at your age, Flynn. It's a beautiful day. Just enjoy it."

"But there is such a thing as hell," Flynn asked.

Anna didn't answer.

"Do you think my mother is gone for good?" Flynn asked.

Anna floated beside Flynn, watched the fog gather and drift across the mountains in the distance. "I think she might be. It doesn't mean she doesn't love you, though. She just has some problems she has to work out before she can take care of you."

"You have been very good to me," Flynn said. A minute or so went by. "Is there fear in heaven?"

"I don't imagine there would be."

"If there is no fear in heaven, then hell must be very foggy." Her eyes rested on the mountain range. "Fog is just a cloud with a fear of heights."

A few weeks ago Anna had called a child psychologist and asked for a meeting. Flynn's facial expressions had been changing. "You mean a lack of affect?" the psychologist had asked, and Anna said, no, it wasn't that Flynn had stopped smiling or laughing. To prove it to herself, Anna wrote down how many expressions crossed Flynn's face in the span of two hours. Roughly the same number as Jack and Stuart each showed; Anna had counted theirs, too, as a control. No, what she meant was the manner in which Flynn's expressions and emotions transited her face—her smile moved from the outside in, instead of breaking open from the center of her face. Amusement began in her eyes instead of her chin and mouth: delight started in the lips and tongue for children, hadn't the psychologist noticed this? Adults, not children, were amused from the top down, from the eyebrows to the mouth. The psychologist, a fiftyish man with one blue eye, one brown, studied Anna as if she were fine print.

"Where does your amusement begin?" he asked.

"Maybe here," Anna had said, then walked out.

"Get your things together," Anna said now, getting out of the water. "We need to get going."

At home, Anna called to Jack and Stuart, who was still here even after Anna postponed Jack's birthday party. Jack had an unpleasant reaction to one of his medicines, but was now steadily improving, either from the re-combination of his meds or Stuart's presence, or both. Anna encouraged Stuart to stay as long as he could. The classes he taught were on Monday and Tuesday only, so presumably he could be here most of every week. Anna liked having him around. She especially appreciated his reliability. Anna could count on the fact that if she overheard Stuart holding a one-way conversation in an empty room, it was always because he was on the phone.

Anna went around back to let Flynn's dog in. He was sniffing all along the cedar fence. Anna whistled, and the dog looked over and wagged. "Hiya, fatso. Wanna come in?"

A voice spoke on the other side of the fence. "Thanks, but I best be ticking on."

"Oh," Anna said. "Violet? Is that you? I was talking to the dog."

"Okay. I do need to whittle my middle, truth be told. Getting on, you know, and picking up flesh."

Anna heard the clink of dog leashes, collars. "Do you happen to know where Jack and his friend went off to?"

"I do not. But they set off near to noon. I was having my lunch when they motored past."

Anna thanked her, and went inside. Flynn was taking a bath. Anna heard the ancient groaning of the pipes. She sat at the kitchen table in the path of the late afternoon sun, made herself a cup of tea and picked up the phone to call Greta, to whom she hadn't talked in nearly a week. "It's me," Anna said, when her friend picked up.

"Hi," Greta said. "Do you know anything about crème de cassis?"

"What is that?"

"That's what I was wondering. I'm making something that calls for crème de cassis, and I don't know if it's a spice or a liquid, or what."

"Hmm. Sounds like a seduction dinner. Who's coming over?"

Greta sighed. "It's hopeless. I've given up on dating, anyway. But even so. What's up with you?"

"Not a lot. Just haven't talked to you in a few days."

"You sound exhausted," Greta said. Anna heard the motor of a blender start up.

"I do? Well, now that you mention it, I am," Anna said.

"How's Flynn?"

"Better, I'd say. She's always going to be peculiar, but many wonderful people are strange."

"Indeed," Greta said. "Anyway, I don't think she's all that peculiar. She's twelve. Who isn't insane when they're twelve?"

"Right," Anna said.

"I remember when I was eleven or twelve, I had this obsessive—and I mean really obsessive—fantasy about a handsome man chasing my naked body around and around my bedroom. I couldn't imagine what I wanted him to do when he caught me, mind you." Greta laughed. "That's twelve for you. You half know things, and you half don't."

Anna laughed. Greta sounded as if she was in a hurry. Anna heard the rattle of pots and pans, the gush of the kitchen faucet. "Who's your date with?"

"Someone I work with. It's not that exciting. I'm already looking forward to the end of the evening when I snuggle with Lily in bed and watch her sleep."

"Are you coming for Jack's birthday in two weeks? Stay as long as you like."

"Absolutely I'm coming. Listen, dear, I have to run, but I think maybe you need a break from Flynn. Why not send her to Boston to see her father? Or send her to me. It'll give you perspective on everything. You sound exhausted and strained."

Anna said she would think about it.

"Really," Greta said. "When was the last time you did something *you* wanted to do?"

Anna considered this after she hung up. What did she want to do? Mainly what she was doing. Except maybe not worry about Flynn so much.

At eleven o'clock, just as Anna was getting ready to turn in for the night, Jack and Stuart came home and wandered into her bedroom where she was watching the news. "Would it have killed you to call?" she said, but she couldn't be mad. They—in particular, Jack—looked so radiant and happy that she couldn't help but smile. Jack jumped in bed beside her and nuzzled against her neck. Stuart sat in the easy chair that had been Hugh's. "We went into Boston," Jack said.

"Were you clubbing?"

"I wish," Jack said. "I don't really feel well enough for that. We went to visit some friends. Wanna come to San Francisco with us? It won't cost you a cent."

"No thanks," Anna said automatically. And then, "What do you mean?"

"Our friend Curtis has three tickets he can't use. Why don't you come? It's only for a few days. Stuart found somebody to cover his classes. So we thought we'd have a hurrah."

"No, I probably can't. But it sounds like fun."

From down the hall Flynn called, "Jack?"

"In here, baby girl," he called back.

Flynn, then the dog, climbed into bed with Anna and Jack.

"I thought you were asleep," Anna said, then looked down at what was fastened to Flynn's red nightgown: one of the hairpins she bought at that auction with Greta.

"Where did you get that?"

"On the floor in the downstairs closet." Flynn looked down at the fine blond hair, outlined the downy circle with her finger.

"What is that?" Jack said.

"It's a hairpin. It was a popular thing in the late eighteenth century to make brooches from the hair of your dead loved ones," Anna said.

"Gruesome," Jack said.

"This is the hair of a dead person," Flynn said, and let her eyes unfocus. "This person was just a tiny baby, who is lost, who has lost her way, and keeps turning the wrong way in the dark. She's afraid she's going to hell where the storms are. There is no thunder in heaven. Only hell has storms."

Anna and Jack and Stuart looked at her. Jack reached for her hand. "Come up here," he said softly, and settled her between him and Anna. "There is no such thing as hell. Only different kinds of heavens. At least, I'm counting on that."

Stuart smiled when Jack looked over, then crept downstairs to the drafty sunroom to call David. He sat on the wicker couch, twisted the phone cord around and around his wrist while he waited for David to pick up. It was late, but Stuart knew David well enough to know that he was in bed with a book, the late show turned low so he could ignore it, and a glass of good French wine.

"It's me," he said, when David picked up.

"Hi," he said, then fell silent.

"Well, I'm still at Anna's."

"Yes. I figured. Are you coming home? I'm not haranguing, just trying to plan."

Stuart felt a pang, imagined the warm flannel sheets with his lover's musky body, his cologne fragrant on the pillows. Stuart's longing to be with him at that moment, to be surrounded by the familiar scents and textures was like an ache all along his jawbone. How could he just leave this behind? David was the man with whom he thought he wanted a future, a string of pleasant and peaceful days unfolding elegantly from his middle years to his late ones. Yet, it was strange how often Stuart's forty-two felt like old-age, stranger still that he could more easily envision their deathbed scenes than he could their next vacation.

"Stuart?"

"I'm here. I'm just thinking. I am coming home, I just don't know when." That was the truth as far as he knew it. He heard David's breathing on the other end, a sigh of anger or unhappiness—he couldn't tell—the faraway sounds of Leno's monologue, and the clink of stemware on a marble coaster.

"Why? You told me you were going to Anna's for the party, fine. Now you've done it, come home."

"Anna postponed the party. Jack wasn't doing great. The party's in two weeks."

"I won't tolerate this."

"Is that an ultimatum?" Stuart looked up, saw a flash of light outside.

Somebody was moving around the perimeter of the house with a flash-light. He stood, peered through the windows but couldn't see anything.

"No. I'm not making it that easy on you. You need to figure it out. Jack continually treated you like shit, and yet you keep going back to him, you keep setting yourself up—"

"I didn't go back to him. I came up for his birthday party."

David fell silent. "You're going to be there two more weeks? What about your classes?"

"Someone covered for me last week. It's under control." Stuart was planning to stay with Pamela in Boston Sunday and Monday nights, then to head back up to Maine Tuesday evening.

"Anyway," David said. "I guess if you're not back here the Monday after the party, that's the information I need."

Stuart snorted. "So it is an ultimatum. You are, you know, invited."

David hung up. Stuart dialed again, but put the receiver back to go check who was outside.

It was the nutty next-door neighbor with her dogs. "Come along, come along, the dark draws nigh."

"Hello?" Stuart called.

The light shone in his direction, and Stuart saw that it was attached to her head. "Good evening," she said. "Just out for our evening constitutional. Glad to see you boys got home safely."

"Oh, goodnight," Stuart said, and headed back in. He sat in the dark, watched the neighbor's light move past the house, then recede. The sensible thing would be to pack up his things this minute and go back to Boston. David was right: Jack was who he always was and staying here only revivified what had always been. If it weren't so, why hadn't Jack come downstairs to find out what he was doing? Jack took his affection and loyalty as a given. It hadn't occurred to him that Stuart might not have made up his mind.

Stuart again heard noises outside. He went out.

"Not to be alarmed, it is still just us," she said. "My dogs are old. It can sometimes take a while for them to say their prayers. You're keeping late hours, young man."

Stuart said that he was. "Working through dilemmas, you know." He stepped outside. The woman looked ghostly in the blue halogen lamplight.

Normally, Stuart found such intrusions offensive, but there was something about her he liked.

"Yes," she said. "Dilemmas, dilemmas. Of course you're working through them. The young always are." She paused. "There are many stations along the pilgrim's path. The way to Santiago is full of peril and false starts."

"What?" Stuart said.

"The truer the journey, the more obstacles you will encounter. In my experience."

Stuart didn't know what the hell she was talking about. Santiago? Chile? But later, years from now, he'd remember this night and see how decisions made at critical junctures weren't what they seemed to be at the time. Certain choices, paths, were as inevitable and as necessary as the rhythm of a beating heart.

At the last minute Anna decided to go with them. Greta was right: she did need some time away. Besides, it was only for a few days. Greta agreed to come up for the weekend, which only left two days of Flynn's being in Violet's care—something Anna wasn't crazy about.

"Flynn is a little overly sensitive to things," Anna said, walking into Violet's house for the first time, a couple of hours before the flight to California. Flynn had come over earlier, to make sure Baby Jesus got along with Violet's dogs. Violet's house was cluttered—years worth of *National Geographics* stacked in the corners—but clean, Anna saw with relief. "She frightens easily. Especially about things like ghosts. And certain subjects, like death and dying, should be off-limits." Anna took the cup of tea Violet offered her, looked around. The place was actually nice. Without the excess stuff it would have been beautiful. The ceilings were vaulted and crossed with heavy beams, and the walls were the original plaster. Above the fireplace were architectural prints from buildings in ancient Rome. The temple of Mars, Anna read on one. The gathering place for Caesar and his armies.

"The lass will be fine. I'll keep her close."

Anna smiled and thanked her. It would be all right. Violet was warm and wise. Her house was inviting and smelled surprisingly good. Anna had expected a doggy smell, dust and mildew, but instead there were the unmistakable scents of lavender, jasmine, and lemon furniture polish.

"You have the number of the hotel, right?" Anna said. "I don't know what room yet, but you can ring the front desk and they'll patch you through. Or call me on my cell phone."

Violet raised an eyebrow. "Anna, zany in dress and habit I may be, but my intelligence is equal to any emergency. I'm in charge of watching a young girl, not rebuilding Jericho."

"Oh, I'm sorry," she said. "I didn't mean to imply—"

Violet cut her off. "The boys are waiting for you out there." Stuart's Jeep angled into Violet's driveway. "The lass is upstairs, going through my old hope chest. Shall I fetch her?"

Anna said no, she'd already said goodbye a number of times. Violet embraced her. "Have a good time. You need this," she said. "Strength comes from pleasure."

In San Francisco, Jack and Stuart stayed with friends of theirs, a lesbian couple, in Nob Hill, just a few blocks from the Nikko Hotel, where Anna had booked a room. Anna was invited to stay in the house, too, but she wanted solitude and quiet, uninterrupted sleep.

She and Stuart spent the entire first day shopping. Linens and bath soaps from an exclusive boutique, and in Chinatown, silk pajamas and matching slippers for Flynn, along with a jade figurine of a dog.

"Enough shopping," Stuart said, his arms laden with packages of his own. "We're never going to get this stuff on the plane."

Anna put a jade bracelet down, then picked it up again and nodded at the clerk. It was small enough to fit Flynn, and it was time the girl had nice jewelry. Jade was good luck.

Outside, an elaborate funeral procession with at least a hundred people was winding down the street. Someone carried a huge photograph of the deceased. All were in traditional Chinese dress. Anna looked away, picked up the bracelet she'd bought for Flynn, and as she did, the beads broke away from the string and fell to the floor.

"Okay, just okay," the woman said. "Just a mistake. I bring another, no problem, okay."

"No," Anna said. "No." She handed over her credit card. "I want my money back. Credit my account."

The woman argued with her for ten minutes, pointed to the sign that said no refunds and finally went off to get the manager when Anna wouldn't budge. "Sorry," Anna said to Stuart, who stood in the doorway watching the funeral march.

"No problem," he said. "Do you think these were all the man's children?"

Anna looked over, counted seven children, all dressed identically, ranging in age from about two to fifteen. "Yes," she said, looking at the woman who was surely his widow, "Probably."

"Madam," the store manager said behind her. "This is a very sad day for you indeed."

"What?" Anna said.

"Please accept my deep condolences."

Anna whirled around. The manager was surely a hundred if he was a day, and blind. The clerk said something to him in Chinese. "I only would like my money returned," she said.

The man cocked his head as though listening to the drumbeat outside then nodded. "Yes. But please accept my sympathy on the loss of something precious. We will not give you additional problems."

Anna was unnerved as she and Stuart walked to the end of Chinatown to meet Jack at Nan King for dinner. "I think he must have thought I was part of the funeral outside. But surely he knew I was just a dumb tourist. Is it me, or is that creepy? The man gave me the heebie-jeebies."

"Who knows. Probably a language barrier thing," Stuart said, opening the door for her. All through dinner the man's comment grew into something like dread. She glanced over at the table beside her—a young couple, a family with two small children—and without knowing why or why she felt this way or under what conviction, she knew she would remember this day, that blind store manager, for the rest of her life.

"Earth to Anna," Jack said.

She looked over, smiled. "You, by the way, look terrific," she said. "Your color is good. I know just by looking at you that your T-cells are rallying."

"You think? Anyway, I must remind you that you are on vacation. Stop worrying. You've barely touched the *meow*-shoo pork. Here, kitty kitty." He pushed the plate toward her.

Anna laughed. "How do you know I'm worrying?"

He handed her his cell phone. "You've got that look in your eye. Get it over with, because you have a long night ahead of you, missy."

Anna stepped outside and dialed Violet's number. Everything was fine. "The lass has had her dinner and is practicing her dancing. You know, bog-stomping, high-kicks. She's a jewel. Do you wish to speak to her?" Anna said no, just checking in to make sure everything was all right, she would call again tomorrow.

Anna lit a cigarette, watched Jack and Stuart through the window. Stuart had never seemed to her like the obvious choice as Jack's partner, but he brought a peace to Jack; it was palpable. It was the way she felt with Hugh all those years ago. Stuart, she suspected, was struggling with what he wanted. Jack hadn't treated him very well in the years they were officially together, had made some comment once about people either having the monogamy gene or not having it, and how could he be faulted for not having what nature left out? To which Anna had said, you're an ass. Still, whatever happened between them, she was grateful for Jack's returning strength; she could have sworn she saw his T-cells increasing, or the effect of them anyway, in the same way when her daughter was an infant the child often seemed visibly bigger and rounder each morning.

She lit another cigarette from the butt of the one still going, wrapped her raincoat tighter around her. The fog had moved into the bay and was hanging low, shrouding the storefronts and shops. The streets were black, glazed with rain.

By the time Jack and Stuart came out, Anna's heart was pounding so hard that it felt like her breath had to move around the pulse in her throat. Maybe it was that damn tea. She'd been drinking green tea all day long, which, she remembered now, was loaded with caffeine.

"Are you ready?" Jack said. "We boxed up the rest of the dinner for later."

"Okay," Anna said. "Maybe we should get a nightcap somewhere. Not in Chinatown, though."

"We have just the cap for your night, dear one," Jack said, with an evil laugh. He walked ahead of her, and hailed a cab just past the gates of Chinatown.

"Jack thinks it's time to broaden your education," Stuart said.

"Oh?"

He shrugged. "The gay underbelly. The places you'd never see except with us."

She glanced over. Stuart looked tired, as though fatigue and illness and anxiety were a baggy gray sweater that they were passing among the three of them and which he now wore.

The cab stopped in front of what was surely some kind of sex club. There was a man in drag standing outside, wearing black leather, a Prince Valiant wig, and eye liner in the shape of wings, extending all the way up to his temples. "You're kidding," she said. "You brought me to a sex club?" But her outrage didn't go as deep as she pretended.

"Don't worry. It's half and half," Jack said.

"What does that mean?"

"Half straight, half gay. Gay play is on the top two floors." He pulled out his wallet and paid all three cover charges.

"Don't leave me alone in here," Anna said, walking into the dark front room where a naked girl stood dancing next to a bouncer.

"We won't."

"And don't fuck in front of me," she said. "If you have to do that, send me off to the bar or something."

The three of them wandered down a narrow corridor. On one side, behind chain-link fencing various tableaus were being enacted. Plywood partitions divided the people within, cutting off their view of what was happening to the left or right of them. It was, Anna thought, like watching a human zoo. She stopped at the first station. There was a young naked Asian man with his hands cuffed above his head. A very overweight woman in black leather, at least in her late forties, maybe older, attached hot feathers to his scrotum. Six men in chairs behind the leather-clad woman watched, presumably waiting their turn. The woman, Anna saw, must be a dominatrix. One by one she yanked the feathers out as the boy winced, pleasure and pain intertwined. The woman kissed him on the lips after pulling out each feather.

"What's the point of that?" Anna whispered to Jack. "Does he get to have sex afterward?"

"If you stand here long enough I'm sure you'll find out," Jack said. "But come upstairs with us. The really interesting stuff is upstairs. This is run-of-the mill schoolboy fantasy crap."

"I don't want to be on the gay floors," Anna said.

"Why?"

"Jack, I love you as I'd love a son. There are certain things I don't want to know about you."

"She's right," Stuart said.

"Anyway, I'm not going to stay in here very long. If I'm not here when you get back downstairs, I'll be back at my hotel, and you can call or stop by later."

Jack asked if she was sure, and Anna said, "Of course." Except an hour later, she was still moving throughout the club. A couple of years ago she and a group of women friends rented Kubrick's *Eyes Wide Shut* and they debated about whether such things existed. Anna had said she doubted it, but now here it all was before her, people having sex everywhere, in every combination and with varying degrees of audience. The club patrons seemed to be primarily men in early to late middle age. Most appeared to be alone. She noticed that the minute a couple so much as kissed and headed toward one of the enclosed rooms, a group of men followed. Voyeurism was as much a part of it all as participation. She had to keep moving, was what she discovered; if she stood in one place too long men approached her. It felt like moving through catacombs, the sticky dark with its bodily smells like a place of the dead. She walked through the hallways, stopping briefly at a station here and there to watch the activities within—people doing things to each other she never would guess anybody would find pleasurable. Why would a grown man want to be spanked by a man with biceps as thick as soup pots? She wondered what kind of lives these people had during the day, what kind of longing and dreaming brought them here at night. What she found fascinating above all was the secrecy of it, the secret subterranean life that ran beneath the surface of the daily one. Her daughter had a secret life, one of drugs and back alleys and hazy dreamlike hours with strangers getting high. She envied these people, really, their desires of the flesh leading them down here from their sunlit hours as stockbrokers or insurance men. She herself had never lived a life apart from the one the world knew her by. Didn't have hobbies that entranced her for hours, or work that was involving enough to keep her in a private world. Jack lived part of his life away from them all—first his numerous affairs, and now, his private memories of those times. Marvin had his art, Flynn had her visions.

She watched as a transvestite worked on two men at once, overweight men in late middle age who Anna imagined were salesmen or cable TV repairmen. There was a jolly floridity to their faces, their cheeks shiny with sweat. What she found fascinating was the unselfconscious immersion in the things that were happening to them, as though it was perfectly normal to be naked and in a state of sexual arousal with a group of strangers looking on. Those watching had expressions of solemn concentration, almost piety, and not the smirking titillation she'd have expected.

For the first time in years, Anna questioned her absent libido. Even watching the heterosexual activity, some of the men beautiful by anybody's standards—hired by the club, she was sure, just as the beautiful young women hanging around the bars must be employees—she didn't feel a flicker of anything.

Anna made her way outside, surprised at how ordinary everything looked once again. She took her cell phone out, but decided it was too late to call Violet. She had no reason to call anyway, except that her granddaughter's face loomed before her with its private mask of secrets, of where she went when she disappeared for hours and the things she knew—how *had* Flynn been able to describe her grandfather so clearly? What kind of nightmares had such force that they consumed her for days on end? How much of her granddaughter lived in that private world? She turned, headed back into the club. She was too restless to stand here, too agitated to go back to her hotel.

Stuart had lost Jack hours ago, just after he saw him duck into the men's room, emerge with a stack of condoms, and then melt into a throng of bodies on one of the dance floors. They'd agreed to meet back at a central staircase at 1:00 A.M., which meant he still had an hour. He circled through the corridors, and found Jack at the entrance to one of the private rooms where he was watching four gay men fulfill some tired fantasy. "Hey," Stuart said. "What are you doing on the sidelines, lad? Shouldn't you be in the fleshy midst?" He was hoping that Jack would swagger back at the end of the evening with nothing but loose change in his pockets, the condoms used up. Certain decisions would have been easier had Jack acted true to form.

"Must be getting old. This isn't doing anything for me. None of these men," Jack said, and led him away by the hand. "Have you seen the theme rooms?" He pulled Stuart into a room bearing the legend "Little Red Riding Hood's Room" above the doorway. Inside, it was decorated like the fairy tale described, complete with brass bedstead and patchwork quilt and nightcaps on both pillows. A red cape hung from a peg, though sized to fit an adult male instead of a girl. Beneath it, a picnic basket held a red check-ered tablecloth and brightly wrapped condoms by the dozens.

Stuart laughed. "Do you want to be the Big Bad Wolf, or should I?"

"I want to marry you," Jack said.

Stuart froze, didn't dare look up.

"That's not part of the fairy tale."

"It's part of mine." He sat down on the bed, pulled out a cigarette. "I don't want any of this anymore." He gestured toward the men who had gathered in the doorway hoping to see a show. "I only want to be with you." He made shooing gestures to the men looking in. "No show tonight, boys. We're a couple of bitches here, talking about our relationship."

Stuart took the cape off the hook. It was beautiful, really, way too nice for a place like this. It was red velvet on one side, black silk on the inside. He wrapped it around his shoulders, capped the hood on his head. "My, Grandmother, what big bones you have. Or was it teeth?" He laughed, but stopped when he saw Jack's stern expression.

"I'm serious, Stuart," he said quietly.

"I know you are. But I don't want to talk about it now. You're not being fair. I have other involvements."

"I am your true heart, and you know it."

Stuart took off the cape, reached for the cigarette in Jack's hand, took a drag, and coughed. He'd never been a smoker. "Yeah? Well, I also know that most of the time your false heart broke my true one. So, I don't want to talk about it right now." He got up and walked out, meandered down the hall, past the Cinderella room, past the men crowding into the room with the Pied Piper, and grabbed the first attractive man who smiled at him, and kissed him. There, he thought. There. I am nobody's pilgrim now. He felt Jack behind him, watching, and kissed the man deeper. He tasted of ciga-rettes and the metallic yeast of beer.

"Stuart," Jack said behind him.

Without taking his eyes off the young man's face Stuart said evenly,

"Why don't you go find Anna. We've been up here a long time. She might have been sold into slavery by now."

The man smiled, his eyes shiny and black as olives, his scent musky and sweet at the same time—newly tilled earth and pineapple. "What's your name?" Stuart said softly.

"Steven," he said, and smiled. "One second," Stuart said to the boy. He turned, walked the few paces back to Jack. "You brought me here. This was your idea. If you say one more word, I'm leaving you forever, and for good."

Jack nodded, and turned away. Stuart watched him walk to the staircase, down to the breeders with their Oedipal or bad Boy Scout fantasies. Jack looked back once, caught Stuart's eye just as he moved into the dark room with the beautiful young man. This, he saw, was the Space Odyssey room, completely black. There wasn't a trace of light from anywhere; even the crack beneath the door had been sealed off. There was no way to tell who was where, or how many people were crammed therein.

Steven was just inside the doorway. "This way," he said, and took Stuart's hand. There was an echo, microphones rigged up to amplify and echo voices. There was murmuring all around him, quiet, throaty noises, the crackling of cellophane, the clink of buckles and snaps.

"Was that your boyfriend?" he asked Stuart.

"Yeah," Stuart said. "One of them."

Steven put his hands on either side of Stuart's face and kissed him. Stuart tasted mint.

"How old are you?" Stuart said, and heard the question bounce along the walls.

"Twenty-five. Why?"

Stuart shrugged, but of course the boy couldn't see this. "No reason. Except that I'm getting old, I guess."

"Haven't been here before, eh?"

"It's not that."

"Don't talk," he whispered, then undid Stuart's pants. "Oh, it's that, then," he said.

"What?" Stuart said.

"It's the honey-honey waiting for you. It's the jealous boyfriend, not nerves. The old guilt wilt."

Stuart heard sniggers all around him. He grabbed the boy and kissed him, forced his tongue into the cool cavern of the boy's mouth, ran his hands over the perfect young skin. Stuart thought of Jack downstairs, with Anna, no doubt, the two of them mocking the puerile fantasies unfolding around them, and felt anger snake up from his gut. Not at this boy, not really at Jack, but at doing what he was doing now and its necessity.

"I have cheated on you," he would tell David on the phone later, admitting first to this boy and then to the indiscretion with Jack. Immorality aside, lying and secrecy never made much sense to him; it only delayed the inevitability of what you had to face.

"Don't ask me what you don't want to know," he would tell Jack later, with the edge of irritation he'd heard so many times from Jack himself.

"Did I ever tell you about the time I fucked this boy in a club, and his skin was so creamy that I swear I tasted butter in my mouth?" To whom he would say this, he couldn't yet imagine.

The boy covered Stuart's body with his own. Stuart hesitated, but couldn't resist, couldn't turn away from the velvety darkness and the smooth hands and silky hair, the gorgeous images blooming in his mind of every summer day of his boyhood, of every lovely thing he'd ever lost coming back to him all at once.

Jack found Anna dancing with three men in the bar closest to the entrance. He walked up to her, smiled, and elbowed his way in. "How's tricks?" she shouted to him over the music. "No pun intended." She looked flushed and happy. He wondered if she'd gotten laid. She looked, anyway, about twenty years younger than the last time he saw her, her face no longer creased and doughy from worry.

Jack slow-danced with Anna when the music changed, from the thumping techno beat to some god-awful grope-song typically played in breeder bars. "I want to get out of here soon," he said, his head resting on her shoulder.

"Okay," she said. "Me too."

"Where's Stuart?"

"Upstairs cheating on me." He felt her startle against him, and he laughed until it felt like the laughter might turn inside out to what it really was.

"Oh," she said. "And so what the hell are you doing down here with me? Isn't this the city of boys?"

"Don't ask." He led her to the bar and ordered them shots of tequila with gin and tonic chasers. "So, what happened to you?"

She turned, her face radiant and glowing. "What do you mean?"

"Did you get laid?"

She made a face of disgust. "God, no. This isn't my thing." She took a sip of her drink. "I've just had some revelations."

"Oh? With whom?"

She smiled, drew her lips in. "I mean, I have figured things out. Figured out certain things."

He nodded, and she said, "This is it. This is all there is. One moment to the next." She looked over at him. "Well, you already live that way. I had this vision of carting around a suitcase that's heavy, but only half full."

Jack leaned in, cupped his hand over his ear; the music was getting louder. "I said, it's stupid to think that you always need to have extra space for what might come."

Jack shook his head. "Heard only about half of that."

Nearly shouting now, she said, "I don't have to worry about the next thing until the next thing comes. Until it does, there is a song by Shaggy to dance to." The DJ announced the songs and singers before he played the track. Over the course of the evening, Anna discovered she liked some of this—hip-hop? urban rap?—music, liked Shaggy and Nelly and Mary J. Blige. And she was going to buy Eminem's CD for her and Flynn's music collection.

He took her hand and kissed it. "You know I love you," he said.

She nodded. "I do know that. And I know that my world is better because you're in it."

She lit a cigarette, nodded for another round of tequila. "This place, anyway, is kind of great. I've spent exactly five dollars all night, and I'm sloshed. People have been buying me drinks all night long."

He took a puff off her cigarette, then moved to a stool where he had a clear view of the staircase so he could see when Stuart came down. Finally, after an eternity, Jack saw him as he threaded his way through the throng, looking this way and that for him and Anna.

The three of them walked out into the early morning air, folded themselves into a taxi where Jack closed his eyes and dreamed of getting back to

RENÉE MANFREDI · 247

Maine, to his quiet and comfortable life with Anna and Flynn and that smelly dog. Stuart coming back to stay, to live with them in Maine, would make his life perfect. He reached for Stuart's hand, and Anna's, on the other side of him. Stuart's hand was lifeless and chilly, but he didn't pull away. Anna's hand was warm. Jack laid his head back, closed his eyes. "Even in reunion there is parting," he said, his dreams opening before his sleep.

"What's that?" Anna said.

"Nothing," Jack said. "It's just nothing."

THIRTEEN

AFTER THE FIRST DEATH THERE IS NO OTHER

Somebody was having a birch log fire. Anna had slept with her bedroom window cracked open and the scent of wood smoke was wafting in from somewhere. It was just after dawn, and the house this early was still quiet. She opened the curtains and looked out. Wintry. The sky heavy-looking with snow, the water at the shoreline gray and marbled with white, like a cheap cut of meat. Still, gloomy as it was, Anna loved days like this, always had.

In the kitchen, she put the coffee on then stepped out on the back porch in her nightgown. The houses along the inlet were doglegged and hidden, but she saw the smoke rising from the stand of spruce to the west, which meant Violet's place. Anna hoped Violet would come to Jack's birthday party tonight; Violet didn't like crowds.

Jack had argued for a small gathering, but Anna's instincts and Stuart's good sense—they'd been back from San Francisco a week now, and he hadn't shown any signs of leaving, which was fine with her—led her to in-vite most of the town. There were people coming in from Boston, old friends of Jack and Stuart's, and Marvin, who hadn't been up to see Flynn in months. Anna hoped Flynn might open up to her father in ways she no longer did with Anna. When she and Jack and Stuart got back from Cali-fornia, Anna questioned Greta, who had come up to Maine and spent two days with Flynn, enough time to form an opinion. Did Flynn seem un-usually quiet to her? Unusually withdrawn? Melancholy or disturbed?

"She's an unusual girl," Greta had said.

"Yes. What have you noticed?"

Greta shook her head. "Nothing in particular, I guess, other than she seems really detached."

Anna pressed her further.

"Well, it was like she didn't remember who I was," Greta said. "Like she was looking at me from the wrong side of a telescope. Or no, actually. The way you look at someone you know from a half a mile away. You're pretty sure it's who you think it is, but not positive until you get up close. Does that make sense?"

Anna nodded. "Do you think she'll be okay?" She paused. "Well, that's not a fair question."

Greta took her hand, squeezed it. "You worry too much. You're like a new mother."

Back upstairs, Anna looked out over the water from her bedroom balcony, sipped her coffee. She took a deep breath, inhaled the scents of brine and wood smoke and the wet canvas from the old tent Flynn had gotten out one afternoon six weeks ago then left in a moldering heap by the wood shed. Anna had The White Glove Maids coming later this afternoon, and Stuart was going to help with the cooking—just basic things, since she had the bakery in town doing a cake and sweets, the town liquor store providing the booze, and the Shimmer Deli putting together party plates of sliced meats and cheeses. She'd hired four or five college kids to take care of the serving, music, and bartending. In fact, Anna had delegated so well, that this might be the first party she'd ever thrown she could actually enjoy.

Anna filled the tub for her bath and got some towels out of the hall closet next to Flynn's room. She put her ear to Flynn's door. There were strange sounds: Pacing, thumping, the sound of moving furniture. Anna walked away, went in to have her bath. She added the salts and oil, felt a pang of nostalgia. She supposed the days of Flynn keeping her company while she bathed were over. As recently as two months ago, Flynn came in when she heard the bath running and stretched out on Anna's bed, chattered through the open door. She'd go through Anna's closet, try on clothes and jewelry, or rummage through her makeup drawer.

Anna rapped lightly on Flynn's door. Maybe what they needed, the two of them, was to go out for Belgian waffles at Sugar Loaf, Flynn's favorite. It was in the next town, a twenty-minute drive on the highway. But there was time, especially with the extra help Anna had hired. The day was already gorgeous, bright but chilly, perfect for a huge breakfast. Maybe Flynn would want to shop, too. She might want something new to wear for the party.

"Flynnie? I have a great idea," she said. The door was half ajar, and it swayed open under the pressure of Anna's hand. The room was dark with the pulled blinds, not a crack of light from anywhere. Anna squinted at the bed, but the rumpled lumps were just blankets and pillows. She turned on the bedside lamp.

In the corner, Flynn was sitting atop a pile of household goods from the shed—a tower of wood and fabric, old draperies and tarps. "What are you doing?" Anna felt something sink inside her. "What are you doing, Flynn? What is all this?"

Flynn looked down at her, pale and wide-eyed. "It's a meditation tower," she said.

"Why?" How—and when—did she get all this stuff in here?

"Because I didn't want to sit on the floor."

Anna opened the blinds, studied the pile of junk, lumber from bookshelves Hugh had started but never finished, the baby gate they used for Poppy when she became too interested in the stairs, old tabletops, quilts. Anna touched one at eye level. She herself had pieced this, Poppy's baby quilt. And here was a huge bag of knitting, yellow baby yarn, twenty-five skeins of it—Anna remembered buying this, too—she was going to make Poppy a blanket, something for the bed Hugh made when Poppy outgrew the crib. Anna quit the project after about fifteen rows. "I had no idea all of this stuff was still around," Anna said, looking up at Flynn and smiling, as though it was perfectly natural to have her granddaughter nesting like a bower bird in a stack of old lumber and discarded hobbies. Flynn looked down at her impassively.

"I was thinking the two of us could go get some breakfast at Sugar Loaf. We haven't been there in a while," Anna said.

"I'm not very hungry."

"You might be, once you get up and get moving. Why don't you bathe and dress and meet me downstairs in an hour?"

But by the time Flynn emerged, a little over an hour later, Anna was already involved in supervising the maids who arrived at ten instead of four—a scheduling mix-up—and polishing the silver. She pulled out the sheets for the guest beds that needed to be laundered. You never knew who might have to stay the night, too drunk to drive.

Flynn found her grandmother in the kitchen scrubbing the floors with strong-smelling soap. "I thought we were going to get breakfast."

"Well, I waited, but didn't think you were coming. I'm in the middle of things now. You'll have to fix something for yourself. But don't eat anywhere where the cleaning people are or have been."

Flynn sighed, went in and fixed herself a sandwich and took it outside, past the maids, to the front porch. It was cold out here—why had Anna said it was a nice day? Everything felt cold to her now, her hands and feet, her bed. She balanced the sandwich on her knee, watched the way the jelly glinted in the light, and took a sip of what she thought was Kool-Aid but which turned out to be margarita mix—Jack was always putting his margarita mix in the wrong pitcher. She wished Stuart would leave. She knew what jealousy was; she wasn't jealous, but she also wanted Jack to herself for a while. She overheard Stuart talking to his friend on the phone, heard them arguing, which meant he was probably going to live here forever.

Two weeks ago when she was rooting around in the shed, she found an old record player with her mother's name printed on it in red nail polish. Three albums, the soundtrack to *Jesus Christ Superstar*, *The Best of Bread*, and *Mac Davis's Greatest Hits*. For two weeks the soundtrack from *Jesus Christ Superstar* had been in her head, though she only played it a couple of times. It was terrible, the line that stuck—*We beseech thee...hear us*—and she felt so sick, sick in a way she couldn't describe, except that it was like something in her head was rubbing away at the skin deep inside her like a blister. The song played over and over in her head, and she thought constantly about what it was like to be dead. She was sure she was going to die, and despite what she told her grandma that day on the train tracks, she was afraid. It felt like everything in her future was rushing toward her, and everything that had already happened was pushing from behind, so that she was stuck in the narrow space between the two, barely able to breathe, living every single minute of her life all at once. She couldn't ever relax.

Even in bed, she felt strained, as if the parts of her body were all boxers and competing for a place on the mattress—if her legs relaxed, her neck craned up, if her head sunk into the pillow, her back arched. The winning parts sent the losing parts off the bed. She couldn't let go, couldn't just let herself drift away. Sometimes she lay at the water's edge in the cool sand and imagined that she was already dead. Sometimes she wished very hard that it was so.

Everything hurt. Her head, her knuckles, every strand of hair. She curled up on the chaise longue in the sun, wrapped herself in a quilt and closed her eyes. She smelled the salt in the air, the fishy water and imagined herself floating, floating away to the middle of the ocean. She squeezed her eyes shut tight against the sun, covered her head with a sweater that smelled of dust and damp. She didn't know why she felt like this, why nothing sounded like fun and nothing mattered. Being alive felt like being dead.

She listened to the crash of the waves against the shore, heard the whistle of the midday train from a few miles away and fell into a light sleep, a dream of her mother waiting for her in a train station after a long trip where she was crammed in a seat with three other people, one very old woman and two men. There was a terrible smell, like too many hot bodies, and a half-full Coke bottle on the floor full of blue-winged flies. The light inside the train got darker and darker. People began to moan and complain. Flynn looked up at the conductor, who was in almost all of her dreams lately. He caught Flynn's eye in the rearview mirror and smiled. His teeth were black and looked like they'd been put in upside down and in the wrong places. She saw tiny faces in them. Just last night he'd sung Spanish songs to her, love songs, and turned the leaves on the trees into parrots to make her laugh. Now this.

Anna didn't know there were so many people in the town—all of whom now seemed to be assembling in her living room in brightly colored clumps. Violet was here, in a typical strange outfit of three skirts, a Shetland sweater, and army boots, and Elmer Thibbodeux III, who went by Tripp, the pharmacist whose father and grandfather owned the drugstore that was now in his hands. Each generation of Thibbodeux druggists, in Anna's view, looked more like used car salesmen. Tripp was hugely fat, an epicurean with delicate hands and a penchant for seaweed facials at the—inferior— salon in the center of town. He didn't care who knew about his skin vanity, the assortment of lotions and unguents in his bathroom (on the sly he dated the facialist's mother, who of course broadcast the quantities of money spent on skin-care treatments). The only visible difference, as far as Anna could tell, between a small town like this one now and fifty years ago lay in what people were willing to reveal; Tripp's father, if he'd had such preferences, would never let it be known that he had forty kinds of body lotion.

"Hey, hey," the tall man in the corner yelled, as he had every time a new guest walked in. He was somebody's nephew; Anna couldn't remember whose. He was about fifty, well over six and a half feet, and held a pizza box in his lap. He was, Anna guessed, a borderline case, with an I.Q. of about sixty or seventy. "I'm Asa, but people call me Toot, and I'm a palindrome," he said, looking up at a group of gay men who had just come in.

"Oh yeah?" one of them said. "Are you out of the closet yet?"

Asa looked up with his slightly crossed eyes, his chin slick with saliva. "I brought pizza. Is this a potluck? I jerk off too much. Huh."

Anna watched her living room fill. The party hadn't been underway long enough for the locals to mix with the gay crowd, who were showing up in astonishing numbers; Anna had no idea Jack had so many friends. Gay people liked parties. Was that too much of a stereotype? The gifts they brought, too, were mounding toward the ceiling. Jack himself was gorgeous tonight in a tuxedo he'd brought from the city, an Armani sharkskin left over from his other life as a rich investments partner. The tux was newly retailored for him and made his thinness not less noticeable, but intentional-looking somehow. With padding and reseaming the tailor had expertly restructured the jacket so Jack's slight camel's hump was nearly invisible. His sparse blond hair was combed and gelled so it shone. He looked, Anna thought, like a Renaissance angel; his straight, columnar body designed to receive the lights of heaven. He'd never looked better or healthier in the time she'd known him. Jack stood in a group of men, some of whom, inexplicably, were in costume. Anna counted three Marilyn Monroes, one Roy Rogers, and a very good Judy Garland—a handsome young man who had Judy down to the thick fringe of lashes and the sleepy, half-lidded languor of intoxication. His hips were as narrow as a girl's in the gold lamé gown. He was the one who'd brought what looked like a huge painting. It was wrapped in Christmas paper printed with demonic-looking elves. He'd left a red imprint of lips on Jack's cheek.

Anna circulated through the crowd toward the bar, a little anxious that Marvin and Greta hadn't shown up yet. Greta had said she was getting an early start out of Boston; Anna had anticipated that she'd be here before noon. Maybe there were last-minute arrangements with Lily. Marvin, too, now that she thought about it, was overdue.

Anna handed her martini glass to the bartender. Stuart was sitting in the bar area like a weary businessman with a high debt-ratio; he looked ha-rangued, anxious. "Are you supposed to be Gene Kelly?" Anna asked, nod-ding at the raincoat he was wearing.

"Excuse me?" Stuart said.

"Your raincoat."

"Oh, no," Stuart said. "I'm not in costume." He realized how ridiculous he must look, wearing this coat buttoned up and belted like the town per-vert. Then again, he was standing next to a crowd of Judy Garlands and Marilyn Monroes, the nostalgic reenactment of the Marilyns they'd all been on the Gay Pride float two years ago. Jack was at the height of both his beauty and his infidelity then, though Stuart didn't know the latter part till later. If he didn't lose his nerve, he planned to present the coat to Jack when he opened his gifts. Most of the men here—well, all—knew of Jack's ex-tracurricular love life. Stuart counted at least five in the group who had in-disputably slept with Jack at one time or another. It was important that it be a public presentation; he'd already considered and dismissed the idea of giving it to Jack in private. The most recent additions were the instructions from the tampon box Jack had modified for Flynn, the stark outline he had colored in and embellished with smiles and jewelry. This technically didn't belong in the coat that documented their life together, but it showed a newly formed side of Jack—compassion—that had begun to creep into their relationship. Not that they were officially together. Stuart didn't know. But at this moment, being with Jack was what he wanted. David had threat-ened and cajoled and issued ultimatums, so Stuart stopped calling and stopped taking David's calls. He just couldn't be back in Boston right now. One of the graduate students agreed to teach his classes for him.

He swallowed down the last of his whiskey, hoped his nervous perspiration wasn't ruining the dried flowers in the sleeves and soaking through the pages of *The Song of Solomon* pasted all around the collar. *I am my beloved's and my beloved is mine; he feedeth among the lilies.*

Two hours into the party the left side of the room had made forays toward the right, the path smoothed by alcohol, perhaps, but still, the Y2K doomsdayist Albert Cyr, who had a bunker full of canned food and bottled water, was speaking to one of the Marilyns as though they were lifelong friends, and Violet was dancing with the man dressed as Judy Garland to "I Believe in Miracles." Jack had been opening gifts for an hour and the end was nowhere in sight.

"Anna, look," Jack called to her. "Robert Mitchum's entire body of work." He held up the DVDs. "Anna will make me watch these upstairs, no doubt."

"Just the second time through. A little Mitchum goes a long way."

"I'd settle for a long Mitchum going a little way."

Anna sat on the ottoman next to Jack so she could look through the loot. Cashmere socks, three Armani shirts, an original Edward Weston photograph, CDs, a hand-carved spice rack and a family-size bottle of Vitabath body lotion and shower gel. "I didn't get near this haul when I turned fifty," Anna said.

"Fags know early on the importance of good gifts," Jack said. "You never know how long the riches will hold out. Don't you agree?" Jack said, to no one in particular. "Today an investments broker, tomorrow a viewer of daytime television and wearer of watch alarms. We're all just this side of selling Amway."

Judy Garland muscled over the huge gift—what could only be a picture or painting of some sort. Anna looked down at his feet, turned inward in the red heels. "Ready for the *Mona Lisa*?"

"What the hell is this?" Jack asked, tearing at the wrapping paper. "Oh," he said, and Anna saw an expression on his face—a recent addition to his repertoire—which she had begun to love, love to an aching degree for its authenticity. It was a look of great intensity that suggested transparency, as though he saw right to the beating heart of things. His eyes widened and crossed just the tiniest bit before dropping down and looking away. There was usually a smile that went with it. "Oh," he said again. Finally, he turned the photograph around. It was a black and white of Jack himself dressed in nothing more than a chef's hat. In his hand was a pair of barbecue tongs clenching a hamburger bun in a strategic location. He was standing at a grill, gazing full into the camera with a cheese-ball grin, surrounded by men and women with blank looks, as though there was nothing unusual going on. They were looking at the grill with open buns in their hands. Jack was breathtaking; Anna had no idea. It was clearly a staged photo meant to be comedy, Anna guessed, but people were studying it now with the solemnity that seemed more fitting for the Edward Weston print. She didn't understand the silence at first—surely a group like this wasn't offended—until Anna felt Violet come up beside her. "Huh. That's some body. Who's he?"

Anna glanced at her, then at the group around Jack who were avoiding looking at one another or the photograph.

Jack himself broke the silence. "Do you remember this, Stuart?" Jack asked. "The redneck handbook Curtis put together."

Stuart smiled, nodded. How could he forget? That was just before everything changed. He looked down at the photo of Jack, then at Jack in the flesh. It didn't look like the same man, though for his money he loved Jack's face better as it was now. Jack was tiring, Stuart saw, a certain tightness around his mouth, tension in the tilt of his head.

Stuart was nervous despite the three martinis he'd hoped would take the edge off his panic. "I have something for you," he said, getting down from the barstool. He took off the coat and laid it flat on the ottoman in front of Jack. "Ever since I've known you, you were the most exciting thing ever, like this great whirl of energy that I never wanted to be outside of. I couldn't imagine not being surrounded by you. This was the next best thing." He opened the coat, explained about the numbers from Jack's running jerseys—more for the benefit of others than for Jack—the flowers they picked together or their first date, feathers from the mourning doves that nested outside their bedroom window in California, but after a few minutes he felt people's attention beginning to wane. Stuart watched Jack's face in earnest, watched the memories come alive in his face as he touched the emblems of them. "Anyway, I give this to you with love and good wishes."

Jack looked up at him, and then away. "I am overcome. I am overwhelmed by this."

"It's just a token of our time together. A scrapbook."

"It's a work of art." He wrapped it around his shoulders. "I'll cherish this forever."

Stuart smiled. Jack kissed him, then kissed him in a way that made the other half of the room stare. Stuart pulled away, but Jack folded him close again, kissed him on the forehead, the mouth, left cheek, then right. "That is my genuflection," Jack whispered in his ear, "I worship you."

By the time Marvin showed up at about ten-thirty, Anna realized she hadn't seen Flynn for hours. She greeted Marvin at the door. A young woman—*young* young woman, nineteen maybe—stood beside him holding a giant box.

"You're way late," she said, irritation rushing in where worry had been. More than any other person in her life, past or present, Marvin had a way of knocking her off an even keel; just when their relationship seemed to be steady and workable, he pulled a stunt like this, showing up three hours late with a woman young enough to be his daughter.

"Good to see you," he said, leaning in to kiss her on the cheek. He smelled of the cold air and tobacco. "This is JoBeth." The woman peeked over the top of the box.

"This is my mother-in-law, Anna." He stepped in and dropped his luggage, took the gift from the girl. "Oh, I need to tell you. Greta called as I was leaving. Her daughter is sick, so she won't be coming in tonight. She said maybe tomorrow. She'll call you later." Disappointment and panic—she didn't know why exactly—sank through her. Something was wrong. Something felt really wrong. She would call Greta at the first possible moment.

Anna left Marvin at the door and escorted JoBeth into the living room where the party was louder, drunker, and more surreal than ever: Judy Garland, with Violet's red skirt on his head, held the giant photo of Jack overhead and had a conga line forming behind him. The line snaked around the living room to the music of Donna Summer. Jack and Stuart were still in their mushy moment, everything but the cartoon hearts above their heads. She was suddenly feeling ungenerous and tired. "There's still a lot of food left if you're hungry, and drinks, of course." To Anna's left Albert Cyr was holding Y2K doomsday court with Violet, whose visible skirt—the red one still being used as a head dress—was now a librarian brown plaid. Asa was still at his station in the corner. His hands were moving beneath the pizza box in his lap. Tripp, the druggist, who had been inspecting Jack's gifts, turned and swatted Asa on the shoulder. He was Tripp's nephew, Anna remembered. "Get your hands off your imagination, boy," Tripp said. "On top of the pizza box, where I can see them."

"I'm a palindrome," Asa said, when JoBeth swept by. Anna watched as the girl turned and bent toward him, puzzled.

Anna waited for Marvin to sidle up beside her. "I have to tell you, I'm a little irritated. You might have called to tell me you were running late, and that you were bringing a date, which by the way is disrespectful."

"Why? To whom?"

"To me. To your daughter, the reason you're supposedly here. The reason you were supposed to be here this morning, as you promised."

Anna watched Marvin's date make her way to the bar. She was exquisite, really, and she had Poppy's coloring and build, though the girl had boobs—augments, Anna decided—and wasn't quite as tall. "And what happened to the lovely Christine?"

Marvin sighed. "What happened. What always happens? Lovers are like pantyhose. Sooner or later they all run." He put his arm around Anna's shoulders. "Come on, Anna."

She didn't dare look at him. "Anna," he said again, in a tone that was patient and cajoling at the same time. Her body had always been traitorous in the presence of Marvin. She could be trembling with rage, but the minute he stood near or touched her, it was like brandy in the back of her throat, a warm and smoky fire. "Take your hand off me," she said finally.

He exhaled dramatically. "Where is my daughter?"

"She's probably hiding out somewhere. She's not much into crowds these days. I'll go find her."

"No. Wait a little while. Don't force her into this group. I'll see her after the party ends. I want you to see what I made Jack. It's something I've had high offers for. A buyer offered me a thousand for it, but I decided to give it to Jack." Anna watched as Marvin reached around JoBeth to get the oversized box, encircled her waist for an instant. He walked over to Jack, who was glowing. Stuart, too, had transformed into something wonderful-looking.

Anna had never thought much of Stuart's looks—he looked to her like an old-egg baby, the short limbs, long trunk, and flat forehead women some-times produced when they bore children in mature maternity—but now she realized that he was a handsome man. Or maybe it was the attractiveness that comes from being in love. The dancers were moving to the corners now, Petula Clarke singing "Downtown." Jack lifted a bust of clay and bronze out of the box. The side facing her was Clinton whose features Marvin distorted to look like a goat's. Half the face was bronzed, the other ordinary clay. She didn't need to see the other side to know it was a serial killer. She'd imagined he would have moved past this by now.

Anna turned away, toward the back door somebody had left open. The air streaming in smelled of the sea and of the damp cedar fencing her garden. Something else, too. Figs. The musky intimate smell of figs, though she was surely imagining that. She walked outside. It was getting very cold. Tomorrow she and Flynn would drive north, stop at a chowder place for lunch, shop for warm school clothes—Flynn was growing so quickly—and walk the beaches in the afternoon. She walked to the porch at the front of the house. Flynn wasn't here, but had been; she'd made herself a little nest on the chaise: rum-pled quilt, a scattering of record albums printed with Poppy's name in her childish handwriting, a nearly full glass of Kool-Aid, and—in the path of the porch light—Elisabeth Kubler-Ross's book about dying.

Anna sat. Something wasn't right. She pressed the blanket to her face, inhaled her granddaughter's scent. It smelled a little sweaty, sour with ill-ness or fear. An animal moved at the corner of her vision. She turned, but saw it was just the wind, not a living creature, moving the leaves and shrubbery. There was something else. A presence, a feeling of being ob-served. Anna walked to the edge of the porch, squinted into the darkness. An insect brushed against her cheek. She smelled roses and lime shaving cream. Anna rarely thought of sex, even more rarely wanted it, but there was something about the night, with its wintry air and the emotions swim-ming around in her—nostalgia, anger, and, inexplicably, fear—that made her want it now. With no one in particular, without any special tenderness, or, God forbid, false expressions of love, just a healthy strong man who could reawaken her body's responses. Once again, she heard something rustling in the bushes beside the house. "Marvin?" she called, but there was no one there.

*

Flynn sat on the railroad tracks waiting for the midnight train. She felt like she was still stuck in a dream, only half aware of what she was about to do. This was best, she knew, because she had seen the future last night in her dreams and it wasn't something she wanted to be a part of: Jack would die soon, so would her grandmother. Last night and early into this morning, she saw the rest of her life. She would marry and live in France, but it would be an unhappy marriage. She would be an artist creating things in blue glass, but even this would not make her happy. She would have a son, but not a daughter, and, most terrifying of all, she would develop a disease in her forties that would slowly paralyze her and confine her to a wheelchair long before she would actually die. She would be completely alone, her son turned against her by her ex-husband, under the care of a nurse who didn't treat her very well because she didn't have to; Flynn couldn't speak but even if she could, no one was there to listen. There were wonderful things before this happened, but not so many to compel her to stay. She knew what would happen after she did it: they would be angry with her, just as in the dream last night her mother was angry when she saw Flynn and said, *what are you doing here, you're not supposed to be here*, and they would put her with the angels for a while, make her sit among them but not be able to experience the joy they had, the place where every living thing had a voice. Her mother was dead, Flynn was sure of this. She'd been dreaming it for weeks.

The angels had come to her last night and showed her things, warned her that time was no better healer of wounds than mercy. They told her in the world of spirits time was measured only by completion, interruption, and violence. She would be sent back, and her next life would be harder but more rewarding. The punishment for what she was about to do was that she had to be in her father's group again, as his mother, which was far worse than being his daughter. He was moving in the wrong direction, toward the dark and not the light, and he had many more lifetimes to learn his lessons. His had been a soul greatly admired: he'd lived twice as a beggar, which was greatly esteemed because it taught people charity and compassion. Before that, when he was new, he was one of the extremely rare beings formed from two separate places: the realm of the angelic and the realm of the human-divine. Sometimes, though, the angels got jealous—they were imperfect, too—and they did bad things. In her dream last night, she saw and understood everything.

Before bodies, souls had colors. Her father had the blue of the angels swirling through the yellow-white of the human-divine. The angelic part of him sang along with the blue flowers, the bluebells and violets, a silvery wet sound in the key of C. Perfect C was what the angels were pitched to. An important task of angels was to escort all souls to the birth tunnel, one on each side, their bodies acting like skin to protect the new being from the dirt and darkness of the human world. There was a small space, a gap, where they had to be extra careful, and that was the border between these two places. This was the place of nowhere. The time of nothing. The place where no heavenly bodies could rule, and no bodies that were human could stay. Underground creatures dwelled here and were hateful.

With Marvin, one of the jealous angels moved just a fraction of an inch, and darkness rushed in. That angel had received the worst possible punishment: it was torn from the angelic realm and forced to become a human spirit. And, even worse, Flynn learned in her dream, the spirit wouldn't be blessed with forgetfulness, it would always remember in a vague yearning way the blue and white happiness of the angels' special place. That's how bad it was to do something unkind and unloving to another being, Flynn was told by a man in her dream. Angels feared one thing and that was becoming human: the worst possible situation for them was to be encased in small spaces like human bodies that demanded to be fed and satisfied. The angel had been Anna, and now she, too, was bound to Marvin. The three of them, Flynn saw in her dream, would be back in the same group, with Marvin and Anna as husband and wife, and Flynn as Marvin's mother. Poppy would be a mentally ill mail carrier who poisoned all the neighborhood dogs. She, a he, in the next lifetime, would go to jail for doing terrible things to children where he—she—would be murdered after ten years. A terrible war was coming and Flynn was to be a soldier in charge of a settlement camp after the fighting ended. Her life would be lonely and she would be blamed and hated for a food shortage and for enforcing laws—who could bear children, and who couldn't; executing people who committed hate crimes—that were designed for the continuation and improvement of the species. In the world to come, only kindness mattered. She would be shot to death eventually, but Flynn would do good in that future lifetime, fulfill her purpose.

In the distance Flynn heard the faraway whistle of the train. It was time, and now she was really frightened, not of dying, but of getting it wrong about being forgiven. Hell was where the unforgiven went. Flynn hadn't seen hell, but she knew there was such a place. This, where she lived now, might be hell. She walked down to the track and lay down. Two Native American men lay beside her. One of them showed her how to make herself small so it wouldn't hurt at all. But something or someone wouldn't let her do this. When the train was close enough so that she could feel the vibrations in the track, she half sat up, about to change her mind. She was so afraid! No one in her dream had told her how afraid she would be; the angels told her there was nothing to fear. She wished she didn't know the things that she did, wished she couldn't see so far or so clearly. What if she was wrong about everything? What if she was just a psycho mental freak like kids at school said?

Lining the track now were all sorts of people—not anybody she recognized—who were staring at her. She didn't know why they would be interested in her or appear glad to see her. *Watch my eyes,* an old man said. Flynn looked at him, and realized he was her grandfather. At least, he looked like the photograph her grandma had on her night table. She kept her eyes on his, felt the Native American men push in closer to her, their soft leather shirts like another person between her skin and theirs. This is wrong, she thought. I don't want to do this. But now she couldn't move and the train was so loud she heard it through every bone in her body. She didn't feel anything, and just at the last minute, when the train was above her she saw a terrifying creature with red eyes hanging on to the underside, a creature from the place of nowhere, the time of nothing. It was like a badger only with a human face and very very angry—the Indian men squeezed against her so hard with such firm pressure that she popped right off the tracks. Now she would have to go home. Now she would have to finish out her life unhappy and crippled and lonely. She began to cry, because she was stuck in this dark dream, this thick darkness and clumsy body of a twelve-year-old girl when she'd been so close to being free of it all. She turned her head to the left and saw the lights from her grandmother's house. She heard singing from somewhere, voices talking with echoes in them. There was a vibration in her chest, a rattling in her and she

knew she probably broke some bones because there was a rattling and a vibration, now moving up to the top of her head and causing a terrible pressure, a pain worse than anything she imagined possible.

Slip out, a woman said. Flynn looked down, saw a pair of red shoes and
a lawn with croquet wickets. *Slip out,* a woman's voice said again, *just like
your body is a sweater you're taking off, and follow me.*

Flynn didn't have any idea how to do this. She couldn't move anything
but her eyes. She felt the waiting presence of this woman, her grandfather
and the others. She had to learn it before they could help her. She watched
as the woman walked toward the wickets. They grew tall as she neared
them, high enough that they cleared her head, then shrank back down
when she passed through. Flynn watched as the woman's red shoes got farther and farther away. She was moving in the direction of the sun, walked
until the white light surrounded her and made her a shadow against it.
Flynn again felt the humming in her head, now worse as she looked at the
light, which she thought might be some kind of food, because in her body
were thousands of buzzing mosquitoes frantic to get at it, so many of them
that they pushed her head out to twice, three, four times its size until it ex-
ploded with a large pop like a gunshot. After that she felt better, could take
a deep breath again. She was going to be okay. She stood up, turned toward
her grandma's house. Turned the other way. Turned back again. There was
nothing there. She looked in every direction: nothing. The croquet wickets
popped up one by one, becoming arches of light. A red soccer ball rolled
toward her. She kicked it, then followed its rolling path; it stopped at a field
of bright green grass where very tall women were wearing shoes the color
of cherries and playing soccer.

Am I dead? Flynn asked the woman, who only smiled, and took her
hand. Her grandfather appeared suddenly on her other side. They began
to walk together. Flynn thought of Anna suddenly, of Jack, and instantly
she was at her grandmother's house, standing with her grandfather
watching Anna sitting on the porch looking out at the sea. Anna snapped
her head around when Flynn moved in close.

Can she see me? Flynn asked her grandfather.

No, but she knows we're here. Kiss her goodbye, she'll be with us soon.

Flynn moved in close, closer. But she couldn't get close enough,
couldn't get Anna to see her. Her grandfather turned her a little to the left,

so she was positioned beside Anna at a forty-five-degree angle, and told her to call her grandmother, call her name. Flynn did so, and Anna turned to answer her. They were on the beach together, walking in raw weather and looking forward to chowder and warm sweaters.

I've been so worried about you, Anna said. Where did you go?

Don't worry. I'm with my grandfather, and new friends. The flowers grow really fast here. We're waiting for you.

I want you to go back to school, Anna said. You've missed so many days you'll never catch up.

I can't go back to school, Anna, I'm dead. Flynn felt her grandmother's shock, and it was so forceful that it pushed Flynn half a mile away. She waved to her, turned, and felt the sand rise up in a giant wall against her back and push against her firmly, not in a mean way, but in a way that told her she no longer belonged. She walked into a swirl of blue and white and looked down to see her feet in red shoes.

Anna sat up in bed sweating, heart pounding from her nightmare. She walked into Flynn's room, and found it was still empty, her bed untouched. Marvin said he'd talked to her on the beach, just after the party ended. He said she told him she'd be back shortly. She checked Jack's room, the bathrooms, downstairs.

She went into the guestroom where Marvin and his girlfriend were sleeping. The woman was so little that at first she thought it was Flynn entangled in his arms. Anna shook him awake. "Something is wrong. Get up. I can't find Flynn anywhere."

"Okay," he said. "I'm coming."

The two of them searched the house again, then walked in opposite directions on the beach. Anna remembered the train tracks, how she'd found Flynn there several times, and turned in that direction. It was still an hour or two before dawn, but there was a full moon, enough light to see outlines and shadows.

She reached the crest of the hill overlooking the tracks, but didn't go any farther. She called Flynn's name several times. If Flynn were anywhere in the vicinity she would have answered. Anna turned to go, but then stopped and looked around again. There was something here, her granddaughter was here, or had been here. The air felt thick, a lacy humidity clinging to her skin. "Flynn?" she yelled again, her heart pounding. She peered down and scanned the tracks. The times Anna had found her here she'd been in this spot exactly, either on this knoll or—twice—sitting on the tracks directly beneath it. She started down the hill.

We don't want your grandma to see you this way, Hugh said to Flynn, as he made the ground swell with tree roots to trip Anna and make her fall. Anna's ankle buckled and twisted beneath her. *I'm sorry, sweetheart.*

"Marvin?" Anna shouted, hobbling back in the direction of the house. Her ankle was useless; it wouldn't hold her weight. She called him three times before he answered.

"Where are you?" he yelled, and she could barely hear him over the crash of the waves and the high wind. He got to her finally. "Did you find her?"

"No. But I fell. I twisted my ankle, and I can't walk. I need you to go and get Stuart's Jeep and drive back to get me."

He picked her up as if she weighed nothing at all.

"This isn't necessary. You can't carry me the whole way back. If you'll just go and get the Jeep—"

"It's no trouble," he said.

They fell silent. Anna closed her eyes, breathing in the salty wet cool smell of the sand and the creatures the tide brought in.

Back at the house he set her on the couch. "Is it broken? Do I need to take you to the hospital?"

She palpated her ankle, already swollen to twice its normal size. Nothing broken. "No. I tore some ligaments, it looks like. I just need some ice and aspirin."

"Where do you think she went?" Marvin asked, bringing in a bowl of ice and some towels.

"When did you see her? What time was it when you talked to her?"

"Around twelve-thirty or one."

"I think something is very wrong. Something has happened to her." She felt all the emotion in her give way. Everything was suddenly working itself loose in her, like old paper that crumbled at the slightest touch. "I want you to call the police. I want you to go up there and wake Jack and Stuart and whoever else is staying here, and I want you to cover every square inch of this place."

In the end, Anna was so hysterical that Marvin took her to Violet's house. He'd never seen her like this, as though whatever bad news she thought was coming had already come. She'd protested, screamed at him that she wasn't going anywhere, but he just picked her up and drove her the short distance to Violet's place. "You'll be the first to know," Marvin said. "I want you to stay here and relax."

Violet's dogs jumped up on the sofa beside Anna. It occurred to her that she hadn't seen Flynn's dog all day. "I'll come back or call in an hour or two with an update. Okay?" He tucked a blanket around her. "I think you're overreacting, I think she's just wandered off somewhere," he said. "Everything will be just fine."

Marvin went out, rejoined Jack and Stuart in their Jeep. He was more worried about Flynn than he let on to Anna. He didn't think, as she did, that Flynn's oddness was indicative of anything more than a highly active imagination, but he did worry she'd inherited her mother's sadness, that, young as she was she didn't yet know how to handle it. Poppy had had problems with depression her whole life, but after Flynn's birth, she had a postpartum spell that her doctor labeled a psychotic break. The Chicken Littles, Poppy called them, a sensation that the world was crashing down, the sky falling, and the shade and intensity of her mood deepening with each episode.

"I don't think there's any reason for us to drive up and down the streets," Jack said, looking at Marvin in the rearview mirror. "I doubt very much that Flynn is in the center of town, which we can search on foot anyway." Marvin saw the lines around Jack's eyes, his trembling hands.

"Do you have an idea where she might be?"

Jack nodded. "Every time she's been missing she's been at the railroad tracks or on the beach. There's a little rocky outcropping about a mile from here, a little cave where she hangs out sometimes. I think one of us should check the beach cave and the other two the tracks. I'm going to drive away, though, because Anna is in there watching every move we make."

Jack parked on a side street and the three of them got out. Marvin started to follow him in the direction of the tracks. "No. Stuart and I will go this way. You go check the cave."

"It makes more sense if I come with you," Marvin said. "I don't know where this cave is."

"I'll come with you to the tracks," Stuart said to Marvin. "Jack can go check the cave."

"No," Jack said. "Please just do this my way." Marvin and Stuart looked at him the same way they had at Anna, like he was a shrill hysterical grandma. But Anna was right; Jack felt it too. Something was really wrong. He'd had a disaster dream last night, too, though he hadn't told Anna this. He and Flynn were riding on a Ferris wheel and they were both very unhappy. She embraced him, straddled his lap and said, *now we are heart to heart.* She kissed him. *I'll call you. Don't forget. Don't forget,* was what she kept repeating, and the next thing he knew he was on the ground, standing in a crowd looking at her body. He was prepared for the worst. He didn't want her father to see her if God forbid something awful had happened.

"You can't miss it," he said to Marvin. "If you walk in a straight line you'll run right into it. It's an outcropping that's in the shape of a dunce's hat."

He and Stuart set off for the tracks. "Why didn't you want me to go with him?" Stuart asked. "And where is this cave? I've never seen any cave."

"There is no cave." He buttoned up his sweater, pulled the navy watch cap out of his back pocket and snugged it down around his ears. "She's dead," Jack said.

Stuart stopped. "What?"

"I dreamed it."

"Oh," Stuart said, with a nervous laugh. "You and Anna both, the witches of Eastwick."

Jack took Stuart's hand, laced his fingers with Stuart's. His legs got heavier and heavier as they neared the knoll of the hill. He stopped, his vision going black for a second. He squeezed Stuart's hand tighter.

"What? What's wrong?" Stuart said.

"Go down there. Go and look around the tracks." He took a deep breath, the serrated edge of a knife in his lungs, the air hot and cutting. He watched as Stuart walked first one way, then the other, stepping carefully over the railroad ties.

He came back up a few minutes later, laughed a little. "You can go home and tell Anna not to quit her day job. Her prophetic gifts have failed. Thank God." He squeezed Jack's hand.

Jack sank down onto the cool grass to catch his breath and to wait for his heartbeat to slow. He drew his knees up and rested his head there. Anna had probably worked him into this state. Her hysteria was contagious. Stuart stood beside him, rubbed his shoulders and neck in slow circles. The minute he felt himself relax was when his vision caught on something down below, about fifty feet away. Something black and small. "What is that?" Jack said, and pointed. Stuart followed his gaze, squinted. "A rock."

"Are you sure it's a rock?"

"Yep." He continued his massage. Jack grabbed his hand. "Go see. Go and check." He watched as Stuart neared the object, watched as he jumped a little then stood still for what seemed like both a second and an eternity. Jack rose and slipped down the hill, nearly falling. Stuart swept Jack in his arms. "Don't, Jack. Don't go any farther." Stuart turned Jack to face the opposite direction.

"What is it? What is that thing? That rock?" Jack said.

"It's a shoe. It's her shoe."

"How do you know it's hers? It could be any shoe at all." Jack started down toward it. "Let me go and see."

Stuart grabbed his arm but he pulled away.

At first he felt relieved. It *was* her shoe, but it was just a shoe, not Flynn. This didn't mean anything—in fact it was probably a good sign. He took a deep breath, stared down at the twigs and branches lying all around it, the glistening pools of rusty rain. Stuart came up behind him. "Let's not jump to every bad conclusion there is," he said. "It's just Flynnie's shoe. She's always kicking them off and leaving them somewhere. She's probably out walking through the hills."

"Jack," Stuart said. "Let's go. We need to go."

"Why? What's the matter with you? She's around here. Her shoe is here. She's around here somewhere."

Stuart took Jack's hand, tried to lead him up the hill.

Jack pushed him away with a forced laugh. "Now you've caught the hysteria flu. It's just a shoe. Flynn?" he called. "Flynn!"

"Jack, I'm telling you we need to go. I am insisting."

"What's the matter with you? Let's start looking." Stuart took him by the shoulders, squared him so he was facing the evidence. "What is that? What do you see?"

"A shoe. A little black shoe."

"What else? What's inside it?"

"A tree branch. A branch from a birch tree."

"Where?" He looked down, then looked at Jack. He didn't know how you could tell if someone was in shock, but he figured this must be one sign: A refusal or denial to see what was there. Overlooking something. Changing it. Making a birch branch out of bone. He let Jack look around for five minutes and then persuaded him that she'd probably gotten cold and walked home, was back at the house, snug in her bed. "We should go back, before they send someone out to find us. Okay? Okay, Jack?"

"Can she get there with just one shoe?"

"Yes," Stuart said.

Somehow, he didn't know how, perhaps because Jack was already exhausted from the party and the exertion of worry, Stuart persuaded him that Flynn was asleep in her room. As Jack stood at the back door taking off his muddy boots, Stuart pretended to cock his head and listen. "I hear her up there."

"You do?"

He nodded. "I'll go up and check. Make some tea, okay?"

He waited on the stairs until he heard the clanging of the kettle, the match being struck to tag the burner, then went back into the kitchen. "She's sleeping like an angel," Stuart said.

"She is?"

He nodded.

"God, what a relief. Tomorrow's she's going to get the lecture of her life."

"Why don't you go on up to bed and I'll go fetch Anna."

After what felt like an eternity, Jack made his slow way up the stairs, Stuart close behind him. By some miracle, Jack didn't open Flynn's door to look in. He went directly to his own bed and was asleep within minutes. Stuart kissed him, then went out and started Anna's Volvo.

Anna sat outside to wait. She didn't know how long she'd been here, propped against the stone pillar on Violet's porch, watching. Her eyes seemed to open wider and wider. She stared at the line of spruces, the very first edge of dawn visible through their branches. She saw birds fluttering in the trees—owls or hawks or chickadees, she didn't know. Then a lot of them, hundreds of them, bending the branches down with their weight. But it was only the wind doing that, making her think it was birds. She'd been here so long. Hours. Maybe they'd found Flynn and they'd forgotten to fetch her. She pressed her cheek against the cool stone and started to dream. She heard her granddaughter's voice, then a whole party of voices. The stone against her cheek became her own hand as she propped her elbow up on the bar, listening to the commotion of the party, the high-pitched voice of the man dressed as Judy Garland, the deep baritone of Marvin, the music of Petula Clarke. "Go find Flynn," she said.

I found her. She's right here with me, a voice—Stuart's?—said from her left.

Anna turned and saw her granddaughter, muddy and rumpled, but fine. "Where have you been? Do you realize how much we've all worried? What's the matter with you?"

Flynn wore a great sorrow on her face.

Flynn said something that Anna couldn't make out. Anna felt the crush of people all around her, the party moving in from both sides, behind and in front of her, the bartender frantic with the mob of people waiting for drinks.

Anna kept her eyes just on Flynn, who looked at her as though trying to memorize her, the look Poppy used to get when Anna and Hugh sent her away to summer camp. The throng of people got thicker and thicker around her, the voices louder and more incomprehensible. There were people here she did not invite. A man with hot angry breath demanding a cocktail, then another and another. She lost sight of Flynn through the crowd. Anna tried to push her way out of the mob but couldn't. All these costumed men! Two men directly in front of her turned in opposite directions at the same time. In the space of their parting bodies, she saw Flynn walking away from her. Flynn turned around once, as though Anna had called her—had she? In the distance was a mountain range. "Where are you going?" Anna asked.

Don't worry, Flynn said. *I need to get out of this storm. I'm going up to where it's warm and calm.* She nodded toward the pink peak. *High up, above the thunder.*

"Don't go," Anna pleaded, but her granddaughter was already a dark dot on the face of the mountain. Anna watched Flynn until she reached the crest then disappeared into a bright white light. But now the light was coming down, into her eyes, glaring and blinding.

Stuart cut the headlights when he saw Anna squinting in his direction. She watched him as he walked up, but she didn't seem to register his presence. He bent down to her. She was so cold; where was her coat, where was that crazy woman who was supposed to keep Anna company?

"Are those doves?" she asked.

"What?"

"That cooing sound. Are they doves?"

He put his arms around her. "I'm afraid I have some really bad news for you," he said.

Anna's attention snapped back. Stuart's face came into sharp focus. "I know," she said. "I know it."

FOURTEEN

GETTING THROUGH THE NIGHT

Anna heard them all downstairs, Jack and Stuart, Marvin and Greta, the neighbors who streamed in with covered dishes and casseroles. She never understood the gathering in that went with grief, the circling of the wagons around the injured and the wounded. She hadn't left her room much in the two weeks since that night, hadn't really eaten or slept except in snatches. She took her tea and a blanket to the balcony off her bedroom. In the distance, she saw a black dog running along the water's edge, but even from here she knew it was too small and frenetic to be Flynn's dog, which had been missing since the night of the accident. A man came up behind it and threw a tennis ball into the water. She looked toward Violet's house, saw the smoke from her chimney. Anna visited Violet frequently, felt secure and protected in Violet's presence. She went over the first time a few days after Flynn's service to ask if Violet had seen Flynn's dog. She hadn't, but the two of them searched the entire length of beach, and in the following days, the woods and acreage around their properties. Violet had put posters around town, slightly unnerving in their size and captions: BABY JESUS IS MISSING followed by Anna's phone number. Anna didn't have any photographs of the dog, so the posters had to rely on descriptions— but Violet often forgot to include them, or they were so vague that it wasn't always clear that a dog was the subject.

Anna had had calls from every Bible-thumping nut in two counties, most of whom offered to help her find her personal savior and not the eponymous Newfoundland. The day Anna had stopped answering the phone was after a call came early one morning from a very pleasant-sounding man. "Hello, Anna?" a rich baritone had asked. "Are you the woman looking for Baby Jesus?" She said that she was. The man proceeded to quote the Gospel of St. John to her, and when Anna interrupted, as she had with the last six callers, to explain that it was a dog, not salvation, she was looking for, the man started to berate her.

"You're a whore who is going to burn in hell," he said. "You live in sin, and allow those who live with you to commit unnatural acts. God took the precious and the innocent from you." Anna hung up and unplugged the phone, laughing for the first time in what felt like years. It could have been worse. Flynn could have named the dog Elvis, and the sightings would have rung in from here to Graceland.

She turned to go back inside. It was stretching into late afternoon now, which made her relax a little. Only in the cover of darkness did she feel anything akin to peace—not peace so much as stillness, which, compared to what she felt most of the day—fiercely angry or the kind of sadness that felt to her like she was drowning from the inside out—was enough for now.

Most of the time she was up all night. While the house and town and world slept, she played her cello, read movie magazines, and took a bath until midnight with a glass of Scotch until midnight. If she could bend her concentration around two celebrity magazines and play another hour of Brahms, then she could often get through the rest of the night. As it was, her attention didn't usually hold out and she ended up just sitting up in bed and staring into space, not watching the television droning on in front of her.

Lighting a cigarette, she sat by the window to watch the dark draw the last of the light in. Well, it was too late to go to Violet's now, too late to drag her out again to look for a lost pet. Violet, anyway, kept her eyes and ears open when she walked her own dogs. If Baby Jesus were around, she and her dogs would know. Now was Anna's hardest time of day, the twilit hour of loneliness and panic. Everything in recent imagination centered on her granddaughter's milestones: high school graduation, college, and the friends Flynn would make. Boyfriends, Flynn's wedding, Flynn's own children. This, more than the sight of the dead girl, was what made her faint at Flynn's memorial service. Anna's whole future seemed erased, as if she was already dead. As terrible as it was to lose Flynn, it was very nearly as terrible to have to suddenly redefine, for the second time in her life, who she was.

There was a knock at her door, and then Greta walked in with a tray of food.

"Howdy," Anna said.

Greta sat on the edge of Anna's bed, picked up one of the movie-star magazines. Greta came in to Anna's bedroom every night, after Lily was in bed. Sometimes an hour or more would pass before either one of them spoke. Greta usually read or sewed if Anna didn't feel like talking. What Anna appreciated most was that Greta didn't try to draw her out, insist that she eat, or, God forbid, try to cheer her up. Only once did Greta give her a piece of advice: "You should try to cry, Anna. It'll help." Anna agreed, but she was afraid once the tears started coming, they'd never stop.

Anna peeked under the foil around the plate. "Lasagna?"

"Of course," Greta said, and laughed a little. "The fifth one this week."

"The food of the grieving everywhere," Anna said, and covered it back up. "People mean well. I do appreciate that. What's everybody doing downstairs?"

Greta looked up. "Jack is organizing the kitchen, cleaning up. Marvin and Stuart are still on the phone. They're calling Bologna, I think."

"Any luck?" Anna unwrapped the plate, took a bite of the lasagna, then put the fork down. Marvin had been on a phone mission to find Poppy. It was good for him, she knew; good to have a task that kept grief at bay for at least a few hours every day. Stuart spoke a little Italian, so he was serving as the translator. "Anyway, I thought she was living in London. Why are they calling Italy?"

"I'm not sure. Somebody gave them a lead that she was in Italy."

"What a complete mess. How did I have a daughter like this? She's a complete disaster. God forbid she checks in once in a while or calls her own daughter on her birthday and Christmas. God forbid she gives the child even a little reason to hang on and to stay alive. The bitch. I'd kill her if I could. I'd shoot her dead through the heart for what she did."

"Anna," Greta said, setting the magazine down.

"Flynn never stopped asking if Poppy was coming home. If she had called just once, just twice a year. If she had sent any kind of message, my girl might be alive right now."

Greta let her rant, then said quietly, "Poppy had nothing to do with what Flynn did. She's not responsible. But of course you know that." She poured a glass of Scotch, handed it over. Anna took a big gulp, then a deep breath. "You don't have to stay with me, Greta. I'm miserable. I'm terrible to be around right now."

"I know," she said. "But it's all right. I don't mind. Anger is a good thing."

Anna sipped her drink, and picked up the phone on her night table. She heard Stuart's halting Italian and Marvin's murmuring encouragement, the hiss and crackle of static. She hung up. "I wanted to call Violet," Anna said.

Greta looked up from the quilt pattern she was studying. "What do you need? Is there anything I can do?"

"I want the dog back. I want that stupid, drooling pet. It's not fair. It's just a dog I'm asking for." She sat beside Greta, picked up a pieced square of the quilt Greta had begun. Pastels with bunny appliqués. "Is this for Lily?"

"Well, no," Greta said, and looked down and blushed.

Anna stared at her friend, incredulous. "No way. You told me you weren't seeing anyone."

Greta shook her head. "I'm not. And I'm not," she said, arcing her hand over her belly. "But I'm hoping to be. I want another child." She looked up at Anna. "I mean, you knew that. This is what I've always wanted. Nothing has changed."

Anna nodded. "Nothing has changed. You're lucky. Consider yourself lucky."

Greta put the work in her sewing bag. "I'm sorry, Anna. I didn't even think you would notice what I was doing. I didn't mean to be insensitive."

Anna opened a bottle of mineral water. "No. You're not. Don't apologize." She glanced at the clock. Nine. Which meant she couldn't start reading magazines now, since she'd have nothing to get her to the midnight hour. Already she'd read all the latest issues of movie magazines, knew more about Jennifer Aniston and Brad Pitt than most teenagers. She'd have to move on to home and garden magazines next, though that was risky; only the news of Hollywood felt safe, remote from ordinary life.

The day they buried Flynn, it had rained and warmed up enough to melt the snow. The little chapel at the edge of town was beautiful, lovely and forgotten in the way of small-town churches. She and Marvin went back to it later, just the two of them, and sat in the darkened room, the morning light streaming through the stained glass. "I wish I believed in God," was all he said. "Do you?"

Anna had shrugged, said not really. "Not a benevolent one anyway." She stared up at the stained-glass angels, the cerulean blues and lemon yellows. "Is this my fault? Is it my doing?" she said, and when he asked what she meant, she said she didn't know; she was barely aware that she'd spoken. Marvin slid over on the bench and draped his arm around her, sat so close that it felt to Anna like they were one body.

By two in the morning, Anna had long since run through her late-night rituals. Wide awake, she went downstairs to look for something to read, prowled through the scant offerings on the shelves in what had been her husband's library, but was now just storage space. She rifled through boxes. Medical journals. Patient charts and long-expired drug samples. She slipped one of Hugh's old lab coats over her nightgown. The cloth felt warm, as though he'd just taken it off, still redolent with his scent, though Anna knew she was imagining all this.

She flipped through a textbook devoted to kidneys, fascinated by the gory overlays of the pictures, the grisliness of disease and the defects of birth. She'd always appreciated the kidneys, their work ethic, found them aesthetically pleasing: like two halves of a heart separated, or two autonomous islands filtering the fleet of toxins that washed up. This, along with *Gray's Anatomy* would have to do for bedtime reading until the next issue of *People* came out. And this one: a slim volume on diseases and malformations of the metatarsal arch—truly fascinating. She didn't remember Hugh being especially interested in feet, but here were whole stacks of clippings about the specialization of the seventy-two bones that made up the foot's architecture.

Anna dug out Hugh's microscope and found the blood and histology slides she'd prepared or collected over the years. There were a dozen or so devoted entirely to Poppy, her viruses and pathologies over the years. There was no medical reason she'd saved Poppy's—or anyone's—samples, just as there was no good reason why people hoarded photographs—it was a matter of preference, whether you wanted the external image or the body's internal narrative. What sagas in a heart histology, what poetry in the bones. She pulled out one marked, "Poppy, May 1st, 1971," a slide prepared for blood-typing. Her daughter was two weeks old, and Anna, in a postpartum haze, had convinced herself the hospital had given her the wrong baby; how else to explain her lack of maternal feelings? And here was Poppy in 1990 with anemia, her red cells as misshapen as rotten tomatoes. And this, Anna's favorite, a highly involved staph infection, circa 1978, after Poppy's return from summer camp in the Berkshires. Anna slid it under the lens, lost herself in the overgrowth of cells as dense as a Serrault painting. She stared at the slide until she imagined she was part of it, a tiny creature camping in the white field, nestled on the icy, jagged edge of a basophil, the dark cocoon of its nucleus as inviting as sleep.

In Anna's desk drawer were a half dozen slides she'd prepared when Flynn was sick, or when Anna wanted to check her white count when mono had spread among the children in Flynn's dance class. But Anna couldn't face those reminders of Flynn just yet. She picked up the textbooks and carried them back upstairs.

At six o'clock Anna woke up and knew where the dog was. She'd dreamed of the quarry, of the place she and Flynn went swimming the day Anna took her out of school. The dream was a reenactment of the afternoon exactly, except that when she turned to look at Flynn floating in the water beside her, it was the dog instead. She went downstairs, grabbed her car keys and, on second thought, walked over to Violet's to see if she was awake. Violet opened the door before Anna knocked, as though she were expecting her.

"Good morning," Violet said. "I have lemon and blueberry muffins, the last of the berries I picked in August."

Anna walked in and took her coat off. "I think the dog is still alive. I think I would know if he were dead, and I don't feel it. He's out there somewhere."

"I'm sure he's alive," Violet said, and handed her a mug of coffee. "He's grieving. He doesn't want to return without the lass. He'll be back."

Anna watched the early sun glint off the copper pots on the wall. Violet's kitchen was cozy. Anna settled into a chintz easy chair next to the enormous table thinking she had no appetite, then ate four of the muffins and drank three cups of coffee. Violet settled beside her in one of the straight-back chairs. She had two summer skirts layered over a pair of thick corduroy pants. "I'm going to drive out to the quarry. I had a dream the dog might be there. Do you want to come with me?"

"Certainly," Violet said. "But it's early yet. Why don't you tarry here for an hour, rest, while I take my dogs out for their morning prayers?"

"Oh, I can't rest, especially after all this coffee. I'll walk the dogs with you," Anna said, but then she closed her eyes and the next thing she knew Violet was returning with the dogs. Violet had covered her with an afghan and a fire was going in the fireplace. Anna had taken such naps at Violet's a few times; something about the house or the comforting presence of Violet always made an hour of sleep here worth five in her own home.

"It's a fine bright day. Cold, but sparkling," Violet said. "I took the liberty of going next door to tell your people what we were up to."

"Thank you," Anna said, and rose to find her coat. Her limbs felt leaden, fatigue settling like fine pollen.

Greta was packing up her and Lilly's things when Anna got back. She knew Greta couldn't stay beyond the weekend—Greta had a new job as a consultant with the school district, Lily had school—but the sight of anybody leaving these days pained her.

"Any luck?' Greta asked, holding Lily's red tennis shoe and searching under the couch, the chairs, for its mate. Greta signed something to Lily, who shrugged.

"No. We searched the quarry for two hours. Nothing. I didn't even see any animal tracks. Anyway, it's silly. I'm being silly. It's just a dog."

Greta looked over, squeezed Anna's shoulder. "I wish I could stay."

"When can you come back? You know, you can leave some of your clothes here. I'll clean out a closet for you and Lily. It would mean you wouldn't have to bother with packing every weekend." She paused to listen to the music coming from the kitchen. David Gray, "Babylon." Anna was indifferent to most things she heard on the radio, but during one of her drives with Jack, who had taken to flipping on Top 40 music stations the second they got in the car, this song had caught her attention. *Friday night*

I'm going nowhere/and all the lights are changing from green to red... She bought this CD, along with Dido and one by Mary J. Blige.

"Jack's baking," Greta said, when she saw Anna look toward the kitchen. Greta's tone made it sound like Jack was doing something dangerous or illicit.

"Okay. Fine," Anna said. "Good." She carried Greta's suitcase to the door. "Truly, why not leave this here? I'll wash your clothes. When Friday rolls around, all you have to do is get in the car."

"I'll be back at the weekend. Maybe as early as Thursday night."

"Okay. I can only count the days. Stuart comes up Thursdays through Monday. He doesn't have to teach until Tuesday. We're hoping he can find a position here."

"So, they are back together?" Greta was still on her shoe safari, checking under a pile of newspapers, around the logs at the fireplace. "Oh, well. She would have outgrown them soon anyway."

"I don't know if they're officially together. They seem like it. I hope so."

Greta helped Lily into her coat, then put her own on. "Okay, we need to be off."

Anna felt as though she might be ill. "Come back as soon as you can. I mean, as soon as it's convenient. And drive very slowly. The roads are slick." She wrapped her arms around Greta. "You're a good friend."

"Everything is going to be all right. You're going to find your way through this."

"I keep thinking...," Anna started. "I mean, I can't figure out what to do now. What am I supposed to do? I can't remember how I filled my days before. Before my girl came along."

Greta started to cry, and Anna pulled her closer. "I'm going to help you get through this," Greta said.

"I don't want the life I had before Flynn. It was empty."

"It'll get easier in time," Greta said.

"And I don't want the life I have now."

"I know," Greta said. "But one day you will. Something will come into it to make it the life you want." Greta looked down at Lily.

Anna kissed Greta, then Lily, goodbye.

She found Jack in the kitchen rolling out pie dough, music blaring. Every surface in the kitchen was covered with baked goods and baking paraphernalia. Anna counted four different kinds of chocolate cakes. She turned the music off, and Jack looked up.

"I have never in my life been interested in cooking. But baking is something different entirely. I'm surprised you don't bake, Anna, as scientific as you are. There is pure scientific precision in the marriage of ingredients. And, here's something you didn't know, I bet." He tipped a bowl toward her, a winter wonderland of beaten egg whites.

"Nice," Anna said.

"The secret is the copper. Copper interacts with the protein in the egg whites, and acts as a stabilizing agent. You don't get this volume in stainless steel."

"What's all this for?" Anna asked, sitting. The light was getting dusky. She poured herself a brandy, though it was a little early for cocktails.

"Is that Grand Marnier?" Jack asked.

He cut one of the cakes, and handed her a slice. "Almond cherry galette. A northern Italian recipe originally, but stolen and adapted by the French."

Anna took a bit. "It's very good," Anna said. "Are we having company?"

"Company has been dropping in and out continuously. You have to have something to serve. You should see what people call desserts. Lime green Jell-O with tiny marshmallows. I had to intervene." He measured out two cups of heavy cream and poured it into a bowl of batter.

"Isn't this a bit excessive?" Anna said. "And, you know in this town...." She read from the recipe he was working from: "Pear and chocolate polenta-crusted tarts with crème Anglais. Well. Pearls before swine and all that."

"This is therapeutic. It helps."

Anna supposed that it would. You measured the ingredients, followed the recipe exactly, and the outcome was guaranteed. "I have my eye on that chocolate raspberry number there," Anna said.

Jack sliced her a generous piece. "My masterpiece so far, my Sistine Chapel." He waited as she took a bite. "Yes?"

"Magnificent," Anna said.

He beamed at her, switched the radio back on. Anna watched Jack work. Years ago, a daughter of a friend of hers and Hugh's came back from Rwanda with film footage of the war. One part showed a young American volunteer sweeping up a hut, shaking out and hanging up clothes while the bodies of the home's six inhabitants were piled in the middle of the floor. Jack's abstracted expression, as he measured and sifted and stirred, as though there was nothing in the world that mattered as much as this, reminded Anna of the woman's face in the video.

"Where is Marvin?" Anna asked, then repeated over the loud music. She reached for the volume knob on the radio. "Jack, where is Marvin?"

"He went to find the dog for you. He left this morning after you did. Somebody gave him a lead on a sighting."

"Oh, well. He can try. I appreciate that he's trying."

Jack turned on the mixer—the old KitchenAid that had been her mother-in-law's. She watched the paddle blades working, remembered the last time she herself used it: the trip she and Hugh made up here on his weekend off, the weekend they conceived their daughter. Anna made a piecrust for the raspberries they'd picked earlier. Everything about that day was still vivid. The hot July sun, the rocky path leading to the raspberry patch, the fronds of fiddlehead ferns brushing her legs as she walked past. Later, she and Hugh went for a swim, then made love on the sand. The whole weekend was sun-ripened and charged, full of promise and clear light. The girl had started in her then, was already splitting the husks of cells and dividing as she mixed the dough for the crust, the size of a raspberry seed by the time, days later, the last slice of pie had been eaten. That afternoon connected to this one, all part of a chain. Her daughter, her granddaughter, Jack, Marvin, Stuart and Greta—all of them linked to her and to each other.

"I'm going upstairs," Anna said.

Jack turned to her, raised an eyebrow. "What, dear?"

"I said, I'll be upstairs." She took her glass and the bottle of Grand Marnier.

It was too early to start reading magazines, too early to get tipsy. She stripped the beds in the guestroom, held Lily's sheets up to her face and inhaled.

Anna gathered the bedding and tidied up the room. Greta was thorough; there wasn't so much as a stray sock lying about. She felt a flash of anger. Why wouldn't Greta leave some of Lily's things here? What harm would it do anybody to leave a few clothes? Anna threw the sheets into the washer, then opened the door to Flynn's room. The blinds were closed. The scent of her granddaughter was everywhere, as if she had just stepped out. Anna turned the light on, looked around. Flynn was messy, just like Poppy had been. Her bed was unmade as usual, clothes spilled out of opened rawers, CDs scattered over the floor. Flynn's overalls were on the bed. Anna fastened the buckles and snaps. Such a slight and delicately made girl, more fine-boned than both Anna and Poppy. Anna sat, held Flynn's pillow to her face. On the night table was the Tinkerbell lamp that had been Poppy's. Flynn's junky treasures cluttered the surface. Two miniature starfish, sea glass, pebbles, the figures from the old nativity set that Flynn remade into Gladys Knight and the Pips. Anna checked the drawers. *The Diary of Beatrix Potter* and a book about Celtic dancing. But she didn't want to do this now, didn't want to rummage around the girl's things for what she both hoped and dreaded she'd find.

It was when she stood to go that she noticed Lily's little shoe, the one Greta had been searching for, on the other pillow. Jack must have been in here. Jack must have come across it downstairs and thought it was one of Flynn's. She put it back on the pillow. Greta could afford to buy Lily new shoes.

Anna went in to run a bath. Only six-thirty, which was a problem, since she was nearly at the bottom of the stack of magazines, down to the trashy weekly tabloids. Marvin or Jack would have to run out later for a fresh stash.

She was just about to step in the tub when she heard a commotion coming from the living room beneath her, the crash and shatter of glass. Was that Violet's voice? Anna walked to the head of the stairs. Violet smiled up at her. "Good evening," she said.

"Hi, Violet."

"Anna?" Marvin called from the living room.

"Over here," she said.

"I have someone who's anxious to see you." Marvin turned the corner, and there was the dog, who bounded up the steps, clumsy and stumbling in his haste. He threw his weight against her, ears back and tongue lolling, smiling in the way only a dog can. Anna wrapped her arms around him, buried her face in his filthy fur. "Hi, Baby. Hi, Baby," she repeated over and over, until she could believe he was really back. "Where did you find him?"

Marvin sat on the step beside her. "Violet and I found him."

Anna looked over at Marvin, saw how pale he was. "Are you okay?"

He nodded. "I got a call just after you left this morning from the groundskeeper at the cemetery. That's where he's been. Sleeping right there beside her. The groundskeeper brought him food and water. He lives in a little cottage half a mile from the cemetery, and he said he heard Baby J. howling for hours every night." She led the dog into the bath she'd prepared for herself, scrubbed him down and checked him over. He was eerily calm for a dog in a tub, even a water-loving Newfie. Anna poured water over his head and he never moved, stared at her in a way she found unsettling. Baby J. had always been an enthusiastic wagger, clearing the coffee table with one sweep, but his tail was lifeless now, even when she cooed at him. He looked at Anna as though she was something worthy of close study and memorization. As if, in the grief-eroded geography of her face, he was trying to figure out where he would go next.

PART THREE

THE MIGRATION OF GEESE: THE HEAVENS

FIFTEEN

The Knights Who Slay the Dragons

Stuart knocked on Anna's door. She was playing her cello, the same piece she'd been playing every day for nearly eight months. It was nearly noon, and she hadn't been out of her room yet. "Anna, it's almost twelve," he said.

Her cello stopped. "Thank you, Big Ben." There was a pause, then the music started again.

"You know the rules," Stuart said. He and Jack and Marvin insisted that Anna leave her room by noon at the latest, for a minimum of five hours every day. After that, she was free to do as she wished. One of them, usually Jack or Marvin, but occasionally Stuart, would sit on her bed with her and the dog—who had attached himself to Anna so completely that Jack renamed him Velcro Jesus—and watch DVDs, often *The Godfather*. In the nine months since Flynn died, Anna's taste in films ran to war movies and thug flicks.

"Anna," Stuart said again. "It's 11:59. You have one minute, Cinderella."

In the beginning, Anna had been infuriated of course, railed against them, told the three of them to get the hell out of her house, who did they think they were, and how dare they tell her what to do in her own home. Marvin simply picked her up, carried her downstairs, and threatened to put a padlock on her bedroom door to keep her out during the day.

"We love you, Anna," Marvin had said. "This is what we've come up with to help you. And you need to stop being selfish. You're not the only one who's grieving."

"Noon on the nose," Stuart said.

"I'm on my way. As soon as I wash my face."

Downstairs, Stuart found Jack in the kitchen. He was finally easing off his baking frenzy, had cut back to just one dessert a day.

Stuart watched as Jack unmolded the cheesecake from the springform pan, then drizzled the mocha raspberry sauce in the loopy figure eight of the infinity sign. Or maybe it was supposed to be a Mobius strip; Stuart would have to puzzle it out before he commented. Jack got irritated when they didn't recognize his designs.

"Are we speaking?" Jack said.

"We are now." Stuart cleared a stack of newspapers off a chair and sat.

"Are we speaking civilly?"

"You tell me," Stuart said. They'd been up half the night arguing. Stuart wanted the two of them to move back to Boston. His commute from the city to Maine every few days was tiring, though it wasn't just that. The time had come, Stuart thought, for him and Jack to set up a household together, preferably in Boston. It was true that he could continue his adjunct teaching while living at Anna's, but going to conventions, networking, interviewing for full-time jobs, was difficult from way up here. "Way up here," Jack had said. "You make it sound like we're living on the moon."

"You're right. It's not like living on the moon. The moon has more nightlife."

Jack said something now that Stuart didn't hear. "Pardon?"

"I said, do I have to let you win? Is that what it will take?" He filled the sink, gathered up the bowls and utensils.

"What it will take for what?" Stuart picked up the newspaper.

"For us to finally make our commitment official. Acknowledged in front of our loved ones."

"You don't have to do anything you don't want to do," Stuart said.

"I just don't think it's a good idea to leave Anna. She's done so much for me. She was with me when no one else wanted to be."

"Excuse me? Are we forgetting how that exile happened?"

Jack turned off the water. "Okay, okay." He dried his hands. "New subject."

Stuart paused. "A guy in the psychology department, Harold James, is renting out his brownstone. Lease with the option to buy. And the best part, the rent is eight hundred. He's leaving the country, and needs someone to live there until it sells. I'm sure, if we wanted it, we could buy it for a song. He's more or less desperate. But there's a catch."

"Oh?" Jack said.

"We would need to move in no later than Tuesday."

"It's the first I've heard of this. Why are you telling me now?"

"Because it's happening now. Harold called this morning asking if I knew of anyone."

"And you thought we might be anyone. Anyway, I didn't hear the phone ring. When did he call?"

"Early. You were still sleeping. Will you at least agree to go into Boston to look at it?"

Jack nodded. "Let's go into town and look at wedding bands. We can take Anna with us so she can shop for a dress. Her clothes just hang on her. A-line needs buffet line."

Stuart sighed. He and Jack had been discussing a commitment ceremony for some time, but Jack had begun making plans at a frantic pace. Stuart wanted a ceremony, but he preferred logical steps: a house, then the wedding, with the rest of it to follow later—the rest being the crazy idea Jack and Greta had cooked up one night not long ago: a baby. How this became a decision, how Jack had gone from someday-wouldn't-it-be-nice to discussing the fertile days in Greta's menstrual cycle, Stuart found utterly baffling. He and Jack had been in bed one night when the phone rang. It was Greta, calling for Anna, but Jack had developed the habit, perhaps as a result of taking Anna's calls for so many months, of picking up the phone regardless of whether or not somebody else had already answered. "I'm on," he'd say, making every call his province. "It's Jack."

The night Greta called, Jack picked up the phone five minutes after it rang. "Jack speaking," he'd said. "Who's this?" Jack waited, presumably for Anna to finish her conversation.

Stuart had gone downstairs to the sunroom to read; Jack's conversations might go on for an hour or more. When he'd finished two chapters of *The Red and the Black*—a novel Jack had recently enthused about—he picked up the phone to see if they were still talking. Stuart heard Jack say:

"the transfer of DNA" as casually as if he were talking about moving money to a different bank account. Stuart felt only a transitory guilt about eavesdropping; nobody would have expected him to hang up in the face of this intrigue. He made himself comfortable in the rocking chair, heard Greta say, "Lily is so wonderful, I can't imagine not having another child. I had a miscarriage with my ex-husband. The only thing I regret about ending my marriage is not trying again for a baby. He had great genes. We would have had a beautiful baby."

"Sweetheart, if it's genes you want," Jack had said, "I'm a virtual Calvin Klein. I'm six-two, Ivy-league-educated, a good athlete, cute as homemade shoes, funny as hell, verbally bright, good at math, and have above-average reasoning skills."

"Which you are not exercising at the moment," Stuart broke in.

"Hi, Stuart," Greta said, as though she'd known he was on the line. Jack was unfazed.

"Stuart and I have been together for over twelve years. It's the greatest sorrow of our life that we don't have a child together."

"Jack, what are you doing?" Stuart said, but both Jack and Greta ignored him.

Forty-five minutes later, Jack and Greta were talking about the possible baby as though it existed, discussing the merits of private school versus public, the rising price of college tuition, and at what age to explain to the child why he or she had two daddies and one mommy. Stuart unabashedly listened, breaking in every now and then to call one of them a horse's ass or a raving lunatic.

"But getting back to nuts and bolts. So to speak." Greta laughed. "How do we get your DNA without your virus?"

"Good question," Jack said. "Maybe Anna can filter it out. Maybe there's a way to get the virus out of the cells."

"Maybe there's a way to get the jackass out of Jack," Stuart said.

"I haven't really thought about that," Jack said. "I have been extraordinarily healthy lately, and it seems the disease is completely remissed, but nonetheless, it will have to be Stuart's seed."

For the first time in over an hour, there was silence on the phone. Stuart hung up. In the following weeks, Jack's enthusiasm grew, instead of fading, as Stuart thought—or hoped?—it might. But the more Jack's intent seemed in earnest, the more Stuart began to think about fatherhood. Objectively, he considered bringing a baby into their lives misguided, but there was a tug, an emotional pull; fatherhood was something he'd wanted his whole life. Stuart's answer to Jack, finally, was a cautious yes.

Jack sidled up to Stuart now. "What do you think? Wanna head into town?"

"Not really," Stuart said. "Were you listening to anything I said to you last night? About taking things in stages? What's your hurry?"

"What's my hurry?" Jack's voice started to shake. "What's my hurry? Do you really need to ask that?"

For a horrible moment he was afraid Jack was about to cry. Stuart sometimes forgot how much Jack loved Flynn, and how he, like Anna, was still grieving for her. "I'm sorry," Stuart said quietly. "I want all the things you want. But I guess I just want to focus on each thing as it comes, even if it all happens quickly. Okay?"

Jack nodded, but didn't look up.

They both fell silent. Stuart counted the ticks from the grandfather clock in the living room, the pendulum tracking the seconds. One hundred and twenty-two. Jack spoke finally. "It's like I've spent my whole life riding backwards on a train. Not seeing things until they passed. I don't want to lose you."

Anna made sure no one was lurking in the hallway before she made her call. She hadn't told any of them yet, but she'd had preliminary talks with a realtor about selling the house here in Maine, about what would be a reasonable price, and told the realtor, Lori, that she'd call back with a decision, which she now had. Two days ago, shopping for a butter dish to replace the one Jack broke, she studied this one and that, debated about Irish crystal or English bone, but then thought: what did it matter? Until now, Anna hadn't realized how much of what she did was pointed toward the future; buying a new watch, a Stueben vase, was in part choosing for her granddaughter, the things that would last beyond Anna and become Flynn's. By the time Anna had left the department store and picked up a cheap Rubbermaid version at the grocery, she had her answer about the house.

She dialed the real estate office, left a voice mail for Lori: "It's Anna Brinkman. I'm ready to sell." There. A decision that would become the right one, even if she didn't completely feel that it was so now. Uncertainty was normal, she told herself, picking up her cello and starting back in on Bach's Suite no. 1 in G major. After Flynn, Bach was all she wanted to play. When grief surged acutely, Suite no. 2 in D minor matched what was inside her exactly. After thirty years with these pieces, mastery had come at last.

There was a knock at the door, then Marvin walked in. "Good afternoon, Anna," he said, elongating the vowels into something menacing.

"Yep. Just a bit slow today. On my way downstairs."

Marvin nodded. "I'll fix your coffee."

Anna sat in the back seat of her Volvo with Baby Jesus, while Jack drove, and Stuart fussed at the dog who was pawing Stuart's jacket. Every few minutes Baby J. stuck his snout in the front seat.

"VJ, no!" Jack said, and reached back to push the dog's head away. "See? He responds to a voice of authority. Good boy, good Velcro Jesus!"

"I wish you wouldn't call him that," Anna said.

Within seconds, the dog was again nosing at Stuart's pocket. "Ha," Anna said. "Baby Jesus! No stealing." The dog gave her a look of reproach, as though he considered himself blameless. "Do you have something in there he would be interested in?"

"I have leftovers from my breakfast, which I was going to finish later."

Anna reached in Stuart's pocket and took out the foil-wrapped food. "Bacon. You have bacon, and you blame my poor dog for his persistence. Sorry," she said, feeding the strips to the dog. "Teasing an animal means automatic forfeiture."

"So, where's the best jewelry store?" Jack looked at Anna in the rearview mirror.

"Boston," she said.

Stuart snorted. Jack gave him a look.

"Though Seavey's on Main and Third has nice bridal sets. Wedding bands, I mean." She leaned forward. "At the next light, left. The college will be on the right."

The three of them rode the rest of the way in silence. Anna felt the anxiety and fear coming from the front seat. Jack had asked her to check his viral load, and to test Stuart.

Earlier Jack said, "I feel so amazing that I'm nearly convinced of a spontaneous healing."

"You know that's not possible," Anna had said.

"Also, we've been extremely careful, but we want to reconfirm Stuart's status." Anna reminded Jack that sero-conversion could take months, and that a false negative was possible. "I know. But we're taking precautions and extra-precautions."

The three of them walked into the lab, the dog trailing behind. Jack, accustomed to needle sticks, barely flinched. But by the time she rewashed and regloved, Stuart was shaking so badly Anna couldn't get a steady draw from the vein. "Take a deep breath," Anna said softly. "Try to relax." Jack, on the other side of Stuart, squeezed Stuart's hand, whispered something Anna couldn't hear. Stuart nodded, and clenched his fist tighter. The blood started to flow. "Done," Anna said. Stuart let out a deep breath, and collapsed into Jack's embrace.

Anna walked out into the hallway to give them a private moment. She read the bulletin board twice. Free kittens, furtniture for sale, typing services, and a bake sale benefiting the Bible Baptist Church Youth Group.

Jack and Stuart walked out, hand in hand. "We'll be back in an hour or so," Jack said.

"That's not necessary. I can have results in fifteen minutes."

Jack shook his head. "We want a little time."

"Okay. Not a problem. Go pick out some beautiful wedding rings." She took her wallet out of her purse. "In fact, I was hoping that you would let me get them for you as a wedding present." She handed Jack a credit card.

"That's very generous of you, Anna," Stuart said. "But truly, it's not necessary. You've done so much for us already."

"Please." The idea hadn't occurred to her until the moment the words came out of her mouth; she'd only wanted to reassure Stuart, to steer him toward positive thoughts. But now she found that she truly wanted to buy their rings. "I really want to do this. I mean, please. I have no other family to buy for. Let me."

Jack took her card, kissed her. Stuart smiled wanly and thanked her.

"Back soon," he said.

Anna prepared Jack's slide first. Something amazing *had* happened. His viral load was nearly nonexistent. She checked his white count. In the high range of normal, what a healthy person might show with a mild infection. The recombination of the protease inhibitors was working beauti-fully. Jack's physicians in Boston had recently started him on a new drug cocktail after the ones he'd been on began to lose their effectiveness, and the results were textbook perfect. "Holy Jesus! He's going to outlive me." The dog, at her feet, thumped his tail. Who knew how long the effective-ness of shuffling and recombining drugs could last?

She shook as she prepared Stuart's slide, then went out to have a ciga-rette while waiting for his results. She imagined calling Stuart's cell phone the second she saw good news. But Jack said they wanted time. Even good news could be a shock when it came before you'd weighed both possibili-ties. And how much sweeter to be called back from the precipice after you'd toed the edge.

From the end of the driveway, Jack and Stuart saw Anna on a bench just outside the lab. Jack drove slowly, held his breath until Anna spotted him. She rose when she saw the car, gathered up her things. "Thank God!" Jack said.

Stuart looked at him, alarmed. "What?"

"You're negative," Jack said, and gripped Stuart's hand.

"Don't say that! You don't know that."

"I do know. I know just by Anna's posture."

And when she smiled at them, they both knew. Jack and Stuart stepped out of the car. "Plan your future," Anna said. "Negative. And Jack, your T-cells are beautiful. The knights have slain the dragons. Well, most of them; your viral load is way down."

"Thank you, Anna," Jack said. "Thank you, thank you, thank you."

"Don't thank me. I didn't do anything." She slid into the back seat, Baby J. hopping in after her. "Did you find some rings?"

"No. Nothing we liked. We did make reservations at Boatwright's for an early dinner. Our treat, of course," Stuart said. "And, as a gesture of goodwill…." He handed a grocery bag to Anna. "For your boy back there." Anna opened it. Two pounds of bacon. "Baby Jesus, manna has fallen from heaven," she said. "From the great space hogs in the sky."

They drove in the bright afternoon. It was a good day, today was a good day—Anna turned the words over in her mind. Jack caught her eye in the mirror and winked. Anna fluttered her lashes in return, a gesture she'd picked up from Flynn, who couldn't manage to close one eye at a time. Sometimes when Anna looked at Jack, she saw his boyhood and youth, the toddler, grade-schooler, and pimply adolescent, as if all his years were layered one over another like the transparencies in medical texts. She knew exactly what he was like at twelve—through his stories and her imagination—almost as if he were part of her own history.

Today was a good day—now she believed it—a dry, sunny patch of grass, just big enough for the three of them, after a downpour that had soaked through everything.

Back at home, Anna quickly listened to the messages while Jack and Stuart were unloading groceries from the car. Two from the realtor, whose voice was so chirpy and annoying that Anna deleted them halfway through after getting the gist: Lori would be over Monday to put a sign in the yard; Anna should stop by the office to start the paperwork; the two of them needed to decide whether to set the price according to appraisal or by market value; please call, earliest convenience. The next two were from Greta: "I don't think I'll be able to drive up before Saturday." And the second: "I definitely can't come till Saturday, but I definitely will be there. Jack, please call me."

Anna relayed the message as Jack and Stuart walked in. "Greta wants you to call her."

"Okay," Jack said, and walked into the kitchen. Anna followed.

"What's up?" she said.

"What do you mean?" He picked up a note on the counter. "Marvin drove into Boston to take his sculptures to the gallery. He'll be back late tonight," Jack said. He pushed the note toward her. "Do you know, those wacky sculptures are selling like crazy. He's getting rich."

Anna raised an eyebrow.

"I'll be upstairs if you need me." He walked out. "Stuart?" Jack called.

"In the sunroom. Reading," Stuart called back.

"Okay, just checking. I'll be down in an hour. I'm going to take a little nap."

"Uh-huh," Stuart said. "Sure you are."

Anna unloaded the groceries, got out a skillet to fry bacon for the dog. Reread Marvin's note, sifted through the mail, then picked up the phone.

Jack was on the upstairs extension. Anna put the skillet on the back burner, covered the mouthpiece with her hand, and listened quietly.

Jack was talking to Greta. Anna put the skillet on the back burner.

Greta's voice: "Did you ask Anna about the possibility of its being your baby?" Greta was saying.

"No. The whole day was about peace and relief. Stuart wanted to be re-tested, and that's always a major trauma. I mean, we were pretty sure, but it's completely nerveracking. I used to absolutely unravel every six months when I tested."

"He's negative?"

"Oh yeah," Jack said. "But anyway, Stuart is warming up to the idea of fatherhood. He's always wanted a child."

What the hell? Anna thought. What in the holy hell?

"I have no problem with Stuart being the biological father," Greta said. "But listen, I called because I can't drive up until tomorrow."

"Yeah, that's what I heard."

"And also to tell you that I'm ovulating. Is Stuart willing to start this weekend? Could we try Saturday night?"

"Are you people completely insane?" Anna said into the phone.

"Hi, Anna," Greta said.

"I don't know about Saturday night," Jack said. "Stuart and I have an agreement we're still working out. One step, then another, quick, quick, quick, but one thing at time. Although, maybe once all the steps are lined up, Stuart would cotton to the idea. I mean, it might be six months before we get a bull's eye, and nine months after *that* before the little fellow—or fella—arrives. By that time, Stuart and I will have been married for fifteen months. I'm guessing it will be all right to start tomorrow."

"No, actually it is not all right," Stuart said from the extension in the sun room.

"Is this a party line?" Greta said.

"It's something, of course, Stuart and I will have to discuss," Jack said.

"This is the most asinine idea I've ever heard," Anna said.

"Ah, the voice of reason. Let's hear it," Stuart said.

"It's wrong to bring a baby into this motley mix, in my opinion," Anna said.

"Why?" Greta and Jack said together.

"Why? Why is it wrong? Because, Jack, at some point Stuart and Greta will be raising this child without you, to be perfectly blunt about it. He or she will have two broken households, one house with a single mother, and the other with a widowed father," Anna said.

"The little fella will have a daddy who loves her, and a mother who loves her. I'm the third parent. How many kids have three parents? She'll have a spare if something happens to one of us. Besides, she'll have you," Jack said.

"No," Anna said, "she won't. I won't be a part of the baby's life, should there be one. I won't be here."

A three-sided silence formed, and Anna made it a fourth, closing the square. Anna felt them waiting. Well, now would have to be the time. "I'm moving. I'm selling the house and moving. The house will be listed on Monday."

"You're what? And where am I going to bring my children for holidays, Mama?" Jack asked.

"Where will you go?" Greta said.

"I don't know yet. Maybe to a retirement home where I can finally learn to play shuffleboard. Where I can live out the rest of my days in a depressing state facility as a bitter old woman in a dingy room with urine-stained carpeting. Maybe there," Anna said.

"Hello and welcome to Maudlin Island, population: You," Jack said.

"But I'm hanging up now. Hanging up in disappointment and disgust at the three of you. But before I do, I'll say this. And this is aimed primarily at Jack, but the rest of you should take it under advisement: Grief is probably the second worst condition out of which to have a baby."

"What's the first?" Stuart asked.

"The first is having a baby because someone else wants you to. And now, if you all will excuse me, I have bacon to fry."

"Anna, am I still welcome to visit this weekend?" Greta asked.

"Certainly. This is Jack's home, too, and he and his partner are always welcome to invite their friends," Anna said.

"*Their* friends? Thank you very, very much." Greta started to cry.

"I didn't mean it like that." Anna paused. "Greta, I'm sorry." She waited. "Jack, can you get off the phone for a second?" Anna asked.

"Whatever you have to say, I want to hear. No buffing the monkey.

Gilding the lily. Spill it," Jack said.

Anna sighed. "Greta, grief makes people go haywire. Jack is grieving as much as Marvin and I are. I think he's way too vulnerable to make a decision like this. And I've yet to hear Stuart weigh in on the subject."

"Well, I agree with you, Anna," Stuart said. "I do want a child. In fact, very much. But my idea is to take things slowly. House, marriage, baby."

Jack drew in his breath sharply. "Wait," he started.

"House?" Anna said. "What house? Mine?" This was all too much. "You know what, I don't want to know anything else right now. I'm hanging up. I'm going to fry Baby Jesus his supper, then I'm going to bed. I don't care what you do, but don't even think about disturbing me before noon tomorrow."

"Anna—" Jack said, but she'd already clicked off.

Greta did come on Saturday, but the unspoken agreement was that they would not talk about the previous night's phone call. Anna peeled potatoes for chowder, Jack diced, and Stuart polished the silver. The lines of tension seemed to arise throughout the day in twos: first Greta and Anna, then Greta and Stuart, then Anna and Jack, and by the time dinner was ready to be served, Greta and Anna again.

Anna wondered what had happened between last night and noon today, when she left her room, and if the way Greta was dressed was a factor in any new development. She wore a pinafore-type thing over a skirt flounced with two ruffles, a peasant-style blouse, and Mary Jane T-straps. Her lips and nails were candy pink. From the way Greta was behaving toward Stuart—solicitous, laughing loud and falsely at Stuart's lamest jokes—Anna suspected that Greta thought this outfit would be less threatening to Stuart than something spangly and beaded or overly vampy. Anna didn't know. Except that if she were Stuart she'd be insulted. Did Greta really think Stuart would want to sire an heir with Little Bo Peep?

"Did I ever tell you the story of how I once broke both my legs in Vail?" Jack was saying. "I was skiing a run that would have been too advanced for me under the best of circumstances, but halfway down I thought I saw Antonio Banderas. I shushed as fast as I could, and the next thing I know, I'm ass over teakettle, looking up at some sixteen-year-old ski patroller who's asking if I'm okay. I was in traction for six weeks."

Greta laughed like it was the funniest thing she'd ever heard. Anna looked over at Stuart, who rolled his eyes.

"Excuse me," Anna said.

"Where are you going?" Jack asked.

"We need more bread." She walked into the kitchen. She dialed Marvin's cell number.

"Where are you?" Anna asked when he clicked on.

"Upstairs. Working. What's up?"

"Oh, nothing really. We're having dinner. Come join us if you want." Anna heard Joan Baez in the background. "Please join us, I mean. I'm drafting you to the battle. I have to call in the reinforcements."

"What's the war?" Marvin asked.

"The war of I can't find anyplace to put what I'm feeling war. Among other things."

The music cut off. "I'll be right down. Meet me on the stairs."

Anna grabbed the breadbasket, dropped it on the table as she whisked by. Only Stuart noticed. The dog followed her.

Anna sat midway up the staircase, Marvin beside her. He had clay in his hair and on his clothes and hands, and smelled of something newly made. "What's going on in there?"

"A kind of love story, I guess."

He shook his head, held out his hand, palm up.

"I think Greta's here to get impregnated this weekend."

Marvin sat upright, crossed his legs. "Excuse me? She's what?"

"You heard me." Anna blew her nose, and Baby Jesus, thinking this one of her niftier tricks, thumped his tail against the wall.

"Impregnated? By whom?"

"Who do you think?"

He paused. "Me?"

"Marvin," she said.

"Well, who? The Spice Girls in there? I'm the only male in the household who isn't neutered or gay."

"I can't deal with them right now. I can't deal with tension very well these days."

"Well, you shouldn't have to." He caressed the dog, who rested his head on the step between Anna and Marvin, and the rest of his body over the four below. "I'll tell you what. Why don't you go upstairs, and I'll bring dinner up to you. We can watch a DVD if you want. I've been working too much anyway."

Anna paused. "That would be nice. Listen, thank you."

"For what?" he asked.

"For always being kind to me, even the times when I didn't deserve it."

Marvin nodded, but was silent. He stroked the dog's silky ears. "God, Flynnie loved this animal. Sometimes I think he's really a person in a dog costume. Sometimes I'd swear I've seen her looking out at me through his eyes."

Upstairs, Anna played her cello while waiting for the tub to fill. Just for the hell of it, she pitched the Bach suite to an F sharp, the key the old pipes were ringing in as the hot water gushed in through the ancient plumbing. It sounded like the soundtrack to a Hitchcock film. She put the cello down, bored. Went in to check tub and turned off the water. She added lavender salts, took out a freshly laundered gown, and wandered out into the hallway. The door to the room where Lily slept was ajar. Anna walked in.

There was someone sitting in the chair beside Lily's bed, a hand on the little girl's back.

"Hi," Marvin whispered.

"What are you doing?" she asked.

"Same thing you're doing. Revisiting the best part of myself."

Anna sat carefully at the foot of the bed, listened to the deep, rhythmic breathing of a sleeping child.

"Come up here," he said, patting the space at the edge of the bed. He took Anna's hand and gently placed it on Lily's back. "Is there anything finer than this? I should have had two dozen. I should have talked Poppy into more." Anna's hand bumped against his, and he laced his fingers through hers. They sat like this until Lily shifted and Anna's bathwater had longed since cooled.

She and Marvin walked out of the room. "Speaking of Poppy," Marvin said in the hallway. "I found her. That is, I found out where she's staying. I left her a message."

"I thought you already did that," Anna said. "When she was in Italy."

"I did, but she never called me back. I couldn't leave the news on an answering machine, I just couldn't. But she'll return my call this time. This time, I said I was willing to divorce her." He sighed, ran his fingers through his hair. "It's pretty fucked up when you have to bribe your wife this way."

"I'd like to talk to her," Anna said.

Marvin looked as surprised as she felt for saying it. "You would?"

"I don't know. Maybe."

"Also, I wanted to tell you that I'm moving to New York. My work is showing and selling well, and I want to be in the thick of it."

Anna nodded. "I'm happy for you."

"And to invite you to stay with me. For as long as you want, until you figure out what you want to do. I have a housesitting gig in a loft on the Upper West Side. Jack told me. About you selling the house. Is it true?"

Anna nodded. "It's sweet of you to invite me to stay with you."

"I'll make sure you have the number before I go."

They walked into Anna's room. "What do you want to watch?" She held up the DVDs.

"Anything. Whatever you want," he said.

Anna chose her new favorite, *Full Metal Jacket.*

Sunday morning, Anna was in the kitchen making breakfast when she heard the sound of luggage being carried down the stairs. A lot of it. She turned off the pan of eggs and went to see. Jack's things mingled with Stuart's, Greta's red suitcase, and a gym bag full of Jack's medication.

Jack walked down the stairs, looked tired and ill—the typical greenish cast his skin took on when he switched medications, though he'd been on the same medicine for six months. "Good morning," he said.

"What's all this?"

"Well, Stuart and I were up all night fighting." He walked into the sun-room.

Anna followed. "And he won," she said.

Jack nodded, his back to her as he uncased CDs. Joan Baez's "Suzanne" filled the room. He sat beside Anna on the wicker sofa, started to sing. Anna sang with him, the entire song, the words she didn't know she knew, waiting right there in her head.

When the song was over Jack said, "I'll come back on the weekends. I'll be back every Friday night."

"Only if you want to. I don't want you to worry about me. It's time for you and Stuart to make a life together."

Jack nodded. "Are you really selling this place?"

"Yeah."

"Are you coming back to Boston?"

"No. Maybe. I don't know."

Jack picked up the remote control, hit the repeat button. "Once more," he said, as the song began anew. "You know, you saved my life."

"I did no such thing. You saved your own life."

"What would you say if I asked you to move in with us? With me and Stuart?"

Anna looked at him. "I'd say your lover would surely leave you for good this time and that you and I would be a pack of two. C'mon, Jack. Stuart's giving you a second chance. He won't give you a third. *Carpe diem*, you know, and all that."

"You will always be a part of my life."

"Of course. And I'm probably not going to go anywhere until I sell this place, which could take a while, or forever, who knows."

It was late afternoon by the time they all left. Anna walked them out to their cars. She and Greta hadn't really spoken since Saturday.

"I'm sorry," Greta said.

"For what?" Anna asked.

Greta's eyes were teary. "I'm just sorry. I'll call you."

Anna said okay, and turned away before Greta could hug her. She got in Jack and Stuart's Jeep and rode with them to the end of the road. She kissed them both goodbye. Jack pulled her close and kissed her again, full on the mouth. "I love you, Anna," he said.

"Take very good care of each other," she said.

"I'll see you soon," Jack said, "probably at the end of the week."

"Whatever you two decide is good with me. I'll be here." She got out. "And I love you, too," she said.

Anna watched them until their car was out of sight, then walked back to the house. For the first time in over two years, she was alone. Marvin had taken an early flight out to New York without even saying goodbye to her, just a note saying he would call later in the week, along with his phone number.

A week passed, each day much like the previous one. There was no one to insist that she leave her room by noon, nobody to vex her into irritation that, in retrospect, was far superior to this dispirited solitude. She filled her days with errands, a day or two at Dr. Naylor's to do blood work, and evening dog walks with Violet, which had become the point of light in her day.

One evening, the instant she stepped into the house, the electricity cut off. She navigated through the dark, found candles in the pantry, and went down to check the fuse boxes. Everything seemed to be okay. She called Violet to see if she had power.

"Nope. I'm just sitting here in the dark, twiddling my thumbs. Storm's coming."

Anna started to hang up but said, "Would you like to come over for a cup of tea?"

Violet said she would, and within a few minutes she was at Anna's door.

"It always seems darker when you're alone and the lights go off, doesn't it?" Violet asked.

Anna agreed. She stared at the fringe of blue flame on the burner, waited for the water to boil. "I have mint, lemongrass, or," she tipped the can to the weak path of light, "jasmine flower."

"Jasmine flower, please," Violet said.

Anna spooned the tea into cups and set out muffins with the last of the blueberries Anna had frozen last summer. That, Anna remembered, had been a shining day, the two of them in the blue abundance, eating berries off the stems. Even the dog's teeth were purple by the end of the day. Flynn had asked, "Other than dogs, you know the only thing I like better than blueberries?"

"No, what?"

"Nothing. Blueberries are the best thing in the world. The more they stain you, the more you can speak their language."

Anna had looked at Flynn's lips and chin. "Well, I guess now we're both fluent. Him, too." She nodded at the dog.

"Isn't it great? You and me and Baby Jesus all fluent in Uly."

"In what?" Anna had asked.

"Uly. The universal language of yum."

Violet spoke now. "Have you heard from the boys recently?"

"Jack called me a few days ago. They're settling into their new home."

"Are they visiting this weekend?" Violet asked.

Anna shook her head. "Not this weekend. Maybe next."

"I hope I see them again. I always thought they made a lovely couple. I enjoyed them immensely." Violet moved the candle closer, peered down into her cup.

"Reading your tea leaves?" Anna joked. When Violet didn't answer, Anna pushed her own cup over. "Tell me," she said.

Violet fished for her glasses in one of her innumerable pockets. Tilted the cup this way and that. "You've been having a lot of bad dreams." She paused. "And what you are unable to embrace, now embraces you. Double what has been taken, with you now abides." She pushed the cup away, took off her glasses.

"That's it?" Anna asked.

"Certainly that's it. Did you expect I'd find the winning lottery numbers?"

"But what does it all mean?"

"Well, Anna, if you want my translation, I'd say this: when in deep water, become a diver." Violet looked away.

Anna felt a cold air around her and Violet, chills snaking up her spine. "Do you believe in ghosts, Violet?"

"Of course," she said. "Don't you?"

"Listen, can I ask a favor of you?"

"Anything," Violet said.

"Would you be willing to stay here tonight? I'm having a little trouble being here alone," Anna said.

"I'd be happy to stay here, dear. Especially if you let me run home and get my dogs. They get so frightened in storms."

"Oh, sure. They're always welcome," Anna said.

In the short time Violet was gone, Anna thought she might be having a heart attack; she was drenched in sweat, tight bands squeezing her chest, at her sides, as though she was standing between two boulders that were pushing so hard her ribs felt like they were bowing in the center, about to snap. Her head was buzzing, full and thick, the ambient room sounds muffled, near things distant: her dog right beside her, though somehow not within reach. He looked up at her with soft eyes; the reflected light in his irises as remote as moons.

"How?" she heard herself say. And in the very next instant the feeling was gone, and the sounds in the room were as they should be: Violet's boot-heavy tread, the click of dog nails on the floor, the thud of a closing door.

"It's us," Violet called, then walked into the kitchen. She stopped. "Is everything all right?" She looked around.

"I'm fine now," Anna said. She did feel calm. Normal, once again, but exhausted. "I'm about ready for bed. But make yourself at home. There's plenty of food if you're hungry."

"Thank you, Anna, but I believe we'll turn in, too. You don't mind if Luna and Haiku are in the bedroom, do you?" Violet asked, pointing to the elderly beagles.

Anna said she didn't, and wished Violet a good night.

Within minutes, Anna was asleep, dreaming that she was sitting in the last pew of a huge cathedral. The windows were floor-to-ceiling stained glass, and a brilliant light kaleidoscoped in. Jack and Stuart were exchanging wedding vows, though she couldn't hear a word from way back here. There was a rustling at her elbow. She turned and saw Flynn.

"Why do you keep calling me? What is it you think I can do?" Anna asked.

Wordlessly, Flynn took Anna's hand and then they were in a hospital, wandering through corridors so narrow and winding Anna had to dodge someone every few seconds.

You can walk right through the people, Flynn said.

They stopped at the nursery. Anna looked in and saw hundreds, thousands, of babies in bassinets. Not one of the infants was crying. No one attended to them.

There. I need to get in there. You need to help me, Flynn kept saying.

Anna looked over at her granddaughter, then back into the nursery. Wolf cubs, all of whom were watching Anna with their yellow eyes, had replaced the infants.

"Those are wolves," Anna said.

No, Flynn said, *some of them are angels. And some are just like us.*

SIXTEEN

SOMETHING LIVING, SOMETHING LOVELY, SOMETHING BETTER

They had a quiet ceremony at the Unitarian church in Boston, just a handful of friends on a midsummer afternoon, with a small reception afterward. Jack thought this was probably the first sign of encroaching dotage: a couple of years ago he and Stuart would have invited two hundred people instead of twenty. Anna was their attendant, beautiful in a pale yellow dress. That was a month ago, and Jack hadn't seen Anna since then, though he spoke to her on the phone nearly every day.

Contrary to her expectations, Anna sold the house almost immediately, for close to double what she thought she'd get. Yesterday when Jack talked to her, Anna sounded almost cheerful. She was spending her days going through decades of accumulation in the attic, the spare bedrooms. The new owners wanted to close as soon as possible.

"Then what?" Jack had said. "Where are you going?"

"Well, I'm still trying to decide."

"Why don't you let me and Stuart come up this weekend?" It had, in fact, been Stuart's idea that they go and help her.

"No. Thank you, but no. I need this distraction. It's perfectly mindless. One of these days, though, you'll have to come and look through what I'm leaving for you in storage. Beautiful antiques. Furniture. I'm leaving four of the beds for you. That's probably more than enough, but you can choose the ones you want. Also, the most beautiful baby cradle that belonged to my husband's great-grandmother. Wait till you see."

"You've done so much for us already. Sell the furniture. Take the money and travel." She had given them a large sum of cash for their wedding, enough to make a huge downpayment on their brownstone with a sizable portion left over to defray some of the costs of renovations.

"Jack, please. I have no one else to spend my money on. You'll get it now, or you'll get it later when I leave it to you. You might as well enjoy it."

There was no arguing with the logic of Anna.

Jack started to dial Anna's number now, but changed his mind. It was probably too early for a Saturday morning. He'd call her later. He walked into his little office off the master bedroom, spread out the stack of folders, the files with the closest deadlines on top. The coffee was brewing. Stuart was out of the house already, at the paint store or Home Depot. Quiet weekends were a thing of the past. Between the sanding and painting and replastering, the continuous stream of carpenters and kitchen refacers and tile men, they never seemed to do anything but house projects.

He shuffled through the papers on his desk, retirement portfolios from a scattering of professionals—university professors, nurses, accountants—who had hired him to sort through the confusion of stock and bond investments, aggressive growth funds and the like. He was reliable and thorough and his consulting business was steadily increasing through referrals. But all of this should have been done Friday afternoon. He had three phone meetings on Monday, with all three clients expecting guidance and advice. He'd gotten off to a slow start, a sluggish awakening to a gray, overcast day heavy with clouds. It had been raining for days.

Back in the bedroom, Jack stretched out to rest for a half an hour before starting to work again. He closed his eyes, inhaled the scent of fresh paint and wood varnish, heard the hiss of tires on the wet asphalt outside. Anna had shown him the beauty in days like this; the gloomier the weather, the brighter her house burned. Birch log fires, soup, soft lights and candles ablaze in every room, even the bathroom. He picked up the bedside phone, dialed.

"Jack," she said.

"How'd you know it was me?"

"Just did. How did your checkup go yesterday?"

"My numbers are in the middle of the acceptable range. And you were right about my fatigue. I am slightly anemic."

"What did they tell you to do?"

Jack heard the screeching of strapping tape. "They put me on prenatal vitamins. Straight iron tablets can be...I forget what they said. Something about too harsh."

"Yeah. Well, what you don't use of the prenatal vitamins, you can give to Greta."

"So, you still think it's bad that we're trying to do this."

"Well, I'm giving you a Chinese Chippendale baby cradle. So, I think the idea is bad, but if a baby manages to get here, the little fella needs someplace to sleep, doesn't she?"

"Of course. No baby of mine is sleeping in anything from the softer side of Sears. Wait, I'll have to call you back, I guess. Someone's downstairs."

Jack walked to the staircase. "Stuart?" he called.

"Cabinets," a voice called back, and Jack backed up, heart pounding. It was the sexy carpenter. Dark and tall, and totally ripped; he wore polo shirts that showed off his shoulders and arms.

Jack washed up, put on clean clothes and went downstairs. "Hi," he said. He couldn't remember the man's name. Why did Stuart do this? Why couldn't he hire heterosexual workers? Why would he hire this man who looked like Antonio Banderas? Wasn't their life enough of a soap opera without bringing Mr. Swinging Tool Belt in? Welcome to this week's episode of *Gays of Our Lives*. On today's show, watch Stuart walk in just as Jack and the Mr. Fix-It Hottie are engaged in a passionate exchange of Tongue and Groove.

"I brought laminates and solids, both in birch, as Stuart requested, and some samples in alder." He looked over at Jack, smiled. "Wanna take a look?"

"You bet," Jack said. "Can I get you some coffee?"

"I'd love some." Jack felt the man's eyes boring into him as he took down mugs, poured the hazelnut French roast that Stuart always made far too weak—and getting weaker, since Greta was often here and complained about the strong coffee. He was aware of everything suddenly, his senses sharpened. He smelled the man's shampoo and aftershave, the wood in the sample book, felt the grit from the imperfectly swept floor under his bare feet.

He put the mug and the sugar and cream on the breakfast bar, then sat on the stool beside the man. "I forget your name, I confess," Jack said.

"Michael," he said, smiling and extending his hand.

Jack took it. Strong and warm, calluses on the palm. Jack felt the heat radiate from the center of his body to his extremities. He bent in close to look at the samples, listening to the litany of price versus quality materials, dovetail joints versus glue or nails. With every page he turned in the book he seemed to move closer to Jack, until finally, now into the high-end hardwoods, the entire length of Michael's arm was against Jack's. There was no mistaking this. The other couple of times he'd been here Michael had flirted with him—well, Jack had to admit that he'd flirted back—but there was no mistaking that this was an invitation.

Michael looked up at him and smiled wider. "What do you think?"

"I like the birch. But I'm deferring all decisions to Stuart and his impeccable taste."

Michael nodded, enclosed his hand around Jack's wrist. "Is this a Rolex?" He took Jack's hand in his, pretended to study the watch.

"That's a Rolex. And this," he said, holding up his left hand, "is a wedding band." He smiled, squeezed Michael's hand once and left the kitchen, shaking. He went into the downstairs guest bedroom and dialed Stuart's cell phone. Out of range, apparently. He sat on the couch with the morning newspapers. He would stay here until Michael left. He didn't trust himself. Didn't trust that his intentions would naturally override his desire—they rarely had before. He felt very much like he did those years ago with Hector, a feeling of physical craving, the drug-like need of the lust Hector inspired.

He'd come very close once in the month or so since he and Stuart had married. It was a man he had met in an all-night grocery. Jack had, in fact, gone as far as getting into the man's car and reaching into his wallet to check for condoms. But something had flashed in his head then, an image of the memorial service they had for Flynn. It was raining lightly that morning, but the light inside the chapel was anything but dreary. There was brightness within, as if the day were sunny and cloudless. The stained glass made it seem even brighter—a few too many haloes, for his taste, though he did like the way the very queenish-looking Saint Augustine held those tablets, like they were his cards at drag bingo—but it was more as if his perception of the light was changing. When the service started, he was impossibly heavy, leaden with sorrow. He had to reposition his body every three minutes because his spine felt so collapsed and brittle under the weight. But little by little a peace settled over him. By the end of the short service he knew everything would be okay—he, Anna, they would all manage. The image that came to him in the chapel was that of an enormous chandelier with thousands and thousands of tiny lights, some of which flickered then burned out. He imagined he could feel Flynn around him, a light that continued with him and Anna and Marvin, switched off somehow, no longer illuminating, but somehow still there. Here.

This was what came to him in the stranger's car and Jack knew he couldn't do it, couldn't ever cheat again. There was the vow to Stuart, of course, though that wouldn't have been enough to stop him then—or now, with the sexy carpenter—despite his great love for Stuart. It was the image of Flynn, of her passing, of her in his thoughts that made him over several brooding days formulate a theory of sorts. Every human being, he believed, must do one of three basic things during his lifetime: leave something living, create something lovely, or make something better. Jack would never father a child—biologically anyway—and he had no talent for anything artistic, so the option left to him was to make something in the world better. He had no great humanitarian instinct, didn't, in fact, even really like most people, so he decided to start with himself. He needed to try to make himself a finer and more ethical person. From that, something else might grow. He might be able to help raise a wonderful child; someone who wouldn't make bad or hasty decisions out of a poor sense of self-worth and the arrogance it engendered. A child who would grow up to be a kind and generous human being who would know, by Jack's example, never to take any loving relationship for granted. And if nature had any role in personality, Stuart's child would have a much better chance of being nice than would a child assembled out of his DNA. Jack had been bitter and miserable so long that it couldn't help but have an effect on his gene pool. Cynicism was a terrible trait, he knew, a kind of immorality all its own.

Hours later, Stuart still wasn't back. When Jack woke up from a nap on the couch in the study it was three-thirty, and he hadn't heard from Stuart all day. He peeked outside. It was raining hard. He started to dial Stuart's cell, but cut the call when he heard a car pull up. He looked out: Greta, minus her daughter, which could only mean one thing.

"Jack!" she said, and rushed in.

"You're ovulating," he said.

"Stuart's stuck in traffic, and I'm fertile."

He took her coat, closed the front door. "What do you mean, stuck? It's Saturday. How much traffic can there be?"

"There's a four-car accident on Storrow Drive, and they have everything blocked off."

Jack dialed Stuart's number.

"I've gone exactly three feet, Greta," Stuart said, without first saying hello.

"Where are you?" Jack asked loudly, above the hiss of the line and the honking horns.

Stuart groaned. "Not you, too. I've been harangued six times in the past hour by Greta. There is nothing, I repeat, nothing I can do about this."

Jack heard the windshield wipers going full-speed. "I'm not calling to harangue you. Greta's about to ovulate."

Stuart sighed. "Oh hey, there's something I haven't heard twenty times."

"And I'm asking you, once again, where are you?"

"Intersection of Beacon and Charles."

Jack hung up. "How long is the egg viable?"

"I recently read a study that said there's a window of just a couple of hours. Nobody knows for sure. But now's the time. I feel it."

"Well, maybe it'll keep." He was going to say maybe she should stand in a cold room to delay spoilage, but realized how ridiculous that was. "Maybe you can stay fertile for a while longer. Can you?"

Greta flashed him a look. "How would I know? You think this is something I have a say in?"

"Testy, testy," Jack said.

"Sorry. But I haven't ovulated like this in months. I'm disappointed. I thought this would be the shining moment."

He thought for a minute. "Okay. I have an idea. It's unusual, and it's risky, but it might work."

"Anything, yes."

"Upstairs in the bedroom are cartons of books. Start ripping them open and look for men's magazines, anything with naked, aroused men somewhere in their pages. Don't ask why, just do it."

From the downstairs bathroom, Jack got out one of the kits made up of the various apparatus to get fluids from one body to the next, without those bodies actually touching. Greta had assembled and left multiples of the kits in both bathrooms, a gesture that Jack found oddly touching, like Valentines left anonymously for strangers.

Greta came down a few minutes later with *The Joy of Gay Sex*. "This is all I could find."

"Well, okay. Better than nothing."

Stuart stared straight ahead, told himself not to be disappointed. They could try again next month. Or maybe if she were as fertile as she claimed the shelf life of the egg would be longer. They had been trying for the past four months, and with each cycle Stuart's certainty that he wanted a child grew stronger. But this time, according to Greta, she was so fertile it wasn't funny; the test strip wasn't a pale pink like it was last month, it was the color of a Mardi Gras float, as pink as a Mary Kay Cadillac.

Stuart put the car in gear when the car horns started honking, but saw that traffic still wasn't moving. There was a man weaving in and out of the idling cars ahead. A man who looked very much like Jack.

Stuart squinted. It was Jack.

"Christ almighty!" Stuart said, as Jack opened the passenger door. "What are you doing?"

"I brought you a little reading material." He tossed the book onto the seat. "I realize they're just line drawings, but you'll have to use your imagination. Here are your works. And, I know this is the wrong thing to say to a man who has to beat off in traffic, but hurry. Greta's in the coffee shop across the street with her panties around her ankles."

"What?"

"So to speak, of course. I told her to lock herself in the bathroom and wait."

"What?" he said again, looking down at the book in his lap, the sterile cup. "What? You've got to be kidding. This will not be happening."

Jack got in and closed the door. "You have to."

"Are you kidding? You want me to do that here? Surrounded by mini-vans and soccer moms?"

"You can do it. I'll block the view on this side." He took off his raincoat and looped it through the handrail above the window. Jack reached over and turned up the music—The Traveling Wilburys, Anna's music, he heard, missing her acutely now. She must have forgotten to take it out of their car.

Stuart started to speak. Jack turned the music down to tell him: "This is a golden opportunity. She might not ovulate next month. Or the month after that. None of us are all that young and fecund anymore. Get busy." He turned the music way up, loud enough so the people in the cars around them would hear, get annoyed, and turn their own radios up. Jack rocked back and forth and sang as loud as he could to give Stuart the illusion that they were alone.

"I don't care about the car I drive," Jack sang, "I'm just happy to be here, happy to be alive...well, it's ALL right!"

"Jack," Stuart said, through clenched teeth. "Shut up."

"Okey dokey." He peeked around the coat: The people in the car be-side them were talking and laughing, paying no attention to what was going on.

Stuart hit the jackpot just as traffic started to move.

"See you at home," Jack said, and kissed him. He put the beaker inside his coat, under his armpit; even a minute at the wrong temperature could make the boys sluggish. "Why the hell don't they make lids for these things?"

"Probably because most people don't treat them as to-go cups," Stuart said, and reached across Jack's lap to open the door. "Don't spill it," he called after him.

Greta was in the front of the line at the coffee shop, which extended nearly to the door with caffeine junkies craving their afternoon fix. Jack pushed and jostled his way up to her, some people shooting him dirty, then suspicious and alarmed looks, as if they thought it was a gun he was holding inside his coat. "Why the hell aren't you in the bathroom?" he said to her.

"Oh God, you're here!"

"Yes, I'm here. Why aren't you in position?"

The woman in line ahead of Greta turned around. Jack stared her down.

"I didn't think you were coming."

He laughed. "Well, strictly speaking, I wasn't. It took a little longer than anticipated. He didn't have a lot to work with, poor boy. Let's go."

The two of them hurried to the back where the bathrooms were and he handed her the cup and bag with the mysterious female paraphernalia. The current guidelines, he'd read, indicated it might be useful to lie flat on her back for thirty minutes with her knees drawn up. It was crucial that she follow all this now, since she was so convinced of the egg's viability.

"Greta? How's it going in there?"

"All the boys are safely in the visitor's center."

"Good. I know the floor in there must be disgusting, but you're following the drill, right? Don't get up."

"Yeah, I know. Can you go get my latté and bring it in?"

Jack turned, faced a line of astonished-looking women. "The ladies' room will be closed for the next twenty-nine minutes," he said.

Later, Greta sat on the couch with a book of baby names while Stuart and Jack painted the living room walls.

"Don't you think you're, well, counting your chickens?" Stuart said.

"I'm pregnant," Greta said.

The paint roller slipped out of his hand and landed on the coffee table. "You are? Already? I must have some strong swimmers."

"She doesn't know that," Jack said. "You don't know that, Greta."

"I do. I felt exactly like this when I was pregnant before. With the baby I lost."

"And how is that?"

"Like something has been plugged in and switched on." She looked back down at the book. "I'm ninety percent sure," she said.

"You know this within six hours?"

She nodded. "The first time, I knew immediately."

Jack and Stuart stared at her. Jack held fast to the notion that this early belief was as crucial as biology. Without a doubt in their minds, the three of them had willed it to be true and in this way faith was as responsible as flesh. In this way, Frances Ella—whom Jack would nickname Fella, to Greta's annoyance—was as much his as anyone's.

SEVENTEEN

STAR CARBON

In under a month, Anna had sorted through everything, from the attic to the basement to the storage sheds around the property. She was leaving most of the big pieces of furniture for the new owners, a young couple with a baby on the way. She watched them as they walked through with the realtor, noticed what they admired, what their eyes lingered on the longest, and left those things. The Duncan Phyffe dining room table, the Chippendale secretary's desk upstairs, the bedstead that had been in her husband's family for two hundred years. She'd already sent two truckloads of furniture to Jack and Stuart. Marvin didn't want anything. Anna saved Flynn's room for last—even after nearly a year, her granddaughter's scent lingered. Violet had spent the morning with her, sorting through and boxing up Flynn's meager belongings. By late afternoon, everything left in the house was either staying, or was what Anna was taking with her.

After Violet went home, Anna sat outside and called Marvin in New York. "Hi," she said when he answered. "I'm getting ready to go, and wanted to double-check there's nothing you want. Violet helped me go through Flynn's room. Mostly girlish trinkets, her clothes and books."

Marvin made a sound deep in his throat. "I don't think I could bear it. The physical reminders, I mean. She's still everywhere."

"I know," Anna said. "I guess I'll donate what's still usable to charity." She stared out at the line of garbage cans she'd filled for Wednesday's pickup.

"Where are you going, Anna?"

"I don't know. I don't have a destination in mind. I'm just going to drive."

"Why don't you come here? I have plenty of room. You can figure out what you want to do. Take a little time, hang out in the city. Relax."

"That's very kind, but no. This is better." A silence hung between them. Anna looked up at the sky. It was a clear, bright afternoon, not too warm. She was planning to leave tomorrow, but there was nothing holding her here, no reason she couldn't leave at any hour of the day or night. There was still a little paperwork to take care of with the sale of the house, and the documents having to do with Poppy's money. Marvin had finally tracked Poppy down in London. She was clean, had been through rehab just in time to go through grief, which, Anna suspected, would probably start the cycle of drug use all over again.

"Anna, I have to say we're worried about you."

"Don't be. Everything will be fine. Tell me the latest about Poppy. There's a trust fund her father left for her. I've signed an escrow release, but I would prefer that this inheritance not disappear into her veins. So I had my attorney name you as executor of funds. Use it at your discretion. And don't give her a penny if she so much as smokes a joint. Is she still planning to come to New York?"

"That's what she says. I hope so. She sounded clean on the phone, but you know."

"Yeah," Anna said. "Well, there's plenty of money. Get her the best treatment available."

"When are you leaving?"

"As soon as I'm done. The minute I'm done with things. You have my numbers."

"I do." He paused. "Look, I have no right to ask this—" he started.

"Ask anyway."

"Especially, the likes of me, with the track record I have."

"Ask," she said again.

"You are all the real family I have left."

"Yes," Anna said.

"And I guess I'm hoping you won't disappear from my life."

"I won't."

"But will you promise?"

For the magic of the word itself, the faith of it and what it might open, she said, "Yes."

She started to dial Jack and Stuart's number next, but stopped midway, then did the same with a call to Greta. She just couldn't right now.

Anna sipped her coffee, watched the water fringe at the shoreline. It felt good just to sit and do nothing. She'd been going nonstop since she sold the house. Which was the way it had to be; she gave herself a deadline of going through and organizing one room per day, but it had gone much faster than she'd anticipated. Most everything ended up in the discard or charity pile. Nostalgia, she began to discover as she sorted through boxes of Christmas ornaments, clay hand-print ashtrays, even most photographs, was actually a state that had nothing to do with preserving the past. It was wistfulness and imagination in equal parts, envisioning what your survivors would want. Which made it easy now. The family snapshots filled two entire trashcans. Anna kept her wedding album, one photograph of Poppy as a toddler, and one of her husband that she loved unreservedly: he was about thirty, sitting on the windowseat in the library looking out at something in the yard. She couldn't remember if she'd taken the photo, or why, or even what year it was. But all his best expressions were in his face and his posture: one leg bent under him, the other on the floor. A book was balanced across his knees, a wine glass in one hand, the other midair, reaching for something outside the photo's frame. His expression was delight and amusement and surprise. Hugh had been a man of great energy, with a way of fully inhabiting whatever he was feeling at the moment. This was what made her fall in love with him in the beginning and what carried through the years. Hugh had, in Anna's eyes anyway, a charming way of not understanding irony or exaggeration. Once, her figure still padded with post-pregnancy weight, Anna said that she was swearing off desserts until she got her weight down from about one hundred and eighty pounds of baby blubber. Hugh had looked at her and said, "Darling, are you sure of your weight?" Anna, clearing dinner dishes, asked what he meant. "I just can't fathom how you could weigh that much. You look to me like you're not much over one forty."

Anna checked her tote bag now, on the step beside her. The usual necessities, some maps, her phone, and, at the bottom, the digital camera she bought just a month before Flynn died. She'd planned to take some shots of Flynn, but never did. Poppy's first letter home after disappearing with Marvin had included a baby picture of Flynn, but Anna couldn't find it anywhere.

Anna heard the rattle of dog tags, then Violet and her dogs appeared. She paused at the trash cans lining the sidewalk. Anna was shocked to see that Violet was wearing only one skirt, and a beautiful one at that. Cotton lawn, printed with delicate blue flowers. Redwing boots peeked from beneath the lacy hem. "Hello, dear," she said as she drew closer.

"You look nice, Violet," Anna said.

"Thank you. Just had a hankering to say hello. Can I help you with anything else?"

"I think everything's done. Thank you again for all your help," Anna said.

"Is this a bad time?" Violet asked.

"Not at all," Anna said. "I'm actually glad you're here, I was just about to start hog-wallowing in dread."

"Ah, I thought as much, which is why," she said, pulling out a silver flask, "I brought this. I myself don't often truck with these kinds of spirits, but I have found that a snout full of whiskey can do wonders for dread."

Anna laughed. "Well, hell. Why not?" She took a sip, passed it back to Violet who herself took a pull, then handed it back to Anna. She felt better almost immediately, the edge of anxiety dulling a bit.

Anna invited Violet in, made a pot of tea. "Actually, Violet, there is something I might ask you to do if you're willing. If you have time, would you mind taking those boxes of Flynn's to the women's shelter? They're always short on children's things."

"Certainly," Violet said, and carried her teacup to the sink. She reached for Anna's cup when Anna was finished. Violet stared into it, then looked up at Anna and smiled.

Anna shook her head. "No predictions, but thanks." Anna rinsed the tea things, and put them in a shoebox for Violet. "I want you to have this teapot and cups. And there are still two cans of jasmine here."

"Are you sure?" Violet said.

Anna said that she was. "Also, now that I'm thinking about it, why don't you walk through the house and take some things. Everything you see, I'm leaving. You're welcome to any or all of it."

"I don't need anything, Anna, but thank you just the same."

"The end tables? They're Chippendale."

Violet declined, and ran her fingers through the fringe of a cashmere throw.

"You can take that with you," Anna said. "And how about that coat rack? My husband had that specially made by a local artist. It's solid birch." Anna stopped. "I guess this is really for me, isn't it?" she said quietly. "It would make me feel better if you took some of this stuff. But that has nothing to do with what you want."

"I surely will miss you," Violet said. "All of you. The boys, Marvin, the dog. That's all. I'll miss you all." They walked out on the lawn. Violet spotted Anna's old bathrobe in the trash can and pulled it out. "This I'll take. You wore it a lot, didn't you? I'll remember you by it." She stood by Anna's new truck—a Toyota Tacoma with a camper shell, which she decided to buy after four sleepless nights of deciding what to do next. She would simply drive, take only the things she needed for a long road trip, and the things that meant something to her personally. Everything else was replaceable.

Violet ran her hands along the shiny black surface. "Is this what they call a testosterone truck?" She blinked behind her glasses.

Anna laughed. "I think it has to be bright red to qualify as that." At the dealership in Portland, Anna had debated between the 4Runner and the Tacoma, leaning toward the former until the salesmen, learning that she alone, without a husband, would be the sole driver, pushed her toward the plusher SUV. That was the deciding moment. She wouldn't play into anybody's notion of what a woman should drive.

Violet peered inside. "Will you have the rest of your things sent on to you later?"

"No. This is all." Clothes and camping gear, her wedding album, her cello, a dog bed and bowls, her husband's good microscope, and every box of slides she found in his study that day. The slides she had of Flynn's were carefully wrapped inside a wood jewelry box in the glove compartment.

"When are you planning to take off?" Violet said.

"Today. Right now," she said, surprising herself as much as Violet. But she couldn't spend another night in this house; even if she only drove to Portland and spent the night in a motel, now was the time to leave.

"Right this minute?"

Anna nodded. "I'll tell you what. I'm going to give you my keys. Go back through the house and make sure there's nothing you want. Take some things, Violet. Even if you take them to sell them. Those light fixtures in the hallway are worth thousands. They're Tiffany."

"Vanity, vanity, all is vanity," Violet said, with a wave of her hand. "We're made of time, and so are our things. I don't need material goods to keep you with me."

"I'll call you. And, wherever I end up, whenever I end up somewhere, I want you to come visit. You are always welcome wherever I am." She gave Violet a slip of paper with her cell phone number, and Marvin's number in New York. "You can leave messages with him, if you can't reach me. I'll check in with Marvin and Jack and Stuart from the road."

She held on to Violet a long time; another second, she thought. If I don't let go in five seconds I'll chicken out. "Thank you for everything. Thank you for being there for me."

"No thanks are necessary."

Anna whistled for Baby Jesus, who heaved himself up into the front seat. In the rearview mirror, she saw Violet standing in the same place, her dogs in perfect sit-stays that Anna hadn't yet succeeded in teaching Baby Jesus. At the stop sign at the end of the road, Anna U-turned, pulled back into her driveway. Violet walked over to the driver's side. Anna rolled down her window. "Your leaves," Violet said. "Your tea leaves...."

"Okay," Anna laughed. "What?"

"Most everything ahead is pure blessing."

Anna kissed Violet goodbye. "I'll call you in a day or two."

Except, as it turned out, she didn't call. The first week went by in a blur. Two weeks turned to three, and before she knew it, a month had elapsed. Sometimes she drove nearly nonstop for three days, then stopped for a week for no better reason than that she liked a certain coffee shop. At least once a day it occurred to her that she should check in with someone.

One morning in Joplin, Missouri, she decided to just get it over with. She pulled into the parking lot of a convenience store, took out her phone, but then changed her mind. What would she say? I'm all right; I've been driving, just driving. Nothing has happened to me, good or bad. She left the car running with the air conditioner on for the dog, and went inside the store. She picked up some snacks, a new road atlas, some dog treats, and bottled water. But by the time she stood in line and paid, she'd talked herself out of it. She imagined how the news of Marvin and Jack and Stuart and Greta would feel rushing in at her. When Jack and Stuart left the house in Maine, it was as if Flynn had died all over again. And Marvin. Just the thought of hearing his voice, the faint echo of Flynn in his phrasing, was enough to start her shaking.

She got back in the truck, handed Baby J. his milkbones, uncapped her soda, and studied the map. She didn't much like these Midwestern states. The campgrounds were full of overfed, overgroomed, and invasively friendly families. She turned her phone on, off, then on again. Maybe Marvin would be at work and she could leave a message. But when did he ever really work outside the home? Except for teaching here and there, he always worked in the studio where he lived. If she could be sure to just get his—or Jack's—answering machine, she would call.

She stared at a group of teenagers gathered around a souped-up truck, smoking cigarettes and drinking sodas. The girls were tarted up in short skirts and sprayed hair, and the boys all in a uniform of baggy pants and T-shirts. She looked at one young woman in particular who was beautiful but seemed not to know it. The girls around her, though, looked at her with tight, distant smiles. She was dark-haired and thin, her hair and makeup were natural. She was fifteen, sixteen, maybe. She caught Anna's eye and smiled. Anna smiled back, felt something catch in her throat, then put the truck in reverse.

For now, driving was what made sense. The more she drove, the longer the intervals of peace were lasting. She'd never been any kind of outdoors person, and she was amazed to discover how much being away from human habitation, sight, sound, and scent soothed her. She liked waking up in her tent. Mornings were the best part of the day, the fragrance of pine trees and dewy foliage, the scuffling of small animals and birds all around her.

The campgrounds were thinning out, since it was nearing the end of summer, and days sometimes went by when she didn't see a single person. "West," she said aloud. "I think we shall go west." Baby Jesus wagged his tail.

Anna liked the terrain of California, the robust pines and Joshua trees, the scrubby desert landscape and somber mountain ranges all in the same vista. She had a comprehensive guidebook that listed the natural hot springs in California, and she spent ten days visiting as many as she could. Most had campgrounds nearby, but they were too crowded for her taste. She wanted solitude and quiet when she crawled into her tent at night, not some mother screeching at her children, or a group of partying teenagers blasting through the night. She typically drove to a campsite ten or fifteen miles away after she finished soaking.

The last one she visited, though, just at the Nevada border, felt like paradise. When she pulled into the nearly deserted parking lot and saw how hidden and remote the mineral pools were—she had to walk in nearly a mile, and even then found them only by the sulfurous odor—she thought she might stay here forever. No one would ever find her.

For two days, she soaked continuously, going back up to her campsite at noon and early evening for a meal, then, after sundown, back into the water. It had become her perfect remedy for sleep. She soaked for an hour while staring up at the stars—beautifully silvered in the sky without the distraction of city lights—sipping wine until she knew that one more minute in the water would leave her too fatigued or dehydrated to walk back up the hill. This was the best her mood had been in well over a year. Not happy or content, exactly, but without the constant nightmares and plaguing guilt that—literally, it seemed, from the way her stomach felt— ate at her until everything she did, even blinking her eyes, was painful. She was afraid to move on, afraid that this new and fragile peace was somehow tied to the place.

On the third evening, after hiking around the surrounding trails, she walked down the path for her nightly soak. She'd grown careless about clothing. She hadn't owned a bathing suit in years, anyway, and wore only a light robe that she took off as soon as she reached the pool. It was dark, but she'd memorized the path, and could negotiate the rocks and roots in just a pair of flip-flops. She didn't even need a flashlight anymore. She hung her robe from the tree branches, settled her customary bottle of wine and glass within reach. It wasn't until she was actually in the water and her eyes adjusted to the dark that she realized she wasn't alone. Two other people. Two men.

Anna introduced herself to them and they to her: Andy, in his thirties from Los Angeles, and George, older, maybe sixties. She was disappointed at first that she had lost her solitude, then found she didn't mind. The men made small talk and neither of them seemed to mind her silence. Anna gathered that they weren't together. She stayed relaxed, which was the amazing thing, and slowly let a thought surface that it might not be a horrific thing to be around people again. She found that she could listen to them talk—mostly Andy, the younger one, about his recent divorce—and not have every other word trigger a painful memory. She was getting better about memories, anyway; what seemed harder now was imagining the future, a terrifying expanse of time made up only of milestones, not ordinary moments. When she thought about the coming year, she couldn't imagine anything other than where and with whom she would spend Christmas, what she would do when Flynn's birthday rolled around. Everything before her seemed like a huge table set for one, a wasteland of sterile apartments, and clear, uncluttered surfaces. These were the thoughts that sometimes kept her awake at night. She might never need to replace things broken by the rush and chaos of domestic life, might never again need to Scotchguard her furniture or coordinate daily schedules.

"What do you do, Anna?" A rich baritone. The older man, George.

Anna reached for her bottle of wine, poured a glass. "I work in health care."

"A nurse?"

"No. A medical technologist." She paused, anticipating the next few questions, and gave a brief bio. "I'm from Boston and Maine, though I am, at the moment, nomadic. I don't have a destination in mind. I don't have any family left." To her horror, she began to tell them the story about Flynn, of her daughter who was supposed to show up but never did. How it all started and where it had ended. She told them about Jack and Stuart, and the baby they were trying to have after committing to each other at long last, talked about her granddaughter and how mysterious and magical she was, how her presence in Anna's life opened up a whole different world. "She believed in reincarnation and that she could communicate with the spirit world. We all thought she was just overly imaginative, you know, but there is something so strange about it all now. Sometimes I would swear that she is right beside me. I feel her. I smell her, and sometimes at night I feel her next to me while I'm sleeping. It's not a dream. I don't know what it is."

Neither of them spoke when she finished. It didn't matter to her what they thought. She felt curiously intact. Impossibly sorrowful, of course, but as if everything in her was unified in this sorrow. One of the most terrible aspects of grief was the sensation that each part of your body produced different, often warring, signals: overwhelming fatigue coupled with insomnia, gnawing hunger pains and nausea upon eating, restlessness and physical agitation along with the hopelessness of completing even the simplest household task.

"That is an amazing story," the older man said. "You must be an exceptionally strong woman."

Anna murmured noncommittally. "Would either of you like some wine?"

"I actually need to get out of this hot water," the younger man said. "I need to push on to L.A."

Anna poured herself another glass. She really shouldn't, but the warmth of the water and a new lightness rising up in her made her want to celebrate a little, get a little giddy.

"I'll try a little of that wine, if you're still offering," George said.

"Sure," Anna said, then realized she had nothing to pour it into. "You can share my glass, or there's the Bowery method."

"The Bowery method?"

"Right from the bottle."

"Oh." He laughed. He reached for her glass. His warm hands brushed against hers. "Ah, a French wine. Let's see. Chardonnay. Probably a '97."

Anna tipped the bottle in the path of the moonlight. "That's right. How did you know? Are you French?" There was an echo of an accent in his speech. Something vaguely European.

"I am a vintner. Born and raised here in California, but of Italian descent." He took another sip. "Nice. A nice choice. Bracing, but elegant. Assertive and tender at the same time."

"You have a vineyard?" Anna looked at him intently in the weak light. He was handsome, as far as she could see. His profile was strong, classically Roman.

"Well, I have part of one. My family has had part ownership for three generations now."

Anna poured the rest of the bottle, moved a little closer to him so they could share the glass. "Tell me," she said. "Tell me about yourself."

He was sixty, a widower with three grown children. An immigrant's son whose father had had a vineyard outside of Siena, in central Tuscany. "In a little village next to Montelocino, where my father was born and raised among the vines, wine in his veins. He came to this country at the age of twenty." George described the summers of his boyhood in Napa Valley, sitting at a long table in the arbor with the newly harvested grapes, a feast for his family of thirteen, and a hundred of the vineyard workers and their families—in those days, his father hired nearly all Italian immigrants, which was how it remained until he made a bad choice with a Merlot in '62 and had to sell part ownership. "Anna, you wouldn't believe how perfect those days were. It was like being back in Italy. We had three feasts a year in the orchard. One after the harvest, one on St. Joseph's Day and another on Easter. Of course every wedding, and there were a lot, was held there, too."

Anna listened as George described the dancing, the tarantellas and waltzes, the day he met the girl who would become his wife. "She was seventeen. I was nineteen. My father had just hired her father as a taster. He was right off the boat, one of the best tasters in Tuscany. There is a word in Italian. A phrase. *Assaggiare luce del sole.* To taste the sunlight, though that doesn't translate so well. My father used to say, the taster, Alberto, knew which vintages had had too much western sun. They were moody. *Doloroso.*" George laughed. "And the sun-drenched southern Cabernets. *Arrabbiato con luce del sole.* Angry with sunshine."

Anna laughed at George's impression of the self-important wine taster and saw him exactly: a little man with a perpetual wine glass in his hand, a golden tongue and a beautiful daughter: his twin blessings and twin curses. Even from this distance, in a memory not even her own, she felt the warmth of the people, the bonds of a tribe. Through his vivid descriptions, she saw George's mother with the ever-present rosary beads in her hand, his sisters crowded six at a time in the bedroom, the excitement of each courtship, wedding, and baby.

"Of course, Alberto took one look at me and knew right away what I was about. He had come over from Italy with his two brothers, who my father put to work in the presses. Alberto had them follow me everywhere. Every move I made had a witness. This, of course, gave me hope. If I were

330 · ABOVE THE THUNDER

not a serious contender for his daughter's affections, nobody would notice where I happened to spend my Sundays. Serafina, the girl who would become my wife, was under the maternal eye."

"Were you deterred?" Anna asked.

"Was I deterred? I am an Italian male. Only death could have deterred me."

Serafina refused to even speak to him, wouldn't meet his eye. "Though I'd seen the *dio lampo*, the divine lightning strike her the same time it struck me. I knew. I felt her heart turn toward me." Finally, at a St. Joseph's Day celebration, he insisted that she dance with him. She agreed after this night to go walking with him the next day. The whole family came along, trailing the couple like pages behind a royal court. This was how they dated for two weeks. One night, miraculously, George got her father's reluctant permission to take Serafina with him to the city for a movie. Two maiden aunts rode with them on the trolley, sat two rows behind them in the theater, muttered in Italian, and knitted their way through *The African Queen*. He hadn't so much as kissed her. He hadn't held her hand. But he said he knew that she was to be his wife. He would not take no for an answer. Not from her father or the flatulent aunts behind him, not even from Serafina's own modest reluctance. After the movie, they strolled along the streets, came upon a jewelry store, closed for the night. In the window were diamond engagement rings. He cupped her elbow and drew her forward. "Pick one out," he said, his heart pounding so hard that he could barely hear his own voice. He held his breath. The wheezing aunts, having finally caught up, were silent. It seemed to him that they, too, were holding their breath.

"That one," she said, and pointed to one in the back, her answer and her choice in one smooth motion. She turned to him and smiled. And he kissed her, without any interference from the *tias*. A month later, they were married.

"Wow," Anna said. "Wow. And are you still together?"

"She died two years ago. We were married thirty-eight years."

"I'm sorry," she said, and fell silent.

A few seconds passed. "So, tell me, Anna. Where are your loved ones now? Jack and...I forget the name of his partner."

"Stuart. They're in Boston."

"Boston." It sounded to Anna's ears like a reprimand. She laughed.

"Will you reestablish with them?"

"Reestablish?"

"I mean, reconnect."

Anna said certainly, just not right now.

"What are your plans? What will you do now?"

"I can't tell you that. I simply don't know. This, anyway, wasn't the life I was intending to lead." He was silent. She felt him watching her. "Well, it was a good life. But a whole phase has ended," she said.

"For me, also. For everybody, eventually," George said.

Anna murmured agreement. She tipped the bottle to the wineglass they'd been sharing, but it was empty.

"Would you like some more wine? I have some in my car. My vintage, of course."

Anna almost said yes. There was something about this man that she found comforting and comfortable. But she felt tipsy as it was, light-headed from the hot water. "That's really tempting. But, unfortunately, I think I've had too much as it is. I'll have to take a raincheck. Are you camping here tonight?"

"Sadly, no. I've been coming here on the weekends to soak, but I have never camped. Had I known there would be a beautiful woman here tonight, I would have transformed myself into an outdoorsman."

"Well," she said. "It's been lovely talking to you." She held out her hand. He took it and kissed it.

In an awkward moment, she realized that she was going to have to walk the three or four feet to the tree to get her robe. She half-stood. "Look at that moon up there," she said.

He laughed, and she got out when he turned his head.

"Anna?" he called.

"Yes?"

"I am going to ask you to have dinner with me tomorrow night."

"Well," she said. "Then I am going to say yes."

"Do you know the area?" She said that she didn't. "There's a good French restaurant. I'll come and get you at seven. But of course maybe you want the option of changing your mind. You might think later I am some sort of *pazzo*, a crazy man."

"No," Anna said, "I'd like to share a meal with you."

"Yes?" He paused. "Then here's what I will do. I'll give you directions to the place, and you can drive yourself. That way, you can decide. Naturally, I am hoping I'll see you, but I'll understand if you think twice. How about that?"

"That sounds good. I look forward to it," she said.

"And as I said," George said.

Anna turned back. "Yes?"

"As I told you, I am an Italian male. So if you say no, I'll just have to pursue you more intently. If you want my advice, you should show up. Even if you're not interested. *Especially* if you're not interested."

Anna laughed, and said he'd just have to wait to find out.

Later, after she heard George drive off, she lay awake in her tent a long time. She got up finally, took out her microscope and her favorite slide of Flynn's. There was a good moon tonight, bright, nearly full. She looked up at the stars, then down through the lens at the milky galaxy of her granddaughter's white cells. She ran her eyes over the monocytes and nutraphils, the basophils and leukocytes until it seemed as though she were moving through them, the white cells as dense and impenetrable as a blizzard. She stared at a cluster of monocytes in the upper left corner until she felt herself relax among the familiar configurations. She had memorized this particular slide the way others memorized passages of poetry. She let her mind wander, remembered the afternoon she checked Jack's T-cells and tested Stuart for the virus, the golden light of that day and the three of them driving through its path. She saw George's devout mother with her rosaries; the beads, too, Anna imagined, saw the old woman's gnarled fingers moving over each mooth cool stone, round as globes, dark as planets, turning now into the jade beads of a broken bracelet that fell to the floor, one by one. Anna looked away for a moment, then repositioned the microscope so that the slide under the lens caught the moonlight. Next to her granddaughter's blood cells was the reflected galaxy, the stars and planets and everything in the night sky. In this way, Anna thought, everything was connected. The carbon in the stars was the same carbon found in human bones. The true shape of everything was a circle. The moon and earth and the cells of a body, a bowl full of berries and a cluster of grapes. Even the future curved back through memory. She watched, in the corner of the slide, as the clouds drifted by, thought of Jack and Stuart and Marvin,

Poppy and Hugh, and of course the girl she cherished above all others—everyone in her past, those still with her, and the people yet to come. She felt the tidal tug of her granddaughter's body in her own pulling her toward some shore, the sea both inside her and out. This, maybe, was Anna's blessing for now: Flynn's cells, little light-years, illuminating the ancient time of stars, the constellations above and below, and the heavens that were everywhere.

ACKNOWLEDGMENTS

Thanks to all who helped me on my journey of writing this book. For enthusiasm and encouragement of early drafts, thank you to Lisa Dush and Anne Caston. Special thanks to Linden Ontjes and Christina Ward for their close readings and insights into character and structure that helped me see the work anew and to push it toward a stronger draft.

Deep appreciation goes to my agent, Eileen Cope, for her faith in this novel and whose good instincts led us to Anika Streitfeld, to whom I am profoundly grateful for her meticulous editing, great counsel, and encouragement, all of which helped this novel turn a corner. Thanks as well to the entire MacAdam/Cage group for their support of my work and for making me feel so welcome in San Francisco: David Poindexter, Scott Allen, Dorothy Carico Smith, Kate Nitze, and Pat Walsh.

Thanks also to Doreen Fitzgerald, for her friendship, support, and innumerable home-cooked meals; to Matt Wharton for his unwavering friendship and loyalty; to Marilyn Rice for her kindness and friendship; and to Tony Ardizzone, whose belief in me and my work over the years has been invaluable. Big thanks to Steven Balistreri and Andrea Steffke for taking care of my menagerie of animals and my house in the year I lived out of state. Finally, to my parents, John and Mary Ann Manfredi: a million thank yous.